WISTERIA WRINKLE

Wisteria Witches Mysteries

BOOK #7

ANGELA PEPPER

CHAPTER 1

THAT SUNNY MONDAY in May, brainweevils were the last thing on Zinnia Riddle's mind. Which was good. Because nobody wanted brainweevils on the mind or anywhere near it. Brainweevils hungered for delicious brains, particularly those of supernatural beings. Being a witch, Zinnia had heard all the horror stories. Ever since a brainweevil had shown up at City Hall a month ago—on a cafeteria plate!— Zinnia had been ever watchful. She'd also been applying a liberal coating of brainweevil-repelling potion to both of her ear canals.

Just before lunch time, Zinnia looked up from her computer screen. She was startled to find she wasn't alone. Her coworker, Dawna Jones, stood silently in the doorway to Zinnia's private office at the Wisteria Permits Department.

Dawna Jones was a slim black woman of thirty. She owned somewhere between two and five cats—nobody knew how many—and she'd apparently picked up their feline ability to suddenly be in a room without anyone noticing her arrival.

That Monday, Dawna wore shimmering bronzing powder that made her clear, dark skin look rich and luminescent. She had her natural, curly black hair pushed back from her face with a bright white headband, all the better to draw focus to her earrings, which were four-leafed clovers. Dawna loved good luck symbols. She had several tokens of luck from different cultures on her desk.

Dawna didn't know it, but her luck came from magic, not her tokens. Zinnia had recently discovered that Dawna was a cartomancer. This explained Dawna's knack for choosing winning scratch-'n-win lottery tickets. Dawna used her winnings to supplement her modest clerk income. She bought designer handbags that she passed off as knockoffs. Funnily enough, Dawna Jones did not know about the existence of magic. The cartomancer believed she was lucky thanks to her positive attitude and good luck charms.

"Hi, Dawna," Zinnia said. "I didn't hear you come in."

Dawna sniffed the air. "Ooh, is that a new perfume I smell?" She wrinkled her nose. "It smells pretty, like flowers, but also a bit like the goopy stuff my auntie used to put on my chest whenever I got a bad cold."

"Oh, that," Zinnia said offhandedly as she searched for an explanation. The witch had added a touch of menthol to her brainweevil repellent that morning. Too much, apparently, if other people could detect it.

"Smells nice, anyway," Dawna said. "Not like regular perfume."

"It's just a new hand lotion," Zinnia said, even though she never wore lotion. Since becoming a witch at sixteen, Zinnia's resilient skin had never needed hand lotion, moisturizer, or even chap stick. She was a pale-skinned redhead who got to enjoy her delicate coloring without the sun sensitivity. She was forty-eight now, so that added up to thirty-some years of time and money saved on moisturizing products. She'd applied plenty of lotions and potions for other things, but that was to be expected. Her magical specialty, being Kitchen Bewitched, involved whipping up various magical compounds in her kitchen. She made lotions for attracting or repelling magical things the way non-magical people made cookies. She had recently made a bookwyrm out of dough for her niece. That particular creation had led to endless trouble, but everything had worked out in the end. Not for the bookwyrm, unfortunately, but at least the little critter had gone out a hero.

Dawna was still in the doorway. She fidgeted with her four-leaf-clover earrings as she studied Zinnia intently.

"Can I help you with something?" Zinnia asked.

"You look puffy this morning," Dawna said. "I know it's not my business, but did something bad happen to you? Did you get in a car accident?"

A car accident? No, but it did feel that way. Zinnia rubbed her shoulder self-consciously. She'd had that arm in a sling the day before, when she'd had Sunday brunch with her niece and grand-niece. She could have used the sling again today, but she'd chosen to leave it at home because a sling would have only led to questions, such as the ones Dawna was now asking.

Zinnia patted her face self-consciously. "I must be retaining water. Too much salt last night."

Dawna raised her eyebrows. "How much salt, exactly? The whole box?"

Zinnia chuckled. Dawna was as perceptive as she was lucky. Zinnia's witch powers allowed her to heal quickly, but they could only do so much, and the injuries had been grave. She'd been the victim of a violent attack, hobbling away with two blackened eyes and deep scratches on her face. And she'd deserved the pain as a reminder to be more careful in the future.

"Maybe it's seasonal allergies," Zinnia said. She was tempted to use a spell to change the conversation, but she had a rule about not using magic at work.

Dawna frowned and leaned into the office tentatively. "How come I never noticed how pretty your eyes are? What's that color? It's not green, but it's not brown."

"Hazel," Zinnia said.

Dawna looked skeptical. "That's a real color? I thought it was just a name for old ladies."

"I assure you, hazel is a real color." Zinnia smiled with relief that the topic had changed. "You can go up to the third floor and check with the DMV. Hazel is what it says on my driver's license."

Dawna tilted her head to the side. "Maybe you should put some cold tea bags on those pretty hazel eyes of yours."

"I'll be fine," Zinnia said. "I simply had too much, uh, *fun* over the weekend."

Dawna sniggered. "Sure, you did. I can just imagine, you wild thing. Did you go to the Chintz Boutique and buy more wallpaper?" She gestured to the floral wallpaper that now covered the walls of Zinnia's redecorated office.

"Something like that." Zinnia tidied the unopened mail on her desk. "Is there anything I can help you with?"

Dawna remained on the threshold, in the doorway. She swished her lips from side to side thoughtfully.

Zinnia prompted her with, "Anything at all?"

Dawna seemed to force the words out. "I was thinking about Annette, and all that crazy stuff she wrote about us in her book."

"Oh?" Zinnia was surprised to hear Dawna talking about their deceased coworker's book. The topic had been taboo around the office, ever since the second tragedy that had happened back in January.

Dawna continued. "Specifically, I've been thinking about all of us in this office having magic powers."

"Not us," Zinnia corrected. "Annette wrote about fictional characters that were only loosely based on us." Loosely based, and yet eerily accurate. Their deceased coworker hadn't known she was a witch, let alone that she'd correctly guessed the magical identities of her friends in the office. It was such a shame Annette Scholem hadn't lived long enough to develop her witch powers.

"Fictional characters," Dawna repeated, nodding. "Yeah, I got that. But you have to wonder, don't you? I've been wondering a lot lately."

Zinnia raised an eyebrow. The redheaded witch also wondered about plenty of things. Being as aware of the supernatural as she was, Zinnia knew just how many things in the world there were to wonder about.

Zinnia cautiously asked, "Dawna, has something happened?"

"Not yet," Dawna said. "But let me ask you a question, Zinnia. I respect your opinion, and not just because you're a mature lady. I think you're smart and wise."

Zinnia felt her barriers rise the way they always did when someone paid her compliments.

Through a tight mouth, Zinnia said, "Ask away."

Dawna took a chest-raising breath and expelled it in one sentence. "Do you think it would be crazy if I got a deck of tarot cards?"

Zinnia felt a tickle of worry wrinkle her forehead. Dawna didn't know she was a cartomancer, but she might discover her powers if she started looking. Would she be better off knowing or not knowing? Powers came with responsibilities, not to mention a big load of trouble.

Zinnia looked down and rubbed her thumb where it ached. Her shoulder twinged. Her eyes really *were* puffy, now that she thought about it. She could actually hear the soft smack-smack of her eyelids sticking together when she blinked.

Dawna Jones was a perceptive woman. Would she be responsible with her powers? Dawna might use tarot cards to win the state lottery, and then quit her job at the Permits Department. Zinnia would miss her. Then again, Dawna might play with tarot cards for years without results. Powers didn't always manifest just from being sought. If it worked that simply, Zinnia's great-niece would have found her own abilities by now. Little Zoey would have stopped moping around the way only a disappointed teenager could.

Zinnia flicked her eyes up to meet Dawna's gaze. Dawna had the loveliest orange, cat-like eyes.

"You ought to do what you feel is right," Zinnia said. "If you're curious about tarot cards, get yourself a deck." Zinnia felt a calm certainty settle over her. It was good to have the wisdom of age, and good to share it with others.

"Really?"

"Dawna, I believe your name means *daybreak*." Zinnia rested her chin on her hand and regarded the woman thoughtfully. "Perhaps you are a true bringer of light."

Dawna let out a surprised laugh. "It's just a pack of cards for fortune telling," she said. "You make it sound like I'm going to start a coven and bring on the apocalypse."

Little did she know! Zinnia felt a smile curl her mouth. "If you do start a coven, I hope you'll invite me." She kept smiling as she added, "And Margaret, too, of course."

Dawna's orange, cat-like eyes widened. Her jaw dropped open. "What? Margaret's a witch?"

Zinnia felt her cheeks flush hot with embarrassment. Joking about forming covens was the exact opposite of being careful. Silly witch!

Zinnia quickly explained, "I was making a joke. Only because Margaret and I were the basis for Nina and Gretta, the two teenaged witches in Annette's book."

The doorway of Zinnia's office darkened with the arrival of a second person. Their coworker Margaret, who was also a witch, appeared next to Dawna as though summoned.

Margaret asked, nostrils flaring, "Did someone say teenaged witches?" Margaret had a highly tuned sensitivity for the word *witch*, as well as other witch-related terms such as brewing, spell, wand, eye of newt, and so forth.

Dawna explained, "We were just talking about Annette's book. Remember that girl who was based on me? Wanda? She was a fortune teller."

"She was a cartomancer," Margaret said crisply. "A card mage."

"Exactly. A fortune-teller. Same thing."

Margaret's whole face pinched toward her scrunched lips. Cartomancers and fortune-tellers were *not* the same thing, and Margaret didn't like to hear an error go uncorrected. Her eyes twitched from the effort it took to restrain herself from explaining to Dawna the difference between a circus-level charlatan and a magic-wielding card mage.

Dawna continued, "Zinnia was just saying it might be fun if I get some tarot cards and see what happens. I've always been lucky with cards. Do you know where I might get a deck? I was reading on the internet that you can't buy them for yourself. It's a superstition thing. They have to be given to you, as a gift."

Margaret's face was still pinched from holding herself back.

Dawna waggled her eyebrows at the shorter woman. "So, what do you say, Margaret? Will you give me a deck of tarot cards?" She winked. "Or should I say *Gretta*? You know, like your witch character in Annette's book."

Margaret's eyes bulged. Her expression reminded Zinnia of a dog's squeaky toy being squeezed in the middle.

"Nothing expensive," Dawna said. "Just a basic deck. Your choice."

Margaret replied vehemently, "No! Why would I ever get involved with something like that?"

Dawna leaned back and raised both hands, waving her manicured orange nails in the air. "Easy, girl. I didn't mean anything by it." She backed away from the door frame. "Time for lunch, anyway." She looked right at Zinnia. "Thanks for the advice. I'll probably let Gavin give me some cards instead of flowers or chocolates, the next time he does one of his annoying Gavin things." She turned and left.

Margaret came into Zinnia's small office and put her hands on her hips. "What was that all about?" Before Zinnia could respond, Margaret said, "You do look puffy. I heard the whole thing, and she's right. You look like you've been put through the wringer."

"Thanks."

"How bad was that attack on the weekend?" She waved a hand. "Never mind. I don't want to know. It's easier for me to stick to the cover story about the gas explosion if I don't know different."

"That's what I figured, on account of how you always need to interrupt people and set the record straight."

Margaret snorted. "I do not."

Zinnia bit her tongue.

"Get up." Margaret waved for Zinnia to rise from her chair. "If you want to heal faster, you need to move around more, get the juices flowing. Come on." She waved again, with more enthusiasm. "Let's walk over to the Gingerbread House of Baking for lunch. I'll buy you anything you want. They do fresh cream horns on Mondays."

Zinnia rose from her chair and joked, "Cream horns? Twist my arm." She winced as pain shot through her shoulder. "On second thought, don't twist my arm. And definitely don't yank it off and punch me in my own face with it."

Margaret's jaw dropped open. "Wha-wha-wha—"

"Joking," Zinnia said, except she wasn't.

Margaret didn't know all the details, but Zinnia had taken quite a beating over the weekend while helping her niece, Zara, with a ghost problem. Zinnia's two black eyes had been delivered by her own fist, after her arm had been yanked off by a demonic force in a borrowed body.

Zinnia had been broken, yet she hadn't been beaten. Anything that failed to kill her only made her stronger. She had survived to fight another day... and to eat a cream horn or two. She grabbed her purse and joined Margaret for lunch.

The forces of evil would have to try a lot harder to keep Zinnia Riddle down.

CHAPTER 2

OUTSIDE, THE SPRING sunshine felt wonderful on Zinnia's pale skin. She'd worn her thick, red hair in a high bun that day, so the sun's rays were particularly warm on the back of her neck, which didn't usually get much sun. The lunch hour had one of the highest UV indexes of the day, but luckily for the witch, her regenerative powers protected her from sunburns.

Margaret Mills had also arrived at work with her hair pulled up in a bun. Several of Margaret's frizzy gray curls had escaped the updo, including the single curl that stubbornly adorned the center of Margaret's forehead like a rhino horn. Margaret was six years younger than Zinnia, and often lamented that it wasn't fair that Zinnia's hair was still red while Margaret's had lost its color already. Marriage and four kids will do that to a woman, they both agreed. Sometimes they joked that Zinnia should take over two of Margaret's kids so they could share the load evenly, but they never could agree on which two. "Because your children are all equally adorable," Zinnia would say, which was an absolute lie. She would take the eldest and the youngest. The eldest was the smartest by far, and the youngest had the most adorable, pinchable cheeks.

Margaret Mills was shorter than Zinnia, especially in the legs, which gave her a short pace. The clip-clop sounds of Margaret's boots on the sidewalk never synced up with Zinnia's footsteps. Margaret took two steps for every one of Zinnia's. Perhaps it only seemed that way due to the noise Margaret made when she walked. The woman could clomp, even on carpet. Why did Margaret sound so much like a hoofed animal? It was anyone's guess. She had a solid build, but she wasn't overweight. Perhaps it was a side effect of her magic.

Margaret and Zinnia were part of a small coven that included two other local witches, Maisy and Fatima Nix. Zinnia had not yet introduced her niece, Zara, to the coven. Zinnia had decided she wouldn't attempt to bring the younger witch into the fold until both she and Margaret agreed Zara was ready, and Zara hadn't even met Margaret yet. Since Zinnia had reunited with her family three months earlier, she had been wildly secretive about her associates, her personal life, and even her place of employment. Both she and Margaret agreed it was for Zara's own protection. The novice witch had to deal with one thing at a time—or at least one *ghost* at a time.

The two coworker witches cast a rolling sound bubble for privacy so they could talk about magical business as they walked.

Margaret asked, "Any sign of young Zoey's powers kicking in?"

"Nothing. I fear she is developing a permanent pout. Like this." Zinnia stuck out her lower lip in an impression of the teenager. "And when Zoey pouts, her kooky mother levitates pastries and sends them flying around the room. She drops bits of custard on the poor child's lower lip. Then the two of them scream hysterically about someone or something named Marzipants." Zinnia shook her head, smiling. "Never a dull moment with those two."

Margaret's round shoulders hunched up and forward. "Sounds fun," she said glumly.

"They can be amusing."

Margaret looked down at the sidewalk, her shoulders hunching even more. "I can't blame you for spending so much time with them. They both sound like a lot more fun than boring ol' Margaret Mills."

"Well, I didn't mean..." Zinnia struggled to find the right words. She couldn't deny that she enjoyed her family. Spending time with the other Riddles was worth the pain of the occasional arm-ripping.

Margaret let out a long, world-weary sigh.

"Poor Margaret," Zinnia said. "I'm sorry you feel so neglected." She'd meant to sound compassionate, but it had come out somewhat sarcastic. What now? Should she put her arm around Margaret? Was that what ought to be done in such a situation? Zinnia wasn't a touchy, huggy person, but she could certainly make some sort of effort when it was socially necessary.

"I'm fine." Margaret kicked at a pebble, still looking down. She sounded anything but fine.

Zinnia gingerly lifted an arm behind Margaret. Zinnia's shoulder screamed in pain, so she dropped the arm before contacting the other witch.

"Oh, dear," Zinnia said, still struggling to find comforting words. Recently, she'd offered so much tea and sympathy to her great-niece. It should have come easier, but she found it so unexpected for headstrong, self-assured —some might say self-righteous—Margaret Mills to be in such a self-pitying state. Zinnia wasn't sure of her role. The two had far more practice fighting with each other than with offering comfort.

"Forget I brought it up," Margaret said wearily. "It's Monday. Let's chalk it up to a case of the Mondays."

"Sure," Zinnia said, but she wouldn't be able to forget.

It was no wonder Margaret was suffering a bad mood. Ever since Zinnia had been reunited with her family, the two coworkers had spoken about little else. Margaret wasn't wrong to see herself as an extra wheel. She had gone from first place in Zinnia's life to third.

Zinnia sighed, though not as audibly as Margaret. For every twist of fate—every action—there was an equal and opposite reaction. The sudden, wonderful influx of Riddles had pushed out Zinnia's other relationships. What could Zinnia do? There was only one of her, only so many hours in the day.

She lifted her shoulder-hugging arm again, experienced a surge of pain like an electrical shock, and dropped it once more.

They turned the corner and soon were on the block for the bakery.

Zinnia snapped her fingers to break the sound bubble as they approached the shop. She could smell the pastries from the sidewalk.

"Here we are," Zinnia said brightly. "And lunch is on me today. I insist."

Margaret didn't refuse, but she didn't cheer up, either. Her posture remained slumped forward and troll-like as they approached the front door.

The exterior of the Gingerbread House of Baking, owned and run by Jordan and Chloe Taub, was decorated to match its name. The front was a gingerbread house, from the giant sugared gumdrops to the white swirls of "frosting" that had been created from Styrofoam and plaster. The "gumballs" were the size of baseballs because they truly were baseballs, dipped in bright, primary shades of paint. The storefront looked good enough to eat. From the outside, anyway. Inside, the shop was all white, bleached wood, gleaming metal, pale marble, and glass. The baked goods—real stuff, made with butter and sugar, not painted sporting goods—were the star of the show.

Zinnia was reaching for the candy-cane handle when the door swung open. She looked up to see the owner, Jordan Taub. He was on his way out with a tiny baby in his arms. Jordan was about thirty, with dark skin and plenty of muscles. The baby had fuzzy black hair and light-brown skin. He or she was awake and wriggling happily in his or her father's arms.

"Good morning, ladies," Jordan said, yawning. "Or is it afternoon?"

Margaret replied in her usual precise fashion, "It's twelve-fifteen, so it's technically the afternoon."

Zinnia said, "Looks like you've been busy with this little one. Boy or girl?"

Jordan gave her a surprised look. "Don't you know already? I thought news traveled fast around certain communities."

Margaret and Zinnia exchanged a look. By *certain communities* did he mean witches? Had one of the coven offended Jordan? Not that Zinnia knew of.

"Small towns," Jordan said in an exasperated tone. "By *certain communities*, I mean small towns." He sighed. "And it's a boy. Jordan Junior." He looked down at the baby's chubby face. An expression of calm tenderness came over the rugged, muscular man's face. "Isn't he wonderful?"

"He's perfect," Zinnia said. "What a charmer!"

Jordan raised an eyebrow. "A charmer? Is that supposed to mean something? As in, *snake charmer*?"

Zinnia blinked rapidly. There were so many ways to insult supernatural people without realizing it!

Margaret stepped in. "Your son *is* a real charmer," she said in a firm tone. "It's something people say. Get used to it." She softened as she smiled at the baby. "With those big eyes, everyone's going to be charmed by this little cookie!"

"Oh," Jordan said. "Uh, thanks."

Jordan stepped back, holding open the door for the two ladies to enter the bakery. He brandished his new baby the way only a proud new father could. They both cooed at Jordan Junior for the appropriate amount of time—about a minute longer than necessary—and then Jordan left with the baby, apparently satisfied by the outcome of their interaction.

Margaret and Zinnia exchanged another look. The baby had looked normal enough, from the waist up, anyway. Both witches knew the newborn's mother was a gorgon, but neither knew what manner of creature Jordan Taub was, assuming he even was one. He might have been, like Margaret's husband, Mike, just a regular, non-magical person who'd gotten lucky.

Both witches relaxed as they looked around and breathed in the smell of the bakery. The scent of fresh bread and cookies was heavenly to Zinnia, who'd been smelling nothing but mentholated brainweevil repellent all morning.

The two were greeted by the baby's mother, Chloe Taub. Despite being a gorgon, Chloe was looking entirely human, her hair snakes hidden away on the magical plane where they normally existed. Chloe was dressed in pale yellow and white.

"Hello, ladies," Chloe chirped brightly. "Today's Monday, so we've just put out a batch of delicious cream horns."

Chloe looked remarkably chipper for the mother of a newborn who wasn't even a month old yet. Chloe had cut her hair since that day in January that Zinnia had seen her crossing the street while visibly pregnant. Chloe's golden curls were now tamed into a short style, shaved at the back with some feminine volume on top. The twenty-nine-year-old's round face was pretty, albeit pudgy from the baby weight. Her magic-wielding blue eyes were a deep, luminous sapphire, lightly tinged with red from sleepless nights.

Chloe was one of three triplets. Her sister Charlize worked for the local top-secret agency. Her other sister Chessa wasn't doing much at all, thanks to being in a coma for the past year. Zinnia wasn't familiar with Chessa's abilities, but she knew that both Charlize and Chloe had the power to turn living things to stone and back again, as well as other powers. Zinnia had a mouse-shaped stone paperweight at home thanks to Charlize, and a crack in her windshield thanks to Chloe.

Zinnia wondered how Chloe's hair snakes were adjusting to both motherhood and their new haircut. Zinnia relaxed her eyes so she could peer through the regular world to see the unseen, the magic that hid itself on another dimension. As Zinnia's witch vision kicked in, the bright white bakery swam around the gorgon's head. Even the scent of freshly baked bread turned to something more like ash. Zinnia's eyes found the other focal plane, and the snakes flickered into view. Their copper heads hung limply, like deflated pool toys. They were much shorter now, their length matching Chloe's trimmed hair. But they weren't as powerless as they appeared. Zinnia knew, from first-hand experience, that the snakes could extend at will. They could fill a room if their owner wanted them to.

Zinnia blinked and snapped her view back to the regular world.

Chloe patted her short hair self-consciously. "Too short? I shouldn't have listened to Morganna Faire. That kook. She thought this haircut would be perfect for my face shape, but... I don't know."

Margaret stared at Chloe. "Did you say Morganna Faire? From the Beach Hair Shack? You mean you go to a regular stylist?"

"Yesssss," Chloe said suspiciously, with just a hint of a gorgon hiss. "Why wouldn't I?"

"No reason," Margaret said in a squeaky voice.

Margaret swallowed and stepped away from the counter, putting some distance between herself and the gorgon. She busied herself studying the pastries in the display case.

"Don't mind her," Zinnia said to Chloe. "She gets a little starstruck around certain people."

Chloe glanced around, frowning. "Who?"

"You," Zinnia said. "Your abilities are amazing. You and your family are tapped into something far more powerful than anything we can imagine."

Chloe frowned. "So, I'm like a rock star or something to you ladies?"

"Exactly."

"That's sweet, I guess." Her expression clouded over. "Did you hear there was another brainweevil sighting?"

Zinnia's ears tingled. She wished she'd applied even more repellent. "I hadn't heard. Where?"

"I can't say where, exactly, but I'd keep my eyes open if I were you." She grinned and whispered, "It was in the archives at City Hall."

"That's a bit close for comfort."

Chloe shrugged. "We've all seen worse. You know, they're not deadly if you get medical treatment right away. I've heard some people feel better after a brief infection." She wrinkled her nose. "Whatever doesn't kill you makes you stronger."

"All the same, I'd rather not find out. Thanks for the warning."

Chloe leaned forward on the counter and stifled a yawn. "It is Monday right? I've been talking up the cream horns all day. Someone would tell me if it wasn't Monday, wouldn't they? Or if my hair is too short?"

Zinnia smiled. "It's Monday. As a couple of my coworkers would say, it's Monday *all day long*. And your hair looks adorable. I can't believe you're back at work again so soon after the baby."

Chloe shrugged. "I had to get out of the house. I was starting to hear phantom cries and see all sorts of things that weren't real."

"You were seeing things? Such as?"

Margaret pulled herself from the pastry display case and came over to chime in, "Like what?"

Chloe took a step back to peer into the back of the bakery. Several noisy mixers and fans were running, but the staff she had working that day weren't within sight. Margaret and Zinnia were the only customers inside the front of the bakery.

In a low voice, Chloe said, "I've seen deer walking through the living room and kitchen. And rabbits hopping down my hallway. Plus something huge, like a snake, but bigger than any snake that exists. More like a whale that goes on forever."

Zinnia and Margaret exchanged a look. Their curiosities had been piqued.

"A big snake?" Zinnia asked. "Could it be a relative?"

"I thought about that, but it's probably just my imagination. When my sisters and I were little, my grandmother used to talk about giant worms that swallowed people whole. She gave me and Charlize nightmares! Not Chessa, though. That girl was never scared of anything."

"Giant worms," Zinnia mused. "That doesn't sound too scary."

Chloe raised her eyebrows. "Have you ever seen that movie *Dune*? With the sandworms? How about

Beetlejuice? Or that nineties movie with Kevin Bacon, *Tremors*?"

"Ah," Zinnia said. She was familiar with the franchises and their subterranean monsters. "I can see how that would be terrifying. And you saw these sandworms in your house?"

"Not exactly," Chloe said. "Oh, I don't know. It was more like a shadow or a movement out of the corner of my eye, then my brain would fill in the rest." She rubbed her temples. "I was probably hallucinating from lack of sleep. People kept telling me that newborns were challenging, but I thought, how hard could it be?" Her eyes glistened. "Plus, I didn't believe them. Jordan and I spent so long trying to have a baby that I thought people were just saying that to make me feel better about not having one. But luckily—" She cleared her throat and looked away.

Margaret spoke up, her voice taking on an air of motherly authority. "A new baby will make you question your sanity, that's for sure. You're doing just fine."

Chloe sniffed. "Thanks," she said weakly. "He's just one little baby. Who knew they could cause so much trouble?"

"Take it from me, a mother of four," Margaret said. "One little baby is plenty of trouble. And may I give you some advice as one mother to another? You don't want to have another baby for a while yet. Space them out. Twenty-five years is about right."

Chloe blinked. "What do you mean?"

"Don't listen to her," Zinnia said. "Margaret adores her children. At least three out of the four of them."

"It's true," Margaret said. "As for which three, they're in rotation."

Chloe's head bobbed. Judging by the unfocused look in her eyes, Zinnia guessed the new mother was barely hearing their words, let alone catching the humor. Even if Chloe was only seeing forest creatures and imaginary worms, she was still hallucinating. Gorgon or not, she would need time to catch up on her sleep deficit.

Zinnia changed the topic back to the business at hand. "We should probably order our food now and stop taking up your time," she said. She and Margaret ordered some grilled sandwiches to go, along with enough cream horns to share with the rest of the office.

As Chloe was packaging everything, she had a faraway look in her eyes. After wrapping up the transaction, Chloe said, "Wait a minute. I've got an extra surge detector here. If I give it to you, then you can keep a lookout for my deer and bunnies. If you happen to see something, you can let my husband know I'm not crazy."

Zinnia said, "What's a surge—"

She was cut off by Margaret saying, "Yes! We'd love your extra surge detector. Yes, please."

"It's in the back office," Chloe said. "I'll just be a minute."

After she left the two witches alone, Zinnia said to Margaret, "You don't even know what a surge detector is, do you?"

Margaret stared up into Zinnia's eyes without wavering. "Sure, I do. A surge detector is for detecting surges."

"Ha ha," Zinnia said dryly. "Very funny."

"I was funny once," Margaret said. "Back in college, I was in an improv troupe. We were called the MacGuffins."

Zinnia bit her tongue. Margaret mentioned her improv days at least once a week. In fact, she mentioned it so frequently that Zinnia had started to wonder if something sinister was going on with Margaret's memories. Had there even been a troupe called the MacGuffins, or was it a false memory placed to cover something else?

Chloe returned with the surge detector, which had a strange yet familiar appearance.

CHAPTER 3

ZINNIA RIDDLE DIDN'T know what a surge detector was, let alone what it might look like, so she didn't know if Chloe was joking when she placed on the counter a round glass ball sitting on a simple wooden base. It looked like something a fortune-teller might use to pretend to see the future. A crystal ball.

She leaned in closer. The ball wasn't solid crystal after all. It appeared to be filled with liquid, as well as floating, snow-like flakes. Was it a snow globe? She kept watching. The flakes weren't simply floating. They appeared to be swimming. Alive.

Margaret, who was standing next to Zinnia, squealed and clapped her hands. "Sea-monkeys!"

"Not even close," Chloe said. "Mainly because there's no such thing as sea-monkeys."

Margaret sniffed. "But my kids have some. They're in a big jar on the kitchen window sill."

"Those are just brine shrimp you have," Zinnia said, elbowing Margaret. "Some marketing genius decided to call them sea-monkeys and sell them as pets."

Margaret tapped on the glass ball. "These are brine shrimp? They don't look like the ones I have at home. These ones are lively."

Chloe said flatly, "They're not brine shrimp." She shook her head. Zinnia caught a glimpse of the gorgon's shortened hair snakes rousing from their slumber to do the snake equivalent of rolling their eyes.

Margaret continued to tap on the glass. The swimming creatures gathered under her fingertips.

"These are way more lively than our sea-monkeys," Margaret said. "Come on, guys," she whispered to them. "Do some neat circus tricks in there."

Chloe narrowed her topaz-blue eyes at Margaret. Her hair snakes flopped around with their forked tongues flicking out, as though laughing at the foolish witch with the gray, horn-like curl on the center of her forehead.

Zinnia elbowed her friend again, trying to get her to stop behaving like a rube at a traveling carnival, but it was too late. The gorgon knew incompetence when she saw it.

Chloe said wearily, "You two have never used a surge detector before, have you?"

Margaret snorted. "Not this *particular* type. Right, Zinnia?" She turned to Zinnia to back her up. Zinnia did not back her up.

Chloe said, "It's simple enough. The creatures in here, the ones that you mistook for brine shrimp, are a paraphyletic class of annelid worms. In this species, the luciferase requires two other cofactors for bioluminescence. One is the energy-carrying molecule adenosine triphosphate, ATP, and the other is..." She frowned. "Do either of you have a background in marine biology?"

Both witches shook their heads.

"Herbs and plants are my field," Zinnia said. "I'm Kitchen Bewitched."

Chloe raised an eyebrow. "How adorable." She looked over at Margaret.

Margaret said nothing. Her witch specialty was something she preferred not to mention. She hadn't even told Zinnia, so it was unlikely Margaret was about to spill it now, no matter how much she admired the gorgon.

"But I do understand chemical reactions," Zinnia said. "Are you saying that these things will glow when a magical cofactor is present?"

"Basically, yes," Chloe said. "That is the gist."

"And did you say they were a type of worm? Any relation to the giant ones you may or may not have seen at your house?"

Chloe appeared to be surprised by the question. "I suppose it's possible they're distantly related. Assuming the latter even exists."

Margaret resumed tapping on the glass ball. The tiny creatures scurried from finger to finger like hungry koi fish.

"This is fun," Margaret said. "What did you say they were called?"

Chloe pushed Margaret's hand away and used the corner of her baking apron to put a shine on the glass globe.

"I won't bore you with their scientific name," Chloe said. "We call them *glowfish*, though technically they aren't fish. Are you familiar with the *Abraliopsis* squid?"

Both witches shook their heads again.

Chloe explained, "It's a non-magical squid that uses bioluminescence for camouflage. It glows to hide from predators."

Margaret raised one hand like a child in school. "But wouldn't making yourself glow be the sort of thing that attracts predators?"

Chloe smiled like a teacher who'd been hoping for that specific question. "It glows on the underside, so it blends with the sky above the water. Then the predators who are swimming below the octopus don't see its shadow as it passes overhead."

"Ooh, that's smart," Margaret said. "I could use a camouflage that makes me look like the inside of my house so my kids can't see me and I can get some peace and quiet. Maybe a glamour that makes me blend with the interior of the bath tub." She reached out to tap on the glass again. Chloe swatted her hand away.

"Don't agitate them," Chloe said. "When the globe lights up, you'll know a power surge is happening. For some reason, these glowfish associate power surges with predators."

Margaret bowed forward, nearly touching the tip of her nose to the globe. "Do they turn different colors for different types of surges?"

Zinnia elbowed Margaret, not that it would do any good. "I'm sure it's not a mood ring," she said.

"The glowfish turn blue for danger, and yellow for mating," Chloe said.

Zinnia leaned in next to Margaret and used her hand to shield the glass ball from the overhead lighting. She asked, "Is it my imagination, or is it faintly glowing blue right now?"

"It's glowing, all right," Chloe said.

Margaret yanked her head back and glanced around nervously. "Are we in danger?"

"No more than usual," Chloe said with a snort. "It's been glowing like that for a month now. And my, uh, friends have detected other anomalies that they believe are connected to power surges."

Zinnia's thoughts rolled around to her great-niece. "About these surges, is it possible they might suppress magical powers?"

"It's possible," Chloe said. "Although it's more likely to force them to manifest. There have been some extra-strange things happening lately. You did hear about Project Erasure, didn't you?"

Zinnia held her tongue. She'd assumed Chloe Taub knew everything that went on in Wisteria, but if she didn't know Zinnia had been present for the dismantling of the mind-erasing machine, then apparently the gorgon didn't know everything after all.

"Yup," Margaret said, answering for Zinnia. "I heard all about that nasty Erasure Machine business. It was a whole big thing." She sighed and rolled her eyes. "Yet another one of Zinnia's hilarious, wacky adventures with her niece. The kind of adventure she never invites me to."

Zinnia ignored Margaret and asked Chloe, "Was the Erasure Machine causing power surges?"

"We thought so, but even after dismantling it, we're still getting readings. We have a few of the surge detectors stationed around the town, with various trustworthy parties."

Margaret gasped. "Are you saying that we're *trustworthy parties*?" She looked down shyly and kicked at the floor with the toe of her boot.

Zinnia asked, "What should we do with this thing? Carry it around? It's a bit large for my purse."

"Take it to City Hall," Chloe said. "Park it on one of your desks and make a call if you see something." She paused and looked steadily at Zinnia, her topaz-blue eyes bright and serious. "Call the water department."

"I understand," Zinnia said. "We can do that." She turned to Margaret.

Margaret winked twice at the gorgon baker. "The water department. Right." She winked a third time. Margaret could be subtle if she wanted to. The problem was she never wanted to.

Both witches understood whom Chloe meant. The town of Wisteria had a group of supernaturals who watched over all things magical. They worked under the cover of the water department. People in the know referred to them as the DWM, the Department of Water and Magic. Zinnia and Margaret both had the phone number to call in the event of an emergency. They had called the number only a month ago, when Margaret had mistaken a brainweevil for a crinkle-cut French fry and nearly eaten it.

Zinnia asked the gorgon, "When did the surge detector begin glowing?"

Chloe blinked at her. "About a month ago." She was quick to add, "After my baby was born. This phenomenon is in no way connected to him. He's just a regular baby."

Zinnia raised an eyebrow. Just a regular baby? She doubted that very much.

Chloe said, "The power surges have nothing to do with me or my family. Nothing." There was a faint hissing as her hair snakes briefly became visible to the witches.

"You seem to be quite certain about what the phenomenon is not, despite not knowing what it is," Zinnia said.

Chloe crossed her arms. "It's got nothing to do with my family now, and it didn't have anything to do with the Wakefuls the last time these surges happened, back in 1955."

Margaret chimed in with a curious, "This happened before?"

Chloe frowned at them both. "There was a whole mess that turned into a witch hunt. My grandfather, Angelo Wakeful, was involved. You won't find any references to it in the local history books. It's all been scrubbed clean." Chloe waved a hand dismissively. "Never mind that ancient history."

Zinnia and Margaret exchanged a look. To an actual witch, the mention of a witch hunt happening in their own town was not something to be forgotten so easily.

In unison, the two women asked, "What's this about a witch hunt?"

Chloe sighed. "If you must know, there was a brief period in 1955 where a couple of monsters were sighted running around Wisteria. People connected it to the Wakeful family simply because my grandfather was the first to see the monsters and report them." She shook her head. "It was so disrespectful the way everyone turned on him. The Wakefuls were one of the founding families! If it wasn't for us, this town wouldn't even exist."

Margaret asked tentatively, "What did your grandfather do to get everyone so suspicious?"

"Nothing!" Chloe's topaz-blue eyes glistened with sudden tears. "Eventually the monsters just walked into the woods and disappeared, back to wherever they'd come from. The whole thing blew over, but the Wakeful name was ruined. My family took their beautiful name off all their local businesses." She chuckled hollowly and glanced around the bakery's gleaming interior. "You know, I actually wanted to turn things around when Jordan and I took over this bakery. I was going to restore it to the original name, Wakeful Bakery." Her pretty faced pinched unattractively as she spat out her words. "But there are still a few stubborn old-timers around who think Wakeful is a dirty name."

Margaret said, "About these monsters who were loose —"

She was cut off by the sound of bells. The front door of the bakery opened to let in other customers. The popular bakery was normally a busy place, especially at lunch time.

It was a wonder the three women had talked privately as long as they had.

Within minutes, the front area was filled with a dozen hungry lunch customers. Everyone was excited about the Monday cream horns.

Chloe pulled on a big smile and said in a cheerful tone, "Nice chatting with you today, ladies! Let me know if you see anything interesting."

She tucked the faintly glowing glass globe into a bag along with their pastries and sandwiches, and sent them on their way.

CHAPTER 4

ON THE WALK back to City Hall, Margaret and Zinnia speculated about the Wakeful family's history in Wisteria.

Margaret did an internet search and read aloud from her phone screen, "To be *wakeful* is to experience the metabolic state of cannibalism."

"Cannibalism?" Zinnia quickly cast the rolling sound bubble to give the two witches their privacy. A sidewalk conversation about cannibalism was the sort of thing that aroused suspicion and could lead to another witch hunt.

"Oops," Margaret said, peering closer at her phone. "Not cannibalism. Something called*catabolism*." She touched the screen and read for a moment. "I'm no biologist, but it sounds like catabolism means breaking down molecules into smaller units. It's what living things do when they breathe air or eat food." She put her phone away. "I didn't find anything else for the last name Wakeful."

"If Chloe said the history was scrubbed clean, I believe her."

Margaret sighed. "She's so powerful. So pretty, and young, and powerful."

"She is all of those things."

"And I acted like a total dork the whole time, didn't I?"

Zinnia hesitated before speaking her mind. "I'm afraid that smearing your nose smudges and fingerprints all over the glass globe was not one of your finest moments."

"I got so excited. I've never seen glowfish before!"

"Me, neither."

Margaret moaned. "Plus being around someone as powerful and cool as a gorgon gets me all wound up."

"That's why I kept elbowing you to control yourself."

"Zinnia, I don't know how you do it. How do you keep yourself all locked down like that? Are you still hung up on the whole Jesse thing?"

Hung up? Margaret made it sound like being kidnapped and poisoned was the typical outcome of an office romance. Zinnia didn't like where the conversation was going. Not one bit. She steered it back on track.

"Margaret, you're usually the conspiracy theory person. Why aren't you suspicious of Chloe the way you are of the other DWM agents?"

"She's not really one of them," Margaret said. "Isn't it obvious? She's a sweet gal who runs a bakery. Anyone who runs a bakery is trustworthy in my book." Margaret waved her hands as though gathering her feelings into words. "She's like one of us, except cooler. Do you think she'd want to join the coven? We've had other members who weren't witches. Like Winona Vander Zalm. Chloe could join, right?"

"Maisy wouldn't like that."

Margaret snorted. "Maisy's not the boss of us. We just need to get Fatima's vote, and then it'll be three against one." She clapped her hands gleefully. "Do you think Chloe would even say yes?" She switched from clapping her hands to wringing them as her mood changed rapidly. "Oh, why bother? She probably thinks we're all lowly demon-spawn. She wouldn't want to be associated with the likes of us."

"Easy now, Margaret. Let's not get ahead of ourselves. Just because Chloe is beautiful and powerful and makes the best pastries in town, that doesn't mean either of us should trust her. Didn't you notice how adamant she was about her family not being connected to these power surges? She seemed awfully sure about that, despite a lack of evidence pointing to another party. For all we know, someone in the Wakeful family might have released that brainweevil you nearly ate last month." Zinnia shook the bag containing their lunch and the surge protector. "We might be smuggling something deadly into City Hall by taking custody of this thing we don't know anything about. This glorified snow globe could be a Trojan horse!"

"You're just saying that because you're jealous."

"Jealous? Of what?"

"You want to be the only one of us with a gorgon best friend. You want to have the other one, Charlize, come over to your house and drink tequila all the time. You two will have your fun, and you'll never invite boring ol' Margaret Mills."

Zinnia knew better than to argue with Margaret. The only way to truly shut her up was to wrap her from head to toe in packing tape, like a mummy. Perhaps Chloe would have an easier time with Margaret's friendship. At least Chloe could turn Margaret into a statue to get her to be quiet.

"You win," Zinnia said finally. "I was probably just being jealous. Be friends with Chloe if you want. She could probably use another experienced mother as a friend."

"She really could," Margaret agreed.

They continued walking without talking. After a few minutes, they both abruptly stopped and peered into the bag to check on the surge detector.

It wasn't uncommon for the two witches to have the same idea at the same time. Margaret had a knack for picking up Zinnia's thoughts, often answering questions Zinnia hadn't spoken out loud. Zinnia's own psychic abilities were limited to perceiving incoming text messages and phone calls a few minutes before they happened. Sometimes she got previews of the distant future, but so far, she'd been powerless to prevent the previews from coming about. What was the point in receiving bad-news-only spoilers of her own life? Alas, there was nowhere for Zinnia to take her complaints. There was no help desk for witches. The DWM had their own network of supernaturals and resources, but they rarely allowed witches into their midst. Many of the agents were shifters, and shifters had a long history of distrusting witches. Zinnia, Margaret, and the other local practitioners of witchcraft were on their own.

Zinnia shielded the sun from her eyes and peered into the bag at the surge detector. The glowfish seemed slightly brighter than they had been in the bakery. Or was the light simply more visible now in the shadowy depths of the reusable canvas carrying bag?

"It's the shadows of the bag," Margaret said, answering Zinnia's unspoken question. As usual, Margaret had done so without even realizing she was being psychic.

"The blue is eerie," Zinnia said. "When we get back to the office, should it sit on your desk or mine?"

"It would attract less attention in your office," Margaret said.

"That's what I thought, but I wanted to give you the option, since it came from Chloe, and she is your new best friend, after all."

Margaret shot Zinnia a dirty look.

"My office it is," Zinnia said.

"I wonder if Gavin will try to get it from you. He's got that gnome ability to sniff out items of value. We'll find out soon enough if it's worth something on the black market."

Zinnia smiled. It would be fun to see if Gavin would be attracted to the device. The office had gotten more interesting as of late. Working with supernaturals was definitely more lively than working with regular, non-magical people.

They started walking again.

A few blocks later, Margaret stopped in her tracks and tugged on Zinnia's arm. "Look," she said, pointing to a sidewalk vendor's table.

There, on top of a threadbare tablecloth, in between a pair of dusty candles and a seventies-era juicer, was a deck of tarot cards. Their coworker Dawna had been asking about tarot cards not one hour earlier. Talk about luck!

Both witches pulled out their wallets.

"Let me pay," Margaret said. "Since you got lunch."

"Plus, I'm carrying this heavy bag."

Margaret gave her a sympathetic look. "You poor, frail little thing," she said, as though speaking to one of her children.

Zinnia smiled. She was glad that whatever had been bothering Margaret had been forgotten for the moment and she was in a joking frame of mind.

Margaret asked the sidewalk vendor, a bored-looking, middle-aged man, "How much for the tarot deck? And what can you tell me about it?"

He shrugged. "I found all this stuff in my grandmother's attic. Give me ten bucks, and I'll throw in this thing." He pushed the cards toward Margaret, along with a piece of costume jewelry. It was a brooch in the shape of a shiny green beetle. The brooch was likely worthless, but it sparkled enticingly in the afternoon sunshine.

"Sold," Margaret said. She paid the man and handed the cards to Zinnia. "You give these to Dawna. I don't want any part in whatever happens next, but I do want to hear all about it."

"Deal." Zinnia slipped the deck of cards into the bag.

Margaret pinned the green beetle brooch to her lapel. "It looks Egyptian, don't you think? Like a scarab."

"It's cute," Zinnia said. "It brightens up your whole outfit." She didn't say that it wouldn't have taken much to brighten Margaret's outfit, which was a drab gray suit.

"You think so?" Margaret flicked at her loose gray curls self-consciously. She angled her body left and right, as though posing for fashion photos. "Does it make the flecks in my eyes sparkle?"

Zinnia raised an eyebrow. "Exactly how many compliments are you looking for today, Ms. Mills?"

"I supposed I did get one measly compliment from you, Ms. Riddle, which is more than usual, so I'll cash in my chips and leave the table."

The street vendor, who'd been listening to their playful insults, was chuckling. "You two are what my grandmother would have called a couple of characters. She would have loved you." He gave them a huge smile. "I'm glad you stopped by. Cleaning up her estate hasn't been easy, but it's been nice to see her favorite things going to people who'll appreciate them."

"Thank you," Margaret said. "And we're both sorry for your loss."

The man turned away quickly, wiping his eye.

Margaret and Zinnia bid him a good afternoon, and continued on their way.

* * *

Dawna Jones was delighted with the tarot deck. She clapped her hands and squealed.

"I have the best coworkers," Dawna exclaimed. "My coworkers are the best of the best! Well, except for that nasty Jesse Berman."

"You're, uh, welcome." Zinnia frowned and rubbed her thumb. Would it ever stop aching whenever Jesse's name was invoked?

Dawna clutched the deck of cards to her chest. "It's going to be hard keeping my mind on work for the rest of the day when I really want to play around with these cards."

"Take it slowly," Zinnia advised.

Dawna raised both eyebrows and stared up at Zinnia from her chair, her orange, cat-like eyes showing curiosity. "Take it slowly? What do you mean? Do you know something about readings?"

"Just what I've seen in the movies," Zinnia said with a light laugh. It wasn't true at all. She'd trained in several witch modalities before finding her specialty in the kitchen with potions. Card magic had been challenging, and she hadn't taken to it. Even just shuffling the deck made her thoughts feel confused, with too many possibilities overlapping each other.

Dawna was still staring up at her with those curious orange eyes, as though she knew Zinnia was fibbing. "You sure about that?"

Zinnia shrugged. "Never mind me. Take it whatever speed you'd like," she said with a smile. "Oh, and Margaret is opening a box of cream horns in the break room right now."

A gruff voice called out from Karl's office, "Did somebody say cream horns?"

"In the break room," Zinnia answered, quickly stepping away from the main traffic path.

There was a chorus of exclamations about the cream horns, and then a stampede toward the break room.

* * *

Two hours later, Zinnia rolled her chair back from her computer and stretched her arms. She licked her lips and wondered if her coworkers had left behind any of the cream horns. Perhaps she would go check. Good pastry should never be wasted. It was time for an afternoon break, anyway. She thought of her niece, Zara, who was probably taking her afternoon break as well. Zara was planning to play a prank on her coworker Frank using a fake jar of peanut brittle that contained pop-out snakes. What a goofball!

The back of Zinnia's neck tickled. She reached up to tidy the stray hair that must have come undone from her bun. Except there was no loose hair. What had tickled her neck? The skin on her forearms contracted into goose bumps. Something was amiss.

She glanced around her office. The walls were no longer the plain white they'd been when Jesse Berman had occupied the space. Zinnia had wallpapered the room, with permission and on her own time, with one of her favorite floral patterns. Everything in the office was where it ought to be. She listened, and heard nothing. Absolutely nothing. Not even the sounds of typing. That was concerning. She had seven coworkers, and it was unusual—no, impossible —for the office to be dead silent during business hours.

She got up from her chair and stepped out of her office. The desks in the main area—two double workstations and two single workstations—were all empty. She proceeded around the corner to the other private office, which belonged to her boss, Karl Kormac. His office was equally empty. She frowned and rubbed her chin. Had everyone gone up to the board room on the third floor for a meeting and forgotten to bring her along?

She returned to her computer to check her calendar and email for notices about meetings.

A flickering light drew her eye to the corner of her office. Something was happening to the surge detector. She'd placed it on her bookshelf after lunch, using it as a bookend. The glass ball was still resting on its wooden stand, exactly where she'd left it. But instead of emitting a pale blue glow, it was pulsating a bright blue and green.

Green?

Chloe had said the glowfish turned blue for danger and yellow for mating. What did green mean? And where had Zinnia's coworkers gone?

CHAPTER 5

ZINNIA PICKED UP her office phone to call someone about the apparent magic surge. She would try Chloe at the bakery first before calling the emergency number for the DWM. She didn't want to be the woman who cried wolf.

Before Zinnia could make the call, she heard the squeak of the main office door swing open followed by the rustling sound of someone walking in. Zinnia dropped the phone, the surge momentarily forgotten, and ran out to see who was there.

It was Liza Gilbert, looking about the same as when Zinnia had seen her at lunch time. Her eyes and nose were a bit red, but she didn't appear to be panicked about any supernatural happenings.

Liza was the youngest person working at the department. She had taken over Zinnia's desk after Zinnia was promoted to Special Buildings. Liza shared one of the two-person workspaces with Margaret, who frequently complained about the younger woman and her irritating cheerfulness.

Liza gave Zinnia a casual nod as she returned to her desk in no particular hurry.

Zinnia caught her breath and waited for her heart to stop racing. When she'd found the office empty, she'd assumed the worst—that foul monsters had slipped through from another dimension and eaten every one of her coworkers. Now, looking at Liza adjust her keyboard tray without fear of being consumed, Zinnia felt a little foolish.

Liza looked up at Zinnia and asked, "Is something wrong?"

"I don't believe so," Zinnia answered. "I was surprised to look up from my computer a few minutes ago and find myself alone in the office. Where did everyone go?"

Liza lifted a hand and counted on her fingers. "Margaret had to run over to the school to see about some trouble her kids got into. Karl came down with the afternoon munchies. Gavin announced that the office coffee maker needed unbleached filters, not the bright white kind. Carrot had a family thing. Xavier went off to make a personal phone call. And Dawna wouldn't say where she was going, but that's Dawna for you."

Zinnia nodded. "That's Dawna for you," she agreed.

Liza looked in the direction of Dawna's desk, which had a new good luck statue on it. It was a *maneki-neko*, a Japanese calico cat with one paw raised in greeting.

Liza asked, "How many cats does Dawna have?"

"Nobody knows," Zinnia said. "Not even Gavin."

The two shared a laugh. Zinnia was surprised to find how comfortable she felt talking to Liza. Zinnia had been avoiding the new employee because Zinnia chatting with Liza made Margaret's eye twitch with jealousy. Now that the two were alone, Zinnia was able to relax and be herself, or as close to herself as she could be with someone who didn't know about magic.

That Monday, Liza Gilbert was dressed in a tasteful tan blazer and skirt. Both articles of clothing were a size too large, which made Zinnia guess the suit was a hand-me-down from a family member. The outfit was conservative and timeless, yet Liza had inexplicably paired the suit with a blouse that resembled a well-used dish cloth, as well as the strangest shoes. They were a cross between boots and sandals. Luckily for Liza, she had a trim figure, so even her bolder fashion choices looked nice, overall. The young woman was also blessed with a face as cheerful as her personality. Her honey-brown eyes were large, wide set, and expressive. Her long, thick eyelashes allowed her to look fully "made up" with just an application of mascara. Her eyebrows were straight and full, almost bushy. She'd recently told the other women at work that her natural eyebrows were so pale they made her look like a ghost, so she'd remedied that perceived flaw by getting semi-permanent makeup tattooed across both eyebrows. The illusion was quite effective, though once you knew some of the light-brown "hairs" were tattoos, it was hard not to stare at them.

Liza had glossy, naturally blonde hair that she wore in a ponytail because she was trying to break her habit of fussing with her hair. It was a trait her grandmother, Queenie, found abhorrent and unladylike. Liza still twirled the end of her ponytail whenever she talked on the phone. Margaret did a great imitation of Liza, twirling her ponytail and biting her lower lip like a lovesick teenager in a vampire romance movie. Zinnia didn't make fun of Liza, partly because she didn't share a desk with her, so familiarity had not bred contempt. But mainly because it didn't seem fair for grown women to make fun of a kid. At twenty-one, Liza was barely an adult. If it wasn't for her office-appropriate clothes and makeup, she could easily pass for fifteen or younger. Zinnia had bumped into her at the grocery store once and not recognized the young woman in her weekend sweatshirt and yoga pants.

Liza sniffed and reached for a tissue from the box that straddled the crack between her and Margaret's desks. She blew her nose, bringing out the redness in her eyes. Zinnia knew that redness. Liza had been crying.

"You didn't mention where *you* went," Zinnia said. She'd meant to sound neutral, but it came out with an accusing tone. Her throat must have been tight from the panic over the glowing surge detector. Panic that was likely unfounded. The thing probably oscillated between green and blue regularly, and she didn't know that yet because she'd only had it for two hours.

"I was just..." Liza trailed off, took in a choppy breath, and made a strangled sound. Tears welled up and rolled out of her eyes.

Oh, floopy doop. "Oh, no," Zinnia said. "Don't cry." What was with her coworkers being so emotional today? Was it a side effect of the magic surges?

Liza's tears doubled in size and velocity. Telling someone to not cry had that exact effect. It was like a magic spell for people who didn't practice magic.

Zinnia leaned into her office to check on the surge detector. The glass ball was back to glowing a pale blue. Whatever it had detected moments earlier had passed. Zinnia brushed all thoughts about magical surges aside and turned her attention to her young coworker, who was now sobbing.

Zinnia grabbed Margaret's desk chair, rolled it around to the edge of the workstation, and sat next to Liza.

"There, there," Zinnia said, patting the young woman on the shoulder tentatively. "You're usually the most cheerful person around here." Too cheerful, as Margaret would say. "Something must be wrong."

Liza hurled herself into Zinnia's arms, where she continued sobbing. Zinnia adjusted her arms to an awkward embrace. She could feel Liza's big teardrops soaking through her floral blouse and wetting her skin. People could be so messy.

Zinnia kept patting. "Liza, is there something you want to talk about?" She lightened the mood with a little joke. "Did someone eat all the cream horns before you could get one?"

"No," Liza sobbed.

Zinnia craned her neck, searching the office for clues. Her gaze came to rest on Dawna's tarot cards, which sat on the crack between Dawna and Gavin's shared desk. "Did Dawna read your fortune and tell you something upsetting?"

"No." Liza caught her breath and then she gushed, "I feel like I don't even exist."

Zinnia took in a deep breath. "You feel like you don't exist," she repeated. "I know exactly what you mean. Just wait until you're over forty. You become completely invisible to some people."

"Huh?"

"Oh, you won't have to worry about that for years. And you're a lovely girl. I'm sure you won't become completely invisible."

"But what if I stop existing?"

"Do you mean... death?" Zinnia's throat tensed. "Liza, have you been having dark thoughts? About harming yourself?"

"Not exactly." The sobbing ceased, but Liza didn't remove her face from Zinnia's chest. "It's complicated and weird."

"Try me. You'll be surprised how well I understand things that are complicated and weird."

Liza sniffed. "Okay." Another sniff. "It's a mistake that I'm here."

"Do you mean in this job? It's an entry-level position. You're more than qualified."

"Not my job. I mean everything. I'm not supposed to *exist*. One day I'm going to disappear, and the world will keep going without me. Nobody will notice I'm gone, because I was never here in the first place."

Zinnia considered this. It sounded like garden-variety existential despair. Liza was young, so it could be her first taste of the bitter fruit of adulthood. Zinnia tried to imagine being in Liza's shoes, and what might be reassuring. Unfortunately, she couldn't lie and tell Liza everything would be okay. It wasn't in her nature. So she said, in her most tender tone, "What you're describing sounds frightening."

"I know, right? It's the worst." More sniffing and more wet tears soaking through Zinnia's blouse. "For a while it was just nightmares, but now I'm feeling it during the day, when I'm awake."

Zinnia considered Liza's predicament. What if her anxiety was about more than the growing pains associated with coming of age in a complicated world? If Liza had magical powers, the nightmares could be premonitions. Zinnia did have reason to believe magic ran in the Gilbert family. It was mainly rumor and speculation, but Liza's grandmother Queenie had been friends with Winona Vander Zalm, who'd confided in Zinnia that Queenie had some very interesting tales to tell.

Zinnia couldn't come right out and ask Liza about powers, not without exposing herself, but she could nudge the conversation in that direction.

"Have you talked to anyone about your nightmares? Maybe an older family member?"

"No. Just you." Liza pulled away from Zinnia's chest. A gooey string of saliva stretched from Zinnia's blouse to Liza's mouth before breaking. Zinnia pretended not have noticed and restrained herself from reaching for a tissue. Distantly, she found it amusing that she could reattach limbs and digits without queasiness, yet a bit of someone else's saliva was so horrifying.

"I had a bad one last night," Liza said. "I was lost inside a dark tunnel."

"Is there anything stressful going on in your life?" Zinnia gave her a playful smile. "Besides having to work with all of us here."

Liza grabbed another tissue and blew her nose. "I like working here."

"Has your boyfriend been treating you well?"

"I don't have a boyfriend."

Zinnia glanced over at the empty desk behind Liza's, where Xavier Batista normally sat. He and Liza had been dating, as far as Zinnia knew. But the younger generation didn't call it dating, did they?

"What about Xavier?" Zinnia asked. "Are you two still..." She couldn't bring herself to say *hooking up*. "Spending time together?"

Liza rubbed her red eyes. "I guess so." She added, "But we're not exclusive."

"Fair enough. You're both just kids."

"The nightmares don't have anything to do with him. It's probably just stress. My grandma is sick."

"I'm sorry to hear that. Is it Queenie, or your other grandmother on the other side?"

"Queenie." Liza smiled faintly. "The first time she collapsed was last month, right after she was here that day for lunch."

"I remember that day. What happened?"

"She needs a pacemaker, but she refuses to get one."

"I'm sorry to hear that. Did she say why?"

"Just that it isn't part of the Big Plan."

"As in God's plan?"

"Something like that." Liza's chin wrinkled. "She's going to die, and there's nothing I can do about it."

Zinnia said nothing. People died. She couldn't refute that.

Queenie Gilbert had looked so healthy just a month ago. Zinnia had an excellent recollection of the day Queenie had visited City Hall. It was the same day a brainweevil had come dangerously close to becoming part of Margaret Mills' lunch.

Could the three things—Queenie's collapse, the first magic surge, and the brainweevil's appearance—be connected? All three events had happened at the same time. Sometimes what appeared to be a coincidence was actually a clue.

Then again, coincidences did happen. Zinnia's perception of connections might be a product of her paranoia. Her detective friend, Ethan Fung, had warned Zinnia she might suffer PTSD following the kidnapping, although it might not manifest for a few months. She'd assured him that witches didn't get PTSD, but she had been on edge these last few months. She'd chalked it up to withdrawal from her emotion-numbing tea, but perhaps she wasn't as tough as she wanted to believe. Also, now that she had her family in her life, she had something to lose, and that changed everything.

Liza sniffed again. "I haven't told you everything, Zinnia."

"Oh?"

"The nightmare is actually really specific. You're going to think I'm crazy if I tell you."

Zinnia gave Liza a playful eyebrow raise. "You know the old saying. *You don't have to be crazy to work here, but it sure helps.* Tell me about your nightmare. I promise not to laugh."

Liza took a labored breath and stared woefully at Zinnia with her large, honey-brown eyes. "If my grandmother dies, I'm not going to exist."

Zinnia didn't blink. "Feelings aren't crazy," she said. "I believe you."

Liza's mouth dropped open. She rolled her chair back, away from Zinnia. "What are you saying?" Her arms twitched. "Is something going to happen to me?"

"I just meant that I believe you that you feel that way," Zinnia said.

Her voice a scratchy whisper, Liza said, "I'm going to fade away."

"No, you won't," Zinnia said adamantly. "I won't let that happen. No matter what, you have me on your side. If someone or something is threatening you, come straight to me. Promise?"

Liza looked confused. "Um. Okay."

"Straight to me. With anything. And if I'm not around, talk to Margaret."

Liza wrinkled her nose. "Margaret? She hates me."

"She doesn't hate you. She just takes a while to warm up to people. When we first met, she hated me, too."

Liza's eyes brightened. "Really?"

"Margaret's not the easiest person to get along with, but she's got the biggest heart of anyone I know. Trust me when I say you want her on your side."

Liza tilted her head to the side. "Since we're talking about Margaret, there's something I've always wondered about. What were the two of you doing that night at Towhee Swamp? That night I was attacked by a cougar?"

Unlike the rest of their conversation, Zinnia was actually prepared for that question. Smart witches always had cover stories ready. Zinnia relayed the cover story she and Margaret had agreed to, about how one of Margaret's children had dropped a beloved teddy bear on the walkway during the day and wouldn't go to sleep that night without it.

Liza seemed satisfied by the explanation. It certainly didn't hurt that Zinnia cast a mild version of her bluffing spell while she was telling the cover-up tale. Being a witch could be handy. Zinnia tried not to cast magic at work, but when used judiciously, it did make life a bit easier.

While Zinnia finished up the tale of the lost-and-found teddy bear, she noticed Liza was stroking a medallion she wore on a necklace. Only the top third of the circle was visible. It was a cream color, like synthetic ivory, and it had an intriguing filigree shape.

Zinnia leaned forward to take a closer look. "That's a lovely necklace."

Liza pulled the collar of her used-dish-cloth blouse up protectively. "It's just a piece of junk I found at my grandmother's house." She adjusted her blouse, further covering the medallion. The more she hid it, the more curious Zinnia became.

Jewelry was one of the most commonly encursed or encharmed items. In fact, right after they had returned from lunch, Zinnia and Margaret had cast several reveal spells on Margaret's new green scarab brooch, just to be careful. If Liza had unwittingly picked up a magical talisman, it could be the thing responsible for her recent nightmares.

Despite Zinnia's policy of not using magic on her coworkers unless absolutely necessary, she considered casting a more powerful bluffing spell on Liza to find out more about the necklace, as well as Gilbert family history. It sure would be nice to know. But did she have a right to know?

Zinnia's internal debate was interrupted by the sound of the office door swinging open.

All at once, everyone who'd been missing filed back in, returning from their various errands.

Margaret clomped over and gave Zinnia an accusatory look. "Your butt's on my chair," she said.

"I know where my butt is at all times," Zinnia retorted.

"It shouldn't be on my chair," Margaret insisted.

Zinnia looked over at Liza and said, "See? Margaret's like that to everyone, not just the new hires."

Margaret scowled. "What's that supposed to mean?"

"Nothing." Zinnia shook her head and got up from Margaret's chair. Softly, she said to Liza, "My door is always open."

Margaret plopped down on her chair and wheeled it around to her side again. She said to Liza in a theatrical tone, "My door is always open, too. Mainly because I don't have a door."

Liza smiled weakly. "Thanks."

Zinnia turned her back on her coworkers and headed toward the break room to check on the cream horns.

She had just bitten into the final surviving cream horn when she heard someone in the main area scream. Two more people had screamed by the time she'd dropped the pastry and run out to see what the fuss was about.

Something dark and bat-like was flitting around the main office area. It flew from the top of one bookshelf to another, then veered off and flapped into Karl's office. There was a ripping sound, and then silence.

Zinnia ran into Karl's office. Everyone else came in right behind her.

Karl was seated at his desk, wearing his yellow-lensed computer glasses. His mouth was agape and he was pointing at the window.

The bug screen that covered Karl's window—the only one in the office that opened—had been slashed open down the middle. Whatever had been flapping around inside the office had apparently slashed its way out.

Nobody spoke. They all looked at each other in shock and disbelief.

Finally, Margaret broke the silence. "It was a bat," she said. "A big one, but definitely a bat." The air sparkled as Margaret's bluffing spell took hold. Margaret flashed her eyes at Zinnia. It had *not* been a bat, but this was one of those times when magic had been deemed necessary, even by rules-touting Margaret Mills.

Zinnia silently cast a minor-key bluffing spell that would harmonize with Margaret's. The air seemed to tighten up around the group, as it always did.

"That was quite the bat," Zinnia agreed. "The poor thing must have been nesting in the eaves and flown in the door by accident."

Most of the coworkers nodded and murmured agreement.

Dawna Jones, however, gave the two witches a skeptical look. "Flown in through *what* door? Nuh-uh. I didn't see nothin' come in." She turned her head and narrowed her skeptical look to just Zinnia. "Zinnia, did you do something when all of us were out on our coffee break? Is this supposed to be a joke?"

"Zinnia didn't do anything," Margaret said. "It was just a bat, or maybe a large robin."

Dawna snorted. "A large robin? I don't think so. I swear that thing had scales. Red ones. Like a dragon."

Gavin laughed. "Oh, Dawna. I'm pretty sure it wasn't a dragon, seeing as how dragons aren't real."

Zinnia said, in her most serious tone, "If you'd like, Dawna, I can put in a phone call to maintenance and let them know that Ms. Dawna Jones saw a dragon with red scales flying around the Wisteria Permits Department."

Karl, whose office they were standing in, spoke up. "It looked more like a wyvern to me. Dragons have four legs. Wyverns have two legs, and their arms are their wings."

Everyone stared at Karl. Everyone except Zinnia and Margaret, who were staring wide-eyed at each other, wondering why their bluffing spells weren't working.

Zinnia turned to look at Karl just as his face turned beet red.

"That was a joke," Karl said. "Of course it was a bat. Not a dragon or a wyvern. I'm not crazy." He banged his fist on his desk. "Everyone get back to work!" He got up from his swivel chair with a loud groan. "Any excuse for tomfoolery," he muttered, waving them toward his door. "If the big, scary bat comes back, I'll let you know, and you can all go home five minutes early. But it won't. Because it's a bat." He waved at the window. "It's probably deep in the woods now, where it belongs."

Still muttering, the group left Karl's office.

Zinnia returned to the break room to finish her cream horn, even though her appetite for pastries had disappeared.

Margaret joined her, and they exchanged a look while Margaret cast a sound bubble for privacy.

Karl had been correct about the flying creature being a wyvern. Both witches knew there were a few wyverns living in the area. The creatures occasionally made themselves known to witches when it suited them— particularly when they were bored and in need of someone to share their unique perspective with.

Both witches knew a wyvern when they saw one, and moments ago they had. That alone hadn't been too shocking, but the color of its scales had certainly made Zinnia's heart race. She'd never seen a wyvern with red scales. She'd only seen males, who were blue or green. Female wyverns were extinct. And yet, the wyvern flapping around the office had been as red as that nutty Realtor Dorothy Tibbits' ruby-red slippers.

The wyvern had been female. And she had ripped her way through Karl's bug screen and disappeared into the nearby park.

CHAPTER 6

AT 5:45 PM THAT MONDAY, Zinnia found herself alone in the office once again.

Right after the wyvern sighting, the two witches had discussed matters and agreed the situation warranted a call to the secret agency. To be more precise, Zinnia told Margaret she was going to make the call, and Margaret spewed conspiracy rants for ten minutes before finally saying, "Fine! Call the Division of Wacky Monsters! But don't be surprised if you wake up tomorrow with your clothes on backwards and your brain erased."

Zinnia couldn't help but smirk. Division of Wacky Monsters was a great alternate name for the DWM.

Margaret had stormed out of the break room while Zinnia stayed behind to make the call from within the sound bubble. An agent who didn't give his name took the call with bored detachment, and said they'd send someone to check the place around six o'clock, after everyone had left for the day.

At five o'clock, Margaret had to go straight home to feed dinner to "the goblin hordes." Zinnia decided to stick around after hours to greet whomever the DWM sent to investigate the wyvern sighting. The agents would have been able to let themselves in just fine, but Zinnia didn't want to be kept in the dark about whatever was happening at City Hall.

There was a knock on the door shortly before six o'clock.

Zinnia unlocked it and greeted two men who introduced themselves as Agent Rob and Agent Knox.

The men did a double take as they looked at her.

"You're a Riddle," said the smaller, skinnier one— Agent Rob. "What an interesting coincidence." He waggled his eyebrows at the larger agent named Knox.

Knox frowned at Zinnia and said nothing.

Rob said, "The big guy here is the strong, silent type." He waggled his eyebrows again. "The emphasis being on strong." He grinned.

Zinnia asked, "And how is my being a Riddle a coincidence?" Her voice cracked, betraying her nervousness. She hoped her niece hadn't found herself in another dangerous situation already.

"We just saw the other one," Rob said. "Your daughter? Sister? I get all of you mixed up, since you look the same."

"My niece," Zinnia said, even though she shouldn't have said anything. "Is she okay?"

Rob guffawed. "Oh, she's fine. It was her coworker, Frank Wonder. He must have gotten the brunt of that last power surge. Can you believe the guy turned into a flamingo? The bright-pink kind!"

Zinnia had no problem imagining it. Frank did dye his hair the color of a pink flamingo, plus he had skinny legs.

"I had no idea he was a shifter," she said.

"Neither did he! He freaked out. We had to conduct a high-speed air chase to catch up with him and get him under control before—"

Knox clamped one enormous hand over Rob's mouth. He gave Rob a meaningful look and slowly released Rob's mouth.

Rob put his hands on his hips and stared defiantly at Zinnia. "Stop with your crafty witcher-i-doo, woman. You won't get any more top-secret information out of me. Not while I have my secret weapon." He reached into his utility belt and pulled out what appeared to be an ordinary ballpoint pen. He clicked it. "There. All good."

As the pen had clicked, Zinnia had felt the pulse of an anti-magic field pass over her. If she had been using a bluffing spell on Agent Rob—which she had not been doing—the pen, also known as a multi-pulse click generator or MPCG, would have counteracted it.

"I know about your MPCGs," Zinnia said. She knew about them from her niece's dealings with Chet Moore, but didn't go into detail. All part of keeping up the mystique of the all-knowing witch.

Knox said nothing. His eyes were already at work, scanning the office from where the three of them stood near the entryway.

"And I know both of you," Zinnia said. "You're the guys who got trapped in that gooey Erasure Machine along with Chet Moore."

Rob cracked a big grin. "Word of our fine services travels fast!"

Knox furrowed his brow. "It's not supposed to travel fast," he said in a deep, resonant voice. "It's not supposed to travel at all." He gave Zinnia a serious stare. "We're secret agents."

"Lighten up, man." Rob patted his associate on his large shoulder before turning to Zinnia. "Don't worry about the big guy. He takes things way too seriously." Rob said to the large black man, "You gotta learn how to not take everything so literally. Lighten up!"

Knox continued to look anything but lightened up. "I follow protocol. Our activities are secret."

Rob sighed and said to Zinnia, "He's just grumpy because someone shot him in the leg during that whole Project Erasure mess, so he had to scale back his workouts to only a couple times per day."

"That was him who got shot?" Zinnia gave Knox a sympathetic look. She decided to volunteer some information to build rapport. "You know, I was also there that night at the Pressman residence."

"No, you weren't," Knox said, shaking his head. "None of us were there. None of us. Because nothing happened at the Pressman residence. Nothing except for an ordinary gas leak."

Rob waved his hand and said to Zinnia, "Just go along with it. Let's say that if the two of us look familiar to you at all, it's because we all happened to be strolling along the beach boardwalk with ice cream cones the night the Pressman residence just happened to burn to the ground in what's been officially ruled as a completely normal accident." He winked.

Zinnia winked back. "That must have been it."

Rob rubbed his hands together and looked around the office. "Now, where are the dragons?"

"It was a wyvern, and there was only one," Zinnia said. "Also, it's long gone. It flew out the window."

Rob looked up. "If it came in here, that means there might be something else nesting in the ceiling tiles."

Zinnia followed his gaze up and shuddered. "I should hope not."

"Don't say that," Rob said. "Think positive! There could be several nests of things up there."

Zinnia caught on. What would be terrifying to a person who worked in that office would be exciting to a couple of secret agents who got their thrills from charging into dangerous situation.

"Several nests," Knox agreed.

Zinnia, who was still looking up at the ceiling said, "I suppose you should at least check, since you're here already."

Rob clapped his hands excitedly. "Oh, yes, we will. That air chase today got me pumped for more action, and I haven't neutralized a nest of something in ages." He jumped up onto the nearest desk—Dawna's—and removed an acoustic tile from overhead. Big clumps of dust showered down.

Knox frowned. "You're making a mess."

Rob retorted, "Neutralizing hellspawn is a messy job, but someone's gotta do it."

Knox shook his head. "We should have brought the dropcloths."

Zinnia asked, "Is there anything I can do to help?"

"Not really," Rob said, tossing aside another ceiling tile and stomping around on Dawna's desk in his steel-toed boots.

"Please don't destroy the ceramics," Zinnia said. She used her telekinetic magic to lift Dawna's good luck objects off her desk and move them to a bookshelf, where they wouldn't be stepped on by enthusiastic Agent Rob.

"That does help," Knox said. "We can compensate you for damages, but some personal effects may have sentimental value. Is this your desk?"

"It's my coworker Dawna Jones' workstation. These are all of her good luck charms."

Rob, who had his head in the ceiling, said, "That's common with cartomancers."

"You know about Dawna's abilities?"

"We have files on everyone," Rob said. He ducked down, looked her in the eyes, and said, "Sorry about the whole thing with Berman. That was some tough luck."

Zinnia pursed her lips. She was less than thrilled about having her personal details in files for anyone at the Division of Wacky Monsters to read. On the other hand, it was nice to get a bit of sympathy from someone who understood the full scope of what had really happened in Jesse's basement.

Rob continued to give her a sympathetic look. "That shouldn't have happened," he said. "What you have to remember is none of it was your fault."

Zinnia stammered, "Who-o-o said it was?" She felt her jaw ache and her eyes sting. The answer was her. Zinnia bore the guilt of feeling that the whole "tough luck" business with Jesse had been her fault. She'd been careless in so many ways. Of course it was her fault.

"It's going to be okay," Rob said. "Everything's going to work out just fine, Ms. Riddle."

She swallowed down the lump in her throat. It did feel good when someone lied to you about everything working out.

Zinnia cleared away the last of Dawna's lucky ornaments.

Rob stuck his head back up into the ceiling along with a device he held up to his eye, apparently to get readings.

Zinnia said, "Dawna began using a tarot deck today for readings. She might be activating deeper levels of her card mage powers. Do you think it's possible she summoned the wyvern?"

Rob grunted as he pulled his body all the way up into the ceiling. His legs dangled down, along with more streams of dust and decades-old construction debris.

"Cartomancers don't summon," Rob called down. "You're thinking of necromancers."

Knox, who'd been so quiet that his deep voice came as a shock, chimed in. "Necromancers summon the dead."

Rob's legs disappeared up into the ceiling. He called down, "It might have been an undead wyvern. Didn't you say it was red? There aren't any red wyverns anymore. Not in this world."

Zinnia walked over to stand under the dark hole in the ceiling. "What do you mean, not in this world? Are you saying this wyvern came through from another world? A full, three-dimensional world? Not just that hidden plane that lies over this one?"

"Sure," Rob said casually. "There are plenty of worlds besides this one."

Zinnia couldn't see Rob's face to gauge if he was joking, so she looked at Knox and asked, "Is he serious?"

"Rob? No. He's never serious."

"I mean about other worlds."

Knox's eyes got big, as though Zinnia's question had spooked him. He backed up toward the door. "I'm going out to the van to get some supplies." He left without another word.

* * *

Agent Rob continued to hunt for whatever was living in the ceiling. Agent Knox returned and then excused himself a few times. He was too heavy to enter the suspended ceiling, and seemed bored.

Zinnia raided the break room fridge to assemble a makeshift dinner, and made sure the falling pieces of ceiling didn't destroy too much of the office.

After a while, Zinnia's cell phone started ringing. She already knew who it was, thanks to her psychic preview, but she checked the screen anyway. It was Zoey, her great-niece, calling.

Zinnia called up to Rob, "Is it okay if I take a phone call?"

He grunted what sounded like *sure.*

CHAPTER 7

ZINNIA RELOCATED HERSELF to her office and answered the phone with a sweet, "Hello, dear. How lovely to hear —"

Zoey launched straight into a story without even saying hello. According to the sixteen-year-old, her mother had been having quite the day. After a kerfuffle at work with Frank Wonder turning into a flamingo, Zara had taken Zoey to the beach. Zara had then stripped off her clothes and walked into the ocean. It wasn't exactly swimming weather, but Zara was apparently possessed by another ghost. Already. And it was a powerful one who had changed Zara's physical properties.

When Zinnia found out the name of the ghost, she clutched her throat. Chessa Wakeful. The woman who was currently in a coma. The news was a shock, and yet it wasn't really a surprise. It had been inevitable. Of course Zara would channel a Wakeful. The woman had a knack for getting herself into the worst kinds of trouble.

As Zoey relayed the story, her usually sweet voice had a hitch in it, as though she was struggling to keep from crying. *What a day*, Zinnia thought. First Liza had been crying, and now poor Zoey was upset. Zinnia was supposed to be able to comfort the people who came to her. She was their elder, and she was supposed to know what was going on. But she'd never felt so powerless as when faced with the tears of a person she loved.

Zoey was saying, "And now she's been underwater for at least five minutes. You need to come here, I think."

Outside Zinnia's office, there was a crash. She peered through the doorway, her free hand cupping blue lightning energy in case she needed to protect herself or Rob. The crash had apparently been Rob, falling through the ceiling and narrowly missing Margaret's desk.

Rob jumped up from the floor. "I'm okay," he said.

Zinnia pulled her phone away from her mouth and asked him, "Any nests up there?"

Rob spat debris from his mouth. "I don't want to alarm you, but there are some nasty creatures living inside your ceiling. That's probably what drew the wyvern."

Zinnia glanced up. The same drop ceiling was over every part of the office. "I'll just stay here in the doorway," she said, as much to reassure herself as to let Rob know.

Zoey's voice came over the phone sounding panicked. "Auntie Z? Are you still there?"

"I'm here," Zinnia said. "I was just dealing with... a tradesman."

Rob snorted. "A tradesman? Way to kick a man when he's down."

Zinnia motioned for Rob to pipe down and fulfill the *secret* part of his secret agent status.

Zoey asked, "What sort of tradesman? Is that a code for necromancer or something like that? Are you out doing exciting witch stuff with your coven that you won't tell us about?"

Zinnia cleared her throat. "Never mind about that. Is your mother still underwater?"

"She just waved at me, so I guess she's all right." Zoey sighed into the phone. "Sorry I called you. It's not an emergency after all. Sorry I bothered you."

Zinnia felt her tender heart break a little at the sound of Zoey's voice. "Don't apologize," Zinnia said. "You were right to call me." In a brighter tone, she asked, "How are you doing? How do you like your new school?"

"I'm fine. School's good. I like school." Zoey sounded chipper, happy to be talking about regular kid stuff. "What more do you want to know?"

Zinnia leaned back and looked at the surge detector, which was still glowing blue with the occasional aquamarine pulse.

Zinnia asked her great-niece, "Have you noticed anything unusual happening around the school? Any sightings of creatures that shouldn't be there?"

"Not me, but some kids were out on a nature walk this afternoon in that forest park, the one where Mom fought off the giant bird, and they saw something."

"Another giant bird?"

"No. Just a bat. But they said it was a red, glittering bat."

"Interesting," Zinnia said. Wyverns were able to use glamour magic to hide their true appearance from non-magical people. Perhaps red wyverns didn't have that ability? Or perhaps the wyvern was injured from its journey between worlds. Either way, Zinnia was pleased to hear outside corroboration of what she and Margaret had seen, even though it wasn't good for the non-magical residents of Wisteria to be seeing mythological creatures. It was the sort of thing that sparked witch hunts.

Zoey asked, "Should I be worried about anything, Auntie Z?"

Zinnia chuckled. "No more than usual, dear."

They chatted for a few minutes about Zoey's teachers and classes, then Zoey said, "Here comes Mom. She's just walking out of the ocean like it's no big deal. She's so weird! Do you want to talk to her?"

Zinnia paused, and the silence was punctuated by Rob cursing at whatever was living in the ceiling.

Zoey said, "You don't have to talk to her now if you're too busy. She looks annoyed that I'm on the phone."

"I'd be happy to talk to your mother," Zinnia said.

"Hang on."

Zinnia waited, listening to Zoey talk to her mother while attempting to dry off her mother's hand and ear with a sweatshirt.

Zara came on the line sounding exuberant. She sounded fine, but Zinnia couldn't relax yet. Zara always sounded exuberant, even when supernatural entities were trying to electrocute her.

"Zara, did you shift into another creature? Zoey said you were underwater for a long time. Longer than five minutes."

"Something happened, but I couldn't have shifted." There was the sound of movement, of the phone receiver dragging across Zara's damp chin. "I'm still wearing my underwear," she said with a chuckle. Something jingled.

Zinnia tried to understand what her niece meant but couldn't. "Your underwear?"

"I mean I'm still wearing my bathing suit," Zara said, sounding very much like a teenager telling a fib. "It would have fallen off if I'd turned into, say, a sea lion."

"Zara, shifting is not an organic change, like a caterpillar turning into a butterfly. It's magic, and magic has a mind of its own. The clothes can shift with you, and then back again." In fact, Zinnia knew that some shifters found themselves wearing a different change of clothing—either their own or someone else's—when they shifted back to human form.

Zara asked, "Are you sure about that?"

Zinnia bit her tongue. Her niece was always questioning her. It was as if Zara knew how insecure Zinnia was about being the mentor in their relationship. Zinnia found herself answering in her own mentor's all-knowing tone. "The only thing we can be certain of with magic is that it's uncertain."

"Maybe I did shift," Zara said excitedly. "Do you think it's permanent? Like, I'm a shifter now? Witch plus shifter. I'd be a double threat."

Zinnia frowned. No shifter would be happy to hear about a witch who had their powers. "We ought to conduct some controlled experiments," she said.

"It's not totally dark yet. I could go dive back in."

"No! Don't!"

"Okay. I'll wait."

"Zara, you must resist your impulsive urges to dash madly into the face of danger. Safety should be your top priority."

"Absolutely," she said, with the tone that meant she was rolling her eyes at Zinnia's perfectly sensible precautions.

"Stop making fun of me," Zinnia said.

"Can you see me?" There was the sound of seagulls in the background.

Zinnia sighed. "Were you even listening?"

"Yes. You were saying it would be a disaster if I accidentally cast two conflicting spells on myself and got killed, like that time you killed me."

Zinnia fought down the guilt that twisted her stomach into knots. "I know you're attempting to give me a hard time, but I'm afraid that particular incident only underscores my point about safety." She rubbed her aching shoulder at the seam where the creature who'd briefly inhabited Zara Riddle's body had yanked it off.

"Safety first," Zara said, sounding agreeable. "Hey, thanks for comforting Zoey today when I went underwater, and thanks for being our mentor. Let's meet up soon, okay?" She must have been shivering, because Zinnia could hear her niece's teeth chattering.

"What's that sound? Are your teeth chattering?"

"No," she said, but her teeth chattered even louder. "Yes," she admitted.

Just then, Rob yelled out something that might have been a cry of danger or a whoop of joy. Something dark and drippy came down from the space over top of Dawna's desk. It plopped with a wet sound, oozed off the desk onto the carpet, and began to slither its way toward Zinnia's feet. Zinnia immediately jumped up onto her desk, her cell phone in one hand and a ball of blue lightning in the other.

Zara was saying something about the sun going down and having human skin. It was hard for Zinnia to focus on her niece's problems with a slithering black pile of goo heading her way.

"Great to hear," Zinnia said with forced cheerfulness. The dark, drippy, slithery thing entered her office. "Go home and get warm," Zinnia said hurriedly. "I have to run. Talk to you soon."

She ended the call just as Rob crashed through a different ceiling tile and launched himself on top of the slithering thing.

Zinnia said, "Roll aside and I'll blast it."

"No need. Just hand me a container. Glass, preferably."

Rob sounded calm, so Zinnia responded with equal calm. "What size? Would a baby food jar suffice?"

"A baby food jar? Sure. Do you have two of them?"

Zinnia reached into her purse, which was, handily enough, sitting on her desk. She pulled out two empty jars and handed them to Rob. He used his hands to scoop the dark, drippy thing into the first jar. He fastened the lid. Some of the entity remained on the carpet, pooling together again like liquid mercury.

Rob laid the second jar on its side and gently shooed the shadowy thing inside, the way a person might capture a house spider for release in the garden.

"There you go," Rob said tenderly as he screwed on the second lid. He tucked both jars into his utility belt.

Zinnia slowly climbed down from her desk. "What was that?"

"Unclassified creature number three hundred and eleven."

Zinnia crossed her arms and tapped her foot. "Is that all you can tell me? Agent Rob, I thought you were the fun one."

He made an exasperated face. "I've told you everything I know. That thing isn't from this world, so it doesn't even have a name. We call it number three hundred and eleven because it's the latest in a long list of creatures that don't have names."

Zinnia glanced up at the ceiling with suspicion. "Are you telling me that in the last month, since we've been having these power surges, you've detected three hundred and ten other unidentifiable creatures?"

His eyes bulged. "I wish! Nah, only about a dozen, but we just keep one list, and our organization has been around a while."

"If that creature is unidentified, how did you know how to deal with it?"

"That's a good question, and I'd love to answer it, if only I wasn't restricted from doing so by certain security protocols."

"I have a right to know what's infesting my office ceiling."

"Your ceiling is clear now. The wyvern, if indeed there ever was a wyvern, shouldn't be back now that its prey has been removed." He looked down at the pieces of broken ceiling tile on the floor as he moved toward the door. "Sorry about the mess. A cleanup crew will be along shortly. You know them already. They put in the new carpet after the Scholem homicide."

"Those were your people? I thought they were sent by the mayor herself, by Paula Paladini."

Rob shuddered at the mention of the mayor's name. "Shh," he said. "That's a name you don't want to say too loud."

They were interrupted by the arrival of Knox. The big guy bounced from one foot to the other. "We gotta go," Knox said. "There's another call. An urgent one."

Rob tapped his utility belt. "Thanks for the jars, ma'am. Call us if you see any more vermin."

And then the two agents were gone.

Zinnia looked down at the busted ceiling tile. She walked around the office, surveying the mess. Bits of ceiling tile, dust, and construction debris were all over everything. She might have cast a dusting spell, except she didn't have the appropriate supplies, let alone a feather duster.

There was a tap at the door, and it squeaked open. "Cleanup crew," someone called out hesitantly. "Okay to come in?"

Zinnia went to the door and waved in a small crew of what appeared to be City Hall's regular cleaning crew, plus a few people she recognized from the carpet installation in January.

"Sorry about the mess," she said.

"It's okay," said the older man who appeared to be the foreman. "It's not a dead lady this time, is it?"

"No," Zinnia said icily. "It's not a dead lady."

"Then it's okay," the foreman said. "We get paid overtime for this. Are all the rats gone now? They told me it was rats."

"Yes," Zinnia said. "It was rats. And they're gone now." She glanced up at the ceiling. "I hope."

CHAPTER 8

IT WAS DARK when Zinnia finally left the office that night. There was a chorus of frogs croaking in the nearby forest's ponds. Their chorus was so loud, it sounded like a generator was running. And then, all at once, the frogs went silent.

Zinnia stared in the direction of Pacific Spirit Park. Was that red glinting over the treetops moonlight bouncing off the scales of a red wyvern? Or just Zinnia's imagination?

She clutched the surge detector to her chest protectively. She could have left it in the office—the cleaning crew wouldn't have disturbed it—but she had an idea about using it for research.

After a moment, the chorus of croaking frogs started up again. Zinnia let out her breath and stopped straining her eyes to watch for the magical creature. If the wyvern wanted to make itself known to her, it would. Wyverns and witches went way back, and even if she couldn't see it, the wyvern certainly knew where she was.

Zinnia strapped the surge detector into the passenger seat of her car, and climbed into the driver's seat. She tuned the radio station to classical music, and drove around the town of Wisteria in random, looping patterns. She kept an eye on the glowfish in the globe, watching to see how the tiny creatures reacted to different areas of town.

After two hours, she'd learned that the globe was the brightest and greenest when she was near City Hall. Whatever was causing the power surges and creature outbreaks, it was centered on her workplace. The agents from the DWM were probably well aware of that, with all their technology and agents.

She considered calling her old friend Vincent Wick to see if he'd picked up any information with his own surveillance system. She even pulled out her phone to call, but decided she was in no mood to talk to Wick. She was still cross at him for electrocuting Zara with his van. The man had a tendency to shoot first and ask questions later. Zinnia didn't need him adding to the trouble at City Hall.

Zinnia returned home, had a light snack to help her sleep, and went straight to bed.

Unfortunately, the events of the day came back to haunt her in her dreams.

The next morning, she awoke early, sweating and agitated, patting herself to make sure she still existed. It seemed Liza Gilbert's nightmare about nonexistence was contagious.

Zinnia got ready for work, dressing in her usual clothes —a dark purple pair of slacks and a pretty floral blouse with blue and violet irises. While checking her makeup in the mirror, she noticed two thick white streaks at her temples. Had those been there yesterday? She had a few white hairs, sure, but didn't remember seeing streaks like these. But then again, Zinnia wasn't the type to spend a lot of time staring at herself in the mirror.

She held the white streaks between her fingertips, closed her eyes, and sent a pulse of energy along the hairs to the roots. Her scalp tingled as the hair pigment blossomed and spread itself down through the hair shaft by magic.

Zinnia opened her eyes and smiled at herself with approval. Much better. If she was going to keep up with the younger Riddles, it wouldn't hurt to look the part. In the back of her mind, she heard her mentor chiding her. *Witches must never use their magic for vanity or to alter their physical appearance!*

In her days as a novice witch, Zinnia had questioned her teacher. Why not fix a couple of minor flaws? Why not remove a few freckles? She would never do more than a good dermatologist with a variety of lasers could do. Her mentor pushed back. Fixing "a couple of minor flaws" was a slippery slope. It could start with freckles but expand to other things. Once upon a time not too long ago, there was a witch who wanted to be taller. Just a few inches. Only the same amount of extra height a pair of heels would give her! For her vanity, the witch had suffered a severed spinal cord, yanked apart in three places. Her body had eventually recovered, thanks to magic, but she was never the same. The story had given Zinnia the caution she'd needed at the time, but she was older now, better able to draw the line.

Zinnia fluffed her long, red locks and smoothed the no-longer-white hairs along her temples back into place. She shrugged off her feelings of guilt. It was just a few white hairs. And besides, almost every witch did it. Margaret Mills, who'd let her locks turn completely gray, was the rare exception.

Zinnia proceeded downstairs, ate a hearty breakfast, and checked the time. She was early for work, so she decided to take the pulse detector for a morning tour of town.

* * *

Zinnia was driving around in more looping patterns when a strangely dressed person on the sidewalk caught her eye. She did a double take. Had she slipped through a time portal and landed in 1955?

The strangely dressed person was a redheaded woman who could have walked off the set for a stage production of *Grease*. She wore a bright-pink blouse tucked into a black skirt decorated with a pink poodle. The skirt flared out voluminously, thanks to the full crinoline underneath.

Aside from the redhead, everything else looked new and modern. Zinnia had not slipped through a wacky interdimensional time portal after all. What a crazy thought!

Zinnia drove by the woman, chuckling to herself about the crazy outfits some people wore. Who craved attention so badly they dressed in a costume on any day besides Halloween? Zinnia glanced up in her rearview mirror and spotted a familiar face. She had her answer about who craved attention so badly. The woman in the poodle skirt was Zara Riddle, Zinnia's niece.

Zinnia kept driving, shaking her head. That Zara! Oh, well. Even if Zara was in a costume, at least she was wearing *something*, and not skinny-dipping in the ocean again.

Zinnia glanced over at the glass globe on the passenger seat. It was no brighter or dimmer than it had been a few minutes earlier. That was good news. At least Zara and her new spirit companion didn't seem to be connected to the power surges. Not directly, anyway.

* * *

Once she got to work, Zinnia kept thinking about Zara's poodle skirts, as well as the catchy, upbeat music of the fifties. Zinnia hadn't been born yet, yet she had a fond memory of the time thanks to countless movies set in that era.

That morning, she found herself doodling the number 5, and then the date, 1955.

Chloe Wakeful had mentioned that 1955 was the year some monsters had showed up in Wisteria. It seemed, based on the appearance of the brainweevil from last month as well as the wyvern and goopy creature from yesterday, that history was repeating itself. Zinnia didn't need to research the history of the entire town, since it seemed the phenomena was focused around the City Hall building.

Zinnia used her new computer network clearance level as the head of Special Buildings Permits to access old records for City Hall itself. The building had been under construction in 1955. She checked the site manager's daily logs from the construction period and found something odd. The records started in 1953, with the initial survey and ground preparation work. All of the daily logs from 1954 were present and accounted for. And then the records jumped to 1956. All the records for 1955 were missing.

Zinnia picked up her phone and made a call to the City Hall archives department.

A happy-sounding man answered. "Hey, Jesse. What can I do for ya?"

Zinnia was shocked to hear Jesse's name, but recovered quickly.

"This is Zinnia Riddle from Special Buildings Permits. Jesse Berman no longer works at this office."

"Oh, yeah? How come? Did he find somewhere better where he could slack off even more?" The happy-sounding man on the other end of the call laughed.

Zinnia rubbed her thumb. "Jesse Berman is deceased," she said.

There was a long silence on the other end of the line, and then the man said, "I, uh, didn't know. Sorry about that. How? When?"

"It happened in January."

"Yeah? What happened?"

"You can read about it in the newspaper archives, if you're that interested." She really didn't want to discuss Jesse's death, especially not with someone who she sensed was going to tell her what a great and wonderful man Jesse Berman had been.

"That's a crying shame," said the man on the phone, no longer sounding happy at all. "Jesse was a great guy. One of the best."

A great guy? Zinnia knew otherwise. She waited the appropriate amount of time before getting back to the task at hand.

"Yes, well, I was hoping you could help me locate some records. I can see from my computer here that the original construction logs for a certain town building don't seem to be digitized. I'm looking specifically for something from the nineteen-fifties."

"Yeah," he said. "Yeah, yeah. So, that's a big project. Honestly, I don't know when we're going to get around to scanning in all those dusty old books. Some of them might disintegrate before we get to them."

"We wouldn't want that. May I put in a request to move some to the top of the list?"

"Uh..."

"It should be simple enough. I'm looking for the daily logs from the City Hall construction, from 1955."

There was a long pause. "A lot of those old books got water damaged. Sorry. I wish I could help you, but that year's not available. My hands are tied."

His hands were tied. The ache in her thumb turned into a sharp pain. You didn't realize how frequently people used the phrase "my hands are tied" until you'd been kidnapped yourself.

"You can just send me the waterlogged books," she said. "I don't actually need them digitized."

"Yeah, I hear ya. But yeah, I can't do that."

Can't? Or won't? She knew bureaucratic laziness when she heard it. She had, after all, been working at City Hall for over a year now.

The guy muttered a few more half-hearted excuses.

Zinnia twisted left and right in her desk chair, her irritation growing. She looked around her office. Her gaze landed on the glowing orb, which was back in its place on her bookshelf. The color was currently pale blue with occasional flickers of green.

She sent a thought at the orb. *Nineteen-fifty-five.* The orb flickered green three times.

She sent another thought. *Is there something in the log book?*

The orb flickered again.

She didn't typically talk to inanimate objects, but she knew that some magical items had enough environmental Animata to give basic responses to simple questions.

She might have been reading more into the flickers than was there, but her gut told her she was on the right track getting her hands on those construction records.

Zinnia returned her attention to the flimsy-excuse-spewing voice on the phone.

"What a shame," Zinnia said into the receiver, pouring on heavy disappointment. The types of spells she could use through a telephone line were extremely limited, or else she'd have already whipped up a bluffing spell. She couldn't bluff the guy without finding him in person, but she could use non-magical techniques. She'd been trying to impress upon her niece how vital it was to not rely on magic, so it would be good for her to practice what she preached. Zinnia had even dosed Zara with power-voiding witchbane to teach the novice a lesson. It had not been easy for Zinnia to use witchbane on a family member, but she had done what needed to be done.

"Yeah," said the man on the phone. "Them's the breaks." His voice was distant now, as though he had the phone halfway to the receiver in his eagerness to end the call.

"Jesse would be so disappointed," she said.

"Oh?" His voice was at full volume again. "Was this for something good ol' Berman was working on?"

"Yes," she said. "It was sort of a passion project for him. He loved this building and was working on something to commemorate its anniversary."

"Oh."

"It was the last thing he was working on before he tragically—" She cut herself off with a choked sob.

"Well, if it's for Jesse..."

The man on the phone took the bait, and the rest of the phone call was as easy as catching goldfish in a bucket.

He promised her he'd put a rush on retrieving the original log books. Unfortunately, a "rush job" in archival records would still take two weeks. The physical copies were stored off-site for safety, in another town entirely, and the transit procedure was labyrinthine. It was no wonder the man had been reluctant to orchestrate the whole thing for a woman he didn't know.

Zinnia thanked the man, hung up the phone, and made a note in her scheduling software to follow up and look for the package in two weeks.

CHAPTER 9

TEN DAYS LATER

THE PACKAGE CONTAINING the construction log book from 1955 arrived earlier than anticipated.

It showed up late Friday afternoon, only ten days after she'd made the request. In fact, when she'd ripped open the envelope along with the rest of her mail, she'd been surprised to see a dusty, water-damaged, leather-bound journal fall out of the padded envelope and land on her desk with a thump.

Zinnia Riddle had forgotten all about her request for the old construction logs. Over the last ten days, she had been busy helping her niece deal with her powerful new ghost. Zinnia had done her best as a mentor. She'd been a good listener when Zara had regaled her with tales of her scuba lessons, and the funny antics of the instructor, Leo.

Zinnia thought she detected a hint of romantic interest in Leo, but any interest in the scuba instructor was overshadowed by Zara's all-consuming feelings for that wolf shifter, Chet Moore. Zinnia had restrained herself admirably from poisoning Zara against shifters. Chet Moore seemed like a decent family man, despite disguising himself as a wolf whenever it suited him. Zinnia hoped Zara would eventually lose interest on her own. The idea of another Riddle woman falling prey to a shifter who secretly despised witches turned Zinnia's stomach.

Anyway, the arrival of the log book was the perfect break from worrying about Zara's affairs.

Zinnia rested her hand on top of the leather-bound book and looked up at the surge detector on her office bookshelf. The orb was glowing bright green now, but that wasn't necessarily from the presence of the log book. The glowfish had been green for days. Chloe Taub didn't know what green meant, but advised Zinnia to continue keeping her eyes open for other strange things.

Other than the stuff with Zara, things had been relatively quiet for the last ten days.

Zinnia had not personally seen any other creatures since the wyvern, though she did hear whispered rumors around City Hall. Something rat-like had been chewing through bags of rice in the cafeteria kitchen. It had thus far avoided capture by rat traps. Also, some moth-like insects had been creating problems for the maintenance crew. They were so powerfully drawn to the security lights around the building that swarms of them blotted out the light completely in the evening, creating safety issues. Last but not least, there was an odd smell coming from the hand dryers in the washrooms. The scent was pleasant and floral, but odd nonetheless.

Zinnia's mind beeped psychically with an incoming text message that would arrive at her phone in a few minutes. It seemed Zara was going out for some celebratory drinks that Friday night with her scuba diving class, and would Zinnia like to drop in and meet the gang?

Zinnia's vision blurred. She blinked back the tears that threatened to come so easily now that she'd stopped guarding her heart with magical tea. She felt like such a silly, sad woman sometimes. To be so easily affected by such simple gestures of kindness! Floopy doop. She was in danger of becoming one of those sentimental old spinsters who collected porcelain figurines of angels and purchased grocery-checkout magazines featuring the royal family.

She waited for the actual text message to come in before responding to thank Zara for the invitation. She declined, vaguely citing "other plans." Her other plans for the evening consisted of going bowling with her office team, the Incredibowls. Zara didn't need to know that. She'd probably crash the game if she knew, and then demand to know everything about everyone present, from their magical powers to their personal histories and love lives.

Zara had a lot to learn about discretion. It was a small miracle she hadn't yet blown the lid off witchcraft for the whole world to see. Being a librarian, she had a natural inclination to want information to be free and available to all who needed it. That was where the two were philosophically at odds with each other. Zinnia didn't share the librarian's love for freedom of information. If all secrets were known, soon every food manufacturer would be adding witchbane to their products, for the "protection and peace of mind" of their customers, the vast majority of whom were not witches.

If the non-magical of the world were to ever find out that people weren't all equal, and some folks enjoyed special perks, it wouldn't be good for supernaturals. Not at all. The phrase "internment camps" often sprang up whenever the topic of "coming out of the closet" was discussed in depth by supernaturals. And, given the social climate of late, unveiling magic was the last thing the world needed.

Zinnia put away her phone, tapped her fingers on the log book, and continued to gaze at the glowing green orb. Staring at the wriggling glowfish was relaxing, like staring at a burning campfire or rippling waters. The creatures were completely sealed within their glass prison, yet they didn't seem to mind. They floated around, growing larger each day. Zinnia hadn't been feeding them—there was no way to access the globe interior without shattering it—so they had to be sustaining themselves on magical energy.

She stared at the glow and fantasized about a future where she didn't have to hide her identity.

If supernaturals became known to the world, the changes would be cataclysmic at first, but eventually a new balance would be found. Perhaps it was time for everything that had been in the dark to come out into the light. If the supernaturals seized control—and who was going to stop them?—they could do things right. New leaders could wipe the slate clean. Humanity could have a fresh start. A do-over.

"Bowling night," came a female voice in Zinnia's doorway.

Zinnia jerked her head up, startled to find Dawna Jones standing there. Startled, but not surprised. Dawna did have that cat-like ability to appear in places silently.

"That's right," Zinnia said. "Friday is bowling night. I'm going. Are you?"

"I have to," Dawna said. "Karl wants to bowl a perfect game. My tarot cards tell me it's possible, but only if everyone's there to cheer him on."

Zinnia smiled. "I didn't realize tarot cards could be so specific." She actually *did* know they could be that specific. It was sort of the whole point of cartomancy, because what good was a vague prediction? But she couldn't let on to Dawna what she knew. The budding cartomancer was doing well on her own, discovering her abilities slowly.

Dawna rubbed the base of her nose. "Did you smell the women's washroom today?"

"Not intentionally, but I do continue to breathe when I use the restroom."

Dawna didn't laugh at Zinnia's joke, which was a shame. People did not get Zinnia's dry humor. She was much funnier than Margaret, who was only funny when she didn't mean to be.

"That smell from the hand dryer is getting stronger," Dawna said. "Something strange is happening around here."

Dawna was joined in the doorway by her pale coworker, Carrot Greyson. Carrot chimed in, "And did you hear about the sneaky rats that have been eating all the food in the cafeteria? They're the size of raccoons."

Zinnia asked, "Do they wear little black Zorro masks?"

Carrot frowned. "I don't get it."

Dawna explained to her coworker, "Because if they wear Zorro masks, that would mean they are actual raccoons, not rats."

Carrot continued to frown. "My cousins Jeremiah and Jebediah are both working in the cafeteria, and they know what a raccoon looks like."

Dawna smirked and caught Zinnia's eye. "I bet they do," she said. She stage-whispered, "Raccoon stew."

Carrot clenched her fists like an angry toddler. "They're both vegans," she said.

Dawna waved her hands in the air. "Whatever! All I know is it's five o'clock and I am getting out of this spooky old building and relocating to wherever it's margarita o'clock."

Zinnia checked the time. It was only 4:55 pm, but that was as good as 5:00 pm on a Friday. She put the log book back into its protective bubble-wrap mailer, slid it into her purse, and got up to leave.

Gavin called out from the main office area, "It's only 4:55, Dawna."

"There you go again!" Dawna said to Gavin with irritation. "That's another one. Every time you correct me, I take away a point."

Gavin made a strangled sound and demanded to know how many points he was currently at, as well as what he could redeem these imaginary points for.

Zinnia smiled. It was a typical Friday at the Wisteria Permits Department.

Everyone gathered their things, made their way out of the office, locked up, and proceeded directly to Shady Lanes Bowling and Ales.

* * *

After the bowling games finally wrapped up, and Zinnia had returned home, she pulled out the old log book.

She used her page-finding spell to do a search on terms like *monsters*, *infiltration*, and *attacks*. She found plenty of material referencing one or all three of those keywords. The only challenge was reading the construction manager's handwriting.

A few hours into her research project, she called Margaret to discuss what she was finding.

Margaret answered, "You can't sleep either? It must be something in the air."

"I've been reading the City Hall construction logs from 1955."

There was a pause, then Margaret said, "Zinnia Riddle, you really make the single life sound wild and carefree. I mean, really. Who wouldn't want to stay up late on a Friday night reading City Hall construction logs from 1955? It's a good thing my life is so perfect already or I'd be jealous."

Zinnia snorted. "Try to contain your excitement."

"I'll try. What did you find out?"

"Either the construction manager went insane or there really were monsters infiltrating the building. Want to take a guess what the construction manager's name was?"

"Was it I.P. Freely? That's a popular one with my kids. Also, Seymour Buttz."

Zinnia chuckled. Margaret's children were always good for a few anecdotes. "It was Angelo Wakeful. The grandfather of the Wakeful triplets. The one Chloe didn't want to talk about."

"Ooh. Let me guess. He tried to tell people about the otherworldly things he was seeing, and they turned against him?" She sighed on her end of the call. "No good deed goes unpunished."

"And get this. He was young at the time, so this all happened before he got married and had kids. And he mentions meeting a pretty young blonde who showed up on the construction site one day, confused, like she had amnesia."

Margaret gasped. "This is good stuff, Zinnia. What happened next?"

"I don't know. Angelo's entries stopped just when things were getting good. Another gentleman took over the record keeping. Someone named Mitch Hamilton."

"Never heard of him."

"I'm not surprised. He's pretty dull. He doesn't write anything about ghosts or monsters, just logs of deliveries and payments."

"Boo."

"And we can't ask Angelo about the past, because he's passed away. I already pulled up his obituary to check."

"Darn. What about the girl with amnesia?"

"Also deceased. But before that, she became his wife, Diablo Wakeful."

"Diablo?" Margaret let out a low whistle. "Diablo is Spanish for devil, right?"

"Yup. And let's not forget that the guy's name is Angelo."

"That is uncanny. Angelo married Diablo. The angel and the devil. Then they had offspring who turned out to be gorgons. It has to be true, because you simply can't make this stuff up!"

"Do you think we should talk to Chloe and see what the family has to say?"

"Hmm. She sounded a bit touchy about the topic. We should wait until she and I are much better friends first."

"And how's that going?" Margaret had been trying to befriend the gorgon without much success.

"We're going to meet up for coffee soon," Margaret said, her voice high and tight.

"If only there were someone else we could talk to," Zinnia mused. "Someone who was around when the building was being constructed."

Both were quiet for a moment, then said, in unison, "Queenie Gilbert."

"Because she worked on-site," Margaret said. "She said she knew the building better than we did."

"She must know something," Zinnia said. "I hope she's well enough to talk to us and we're not too late."

"We shouldn't wait. Let's go see her tomorrow. My husband has the kids for the weekend."

"What do you mean? Did he take them somewhere?"

"Yeah," Margaret said. "Camping. I, uh, didn't want to go. I can protect my house from brainweevils, but not a whole campsite." She cleared her throat.

"I understand," Zinnia said. She didn't care for camping, either. "What time tomorrow morning do you want to meet up?"

There was a long pause, and then Margaret said, "I'm coming over there right now. I need to see that log book myself. I'll stay overnight."

"You will?"

"Sure. Thanks. Your guest room will probably give me nightmares, but I don't think I'll sleep much here at the house by myself."

"See you soon," Zinnia said. She wasn't sure why Margaret was so eager to come over, let alone how a beautiful guest room decorated in cheery florals would give anyone nightmares, but she was excited to share the log book with another witch.

CHAPTER 10

ON SATURDAY MORNING, Zinnia Riddle yawned as she slid into the driver's seat of her car.

Margaret Mills, however, was anything but tired. Her gray eyes were bright, and she had a bounce in her step as she rounded the car and hopped—literally hopped—into the passenger seat.

"You sure have a lot of energy," Zinnia commented.

"Why wouldn't I? This is so exciting. We're actually doing something, Zinnia, not sitting around in the back of Maisy's coffee shop *talking about* doing something."

Zinnia yawned again. After they'd spoken on the phone the night before, Margaret had arrived at Zinnia's house quite late. Rather than going straight to bed like sensible women, they'd stayed up reading the 1955 construction log book kept by Angelo Wakeful.

When they did finally head upstairs for bed, Margaret kept Zinnia awake until dawn, talking and giggling like a pre-teen at her first slumber party. Separating Margaret in the guest room hadn't helped, because Margaret simply yelled down the hallway about whatever thought had just popped into her head. The only way Zinnia could get to sleep was to surreptitiously cast a sound bubble spell around her bed.

"I just wish we were more rested," Zinnia said as she started the car engine.

"Who cares about sleep! We actually have a mission, Zinnia. A mission! How long has it been?"

"Since we had a mission? We did that location spell in January, and then we had our trip to Towhee Swamp. That was quite the mission."

"Exactly. It's been months. Way too long." Margaret fastened her seatbelt with a loud click. Even the click sounded cheerful.

For the first time since Liza Gilbert had started working with them at the office, Zinnia could understand why Margaret found the blonde so irritating. Cheerful people were irritating. Especially in the morning.

Zinnia put the car in gear but paused to yawn.

Margaret filled the lull in conversation with more cheerfulness. "The swamp was so much fun!"

"That's not how I remember it, and certainly not what you said about it at the time."

"Sure, it was dark and cold and damp, but didn't it feel great when we combined our forces and zapped that mean ol' cat with our invisible powerball?"

Zinnia recalled how powerful she'd felt in the hours following the attack in the swamp. It had felt good to zap the cougar. The power had gone to the witch's head, though. She'd gotten cocky and fooled herself into believing she was invincible. First came pride, then the inevitable fall.

Margaret punched Zinnia on the upper arm. "Stop overthinking, already! It's good to feel powerful."

"Get out of my head, Margaret Mills."

"Admit that we make a good team," Margaret said.

Zinnia sighed. "Fine. We make a good team. That invisible powerball was perfect."

"That's right." Margaret bounced in the passenger seat, making the springs squeak. "Me and you, forever."

Zinnia turned the corner and drove in the direction of the hospital. They'd made a few phone calls before leaving the house to locate Queenie Gilbert. One nice thing about a small town was it didn't take too long to track someone down.

Zinnia hoped that Queenie was feeling well enough for visitors, and that they weren't too late. One person they'd called was sad to inform them the woman had died already, only to be corrected by a friend who was standing nearby. Queenie must have been close to the end of her days.

* * *

They arrived at the hospital and found out which wing and room the eldest Gilbert was in. Then they stopped by the gift shop so they wouldn't show up empty-handed.

As they picked out gifts, Margaret said, "I can't say I blame the ol' gal for refusing a surgery to put in a pacemaker. How would you like one of those things inside your body, zapping away at your heart?"

"Shh," Zinnia said, mindful of the other hospital visitors shopping for gifts. "I'd be fine with the surgery if I needed one. Modern pacemakers are very small, and the recovery is fast. Besides, it beats the alternative."

"Stop being so stoic. Admit that you wouldn't like it one bit."

"Just because I don't like something doesn't mean I won't do what ought to be done."

Margaret looked up from the patterned socks she'd been digging through. "But how do you know what's supposed to be done if you don't feel like doing it? Do you have a little voice that tells you?"

Zinnia raised both eyebrows. "It's called a *conscience*, Margaret. Don't you have one?"

Margaret snorted and went back to browsing the socks.

Once they'd selected some gifts for Queenie Gilbert, they paid, and then applied more hand sanitizer. Being witches, their hands were already naturally antibacterial, and their saliva was probably a better disinfectant than whatever was in the sticky foam, but the dispenser was in a conspicuous place and not using it would have called attention to themselves. They finished rubbing the foam on their hands and proceeded to the elevator.

Once they were inside the elevator, which was empty except for the two of them, Margaret lightly ran her fingertips over the buttons on the control panel.

"Seven floors," Margaret said.

Zinnia waited, sensing there was more.

Margaret continued, "When I was growing up, I always imagined that one day I would live in a luxury penthouse on the thirteenth floor. I shouldn't have come to Wisteria, where the tallest building we have is seven floors."

"You couldn't have lived on the thirteenth floor anyway. Most tall buildings skip the thirteenth floor due to superstition."

"Do they really? I thought that was just a movie thing." Margaret continued to trace the buttons with her fingertips. "I'll just have to find a proper building that has a thirteenth floor, then. A real one, not a thirteenth floor that calls itself the fourteenth."

"Oh? Are you planning to move away? I don't know if a penthouse is the ideal place for raising four kids."

Margaret straightened up and stared at the floor indicator. "Let an old woman have her daydreams."

Zinnia scoffed. "You're not old, Margaret. You're younger than I am." The elevator dinged and the doors opened. "Besides, you can't leave me here in Wisteria all by myself."

"You won't be alone. You have your shiny new family."

"But they might not stick around, and then what?"

Margaret stepped out and shot a sly look over her shoulder at Zinnia. "You can buy the penthouse next door to mine."

"That sounds like an awfully large commitment considering I don't even know what city this imaginary thirteen-story building is in."

Margaret shrugged. "Fine. If you want to be cautious, you can rent for a bit before you decide to buy."

"Sure," Zinnia said, though she was anything but sure about what she was agreeing to.

The elevator dinged again as its doors closed behind them. The two women made their way to Queenie Gilbert's room, walking quietly out of respect for the patients and staff. Well, Zinnia walked quietly.

Zinnia got a flash of déjà vu. The hospital room at the end of the hall was the exact same one Zinnia had visited earlier that year, when Detective Ethan Fung had been recovering from his injuries. She felt a pang of guilt for having all but forgotten about the man lately. Between the strange occurrences at City Hall and the antics of the other Riddles, Zinnia had not thought about Fung much.

In a whisper, Margaret asked, "Have you heard from Ethan Fung lately?"

"Stop reading my mind," Zinnia said. That was the second time that morning. Did it come easier to Margaret when Zinnia was tired?

"But have you heard from him? Did he go to Venice?"

"Yes, he did. He sent me a postcard in March, or maybe April."

"I hate getting postcards," Margaret said. "I always put them up on my fridge like a normal person, but I don't like them one bit."

Zinnia was surprised by her friend's bitterness. "I'll keep that in mind."

Zinnia wondered, did *she* like receiving postcards? She gave it some thought. The answer was no. Not really. They were just a reminder of the fabulous adventures other people were having. Did *anyone* like getting postcards?

"Nobody likes getting postcards," Margaret said. "Nobody."

Zinnia didn't bother telling Margaret to stay out of her head. There was no point.

They reached the room and stopped at the doorway.

Inside the room was the usual hospital furniture—some tables on wheels, a visitor's chair, and one bed. The patient, Queenie Gilbert, lay on the bed. She was, contrary to at least one friend's impression, still alive.

Someone was sitting next to her in the visitor's chair. A woman. When she looked up at the two witches, Margaret made an air-gulping sound. Zinnia felt her throat suddenly constrict.

Sitting in the visitor chair was the mayor of Wisteria, Paula Paladini.

Zinnia's mind reeled at seeing Mayor Paladini outside of City Hall, as though someone had made a continuity error while editing Zinnia's life and spliced a frame where it didn't belong. She had never seen the mayor outside of their work building, not even at parades or the openings of new parks. For public events, the mayor always sent a delegate, along with the unspoken message that she was much too busy with important town business to pose for photos with comically large scissors.

Ms. Paladini was over sixty, and attractive in the way people used to call *handsome*, due to her poise and dignity. She had icy blonde hair streaked with white, or possibly white hair streaked with blonde. She had an aristocratic nose, narrow with a high bridge. The contrast between her light hair, pale skin, and other features was startling. Her lips were a deep mahogany red the color of dried blood. Her eyes were such a dark brown they seemed to be, at least in the dim light of the hospital room, entirely black. As the ice-haired woman looked over the two witches, she bared her teeth in something of a smile, revealing more black and white contrast: bright teeth with a single dark gap in the center.

Even seated, Paladini gave the impression of height and strength. The mayor always wore a pinstriped pantsuit with a crisp white shirt—every day, every season. She paired her suits with flat, soft-soled shoes. Even without heels she was still taller than most of the men at City Hall. As for her work, it was as impeccably black and white as her appearance. The mayor was highly respected by town residents, even the ones who disagreed with her policies. She worked tirelessly, putting in long hours and running through assistants and interns every few months. Sometimes it seemed Paula Paladini might not even exist outside of her office. She was the sort of exceptional mayor who deserved a much larger town.

"I'm glad you're here," the mayor said, getting to her feet. "You can keep our friend company while I take care of some business."

She left without bothering with introductions, as though she knew exactly who Zinnia and Margaret were, as well as what they were up to, and had simply been biding her time until their pre-ordained arrival.

"That was surprising," Zinnia murmured to Margaret. They were still in the doorway, not yet in the room. Queenie hadn't seemed to notice them yet.

Margaret made a nonverbal choking sound, then asked, "Did that just happen, or am I hallucinating? You saw her too, didn't you?"

"Yes. I saw Mayor Paladini. In black and white."

Margaret grabbed Zinnia's arm and squeezed her elbow. "That woman scares me. I know the whole town loves her, but I wouldn't be surprised if one day it comes out that she kidnapped a bunch of Dalmatians to make fur coats."

Zinnia pulled her elbow from Margaret's tight grasp, and patted her on the shoulder. "There, there. I'm sorry that watching Disney's *One Hundred and One Dalmatians* was such a traumatic experience for you." This was familiar conversational territory for the two witches. Margaret had been comparing the mayor to the cartoon villainess Cruella De Vil for years.

Margaret shuddered. "People shouldn't wear fur coats. It's just plain wrong."

"The mayor wasn't wearing fur," Zinnia said. "She was in one of her pinstripe suits, as usual."

"Even so, we don't know what's in her closet at home. Fur coats are murder."

"I know, I know," Zinnia said soothingly. "I assure you, I would *never* wear a fur coat." She had not gotten all of the details out of Margaret concerning her traumatic movie-watching experience. All Zinnia knew was that Margaret's phobia involved the classic Disney animated movie from 1961 about lovable puppies being pursued by a nasty fashionista named Cruella De Vil. Margaret wasn't old enough to have seen the film during its original theatrical release, so she must have watched a home video of the film at an impressionable age. A *highly*impressionable age.

Zinnia glanced over her shoulder to make sure the mayor wasn't in hearing range before whispering, "I haven't seen the resemblance until now, but I must admit the mayor would look exactly like Cruella De Vil if she dyed one side of her hair black."

"Maybe one side of her hair is already naturally black, and she goes to the hairdresser to make it all white and blonde."

That didn't seem likely to Zinnia, but she knew better than to argue with Margaret. She asked, "What do you think she was doing here?"

"Maybe she's a friend of the Gilbert family." Margaret shuddered again. "I have the strangest feeling she was sitting in here waiting for us."

"Either I have the same feeling or one of us is picking up on the other one's thoughts again."

There was a soft, polite cough inside the hospital room. Queenie Gilbert called out sweetly, "Hello? Is it time for lunch already? I've barely finished breakfast."

The two women entered the room and introduced themselves.

"We both work with your granddaughter, Liza," Margaret said. "I sit across from her."

"Liza is such a lovely young woman," Zinnia said. "You must be so proud of her. She does excellent work."

"Well, she does *some* work," Margaret said. "I'm not sure if I would call it excellent."

Zinnia elbowed Margaret to behave herself.

Margaret presented the older woman with their gift shop purchases: a bouquet of flowers, a puzzle book, and a basket of miniature toiletries. The woman looked over the gifts with polite interest.

Queenie Gilbert didn't seem very regal in her blue gown and adjustable hospital bed. Her snowy-white hair was curled on one side and flat on the other. She looked small and fragile in the bed, barely a bump under the thin covers. She thanked her visitors for the thoughtful gifts with a sweet smile that almost—but not completely—masked her pain. Her big eyes flicked back and forth between Zinnia and Margaret.

"You're probably wondering why we're here," Zinnia said.

Queenie replied with a vague, "Yes, dear?"

"When you were at City Hall last month for lunch, you mentioned you knew your way around the place."

"Yes." She blinked at them with her honey-brown, wide-set eyes. Her eyes were so similar to Liza's that looking at her was like seeing Liza in movie special-effects makeup and a white wig.

"Can you tell us about those days?" Zinnia asked.

"I was there when they built the place," she said. "When all of the exciting things happened."

Margaret slipped into the chair next to the bed and leaned in close. "What kind of exciting things?" Margaret couldn't conceal her excitement. "Do you mean flying things that look like bats but aren't bats because bats don't glitter?"

"A few of those," Queenie said. "Mostly people saw ghosts. Especially the fellows working on the third floor."

Zinnia asked, "Did anyone get hurt?"

"Goodness, no. Ghosts don't hurt the living, dear."

Ghosts didn't hurt the living? Margaret and Zinnia exchanged a look. They both knew otherwise.

Margaret said, "What about the construction manager, Angelo Wakeful? What can you tell us about him?"

Queenie's eyes lit up. She pushed herself so she was more upright in the bed. "Angelo was a wonderful man. He was a handsome one, all right! If my friend hadn't fallen for him, I might have..." Her expression clouded over. "If she hadn't loved him, I suppose I might have, and then everything would have been ruined. If she hadn't crossed over..." She broke into a coughing fit.

Zinnia poured a glass of water from the nearby pitcher and handed it to Queenie. The elderly woman struggled to get the water down, but seemed eager to continue the conversation.

She licked her lips and said, "Angelo was just *mad about* my friend, Diablo."

"That's such an unusual name," Margaret said. "We read in some old log books that one day a beautiful blonde showed up on the construction site, from out of nowhere. No memory and no idea who she was. She picked her own name and called herself Diablo. What did you mean about her crossing over? Do you know where she came from?"

Queenie's eyes twinkled. "Far away," she whispered. She straightened up even more, and craned her neck to look behind them. "Is he with you? Did you bring him?"

Margaret asked, "Who? Are you expecting someone?"

"The fellow. The one who tries too hard to be handsome," she said. "You didn't bring him? But we're running out of time!"

The witches exchanged a look. They knew one man who tried too hard to be handsome—their coworker, Gavin Gorman.

Zinnia asked, "Are you talking about Gavin Gorman? He's someone we work with."

Queenie's dry fingers rustled as she made a snapping gesture. "That's the name. Yes, I believe he's the one."

The witches exchanged another look.

Zinnia asked, "The one who does what? Is Gavin responsible for the recent events at City Hall?" If this mess was all Gavin's doing, Zinnia was going to cut off her supply of the gnome's favorite potions. If there was one thing she hated, it was being used and getting played for a fool!

Queenie's eyes kept twinkling. "You don't know," she said playfully. "You don't know, and I'm not allowed to tell. It would mess up everything. Diablo made me promise. It's all part of the Big Plan."

Margaret turned to Zinnia and said flatly, "She doesn't want to tell us. Don't you hate it when people won't tell us stuff?" She gave Zinnia a double eyebrow raise. "Perhaps we'll have to sit here *for a spell* and see if she changes her mind *after a spell*." More unsubtle eyebrow raises.

"We ought not," Zinnia said, giving Margaret a stern look. They couldn't responsibly cast any spells on a woman whose health was already so fragile. Not even a relatively harmless bluffing spell. All spellwork had side effects, which could put a strain on the body of both its spellcaster and recipient. Witches were highly resilient, so they barely felt it, but a strongly worded spell could kill the frail woman sitting in the hospital bed.

Queenie tilted her head to the side and gave them a curious look. "Why are you asking about Diablo and Angelo? Have you two found my key?"

The witches asked in unison, "What key?"

Queenie coughed some more, then looked around the room, her curiosity replaced with confusion. "Where am I? Who are you?"

"You're in a hospital," Zinnia said. "We're visitors. We both work with your granddaughter, Liza."

Queenie wrinkled her nose. "I don't have a granddaughter. Stop fooling around, you two. I'm the queen. I'll have you both executed."

Zinnia leaned over and hissed at Margaret, "Did you do something?" She didn't sense a spell in the air, but Margaret could be sneaky when she broke the rules.

Margaret gave her an innocent look. "Not this time. I swear. My word is my bond."

Zinnia gently asked Queenie, "What were you saying about a key?"

The white-haired woman gave them both a wide-eyed look as she scrambled backward in her bed, clutching her covers over herself and generally making Zinnia feel like a monster. Her voice trembled along with her hands. "What's happening? Are you a nurse? Is it time for lunch already?" Her gaze flicked up to someone who was entering the room. It was a nurse, dressed in pink-sherbet-colored scrubs.

"Two more visitors," the nurse cooed. "Aren't you lucky today, Queen Bee!"

The patient looked around, still visibly rattled. "Who's Queen Bee? I'm Elizabeth. Everyone calls me Beth."

The nurse said to Margaret and Zinnia, "Let's call it a day, ladies. She might be up for visitors again tomorrow, but our patient needs her rest right now."

Zinnia, who was still feeling like a brute, said to the nurse, "We both work with her granddaughter, Liza. I'm afraid Queenie doesn't know us very well. It's our fault she's upset."

"It's still good of you to stop by anyway," the nurse said. She not-so-subtly nudged them toward the door.

They left. As they walked down the hallway toward the elevator, Margaret said glumly, "So much for our mission. We didn't find out anything."

"What's with your mood swings today? Are you having a mid-life crisis?"

"No." Margaret pouted and kicked at a stray plastic bottle cap littering the hospital floor.

"Well, cheer up," Zinnia said. "Our mission was a success. We found out plenty." She counted the facts on her fingers. "We saw the mayor here, so we can assume she's connected. We know that Queenie was friends with the triplets' grandparents. We know that the strange events of 1955 were concentrated on the third floor. And best of all, we know that there's a key of some kind. A key that may unlock this whole thing."

"I bet Mayor Paladini is already after the key."

"So, we'll just have to get to the key first. What do you think about asking her directly what she knows? We could see if she wants to hitch up to our wagon, so to speak. I mean hitch her wagon to our horse. Is that right? I'm so sleep deprived. Anyway, maybe she wants to join forces with us. Just me, you, and Cruella De Vil."

Margaret squealed in horror.

CHAPTER 11

AFTER LEAVING THE hospital, Margaret and Zinnia went for lunch at Kin Khao, then picked up some groceries before returning to Zinnia's house. Margaret was planning to stay overnight again, which was fine with Zinnia. Perhaps they would get to the root of Margaret's mid-life crisis.

Later that afternoon, Zinnia spoke to her great-niece, Zoey, on the phone. Zinnia was surprised to hear that the teenager's mother would also be attending a sleepover that night—with the two Wakeful gorgons, Chloe and Charlize.

Upon hearing the news, Zinnia felt a pang of jealousy. Charlize had been *her* friend first, not Zara's! Had it been so easy for Charlize to cast aside Zinnia for the younger model of Riddle? As Zinnia considered her petty emotions, she suddenly felt empathy for poor Margaret. No wonder Margaret's nose had been out of joint. The same thing had happened to her.

Zoey said into the phone, "You don't think they'll turn her into stone, do you?"

"If they'd wanted to, they would have done so by now. They're both very powerful women. They don't need to invite someone over for a sleepover before stoning them."

"I think you may be right, Auntie Z." There was a clinking sound. "At least we found out the secret behind all those tiny pebbles we kept finding in the back yard. The ones that look exactly like hornets."

"Gorgon pest control," Zinnia mused. "Where did you say this sleepover is taking place?"

"At the coma lady's house. I haven't seen it, but Mom says it's an adorable cottage that sits behind one of the sisters' houses."

"Since you seem worried about your mother's safety, I ought to stop by and check on her," Zinnia said. She could also question the gorgons about their grandparents and what exactly happened back in 1955.

Zoey gasped. "Don't do that! I shouldn't have even told you she was going. Mom will kill me if she finds out I blabbed to you. Well, not kill me, because she's a pretty good mom, but she'll make *that face*."

Zinnia knew the face. It was the universal I'm-so-disappointed-in-you parental expression that induced shame without fail.

Zinnia really wanted to ask the gorgons about their ancestors as soon as possible, but she didn't want to humiliate her entire family by showing up to a party uninvited. It was a shame she hadn't been included, but she had only herself to blame. If only she'd accepted her niece's Friday invitation to the post-scuba-lesson gathering, she might have been invited to the next social event. She'd made her own bed, so to speak. Zinnia resolved to try being more flexible about socializing.

"What are you doing tonight?" Zoey asked.

"I'm not sure." Zinnia looked across the living room at Margaret, who was sprawled across the couch, fast asleep. "I have a few options," she said.

"You could come over and watch scary movies with me. Nothing with gorgons, though."

Zinnia frowned at Margaret. Even unconscious and snoring, the woman was effectively blocking Zinnia from spending more time with the family members that Margaret was so jealous of. Two points for Margaret.

"I shall have to take a rain check," Zinnia said. As she spoke, she received one of her rare distant premonitions. In the vision, she was staying at the other Riddles' residence, the Red Witch House, and cooking dinner with Zoey while Zara was... the vision was less clear, but Zara seemed to be in a hot tub with two other women. "Is your mother planning a spa weekend soon?"

"Not that she's told me about, but I could see that happening. Thanks to Mom's Mr. Finance Wizard ghost, I think there's more money in our budget these days."

"That's wonderful news," Zinnia said, keeping her tone cheerful to cover for her revulsion at the ghosts having so much influence in Zara's and Zoey's lives. "And how are you? Any changes?"

"If you are referring to the W word, the answer is a resounding..." She made a raspberry sound with her tongue.

Zinnia thought about her great-niece's lack of witchcraft powers. They still hadn't manifested, and her sixteenth birthday had been months ago. Zinnia's feelings on the matter were mixed. On the one hand, she wanted Zoey to be a witch so that they had more in common. On the other hand, the young redhead's life might be better without magic. Being a witch wasn't necessarily a fortunate thing in everyone's eyes. The girl's own grandmother had renounced her witchhood, after all.

Zinnia left Margaret sleeping on the couch and walked upstairs, where she spoke to Zoey a while longer about regular, non-magical matters.

* * *

That Saturday night, Margaret kept Zinnia awake late once again while they pored over Zinnia's magical reference books. They were looking specifically for information about creatures that came through from other worlds.

Some of the older books acknowledged that it was, indeed, a thing that happened from time to time, but they gave no information about how to deal with such incursions. The witches did find a diagram for building a surge detector, similar to the one that sat on the bookshelf in Zinnia's office, softly glowing blue and green. The book stated that when rifts between worlds occurred, the glowfish were part of the first wave of creatures to come through. They could be captured easily, using special traps baited with peanut butter. Zinnia was surprised to find that the glowfish swam through air, not water. What had appeared to be liquid inside the glass globe was actually air.

* * *

Sunday morning, the witches both rubbed sleep sand from their eyes. It was not the typical dried thin mucous, also known as *rheum* or *gound*, that might be found in a non-magical person's eyes. It was actual *sleep sand*, a magical ointment that refreshed the eyes and attention after a late night of reading.

While the witches were making breakfast, Zinnia received a phone call from her niece. Zara Riddle excitedly informed her aunt that she'd had a major breakthrough with the Wakeful spirit, and was going scuba diving with some people from her class. Zinnia told her to be careful—not that it would do much good.

After the phone call, Margaret announced, "I'm ready to meet your niece."

"I'm not sure she's ready to meet you."

Margaret snorted and pulled the breakfast quiche out of the oven. Witches didn't need oven mitts in their kitchen, thanks to their telekinesis powers. Margaret floated the hot pan over to a trivet. Witches still needed trivets to protect their counters.

"I don't know what you're implying," Margaret said. "I'm utterly delightful." She sniffed over the dish. "And I do make a lovely quiche."

"True," Zinnia said. "But as soon as Zara meets the whole coven, they'll inevitably want her to help them with the spirits they encounter. And Zara has so little control over the spirits that already come to her."

Margaret frowned thoughtfully as she sent a parade of dishes and utensils sailing around the kitchen, performing a synchronized dance before settling on the table. Margaret enjoyed using as much levitation as possible whenever she was away from her family. The children's father had no supernatural abilities, and so far nothing had manifested in the children. They were all blissfully in the dark about magic. When it came to matters of marriage and secrecy, and whether or not a witch told her spouse about her powers, opinions were mixed. It was up to the individual. Margaret had chosen to keep her powers secret from Mike.

The toaster popped, and Margaret made it appear as though the toaster had ejected the toast in a perfect arc aimed at the side plates. The quiche itself had a hearty crust, but Margaret had insisted they needed extra carbohydrates that morning. She sounded a bit like Gavin Gorman, with all his talk about macronutrient ratios, except Gavin would never double up on carbs.

"Such a shame about your niece's specialty," Margaret said finally. "I wish I had a solution, but there's not much a witch can do to protect herself once the spirits know they have a way in."

"Not much, no, but I have been working on something." Zinnia retrieved a jar from her hidden cupboard and set it in front of Margaret as they both took their places at the kitchen table.

Margaret clapped her hands. "Ooh! Delicious homemade jelly?"

Zinnia smirked. Despite appearances, the substance in the jar wasn't delicious homemade jelly. If anything, it was the exact opposite.

"Don't put that on your toast unless you want to be sick," Zinnia said. "It's actually something I've been working on for Zara. I thought of it when I was whipping up the last batch of brainweevil repellent. It should, in theory, block ghosts from infiltrating via the nostrils."

Margaret removed the jar's lid and took a sniff of the gel. She immediately made a retching sound and frantically replaced the lid.

"That's nasty," Margaret choked out. She pinched the tip her nose. "It smells exactly like the stuff you get on dental floss after you've skipped flossing for a few days."

"As it should. It contains periodontopathic bacteria from the banded tree-hoppers."

"Really? I didn't know that banded tree-hoppers had teeth."

"They don't," Zinnia said, making a squeamish face. "It's extracted from a set of glands."

Margaret made more retching sounds.

Zinnia tightened the lid on the jar and tucked it away again. "I have a few things I can use to lighten the compound. I could turn it a pretty lavender shade, and we all know a pretty color makes everything smell better."

"A pretty color can only do so much." Margaret rubbed her nose. "I can still smell that stuff. Ugh. The molecules are way up in my sinus cavities now."

"I'm sorry if I've put you off your breakfast."

Margaret dropped her hand from her nose. "Nonsense," she said, reaching for her fork. "I have four children I dine with regularly. Nothing, and I do mean nothing, can put me off my food."

It was true. The very next day after Margaret had nearly eaten a brainweevil that resembled a crinkle-cut French fry, Margaret had ordered the same fries for lunch.

* * *

On Sunday night, after Margaret had returned to her own house, Zinnia called her niece to get an update on the scuba diving adventure. It had sounded as though Zara was on a quest to find something at the bottom of the ocean.

The call went to voicemail.

Zinnia called her great-niece next. Zoey sounded both deeply concerned about her mother and bored at the same time—the way only a teenager could.

"She's doing something tonight with Mr. Moore," Zoey said.

"A date?"

"There's absolutely no chance of them dating," Zoey said. "Not since Mom found out about the coma fiancée and all that sneaky stuff."

"Good," Zinnia said.

"Why? Is there something wrong with Mr. Moore?"

"Uh..."

"There's something wrong with shifters, right? Nobody will come right out and tell me, but I get the sense that witches and shifters don't play nice together."

"There is a long history of distrust," Zinnia admitted. "But we ought not let old prejudices color our perceptions."

"Prejudices are wrong."

"Well..."

"Auntie Z?"

"Far be it from me to perpetuate the longstanding feud between our people, but some sorts of prejudices do exist for a reason."

"That's not how my generation thinks," Zoey said. "But luckily for me, I'm a freethinker, and I make up my own mind!"

Zinnia smiled. "And you're very good at it." Sometimes when Zoey spoke, it gave Zinnia so much hope for the future. "Did your mother mention when she'd be back?"

"She told me not to wait up. Do you think they're getting fake-married again?"

"With your mother, we can never rule out anything."

"No kidding. She went to that sleepover with a couple of gorgons."

"Don't worry about those two. They mean well."

"What about them? Are they considered shifters?"

"No. They're something else."

"Are they descended from gods and goddesses? That's what Mom's Monster Manual says. I can't read the text myself because I can't make my eyes do that thing, but she read out some parts to me."

"We must take everything we read in books with a grain of salt," Zinnia said. "Because books are written by people, and people are fallible."

"You can say that again."

"Is something bothering you?"

Zoey let out a sigh that sounded both deeply worried and also bored. "I think everything's okay. I've been working on my Witch Tongue drills, just in case."

"Excellent. When your powers kick in, you'll be far more ready than I ever was."

"Do you think it will ever happen? Be honest. Don't just tell me what you think I want to hear."

Zinnia rubbed her temple. Her mind ached with another incoming long-range premonition. She felt the awful sensation of herself suffocating, and then she saw flashing white teeth. There was a beast of some kind rescuing her, and she sensed the beast was under Zoey's control. Its sharp teeth were giving off blue sparks. She'd never seen anything like it.

Zinnia gasped for breath, and the vision was gone, thankfully along with the sense of suffocation.

"Be patient," Zinnia said softly into the phone. "I know in my heart that magic will find its way to you when you need it most."

CHAPTER 12

MONDAY MORNING, ZINNIA kept getting distracted from her work by the pulsating surge detector on the bookshelf. Since her arrival at the office, the glowfish "swimming" inside the air-filled globe had been glowing a steady bright green. Not blue.

At ten o'clock, she closed her office door for privacy and called Chloe at the bakery to compare theories.

Chloe replied with a chirpy, "Isn't it the greatest day ever?"

"Because it's cream-horn day again?"

"No, I mean because of what your niece did! Our whole family has had this horror hanging over our heads for a year, and now it seems like finally everything's going to be good again."

"I believe you're referring to some new development that I haven't yet been made aware of."

"It's my sister," Chloe said, sounding positively giddy. "She's back. Chessa. Isn't it the greatest day? Chessa is back!"

"She's woken up from her coma?"

"You didn't know?"

"Not until now, but congratulations. Are you able to tell me a little more about what happened? I haven't spoken to my niece yet."

"Sure. Hang onto your hat!"

Zinnia wasn't wearing a hat to hang onto, but she did listen in stunned silence as Chloe told her everything that had happened over the weekend, between the sleepover and now. Zara Riddle had played a vital role in uncovering a dark conspiracy at the DWM.

When Chloe was done, Zinnia said, "I'm so happy for you. I'm concerned about Zara, though. She won't suffer any lingering effects from the possession, will she?"

There was a hiss on the line. "What are you saying? Possession? My sister is not a demon." There was a rattle that joined the hiss. "We are not demon spawn. We are descended from ethereal beings, unlike *some* people."

"Possession was too strong a word," Zinnia said. "I'm sorry if I offended you."

The hissing died down. "My bad," Chloe said. "And I shouldn't have brought up your inbreeding. I apologize."

Zinnia nearly choked. Inbreeding? As far as apologies went, Chloe's was not the best Zinnia had heard. Even Karl Kormac gave better apologies, and that was saying something.

"Zara should be fine," Chloe said. "And if she has any lingering effects from being temporarily blessed with my sister's ethereal powers, I'm sure you'll help her." Chloe's tone became casual and friendly. "She says you're a very thorough mentor." Chloe giggled. "We went through a lot of wine on Saturday night. She told us all about your training methods. Did you really dose her with witchbane?"

Suddenly, Zinnia wanted to end the phone call. The only thing worse than being talked about at events you weren't invited to was hearing reports about how much fun the event had been and how much you'd been talked about.

"My training methods are private," Zinnia said icily. "The reason I'm calling you is because the surge detector —"

Chloe cut her off with a laugh. "That old thing? Let me guess. It's gone yellow on you?"

"Green." Zinnia squinted at the glowing orb to isolate the color. "Maybe a bit yellow? It's a shade that one might call *mustard*."

"Oh, just ignore it. The glowfish are probably going into mating mode. I wouldn't worry about these silly power surges. This town is crawling with magic, thanks to all the tunnels and weird stuff below us. It's something we'll have to live with. No point in worrying about a few surge readings here and there."

"Chloe, something is going on. We had a red wyvern appear in the office two weeks ago. A female."

"These things happen," she said lightly.

"Is the Department still looking into the source of the surges?"

Chloe paused before answering, "The Department is kind of busy right now. Ever since Zara, Chet, Rob, and Knox cleaned house last night, everyone's scrambling to cover their butts before the internal investigations. Their external operations might be down to a skeleton staff for a while." There was the sound of a baby crying on the other end of the line. "I'm so glad I work here at my peaceful little bakery," Chloe said. "I'd hate to be in Charlize's shoes right about now. The politics in that place have always been insane, and they're only going to get worse now."

"I can imagine."

"Like, seriously insane."

"Speaking of politics, is Mayor Paladini aware of everything that goes on in town? Surely she must be in the loop."

"Oh, Zinnia. You know I can't tell you absolutely *everything* I know."

"All right. Then what about your own grandmother? What can you tell me about Diablo Wakeful? And how it came to be that she arrived here in 1955 during a wave of monster invasions from another world?"

There was a hiss on the other end of the line. "Never mind about my grandmother. Stay out of our family business."

"But I believe your family history is relevant. I believe everything might be connected to the power surges."

"Stay out of it," Chloe said sharply.

"I know about the key," Zinnia said, bluffing.

"What key?" Her reaction seemed genuine. If there was a key, Chloe didn't know about it.

Zinnia kept up the bluff anyway. "I'll tell you about the key if you tell me what kind of magic runs in the Gilbert family. Or what Mayor Paladini is."

The hissing sound grew louder, as did the baby's wails. "I have to go." She ended the call.

Zinnia hung up her phone and looked over at the orb. It was still glowing mustard.

She queried the glowfish, "What do you little critters know about a key?"

The glow remained mustard.

"Come on. Give me a hint. Do you know the Gilbert family?"

The globe pulsed a brighter yellow.

"Good to know," Zinnia said. "Let me know if you happen to remember anything about a key. I could reward you by... Never mind. I don't know what you might want." She thought about it for a few minutes. "How about your freedom? I could let you out if you help me first with some information."

The color of the glow didn't change. It had been worth a shot. When things got strange, you never knew who or what might become your ally.

* * *

After her phone call to Chloe, Zinnia tried to focus on her work, but she couldn't settle in.

If the Department of Water and Magic was currently embroiled in internal investigations following a scandal, they wouldn't be trying very hard to figure out what was happening at City Hall.

Zinnia spent the rest of the morning poring over Angelo Wakeful's log book from 1955. The thing read more like horror fiction than a report. There were multiple rambling passages about breezes that carried pleasant yet unusual odors, not unlike the ones currently coming into City Hall through the washroom hand dryers. Workers reported having their lunches stolen by rats the size of raccoons. At times, the crew would be swarmed by moth-like insects that were drawn to their work lamps. The insects were harmless enough, but it slowed work on the site. Most of the phenomena occurred on the third floor, but then it spread throughout the building and surrounding parts of town.

Angelo also wrote more personal passages dripping with paranoia. He felt he was plunging into madness, seeing things that wriggled at the edge of his vision but disappeared when looked at directly. There was only a single page about the arrival of a beautiful young woman with amnesia, and then the writings ceased.

City Hall had been plagued in 1955, all right, but by what? And why was it coming back now?

As Zinnia closed the book, something being spoken outside her office caught her attention.

Xavier was saying, "Give me the key and I'll meet you there."

The key? What key? Zinnia listened with bated breath.

"No way," Liza said to Xavier, sounding annoyed. "It's my key. Only I can use it."

Zinnia straightened up in her chair so quickly her neck cracked. If Liza was in possession of a key, it could be the same key her grandmother had mentioned on the weekend at the hospital. It could be a magical key. If only Zinnia could get her hands on this key, she could run some spells.

Xavier said, "Then let's go now, and you can use your precious key to get us in. Make an excuse and I'll wait and leave a few minutes after you so nobody knows."

Zinnia leaned to the side so she could see the two young employees. It was ten minutes past noon, and the others were in the break room already for lunch. Judging from the way Xavier and Liza were talking, they thought they had their privacy. They'd forgotten about Zinnia in her office. Sometimes it was handy to be a wallflower.

From where Zinnia sat, she could see Liza's upper body in profile. Liza was half turned in her chair to talk to Xavier, whose desk was behind hers. Liza was stroking the pendant she wore on her necklace. It was the same medallion Zinnia had asked about the day Liza had confided in the older woman about her nightmares. Liza lifted the necklace slightly, and Zinnia saw that the bottom wasn't round like the top. It wasn't a filigree medallion after all. What Zinnia had seen that day was the top of a key!

Zinnia clenched both hands in silent triumph. The witches' trip to see Queenie Gilbert had born even more fruit, and that fruit was a key, currently being worn by Liza Gilbert.

Liza said to Xavier in a flirtatious tone, "Since you're so cute, sure. Give me five minutes, and then meet me by the elevator."

"I'm what? Cute?" Xavier pretended to be offended. "I'm a man. You don't tell a man he's cute."

Her voice sing-song, she said, "I'll call you whatever I want, soldier!"

"Soldier?" His voice got deep and gritty. "I like the sound of that."

"Five minutes," Liza said. She got up from her chair, and stopped at the break room to tell the others she had to leave the building to run some errands.

Zinnia noted that Liza was a smooth liar. It was always good to note when someone was good at lying, even if they were your friend. *Especially* if they were your friend.

As soon as Liza was gone, Zinnia emerged from her office, pretending to yawn. "Is it lunch time already?" she asked Xavier.

He looked up at her with large, startled eyes. "Zinnia! Have you been sitting there in your office the whole time?"

"In here?" She waved behind herself and played dumb. "Why, yes. My office is where I do my best work." She walked over to his desk and asked, "Where are you planning to meet Liza in five minutes?"

He blinked repeatedly. "Nowhere."

She stared at the young man with a look that said I'm-your-friend-but-I'm-also-your-elder-and-you-should-respect-me. It was a look she'd been using a lot on her niece—not that it did much good, but it came to Zinnia's face easily thanks to muscle memory. She was tempted to use magic on the young man, but she did have that rule about spells in the office. Sound bubbles were fine, because they didn't affect other people directly. Bluffing spells, however, were on her do-not-cast list.

Xavier swallowed hard under her shrewd look.

Xavier Batista was, along with Liza, one of the office's two new hires. The twenty-five-year-old's Mexican father pronounced his name HAV-ee-ay. Everyone else, including Xavier himself, pronounced the name with a Z at the beginning, rhyming with savior. Whenever people pronounced his name the wrong way, such as Ex-avier, like Professor X from the X-Men, the young man didn't correct them, but he did smirk in that cocky way of his.

Xavier had a long face, a broad nose, full lips, and bushy, dark eyebrows. His hair was black, and his eyes were a surprisingly light green, in contrast to his tan-colored skin. The light-green eyes were inherited from his Irish mother—a fact he never failed to mention on Casual Fridays, when he wore one of his many Kiss-Me-I'm-Irish T-shirts. Xavier relished the attention he got as a Latino-looking young man making such a fashion statement. He did occasionally refer to himself as a "skinny Irish boy," such as during retellings of his bravery that night in Towhee Swamp, when he'd shown an attacking cougar how tough he was. Never mind that the cougar had been retreating already when Xavier nicked it with his blade. To Xavier's credit, it was no small thing to face a wild animal. He truly had been brave. And later that night, he'd also been brave when he'd challenged various paramedics to fight him. Not very bright, but brave.

Despite Xavier's T-shirts and explanations about his family tree, some people in the office were still confused about the young man's ethnic background. Karl Kormac, the supervisor of the department, kept insisting Xavier was Pakistani, because he resembled a certain Pakistani-American actor whose name Karl couldn't pronounce.

Since Xavier had started working at the Wisteria Permits Department, sitting in Annette Scholem's old desk, he'd proven himself to be a reliable and courteous coworker. As a special bonus, he was adept at figuring out computer hardware and software issues—even better than Dawna. In the two months Xavier had been working there, the department hadn't needed to call in outside technical support once. Xavier had even, on his own free time, upgraded the office laptop. The sturdy old thing was able to boot up in record time. Less than a minute! The laptop had become so popular with staff that they'd needed to create a signup sheet.

Zinnia continued to give Xavier her shrewdest look. "You can tell me," she said. "Is your secret meeting place somewhere on the third floor?"

The whites flashed around his light-green eyes. "How did you know?"

"I've been around this place longer than you." She'd actually been around *everywhere* longer than him.

"What's it all about?" he asked. "Why is the third floor like that?"

She didn't know what he meant, but couldn't let on that she was bluffing.

"Tell me your theory," she said. "What do you think?"

"Politics?" He shrugged. "Or budgets. Or maybe superstition?"

She held her hand to her chin and tried to give the impression she had more than half a clue about whatever he was talking about.

"Hmm," she said. "And what makes you say that?"

His eyes narrowed. "I, uh, have to go."

"Go," she said with a hand wave. "You don't want to keep your girlfriend waiting."

"She's not my girlfriend." Xavier got to his feet and paused, frowning. His dark, bushy eyebrows nearly became one. "Why? Did Liza say I'm her boyfriend?"

"Would you like it if she did?"

He eyed her with suspicion. "Did she put you up to this?"

"Just go," she said with another hand wave. "Go and meet her, then ask her yourself.*Soldier.*"

Xavier left for the door, looking back over his shoulder as though he expected Zinnia to follow him to whatever secret place on the third floor the two young employees had been using for their meetings.

Zinnia didn't have any intention of following him. But she did have every intention of finding their secret meeting place, and she even had a plan. Step one was to make a copy of Liza's key. Well, technically step one was to talk to Margaret and get the other witch's help making the switch, and then step two was to make a copy of Liza's key.

If everything went according to plan, the two witches could have the mystery of the power surges solved before dinner time.

CHAPTER 13

LIZA GILBERT RETURNED to the Wisteria Permits Department office at 12:55 pm with her sporty blonde ponytail perfectly smooth and her light makeup perfectly fresh.

Xavier Batista didn't return with her. He would likely be along in a few minutes, as per the young lovers' plan. Zinnia and Margaret sprang into action, as per their own plan. The witches would need to steal Liza's key and swap it for a duplicate before Xavier got back to his desk.

Using a combination of non-magical distractions plus minimal levitation, Margaret and Zinnia successfully got Liza's necklace off the young woman's neck. They copied the key using a duplication spell that required two witches to cast, plus several costly ingredients, and then returned the fake key to Liza's neck without her noticing.

"Not bad," Zinnia said, complimenting her partner in crime once the deed was done.

Margaret beamed. "We should take our show on the road. Vegas is always looking for magicians."

"Are they? Really? I mean, aren't there far more people who'd love to find full-time work as magicians than there are people willing to pay eighty bucks to watch a forty-minute show of prop-based illusions and sleight-of-hand?"

Margaret thought about it. "Vegas is probably not looking for new magicians, but I still like the idea."

"Maybe someday," Zinnia said with a smile. "Let's keep the dream alive."

* * *

At 5:30, after everyone else had gone home for the day, the two witches met in Zinnia's office. Both sat in silence, solemnly staring at the stolen key.

Margaret frowned. "Are you sure this is the original? It looks exactly like the duplicate we made."

"That's sort of the whole point of making a duplicate," Zinnia said.

Margaret poked at the key. "What is this material, anyway? It's like something halfway between bone and plastic. It looks exactly like the synthetic compound we used to make the duplicate. And that stuff is only used for duplication spells, as far as I know, so what the heck is this?"

"It must be otherworldly."

"What does that mean?"

"It's a fancy way of saying I have no idea what that key is made of."

"You could have just said you didn't know."

"And you could have cast a spell to find out the material in the same time you've taken to badger me."

"Good point. Hang on." Margaret plopped her purse on the desk next to the key and started rummaging around. Her purse was packed full of disguised items. Margaret had four nosy children who didn't know their mother was a witch, so she didn't carry nearly as many eyeballs in her purse as Zinnia did. Margaret pulled out a tube of what appeared to be red lipstick—a shade she never wore—twisted it in reverse to open a secret compartment, and then sprinkled powder in a circle around the key. She muttered some words in Witch Tongue, frowned, and reported back, "Composition unknown."

"Do you think it's jinxed? That could hide the nature of the materials."

"I'll check." She took out a roll of sticky-looking cough candies and popped one in her mouth. She sucked off the outer candy coating and then spat the core of the candy—the magical compound part—onto the table, next to the key.

She said to Zinnia graciously, "Would you like to do the honors?"

Zinnia waved a hand equally graciously. "Be my guest."

Margaret nodded. "I do believe I'm up to it."

"Oh, Margaret. You do believe you're up to it? Please. You could do a reveal spell with a Popsicle in your mouth and both hands tied behind..." Zinnia's eye twitched as she trailed off. She didn't have PTSD, not really, but she did have a problem using everyday expressions that involved hands being tied behind one's back.

Margaret didn't seem to have noticed. She was already whispering the reveal spell in Witch Tongue.

They waited.

If the key had any magical enchantments designed to cause harm to the user, the reveal spell would give them a warning. In theory, anyway. The witches who failed to detect harmful spells also failed to report reveal-spell failures, due to being deceased.

There was no puff of ominous smoke in the shape of a skull, no spooky warning howl, and no glowing red light. The key seemed to be a perfectly ordinary key, albeit one made of an unusual material.

Finally, Margaret swept up the key in one decisive movement. "To the third floor," she announced.

"That's it? You don't want to do any more tests?"

"Oh, I'll do more tests, all right." She headed for the door. "I'll test it in everything on the third floor that looks like a keyhole."

* * *

The two women hadn't spent much time on the third floor, other than for the meetings they took in the boardroom. The most exciting part of those meetings was usually the elevator ride. Then they sat around a big table discussing the reports they made about other reports. The only interesting boardroom meeting had been the time Karl Kormac accused an employee of being a witch and then tried to fire them all. In hindsight, his behavior hadn't been that strange after all, since the woman really had been a witch. Karl had been on good behavior ever since, and thus hadn't been slapped by anyone.

Other than the route to the boardroom, the witches didn't know their way around the third floor, but navigating the departments was simple enough. All the employees had gone home for the day, so the two partners in crime had their run of the place. Most of the doors were locked, but that wasn't a problem. To a witch, there was no such thing as a locked door. They used Liza's key everywhere they could, and when it failed to open a door, they opened it the witch way.

They breezed in and out of every division, trying the key not just in every door, but also in every desk drawer, filing cabinet, and storage closet. It seemed unlikely that Liza and Xavier had been meeting for makeout sessions inside the storage closet belonging to Property Taxes Arrears Collection Services, but Margaret was determined to leave no keyhole untested.

By the time they had exhausted all of their options, it was hours past supper time.

Margaret handed the bone-white key back to Zinnia.

"So much for our mission," Margaret said glumly. "We didn't find anything useful."

"You've got to look on the bright side," Zinnia said, replaying the role of cheerleader, just like she'd done two days earlier after their meeting with Queenie. "We did find out that none of the keyholes on the third floor lead to a magical other world."

Margaret gave one of her laughter snorts. "You make it sound like we're hunting for unicorns and leprechauns."

"Honestly, I don't know what we're looking for, but I am reminded of a certain Sherlock Holmes quote. Something about how when you eliminate the impossible, whatever remains must be the solution." Zinnia rubbed her chin. "If only my niece were here. Zara would know the exact quote, I'm sure of it."

In a sing-song voice, Margaret quipped, "Zara would know just what to say. Zara's so smart, and she has such a good memory. Zara would make some lucky man a very fine wife."

Zinnia stared at her friend. "And if she were here right now, Zara would tell you to stop feeling sorry for yourself.

My niece has a wonderful gift for telling people what they ought to hear, whether they appreciate it or not."

Margaret crossed her arms. "Stupid key," she said. "Are you absolutely sure we got the right one? Are you one hundred percent sure we didn't double-swap it back and give ourselves the copy?"

They both looked down at the key.

"I am starting to have my doubts," Zinnia said. "Everything happened so fast. I was so worried about Xavier coming back and catching us."

"Maybe you should call your dear friends at the Division of Wacky Monsters and see if they can do some high-tech analysis on this key."

"No," Zinnia said vehemently. "They're busy right now, and besides..." She was reluctant to admit her true feelings.

Margaret jabbed a finger at Zinnia. "Hah! You don't trust them, either! I knew it. You always say I'm the crazy conspiracy nut, but now that you've gotten to know more about how they operate, you don't trust them, either."

Zinnia said nothing. She regretted telling Margaret about everything that had happened at the DWM's underground facilities over the weekend. Especially about what their esteemed doctor had really been up to.

Margaret gloated while performing a victory dance. "You don't trust them, either," she chanted. "You don't trust them at all!"

"They haven't exactly earned my trust." Zinnia glanced around the hallway between the third-floor offices. "And they've got all that high-tech stuff at their disposal. They've probably tagged us all with tracking devices."

Margaret stopped dancing and pointed a finger in the air. "That's it! We can put a tracker on Liza."

"A tracker? Do you mean a magic one? I've never heard of a spell to do that."

"I've got one." Margaret looked down at the floor. "It's not a spell, though. It's a high-tech hybrid device. I got it from Griebel Gorman."

"Griebel? You've seen him? I thought that little gnome was supposed to be keeping a low profile."

"He owed me a favor."

Zinnia narrowed her eyes. "Why would you happen to have a high-tech hybrid tracker device?"

Margaret waved a hand. "You're missing the point, Zinnia. I have one, and when we swap Liza's key back tomorrow morning, we can slap it on her and find out exactly where she goes."

Zinnia didn't like the sound of that. They'd already stolen and copied Liza's key. The operation had felt like madcap, zany witch fun earlier that day, but now the guilt was setting in. This was exactly why Zinnia had her rule about not casting spells on coworkers.

"We have to finish the mission," Margaret said, dead serious.

"But putting a tracker on her? I don't know. We could try following her."

"Oh? Are you going to disguise yourself as a bush?" Margaret snorted. "I'm sure Liza won't notice when a weird-looking shrub gets in the elevator with her."

"I could use my old-man glamour."

Margaret wrinkled her nose. "You are always way too eager to use your old-man glamour. I don't like him. He gives me the creeps. You can't do that. Liza is a sensitive girl. She'd know something is up, and she'd panic and destroy the key!"

Zinnia put her hands on her hips. "You're just looking for an excuse to use your tracker."

Margaret pressed her palms together in a prayer gesture. "Please can I use the tracker? Pretty please?"

"Sure. Fine. We'll use your tracker." Zinnia hadn't liked the idea of following her coworker anyway. Not that putting a tracker on Liza was much better, but at least it would make Margaret happy.

Margaret clapped her hands. "This is totally going to work," she said. "You won't regret it."

Zinnia felt her stomach fall. There was nothing quite like someone telling you that you wouldn't regret a decision to instantly make you regret it.

The two witches carefully checked that they'd locked all the doors on the third floor and left everything how they'd found it. Then they took the elevator down to the main floor, walked out to the parking lot, which was now dark, and spent a few minutes in a sound bubble planning the next morning's cloak and dagger activities.

CHAPTER 14

WHEN ZINNIA ARRIVED at work on Tuesday morning, she entered via the staff entrance at the side as usual.

Once inside the building, she heard the nearby din of several agitated people talking at once. She circled around to the front lobby and found a group of people in jeans and T-shirts gathered in a clump. The group was comprised of close to thirty people, the entire crew who maintained the premises. She recognized a few of them as the cleaning crew who'd arrived at the Permits Department two weeks earlier. They had efficiently cleaned up the dust and broken ceiling tiles after Agent Rob had captured the goopy, dark thing that had been living in the ceiling.

Zinnia scanned the crowd until someone met her eyes. It was a diminutive woman of about sixty, with dyed black hair and deep-set eyes ringed with dark circles. She'd been one of the cleaners who'd attended to Agent Rob's mess.

Zinnia introduced herself to the woman as the manager of Special Buildings Permits, and then asked, "What's going on?"

The woman, whose name was Ruth, looked up at her with small, dark, rat-like eyes. "We're not supposed to talk to management," she said.

Zinnia listened to the rumbling voices around them. The cleaners were talking in different languages, all at once, but one word did stand out: *strike*. They were threatening to go on strike. No wonder Ruth didn't want to speak to management on her own.

Zinnia smiled warmly at the small woman. "I'm not really management," she said. "My entire department is only one person, which is me."

Ruth frowned up at her. "That's nice for you, but I still can't talk about it. And not just because we're all waiting to get to talk to the mayor. If I told you what happened, what really happened, you wouldn't believe me."

"Oh, you'd be surprised. I've seen a lot of things."

Ruth shook her head, turned on her heel, and walked away.

Zinnia silently bid her a better day and walked toward the Permits Department. She clenched and unclenched her fists as she walked. It bothered her that she didn't know the housekeeping staff well enough to be trusted by them. She also wanted to know what had happened. She'd sensed that Ruth had good information. If Zinnia had simply used a bluffing spell on the woman at the start of their conversation, she could have easily compelled the woman into telling her what happened, and now she would be in the know instead of wondering.

Even as she admonished herself for not acting more quickly to cast a bluffing spell, she also congratulated herself for not whipping out magic at every whim. Just because she had powers didn't mean she was justified in using them whenever she felt like it. Cops couldn't just search any premises as they pleased. They had to get a search warrant from a judge. There were rules. Procedures.

Unfortunately, witches didn't have the equivalent of a judge they could consult for a search warrant, let alone a warrant to search around inside a person's mind. All witches and supernaturals had were each other, and their own judgment.

Instead of walking into the office, Zinnia detoured to the ladies' washroom on the ground floor to buy some time to think before facing Margaret.

The washroom smelled strongly of an odd fragrance, the smell that emanated from the hand dryers. It had smelled that way for so long that Zinnia scarcely noticed the blend of cinnamon, flowers, and something unidentifiable. A cactus fruit, perhaps?

The ladies' room was empty. However, the large mirror over the sinks was flecked with a full day's worth of water droplets. The garbage receptacles were full of crumpled brown paper towels. The cleaning staff must have been spooked or upset before they'd completed their overnight cleaning. What had it been? More raccoon-sized rats? More moth-like insects that covered the lights? A red wyvern, or the goopy thing it fed on?

Zinnia rested her palms on the soap-spattered counter. The marble was cool under her hot hands. She stared at herself in the mirror. *Well, hello there, Zinnia*, she thought. *What can I do for you, Zinnia? You look like someone in need of a mentor.*

That was exactly how she felt. She considered calling her niece, but this wasn't really Zara's department, since the situation didn't appear to involve a ghost.

Zinnia set her purse on the counter and went about reapplying her makeup. She kept glancing down at the hidden purse compartment that concealed the counterfeit key. *No.* It was the genuine key. Liza had the counterfeit, and the witches needed to swap the real one back this morning, so they could follow Liza using Margaret's tracker. Zinnia shook her head. Life got so confusing when you started stealing people's things and duplicating them, prying into their private business.

Then again the key wasn't Liza Gilbert's private business. Not entirely. If she was doing something with the key that allowed monsters from some other world to infiltrate Wisteria, the town's supernaturals had a right to investigate.

Zinnia's actions had consequences, like the ripples in a pond spreading from drops of rain. But, by the same reasoning, her inaction also had consequences.

Zinnia's thoughts turned back to the cleaner, Ruth. That woman hadn't been up to anything nefarious. She was a victim in everything that was happening. If Zinnia were to use one small spell to charm Ruth into sharing information, it would be for the woman's own benefit, as well as for the benefit of her whole crew. By threatening to go on strike, all of those cleaners had put their livelihoods in jeopardy. If they lost their jobs, or even a few days' pay, it would affect their families. What about the workers' innocent children, who needed to be fed and clothed? If Zinnia didn't cast her spell and get the information out of Ruth, she'd practically be taking food from the mouths of all those children!

If she Zinnia didn't find out what was happening at City Hall, who would? The DWM was busy with their scandal. And even if they weren't, what guarantee did she have they were even interested in stopping the phenomenon? More monsters meant more emergency phone calls and more work for the agents. In fact, the existence of monsters was their only job security. Zinnia didn't like to think such a thing, especially after meeting Agents Knox and Rob and finding them to be so personable, but she had to consider all the possibilities.

She removed and reapplied her lipstick for the third time.

Was she succumbing to conspiracy-theory paranoia? Was it insane to suspect the DWM was summoning monsters just so they could swoop in and save the day, thereby justifying their existence? She frowned at her reflection. It wasn't a very pleasant idea. Fire fighters didn't go around setting fires—except for a few sick individuals.

Even so, she had to wonder. Was this power surge phenomenon the work of one sick individual who worked within the shadowy organization? Something bitter roiled in Zinnia's stomach. It had been less than twenty-four hours since she'd spoken to Chloe and learned of the twisted atrocities committed by one of their own, one of their most trusted.

Zinnia blotted her lipstick and applied it a fourth time.

Two women came into the washroom, chatting about what a mess things were. They paid her no attention before disappearing into two toilet stalls.

Zinnia made up her mind. She was going to break her vow to not do magic on people at work. Again.

She left the washroom, detoured by the cafeteria to get two cups of coffee, and returned to the lobby.

She found the woman she'd spoken to fifteen minutes earlier, and offered her a hot drink.

The woman yawned and reached for the coffee but stopped herself. She looked down at Zinnia's clothes.

"Those flowers," Ruth said. "Are you the crazy lady who put up the wallpaper in her office?"

Zinnia swallowed hard. Now was not the time to be offended by being labeled a "crazy lady" simply for having some style.

"That's me," Zinnia said through a forced smile. "I'm the crazy lady with the wallpaper in my office."

Ruth smiled through her apparent exhaustion. "I like that room. It's my favorite." She snapped her fingers and pointed at Zinnia's chest. "And you have that funny thing. The snow globe that glows in the dark."

Zinnia's lips pinched at the notion of this relative stranger being in Zinnia's private office when she wasn't there. Of course Ruth was only doing her job, cleaning the dust from the shelves and vacuuming up muffin crumbs, and yet there was something about it that felt violating. As Zinnia considered this, she heard her conscience in her head. *Violating? You mean like dosing someone with magical mind-control potion so you can dig around in their head?*

Zinnia shook the thought away. She was doing this for the right reasons. And she would inform Margaret about everything the minute she got to the office—to ease her conscience, and also to prevent Margaret from casting a second spell on petite Ruth, thereby causing all sorts of spell interaction trouble.

Ruth was saying, "I like your snow globe. Very relaxing."

"I'm glad you like it," Zinnia said. "That little wallpapered office is my whole department. Just me. I'm not really management."

Zinnia lifted both cups of coffee again. *Come on*, she thought. What good was being a witch if people wouldn't take the bait?

The woman licked her lips and stared at the cups hesitantly. She had layers of puffy bags under her eyes. She'd been there all night with no sleep, so the coffee shouldn't have been a hard sell. Zinnia wondered if she should have gotten tea instead, or tried with another one of the cleaners.

"Sure," the woman said at last. "Thank you."

Bait taken! Zinnia raised one cup and then the other. "Cream or no cream?"

"Black," the woman said, and accepted the second cup.

"Perfect," Zinnia said, even though either choice would have been perfect. She had dosed both cups with a liquid potion that would compel the woman to open up her mind for about ten minutes. The potion was similar to one of her bread and butter spells, the bluffing spell, but in liquid formula. Most Witch Tongue spells could be cast via a compound, but not the other way around. There were many, many potions and compounds that couldn't be re-created verbally—not even with a dozen witches and a solid week of rehearsal.

Zinnia pulled from her purse what appeared to be a packet of artificial sweetener and shook it into her own cup. It was actually a general antidote to potions. The powdered compound was also a rather good low-calorie sweetener, though a witch wouldn't want to use it too frequently as it could cause the growth of nose warts.

As the woman took enough sips for the potion to take hold, Zinnia squashed the last of her lingering moral objections.

Ruth asked, "What's inside that snow globe of yours, anyway? It looks like bugs swimming around in there. My kids got sea-monkeys once. They didn't look anything like they did on the package. Have you got sea-monkeys inside that thing?"

Zinnia could see by the shape of Ruth's pupils—they were slightly oblong, like those of a goat—that the potion had taken hold.

"You're not concerned by the contents of my snow globe," Zinnia said.

Ruth didn't blink. She repeated back, "I'm not concerned by the contents of your snow globe."

"That's right. But you do want to tell me about what happened here last night."

"I do want to tell you." Ruth nodded. "Everybody saw ghosts last night. On the third floor. It was full of ghosts. They had a campfire, and there was a giant snake, and an ugly statue of an angry lady."

"The cleaning crew saw the ghosts of people, plus a snake, a campfire, and an ugly statue?"

Ruth nodded. "I didn't see it myself, but that's what the others said."

"How can a campfire have a ghost? Ghosts are usually people."

"The fire was there and also not there. They walked through it and it didn't burn." Ruth's pupils were completely horizontal now, like sideways keyholes. Even if Ruth's coworkers had been fibbing, Ruth wasn't. No one could lie when under the potion's spell.

Zinnia asked, "What time was this?" She had been on the third floor with Margaret, and they'd left around sundown.

"At midnight." Ruth closed the space between them and clutched Zinnia's forearm. Hoarsely, she said, "But that wasn't the worst thing. I would be glad if I was them and all I saw was the ghost of a campfire and a statue."

"Oh? What did you see?" Now they were getting somewhere.

"This week, I'm supposed to clean the top floor. That includes the mayor's office. You know her?"

"Mayor Paladini? I know who she is."

"Normally it takes a few hours to clean up there if you do a good job, and I always do a good job. Thirty-five years working here and nobody complains about my work."

"That's good," Zinnia said. "And did you see something unusual on the top floor?"

"Not the first time," she said. "But the whole time I was cleaning, I felt like someone was watching me." She took a timid sip of her coffee while her free hand mimed clawing at her throat. "That feeling, like I was being watched, it made me move so fast. I worked up a sweat. And I got everything done in less than two hours."

"And then what?"

"Then I came downstairs. Right here. The lobby. I thought since I was done so early, I would lie down on the couch and rest for a bit." She blinked. "You won't tell anyone about that."

"I won't," Zinnia said.

The woman craned her neck, looking around the two of them to make sure nobody was paying attention.

Zinnia prompted her to go on with the story. The spell's effectiveness would wear off soon.

Ruth took a few more gulps of her coffee and continued, her voice sounding less hoarse now. The caffeine in coffee dried the vocal chords, but the potion had a nice side effect of lubricating them.

"I was just about asleep on the couch when my supervisor came by and yelled at me. Oh, he was mad. I told him I finished the top floor, but he was so mad. He said there was no way I could clean the whole floor in five minutes. I thought to myself, oh, he is the crazy one! I was up there for two hours, not five minutes. What is he talking about? Five minutes?" She shook her head. "So I took my cleaning cart, and I took the elevator up to the top floor. I thought maybe I could lie down on the couch in the mayor's office. The mayor's couch is the best place for napping. You won't tell anyone about that, I hope."

"I won't tell anyone who would get you in trouble," Zinnia assured the woman. Margaret would be delighted to hear about all the couch naps that happened after hours.

"So I get to the top floor, and I hear something."

Zinnia's neck was starting to ache from leaning down to better hear the short cleaning lady. "And?"

The woman's face abruptly went pale and ashy.

"It wasn't a ghost," she said. "It was me." She thumped her chest. "It was Ruth." Another thump. "I'm Ruth. I was watching myself."

Zinnia had been prepared to hear about ghosts or monsters, so this revelation took her by surprise.

"You were watching yourself," Zinnia repeated back. "Are you saying you floated out of your body? As though you were a ghost, and someone else was in your body?" Something similar had happened to Zinnia's niece recently.

"No, I was there," Ruth said. "I was here, inside of me, and I was also there. Two places. Two of me. That's why I felt like someone was watching me. It was me." Her eyes grew big and round, which made the magically flattened pupils look even more strange.

"What did you do? Did you talk to yourself?"

Ruth shook her head vehemently. "No. I crouched down. Oh, you better believe I didn't talk to myself. Oh, no. I crouched down and I stayed where I was in that hallway with the glass walls. The lights weren't on there, so she didn't see me." She thumped her chest again. "I didn't see me."

"I understand, and I believe you, Ruth."

"I stayed there for two hours, and I didn't make a peep. I watched myself dusting all of the desks, and emptying the recycling. I stayed crouched down there the whole time, watching myself from the shadows."

"And then what?"

She blinked. "And then I woke up on the couch in the lobby."

Zinnia straightened up and gave the woman a frown. So much for the bluffing potion as a truth serum.

"So, it was just a dream?" She shook her head.

"No, ma'am. It was not a dream. I know what dreams are. When I woke up, it was my supervisor shaking me. His eyes were so big. I've never seen him like that. He was scared, you know? And he's a big man. He doesn't get scared over nothing. He said he was just sitting on the couch a minute ago, and he didn't hear me or see me come in. Then he turned around, and there I am. Oh, he was mad again. He yelled at me and said I was a witch. He said I cast a spell to get back at him for yelling at me."

"Are you a witch?" Zinnia asked. It was the height of rudeness to inquire about another supernatural person's powers, let alone dose them with a truth-serum-like potion and ask, but Ruth was already under the spell, and it had been her supervisor who'd first accused her of being a witch.

"Am I a witch?" Ruth's pupils snapped back into circles. She blinked and stepped back. She made the sign of the cross. "Of course I am not a witch. How could you say such a thing? Disgusting!"

As Ruth got louder, a few of the other cleaners in the lobby looked their way with mild interest.

Zinnia ducked her head forward to let her hair cover her face, muttered a thank-you to Ruth, and quickly made a beeline for the permits office.

CHAPTER 15

WHEN ZINNIA ENTERED the office, she found Margaret pretending to do her computer work while actually staring, goggle-eyed, at her deskmate, Liza Gilbert.

Liza had her earbuds in, and was paying no attention to the gray-haired witch. Liza was sipping coffee from her favorite office mug—a pink, chipped cup that read World's Best Secretary—while looking over her email inbox.

Zinnia tapped Margaret on the shoulder. "Looks like you could use a refill," Zinnia said, even though Margaret's plain white mug was three-quarters full. Margaret sucked back the coffee in one go, and followed Zinnia into the break room. They entered as Karl Kormac was leaving. He made one of his signature HARUMPH sounds, which he often used to cover fart bombings. Sure enough, the break room had a malodorous presence.

Margaret said in a low tone, "That man is not human. I don't know what he is, but those blasts he lets out are a side effect of some unholy inner combustion."

Zinnia cast a sound bubble spell for privacy.

Margaret made a choking sound and waved her hand under her nose. "Ugh. You've trapped us in here with Karl's infernal gases. Are you trying to kill us?"

"The sound bubble doesn't hold in odors, and you know that, Margaret." Zinnia pulled out a chair. "Now sit down and brace yourself. I have news. I believe the power surges and monsters are all connected to something powerful."

Margaret pinched her nose with her fingers. "More powerful than Karl Kormac's noxious winds?"

"Yes. What do you know about..." she paused for dramatic effect, "time loops?"

Margaret dropped her hand from her nostrils and took a seat, the smell forgotten. The truth was, it had dissipated almost immediately anyways.

"Time loops?" Margaret grabbed the single gray curl that poked out over the center of her forehead like a horn, and twirled it nervously. "Like from science fiction movies? Is that what's going on? How do you know?"

"Did you happen to come in through the front and see the cleaners gathered in the lobby? The ones threatening to go on strike?"

"I came in through the side door. Is that what that noise was? It sounded like the local scouts and guides were selling cookies in the lobby."

Zinnia thought that was an odd conclusion for a person to have jumped to, but not that odd for Margaret. The woman prided herself in being keenly observant, even though she wasn't. In January, she had walked past the dead body of a coworker without noticing.

"The cleaning staff were all spooked last night," Zinnia said. "Some very strange things occurred around here after we went home."

Margaret pouted. "I miss all the good stuff."

"I detoured by the lobby on my way in, and I spoke to a woman named Ruth."

"I know Ruth," Margaret said. "Tiny lady? Eyes like a rat?"

The description was as unflattering as it was true. "That's her."

Margaret smirked. "Maybe she's the one who's been eating bags of grain in the cafeteria."

"Would you just listen to me for a minute? Ruth didn't want to talk to me about what she saw, but I, uh..." Zinnia looked down at her shoes.

"You broke your rules," Margaret said, her voice jubilant. "Zinnia Riddle! You broke your little rules about casting magic at work, and now you can't stop yourself."

"Stop your gloating. It's okay to break the rules when it's necessary."

"You mean when the end justifies the means."

"Yes, Margaret," Zinnia said in the tone of someone admitting defeat. "You're right. I'm a rule breaker. Shame on me. Now, do you want to hear what Ruth saw or shall I keep it to myself?"

Margaret leaned forward over the table, resting her chin on her hands. "Tell me quickly before someone comes in."

Zinnia relayed the story about Ruth sensing that she was being watched as she cleaned the top floor, and then looping around to be in two places at once, watching herself while being watched. And then how she'd skipped back to sleeping on the lobby sofa with no recollection of traveling there, only to be yelled at by her supervisor and accused of being a witch.

"And?" Margaret blinked expectantly. "Is she? We could use another member for our," Margaret winked three times, "book club."

"She's not a witch," Zinnia said. "Ruth responded to the bluffing potion the way any normal human would."

"Did her eyes do that creepy goat-eye thing?"

"Exactly."

Margaret rubbed her cheeks with both hands, making her lips smack noisily against her gums. After a dozen smacks, she said, "There is some seriously bad juju going on in this place. We're talking messed-up, science-fiction, *Stargate*-meets-*Dr.-Who*, comic-book-movie stuff. Time loops? Seriously?"

"That's what Ruth told me, and she believed it to be true."

"Maybe Ruth is a demon. She is weirdly small."

"Demon or not, she was telling the truth. I gave her a strong dose of the potion."

Margaret rubbed her cheeks and smacked her lips some more. "What do we know about time loops?"

"Not much. I've never seen anything in any of my magic books about time loops."

"Do we happen to know any genius physicists?"

Just then, their coworker Gavin Gorman came into the break room.

Both witches popped the magic sound bubble, exchanged a look, and said nothing.

"You two," Gavin said, shaking his head. "You're clearly up to no good."

Margaret asked him, "Do you know anything about physics? Or about time travel?"

He poured himself a cup of coffee, shook his head at them, and left without a word.

Margaret shrugged and said to Zinnia, "It was worth asking. He's a gnome, so he can do that teleportation thing, which is sort of like time travel, in the sense that it's also impossible according to the laws of physics."

"Some physicists do believe time travel is possible, but only to the future, not the past."

Margaret got a far-away look in her eyes. "Ah, the past," she said dreamily. "If only we could go back and get a do-over."

"Be careful what you wish for. Ruth didn't seem very thrilled with her experience."

They were pondering Ruth's experience when Liza came into the break room.

Margaret snapped to attention and gave Zinnia a furtive, desperate look. If they wanted to uncover the mystery of the key and the third floor, they had to swap back the original key and place the tracker on Liza so she could lead them to the exact location.

Oblivious to the witches' plotting, Liza hummed a somber tune as she retrieved one of her bananas from the refrigerator. Nobody liked seeing Liza's bananas inside the communal fridge become gray and zombie-like, but Liza insisted refrigeration didn't harm the bananas' taste at all, while preserving them at peak ripeness.

Margaret gave Zinnia the signal, and they swapped Liza's fake key with the original. Margaret adeptly planted the tracking device, which was either a magical twig or an electronic-magic hybrid device disguised as a twig. Either way, if Liza discovered the tracker, the worst she could do was toss it in the nearest trash.

CHAPTER 16

ALL MORNING, RUMORS buzzed around the office about the City Hall cleaning crew and what they may or may not have seen.

"It's just a ploy to get another raise," Karl Kormac said. "People at the bottom are always trying to get more than they deserve."

Carrot Greyson accused Karl of being aligned with a certain political party, then people in the office took sides, and things progressed in the usual fashion for the rest of the morning, with passive-aggressive sniping and extra-loud file drawer openings and closings.

And, as per the usual fashion, the political dispute had all blown over by lunch time.

Shortly after twelve o'clock, Zinnia waited silently in her office. She listened as the exact same events she'd overheard the day before replayed. Xavier offered to take the key and go ahead. Liza refused to give up the key, and told him to wait five minutes while she went first. She left the office, stopping by the break room to announce she'd be out doing errands. Five minutes later, Xavier also left.

As soon as the door closed behind Xavier, Margaret crawled out from her hiding spot underneath Zinnia's desk. She put her phone on top of the desk so the two of them could watch where the branch-shaped tracker went, using a custom app on Margaret's phone.

"This is really quite sophisticated," Zinnia said, admiring the app's three-dimensional functionality. "This tracker is the real science-fiction, *Stargate*-meets-*Dr.-Who*, comic-book-movie stuff."

"It's okay," Margaret said begrudgingly. "Shh. They're in the elevator now."

Both watched in tense anticipation.

"They're moving up in the elevator," Margaret said.

Zinnia could see that, thanks to the 3D visualization on the phone's screen, but she let Margaret narrate anyway.

"Second floor," Margaret said. "The elevator's stopping, but they're not getting off."

"The elevator might be picking up someone else."

"Good point. And now they're traveling up. Up. Top floor. Number five." The witches leaned in close enough to bump heads. "They're still in the elevator, though. They didn't get off on the fifth floor. Going down now."

"Why wouldn't they get off on the third floor? Why go all the way up just to go down again?"

"I don't know." Margaret frowned at the screen. "Do you think maybe we were wrong? It's possible they just ride up and down the elevator for an hour."

"That's a strange way to spend lunch break."

The app showed the tracker and the elevator stopping on the third floor. The glowing light that represented the tracker on Liza jiggled, almost imperceptibly, and then abruptly blinked off. The program on the phone flashed a yellow text alert: *Signal lost.*

Margaret made an angry rhino noise.

"We lost them," Zinnia said. Unlike Margaret, she hated stating the obvious, but there it was. The signal was lost. Liza and Xavier were lost.

They would be back again before one o'clock, and the witches could try another tactic. They'd probably resort to questioning Liza directly with the help of a potion. They had more options, but it was still disappointing the tracker hadn't worked.

Margaret shook her phone. "That gnome had better give me a full refund."

Something bright in the corner of the office caught Zinnia's eye. She elbowed Margaret and pointed at the surge detector. "Look! It's brighter now."

Margaret looked. Her face went slack. "It is brighter. And lemon yellow."

"Chloe said it was meaningless, that it meant the glowfish were just phasing into their mating cycle, but I swear that thing surged at the exact same moment we lost the signal in the elevator."

"It's connected," Margaret gasped. "Everything's connected. It's all a huge conspiracy."

"As much as it pains me to admit this, you may be right. The Gilbert family. Mayor Paladini. The monsters. The time loop. It could all be related."

"We have to get the truth out of the Gilbert girl. I don't care if she finds out we're onto her. We need to know what she's doing. Lives are at risk!" Margaret dug into her purse and pulled out a vial of dark sludge. "We're doing Trinada's Confession Hex on her."

Zinnia couldn't shake her head hard enough. "No way! No! That's a terrible plan."

"Fine. I'll do it myself."

"Do I need to remind you of what happened the last time you performed Trinada's Confession Hex? Karl still isn't back to normal. He hasn't mentioned his retirement date countdown since you forced that false confession out of him."

Margaret stuck her nose in the air. "My spell was working perfectly fine, right up until you jinxed it with your sloppy syntax on that second spell."

"No, it was not working perfectly fine. It wasn't working at all. The only thing your spell did was give him the munchies, and even that's debatable."

Margaret shook the vial of dark sludge. It was not one of her better-disguised purse supplies. The vial had simply been labeled, by hand, as *sourdough fudge starter.* As far as Zinnia knew, there was no such thing as sourdough fudge starter. It looked more like a medical sample.

Margaret was still clutching the vial, her expression earnest. "We have to step up our game," she said. "That darn perky Gilbert girl is hiding something, and now she's got poor, sweet Xavier mixed up in it."

"Since when do you care about Xavier?" Zinnia swiped the vial from Margaret and examined it. "And since when is half of your koodzuberry enzyme used up? This was full last month when you bought it from Tansy Wick. I knew I should have stopped her from selling it to you. What have you been up to?"

Margaret snatched the vial back and buried it in her purse. She hissed, "None of your business, witch."

Zinnia raised her eyebrows. "Oh, no you didn't." Margaret did not just call her a witch. And after everything Zinnia had done for her over the years.

Margaret bobbed her head from side to side. "Oh, yes I did."

"Margaret Mills, do not make me take you into the office supply closet and whoop your butt again."

The gray-haired witch closed her mouth, scrunched her face, and made a scolded-rhino sound.

"No more hexing," Zinnia said, shaking a finger. "We need to stay cool and use our heads." She pulled out the fake key that was a perfect copy of the one Liza had, and dropped it on the desk next to Margaret's phone. "We've got an hour until they come back. Maybe we can use that time to find out more about this key."

"Not that key. That one is the copy."

"Even so... Hang on a minute." Seeing the key next to Margaret's phone gave Zinnia an idea. She used the phone to snap a photo of the key, and then used the photo to do an image-matching search on the internet.

A minute later, they had an answer, and not one single drop of koodzuberry enzyme had been used to force a confession.

It was so simple, so stunningly simple, the two actually stopped arguing.

"It's an elevator key," Zinnia said, stating the obvious and hating herself for it.

The two witches looked up from the diagram on the phone and stared into each other's eyes.

"An elevator key," Margaret repeated. "But according to this page, it only opens the control panel for that particular old model of elevator." She jabbed her finger at the screen. "This doesn't explain anything. It doesn't explain where they went."

"Doesn't it? We searched the entire third floor for a keyhole that matched the key. But we didn't find it, because it was inside the elevator the whole time."

"Are you saying that Liza and Xavier opened the elevator control panel and crawled through to some hidden space within the building? Somewhere with enough solid material that it blocked the tracker signal?"

"That's one possibility," Zinnia said cryptically.

Margaret turned her head and gave Zinnia a sidelong look. "What's the other possibility?"

Zinnia smiled knowingly. It had become so obvious, now that they had the right clue, thanks to Margaret's high-tech tracker.

Agent Rob had said the creatures infesting City Hall were from another world. And the glowfish in the surge detector were, according to Zinnia's magic reference books, also not from Earth. And then there was the powerful Wakeful triplets' grandmother, who'd appeared from "out of nowhere" back in 1955. That woman had been friends with the eldest Gilbert. Now the Gilbert family was in possession of a special key. It seemed the Gilberts were just as connected to the historical and current phenomena as the Wakeful family.

Most importantly, regardless of which family was behind the incursions, was the fact that if the creatures from another world were getting to Earth, they were coming in through some type of passageway. And, thanks to Margaret's tracker, the witches had located the entry point to that passageway.

Zinnia could barely contain her excitement as she said, "The other possibility, which I believe the correct one, is that Liza's key opens a portal to another world."

Margaret's eyes bulged. Portals were the domain of science fiction movies. And yet, to most people, witchcraft was also make-believe. If witches and gorgons and shifters were real, why not portals to other worlds?

They both looked down at the duplicate key.

After a long moment, Zinnia said, "We must be brave and do what ought to be done."

Margaret swung one fist in a let's-do-it gesture. "We must get the real key from Liza and destroy it before she releases hell on earth."

"Actually, I had a different idea."

Margaret's eyes bulged again. "You're just full of ideas, aren't you?"

Zinnia grinned. "Like Karl Kormac is full of noxious gases, I am, indeed, full of ideas."

Margaret rolled her eyes. "What?"

"Margaret Mills, do you have any fun plans for this evening?"

"No." She pouted. "You know I don't. Four kids, remember?"

"How would you like to accompany me on a research expedition to another plane of existence?"

Margaret's mouth didn't answer. Her eyes did.

Her eyes said yes.

CHAPTER 17

WHEN LIZA GILBERT and Xavier Batista returned at the end of the lunch break, neither gave any indication that they'd been up to anything exciting, let alone traveling to another plane of existence. That didn't stop Margaret from watching them like a hawk instead of getting any work done.

With Zinnia's assistance, Margaret switched Liza's key again during afternoon coffee break. The two were getting very good at swapping out the key. The switcheroo went off without a hitch.

Five o'clock took forever to roll around. Even longer than it did on the Fridays that came before a long weekend.

At last, the office finally emptied out. The witches could get down to their secret business.

At 5:15 pm, Zinnia and Margaret stood in the elevator. Margaret clutched the key in her hand. The two rode up and down the elevator as it groaned between floors. What had they been thinking? There was no way they would get a moment alone in the single elevator that served the whole building, not at that time of day. Just when it seemed like they might get the elevator to themselves so they could test the key in the keyhole next to the control panel, the elevator would ding and rise again to get more passengers.

After twenty minutes of riding the elevator up and down, Zinnia was getting bored. Margaret's stomach growled.

The two decided to leave the elevator, hit up the cafeteria for a wrapped sandwich and beverage, and then return to the elevator once the crowds had thinned.

While they ate cold sandwiches, left over from lunch time, and drank hot tea in the nearly-deserted cafeteria, Zinnia said, "I feel like we should be doing something to prepare for our trip."

Margaret gave her a quizzical look. "You mean pack a bag? With sunscreen, spending money, and extra socks and underwear?"

"I was thinking more along the lines of letting someone know where we're going." She paused. "Just in case we don't make it back."

Margaret shook her head. "Don't even think about it," she said. "If you call the DWM, they'll confiscate our key, and—"

"It's not our key."

Margaret waved a hand. "They'll confiscate *the* key, and you'll never hear anything else about it ever again."

"You're probably right. What do you think about telling my niece? She's not possessed by anything or anyone at the moment. It might be a good time to let her know more about what I do. What we both do."

"No way." Margaret shook her finger at Zinnia. "Don't you dare invite her along with us tonight. No third wheels. This first trip for Monsterland is just for me and you. Just us. We don't need a younger woman trying to horn in on what we have."

Zinnia stared at her friend. "What's going on with you?"

"Nothing," Margaret said indignantly. "It's just that some things are sacred. I've never gone through a magic portal before, and I want my first time to be with you. Only you."

"And it will only be me," Zinnia said. "Forget I dared to bring up the topic."

Margaret chomped into her sandwich. "But we could leave a note. Just in case." She looked thoughtful while she chewed her sandwich. "We could write a note and put it on Gavin's desk."

"Gavin? How would he be able to help us?"

"He's a gnome. I know that doesn't mean much, but it's better than nothing. He's the only one in the office who definitely has powers that he knows about."

"Very well, then," Zinnia said. "As much as I detest the idea of making Gavin Gorman our safety lifeline, you make a good point."

Zinnia thought about it for a minute.

"I know," Zinnia said. "In the note, we should mention that we're going through the elevator portal on a quest for treasure. That'll get him interested."

"Ooh. Good idea."

They borrowed a pen and paper from the cafeteria staff and worked on the note while they finished their sandwich dinner.

* * *

Zinnia and Margaret stood in the elevator alone. It was six o'clock now. The crowds had thinned, but someone was bound to press the call button sooner or later. For the time being, though, the cage wasn't moving.

Margaret handed Zinnia the key. It was damp with sweat.

"You can do the honors," Margaret said. "I'll stand back and cover you." She pulsed a thread of green plasma with one hand and wove it around her fingers.

The idea of needing backup gave Zinnia a nervous shiver, but she said with confidence, "I'm glad you have my back."

Zinnia took one more look at the key. It looked so ordinary, the color of a bleached bone and the texture of hard plastic.

"I have a theory," Zinnia said. "About the key."

"The original is a copy and we made a copy of a copy," Margaret said.

"Did you read my mind again?"

"No. I thought of that myself."

"When?"

"Just now."

"At the same exact time I thought of it?"

"Actually, I thought about it in the cafeteria, when I was looking at the plastic utensils."

Zinnia narrowed her eyes. "Really?"

"Stop stalling," Margaret said. "It doesn't matter if that key's also a copy. Liza wouldn't have been wearing it around her neck if it didn't do anything."

"She might have. It is rather pretty, as a decorative item."

"Stop stalling," Margaret repeated.

Zinnia sighed. She had been stalling. She carefully held the key by the bow and slid the bit into the elevator's control panel. The key fit perfectly and slid in up to the shoulder. A tingle of magic wrapped around Zinnia's arm. She swallowed the lump in her throat and turned the key.

The elevator made a ding sound that was both comforting and otherworldly at the same time. The cage began to move, though whether it was moving up or down, Zinnia couldn't tell.

The floor beneath their feet trembled.

And then, with another ding, the doors opened.

"Oh," Zinnia said.

The green lightning twining around Margaret's fingers blinked out as she dropped her hand to her side.

"Oh," Margaret said. "That's not what I expected."

CHAPTER 18

"WHAT WERE YOU expecting?" Zinnia asked.

Margaret said, "I was sort of hoping for an alien landscape with purple trees and triple moons."

The view before them was anything but an alien landscape.

Zinnia said, "I know it's not much at first glance, but if you look closely—"

Margaret cut her off. "This totally sucks!"

"If you look closely—"

"I'm paying for a babysitter tonight, too. Not worth it." Margaret shook her head. "Are you sure we used the right key?"

Zinnia sighed. "Yes. The key worked. Don't be so disappointed. I know it's not an alien world, but look on the bright side. At least it's not a burning hell dimension with lava bursting from fiery volcanoes, and little red demons poking tortured souls with pitchforks."

Margaret grumbled that she'd like to have seen just a bit of soul-torturing for her money.

Zinnia said, for the third time, "If you look closely, you'll see this is—"

"The third floor." Margaret walked ahead, leaving the elevator. "It's the third floor."

"No. It's similar to the third floor, but it isn't the third floor that we know."

They'd both been to the third floor just the day before. The third floor of City Hall had a hallway, offices, and a big boardroom with glass walls.

The space Margaret was now wandering through was what the third floor might look like if a renovation crew removed all the interior walls and furnishings, and stripped the carpet. This floor was just a vast, empty space. The ceiling didn't have any lights installed, but there was enough light coming in from the windows for the witches to see clearly.

"This is a perfectly good floor," Margaret said. "I guess they never finished building it." She looked around at the plain concrete floors and bare walls. She looked up at the exposed wiring on the ceiling. "They must have abandoned it back in 1955, when all the spooky stuff started happening."

Zinnia stuck her foot in front of the elevator's door to keep it from sliding shut while she retrieved the key from the control panel. As she rotated and removed the key, it gave her another tingle of magic running up her arm. She tucked the key into her purse, and followed Margaret out into the raw construction space. The elevator doors closed quietly behind her.

"How did we not know about this floor?" Zinnia asked. "I've been working here for almost a year and a half and I never noticed." She unbuttoned her jacket. The space was much warmer than the rest of the building, probably due to the air conditioning not being hooked up.

"I'm shocked that even I didn't notice," Margaret said. "I don't miss much, but somehow I missed the fact that there are six floors to this building, but only five floors on the elevator panel."

Zinnia tilted her head, looking up at the shadows, and tried to visualize the exterior of City Hall. Her mind's eye flickered between an image of the building with five rows of windows, and an alternate vision with six. It was surprisingly difficult to remember how the building appeared. She couldn't even recall the color of the exterior. Was it gray concrete, or red brick? Was the appearance of the building altered by some powerful glamour, or was she simply not that observant about the building she entered five days a week?

"Is this normal?" Margaret asked. "Before they started labeling the thirteenth floor in tall buildings as the fourteenth floor, did they build a thirteenth floor anyway, and just leave it empty like this?"

WISTERIA WRINKLE

Zinnia chuckled. "If I know anything about real estate developers, the answer is no."

Margaret walked over to a concrete pillar, where she picked up a dusty hammer. The floor wasn't as empty as it had appeared at first. The area was littered with piles of timber, buckets of plaster, and construction tools.

Margaret used the dusty hammer to lightly tap on the concrete pillar. The tap-tap sounds reverberated through the cavernous space. Nothing stirred. The floor was quiet. Too quiet.

Zinnia felt a chill, even though the air was quite warm.

"There must have been a reason they abandoned this floor," Zinnia said. "Maybe we shouldn't be here."

"What's your hurry? I pre-paid the babysitter for the whole night. She'll stay on the fold-out bed if we're out late."

"Why did you need a sitter, anyway? What's Mike doing?"

"Working late." Margaret used her toe to nudge a pile of power tools, disturbing ancient dust that drifted upward.

"Those tools look very old," Zinnia said.

"Nothing modern and battery operated, that's for sure." Margaret lifted a bladed tool, groaned, and set it down again with a noisy thunk. "Heavy."

"We shouldn't touch anything," Zinnia said.

"Don't be such a worrywart. Nobody's been here for years." Margaret picked up a newspaper, blew the dust off in a billowing cloud, and examined the front page. "This paper is from 1955."

"That's not much of a surprise."

Margaret turned the newspaper over. "They really were excited about canned foods in the fifties," she said. "And Jell-O. I guess it was new."

"Jell-O was already well established in 1955. Portable gelatin, as it was called, was patented in 1845. The inventor was more interested in making glue than desserts, though, so it wasn't until 1904 when the new patent owners started advertising in *Ladies' Home Journal* that..."

Margaret was grinning.

Zinnia said, "What's so funny?" She glanced over her shoulder. "Is something behind me?" She didn't see anything in the shadows.

"It's just that you're *soooo* Kitchen Bewitched sometimes. You're like a walking cliché."

Zinnia snorted. "I'm glad I'm able to provide you with the entertainment you so desperately need."

The two witches chuckled and went back to exploring the space. The windows were coated with some substance that made it impossible to see outside. The substance couldn't be scratched or wiped off. It seemed to be a magic-based substance. Other than that, the rest of the materials within the abandoned floor were fairly mundane.

"Talk about a waste of good space," Margaret said after a while. "We should see about getting the whole Permits Department moved up here. We'd have so much room to ourselves. No more shared desks. Every single one of us could have our own window."

"That does sound appealing."

Margaret put her hands on her hips and made a tsk-tsk sound. "It's a darn shame nobody's been using this perfectly good floor for sixty-some years."

Zinnia approached a pile of lumber that was different from everything else in that it wasn't covered in dust.

"I wouldn't say *nobody's* been using this floor," Zinnia said. "Remember, Liza and Xavier have been coming here. It looks like they cleaned the dust off this pile of wood."

Margaret came over and frowned. "That doesn't look very comfortable." She waved a hand over the stacked lumber. "Not for doing whatever it is they've been doing up here."

They both chortled, then Margaret sighed. "Ah, to be young and have a man be interested in you like that."

Zinnia said, "Lust is not necessarily limited to the young, my dear."

Margaret sighed again.

Zinnia took a seat on the pile of wood. It was the perfect height for a chair. "Perhaps they were simply eating lunch up here, away from the likes of us, or the crowds of the cafeteria."

"Sure, they were." Margaret smirked as she picked up a dusty aluminum lunch box and blew off a cloud of dust. "Look at this old thing."

"I haven't seen one of those in years," Zinnia said. "Does it have the matching vacuum flask inside?"

Margaret snapped open the metal buckles and flipped open the lid. "Sure does." She pulled out the squat vacuum flask, shook it, and unscrewed the lid. A wisp of steam floated up from its contents. "Um," Margaret said.

As the steam continued to wisp up from the open flask, the silence around them felt even more eerie. There was more to this floor than met the eye. They should have been able to hear the hum of the adjoining floors, or at the very least, the building's central ventilation system.

"Um," Margaret said again.

"I saw." Zinnia leaned in close to Margaret and waved her hand over the open container. Steam clung to her fingers. If it was an illusion, it was the kind that came with a sensory component.

Zinnia said, "I don't know if that's soup or coffee, but clearly it's still hot. How can that be?"

Margaret plunged her hand in through the wide rim. She grimaced, removed her hand again, and immediately licked her fingers.

"Soup," Margaret said. "Tomato soup."

Zinnia wasn't too surprised by Margaret's taste test. Witches, blessed as they were with resilient fingers and germ-killing saliva, could be very bold about tasting unknown liquids.

Zinnia said, "Since it's still hot after sixty-some years, the vacuum flask must be charmed in some way."

"To keep tomato soup hot for decades?" Margaret shook her head. "No way. If magic worked that well, we witches would have solved the planet's energy crisis years ago. Actually, we'd all be enslaved in some underground geothermal production facility by now."

"Thanks for that mental image. As if we witches didn't have enough to worry about."

Margaret screwed the lid back onto the vacuum flask, and tucked it back into the lunchbox. She returned the box to the spot where it had been, matching the base to the rectangular-shaped clean patch of concrete floor.

Margaret said, "I wonder what the mayor thinks about this floor."

"Mayor Paladini? That must be why she was at Queenie Gilbert's hospital room. She must have been trying to get the key from her."

"Why? She's the mayor. She could have ordered someone to make the elevator start going to this floor again. She could have gotten it fixed in a day. She wouldn't need a key."

"Actually, I was thinking more along the lines of she didn't want *anyone else* to have access."

"Like us."

Zinnia nodded. "Like us."

They both turned their heads at the same time to stare at the cloudy windows.

Time passed.

Zinnia kept coming back to the idea of City Hall having six floors, not five. She listened for the sounds that should have been coming from the other floors, and heard nothing. Surely the floors weren't insulated from each other that well? After a while, she even scuffed the sole of her shoe on the floor to make sure her ears were working properly. She heard the scuff but nothing else.

She leaned forward, resting her chin on her hands, and tried again to remember what the building looked like from the outside. She tried to hold the image in her head so she could count the rows of windows, but she kept coming up with five.

Margaret said, "I'll pull up a picture on my phone."

"Good idea." Sometimes it was nice that Margaret picked up on Zinnia's thoughts, at least when doing so helped solve problems. It was like having a computer with an extra processor.

"No signal," Margaret said, looking at her phone screen. She grunted as she hopped off the pile of timber. She held her phone up and walked around the space. "Nope. No bars. There must be a dampening field in here."

"That could explain why Liza and Xavier seemed to wink out of existence when they came here."

"Still no bars." Margaret put away her phone. "And I'm starting to get bored now."

"We can go in a minute. I just want to see something." Zinnia hopped off the timber. She stepped carefully around the lunchbox with the eerily warm tomato soup, and walked toward the fire exit stairwell.

Margaret clomped behind her, taking two steps for every one of Zinnia's, her hard-soled boots sounding like hooves.

"Wait up," she cried. "Don't leave me behind. What are you doing?"

"I'm doing what we ought to have done in the first place," Zinnia said. "I'm going out to the front lawn where I can count the floors from outside. It's driving me nuts! How could there be an entire floor that's been closed off for over six decades and this is the first we've known about it?"

"Fine, but I'm coming with you."

"I can count floors all by myself," Zinnia teased. "I can count all the way up to ten, you know."

Margaret used her tongue to make a raspberry noise.

Zinnia expected the concrete stairwell to be cool, as it always was, but it was actually hot. Hot like a summer day. They walked down three flights of stairs, and let themselves out through the fire door.

Blazing-hot sunshine and even warmer air hit their faces. They hadn't left the building for lunch, and Zinnia was shocked by how much hotter the day was than when she'd arrived at work that morning. She took her jacket all the way off and slung it over her shoulder.

The two turned right on the concrete pathway to make their way around to the front of the building. They'd only walked a few feet before they were stopped by a pile of rubble.

"That's rude," Margaret said. "Who put this on the sidewalk?"

Zinnia realized that the small details she was noticing didn't add up. The air was too hot. The lawn at the side of the walkway was dirt, not grass. And the walkway itself was practically gleaming, it was so clean—as though the cement had been poured yesterday.

Zinnia looked around. Really looked around. She gasped and grabbed Margaret's arm.

"I know, I know," Margaret said. "I can see the giant pile of dirt right in front of us. I wasn't going to walk through it."

"That's not why I grabbed you. Look." Zinnia pointed to the parking lot, which was actually a bare dirt area that hadn't been paved yet. "Look at those cars," she said.

Margaret pulled her head back, giving herself a double chin. "Is it Show and Shine day already?"

Zinnia shook Margaret's arm impatiently. "It's not Show and Shine day." She waved emphatically at the collection of shiny, colorful cars from eras gone by. There was a shiny red 1951 Mercedes-Benz Type 300 Limo, and a 1954 Buick Skylark, along with a couple dozen beat-up trucks that might have belonged to the people who worked for whomever drove the Mercedes.

Zinnia said very slowly, "It's not Show and Shine day, because the people who live here drive those kinds of cars every day."

Margaret snorted. "Maybe in 1955 they did. Nope. It must be Show and Shine day." She wiped some sweat from her brow with the back of her hand. "Why's it so hot out all of a sudden?"

Zinnia looked down and rubbed her temples with both fingers. Very loudly and clearly, she thought, *Margaret, we are in 1955.* She repeated it in her head for good measure.

When Zinnia looked up again, Margaret's eyelashes were fluttering.

Suddenly, she gasped, "Zinnia! I just figured it out! We're in 1955."

CHAPTER 19

WHEN ZINNIA RIDDLE and Margaret Mills found themselves smack in the middle of the town of Wisteria, circa 1955, they were torn between the idea of exploring versus turning around and running back to where they'd come from. Well, Zinnia was torn. Margaret had no qualms about exploring, even if it did mean causing paradoxes and other calamities.

"We're here already," Margaret said in a cajoling manner, as though talking to a shy toddler. "We might as well go for a milkshake at the soda shop."

"You must be joking."

"I never joke about milkshakes."

Zinnia looked around. It was the same City Hall, all right, but the surroundings were different in small ways. The mighty oaks that lined the street were mere saplings. The nearby traffic was lighter, and each vehicle was louder.

"This is all very unexpected," Zinnia said, holding her jacket under her arm while she wrung her hands. "I thought we were going to the place the monsters were coming from." She scanned the sky and saw only a few fluffy clouds. "But if they're coming through from here, from the past, then I suppose we've solved the mystery."

"Great! Let's celebrate."

Zinnia shook her head. "We ought to head back inside the building and return to where we belong. If we stay here, we could mess up the past and create problems in the future. You've seen *Back to the Future*. We could run into an ancestor and prevent ourselves from being born." She rubbed her temples, remembering what Liza had said about her nightmares, about not existing. Had Liza done a *Back to the Future* on herself?

Zinnia explained this theory to Margaret, who listened patiently before stamping one foot like a billy goat pawing the earth. "But I want a milkshake."

"So did Marty McFly, and look what happened!"

Margaret grinned. "Marty McFly tried to order a Tab, and then a diet Pepsi. See? I know what I'm doing."

"I see," Zinnia said flatly. "Because memorizing lines from a 1980s movie about time travel is exactly what qualifies you to be a time traveler."

"Please, Zinnia? Pretty please? I promise not to mess up anything with the timeline." She pleaded with her eyes. "Let's not be the boring women who traveled back in time, got sweaty standing next to a parking lot, and went home ten minutes later. Let's not be those boring women."

"We can get milkshakes in our own time, Margaret. We don't exactly live in a post-apocalyptic wasteland where cows have gone extinct."

"Sure, we can get milkshakes, but not authentic 1950s soda shop milkshakes."

Zinnia frowned. Darn it all if her mouth wasn't watering just thinking about it. And darn it all if she didn't want to avoid being boring, like Margaret had said.

"And how are you going to pay for this milkshake?" Zinnia asked. "With brand-new dollar bills that haven't been minted yet? Or perhaps with the handy-dandy chip embedded in your bank card? Oh, that's right. They don't have machines in the 1950s that read chips in bank cards."

Margaret shrugged and clomped over to the parking lot. She leaned from side to side, admiring them the way someone would view the vintage cars at a Show and Shine. "I'll pay cash," she said over her shoulder. "What does a milkshake cost in 1955?"

"About ten cents." Zinnia followed Margaret over to the cars. They were all rather remarkable to her modern eyes. The windshields were flecked with genuine bug splats from 1955. It didn't get more authentic than this.

Margaret said, "I'm sure I have more than enough coins with old dates that I can use to buy us a full meal. Not that people are going to look at the dates on my pennies. Who would do that?"

She did have a point. But something was amiss. It was so hot, and Zinnia's hair was sticking to her face at the sides. Zinnia lifted her chin and shielded her eyes as she checked the position of the sun in the sky. It was directly overhead.

"Margaret, don't panic, but it appears to be lunch time."

"Perfect. I'll buy you lunch. We'll go to Lucky's Diner. They're always bragging about how they've been in the same location for seventy years, so they must be here already." She rubbed her hands together. "I'm getting a strawberry milkshake."

"We just ate dinner."

"So? Get a milkshake and call it dessert."

"What I mean is it's noon here. Look at the sun."

The short, gray-haired witch peered up at the sky. "Yup. Looks like noon to me."

"It was past six o'clock when we came through. Time of day must not be in sync here with where we came from. It might even be running at a different rate."

"I guess we'll find out when we get back."

"Which really ought to be right away." Zinnia glanced around. She turned and looked at City Hall.

"Five floors," Zinnia said.

"Five floors," Margaret agreed. "See? We've already been in 1955 for a while, and nothing bad has happened. We've been here since the minute we stepped out of the elevator."

Zinnia said nothing as she looked over the building. It was made of gray concrete. The main structure had been fully constructed, but the windows were missing from the upper stories. She looked around for construction workers but didn't see any.

"Either the crew is on a break or it's the weekend here," Zinnia said.

"Perfect," Margaret said. "Nobody will notice when we come back later. How about one hour?"

Zinnia looked at her friend and then back at the tall, familiar building. "I don't know," she said hesitantly.

"That's the exact tone I use with my kids when they've broken me down," Margaret said, pumping her fists.

"We can stay for one hour." Zinnia licked her lips. "I could use a strawberry milkshake."

Margaret dug into her purse, popped open her coin purse, and frowned. It was empty.

"Darn kids," she said, and then, "Oh, well. At least we're witches. I'll just charm the soda jerk into giving us a freebie." She grinned up at Zinnia. "I'm not being mean, you know. They were called soda jerks. See? I know the terminology. I'll fit right in here."

Zinnia pulled some coins from her purse. What would a 1955 soda jerk say to a coin dated the next millennium? He'd accuse them of trying to pass counterfeit currency. Luckily, Zinnia had more than enough backdated change for them to buy a few treats without causing anachronisms.

Zinnia handed all of her loose change to Margaret. "Here."

"Ooh! An allowance."

"Buy whatever you want with this money, but promise you won't use any magic. This might not be the real 1955."

"What?" Margaret gave her a skeptical look. "Do you mean it might be 1956?"

"No. I mean we could be inside a hell dimension that only looks like Earth on the surface. And, as we learned in those books you made me stay up all night reading, hell dimensions are highly combustible. Even a tiny spark of magic could set off a cataclysmic event."

Margaret wasn't listening. She was already wandering off in the direction of the soda shop they knew of, Lucky's Diner.

Zinnia caught up with her friend.

They walked into the busier part of town, the main shopping streets. Zinnia couldn't help but stare at the people around her, going about their business. She was in the past! Half of the people she was walking by were dead by now. It was not unlike walking among ghosts.

After a while, Zinnia leaned over and said, "I'm concerned that our clothes might make us look out of place." Her jacket, in particular, looked too modern, so she'd folded it up in a small square.

Margaret looked both of them up and down. "Actually, we fit right in." She frowned. "That doesn't say much for our fashion sense, does it?"

Zinnia frowned. A woman wearing a jacket exactly like the one Zinnia was clutching in a bundle walked by. Perhaps Zinnia's jacket wasn't too modern after all.

They passed a group of women their age on the sidewalk. The women gave them friendly looks and returned to their conversation about recipes.

Out of the side of her mouth, Margaret said, "Next time we come here, we need to wear hats. Look how many ladies are wearing hats. And the men, too. Hats everywhere."

Zinnia looked around. It was true about the hats, but her mind balked at the idea of there being a next time. Zinnia couldn't fathom coming to the past again. She wanted to, yes, but her mind boggled at all the infinite ways they might screw up the future.

CHAPTER 20

HOURS LATER

MARGARET MILLS WASN'T known for being punctual. It came as no surprise to Zinnia when their "one hour" stay in 1955 turned into several hours. Their visit to the past showed no sign of ending soon. Margaret insisted on spending every single penny of the pocket change she'd been given, so they'd visited every chocolatier and bakery in the much smaller yet still familiar main streets of Wisteria.

Margaret was down to her last nickel at five o'clock, when they entered a charming, old-fashioned candy shop that was, to the people of that time, simply a candy shop.

"I can't decide," Margaret said. "Everything looks so yummy." She leaned forward over the display case, studying the colorful gumballs and rainbow suckers. She accidentally brushed against an upright display kiosk. The green scarab pendant she'd been wearing lately popped free of its pin and dropped onto the counter with a light clink.

The woman working behind the counter squealed. "My brooch!" She swept up the pin and whooped with joy. The woman had long, dark hair, and an Italian accent. In her exuberance, she almost sounded like she was singing. "My darling little beetle! Oh, my baby." She said to the women, "I've been looking for this everywhere. Where did you find it?"

Margaret and Zinnia exchanged a look. They'd bought it from a street vendor two weeks earlier, along with a deck of tarot cards for Dawna. Or, to put it in current terms, they hadn't bought it *yet*, but they would buy it in sixty-some years.

The woman asked again, more insistently, "Where did you find my darling little beetle?"

"Oh, it was just out on the street not far from here," Margaret said. "I, uh, figured I'd wear it on my lapel until the real owner identified it."

The woman, who appeared to be in her forties, about the same age as the two witches, beamed happily as she pinned the brooch onto the top of her apron. "You're both angels," she said.

"We're not exactly angels," Margaret said.

Zinnia snorted softly.

"Here," said the woman, setting out trays of candies before them. "Help yourself to as much as you can carry. Consider it your reward." She regarded the green scarab brooch with a smile. "This old thing isn't worth more than a dollar, but it does have sentimental value." She called over her shoulder, "Piero, come quickly! You have to meet these two angels who found my pin!"

Margaret, who had restrained herself to choosing only six pieces of candy, nudged Zinnia toward the door. "Actually, we should be going," she said to the Italian woman.

Zinnia raised her eyebrows. Now? Now Margaret was concerned about the time?

A man emerged from the back of the shop. He was shirtless and flecked with dabs of paint. He had shiny dark hair, pulled back in a ponytail. His face and his sly grin were devilishly handsome. He looked about fifty, perhaps, but with youthful eyes and a lean, muscular physique that took Zinnia's breath away.

Margaret tugged at Zinnia's elbow. "Come on," she said. "It's time to get home before things get all tangled up."

"Not so fast," Zinnia said. Her eyes didn't want the rest of her to leave just yet. Not before they'd all been introduced properly.

The candy-store owner said, "This is my cousin, Piero. Piero, these are the two angels who found my brooch! Aren't they wonderful? I adore them both."

Piero came around the counter and strode toward the women, his flashing dark-brown eyes locked on Zinnia's.

"Yes, yes," Piero said, turning his face toward his cousin. "This one," he said of Zinnia. With his Italian accent, it sounded like *this-ah one-ah*. "She does have the face of an angel." He took Zinnia's hand and kissed it. "You have shown great kindness toward my family. Now, let us return the favor."

"Uh, we have to get going now," Margaret said.

"Nonsense!" Piero grabbed Margaret's hand and kissed it as well. "Another angel. You, my little one, have the curls of a cherub."

Margaret giggled. "Really? I'm an angel? A cherub?"

"Yes, yes," he said in his charming way. "Come with me. Come to the back. It's where I paint, in my studio. We will have wine and food."

The woman laughed. "Oh, Piero. You always come on so strong!"

"There is only time for the strong," Piero said. "No time for the weak." He said to Zinnia, "Never mind my cousin, Francesca. She's a good woman, but she's not so much fun."

Francesca swatted him playfully. "I can be fun!"

Piero grinned. "Then lock the front door and put up the sign. Be done for the day. Let us relax and have wine. We have much to celebrate."

Zinnia said, "Oh? Is it a special occasion?"

He kept grinning. "It's the occasion of two beautiful angels coming into our humble candy store. Come, come." He tugged at their hands.

Zinnia and Margaret looked at each other. Now would have been the right time for one of them to be the responsible, grown-up one and insist they return to City Hall and their own time immediately.

Neither said a word as they followed their new friend Piero into the back room for his promised hospitality.

CHAPTER 21

APPROXIMATELY NINE HOURS and several bottles of wine after entering 1955, Margaret and Zinnia started making their way back home.

When they arrived at the City Hall building, it was very difficult to see their surroundings, as the safety lighting along the perimeter wasn't working.

Zinnia squinted up at the light fixtures, trying to see if the lamps were lit but covered in the same moth-like insects that had been plaguing the present-day City Hall. There didn't appear to be any insects. The lamps were simply not switched on, which made sense, given the building wasn't yet occupied.

As for the other creatures that had been reported in both the present-day and Angelo Wakeful's log book, the witches hadn't seen anything unusual. Not even a large rat, let alone a raccoon-sized rodent. According to the "locals," Francesca and Piero, nothing inexplicable had been happening lately. Nothing but one small thing. Why was the building called City Hall when Wisteria was barely a town? Shouldn't it have been called Town Hall? The two witches had laughed at the question and agreed that people would probably be asking that question for years into the future, at least until the town grew enough to be called a city.

The two Italian-Americans had been so much fun to share wine and food with. Zinnia missed them already. But she couldn't be distracted by emotions. She and Margaret had to get back to the third floor and through the elevator to their own time.

Margaret was stumbling around like a drunken fool. For that matter, so was Zinnia. They both forgot about the dirt pile on the walkway, and both fell into it, face first. They got themselves extracted, still carrying on like drunken fools, and managed to find their way in the dark to the fire exit. They found it locked.

"Oh, no," gasped Margaret. "We're locked out."

Zinnia pushed her friend aside and used simple telekinesis to push open the door from the other side.

Margaret squealed. "You did magic," she whisper-yelled. "You broke the rules!"

Zinnia clamped her hand over Margaret's mouth. "Woman, control yourself before I wrap you from head to toe in something sound-dampening, like insulation, or another pile of dirt."

Margaret mumbled through Zinnia's hand that she would behave.

"It was just a little magic on the door handle," Zinnia said. "It was absolutely necessary, and I promise I won't do any more."

"That's too bad, because we could use some light."

"Hang on. I've got that covered." Once inside the stairwell, Zinnia took out her cell phone and turned it on. There was no cell phone service here, but she could use the flashlight app to generate light. Considering they were in 1955, it might have been less dangerous to be caught using magic than using a modern phone, but Zinnia was still concerned about sparks and the flammability of this world.

They stumbled all the way up to the third floor, which was no small feat considering the amount of wine they'd had. A witch's regenerative powers did typically include the liver, as well as the processing of non-magical toxins, including alcohol, but there was a funny quirk that happened under the right circumstances. When a witch was enjoying her alcoholic beverage, the regeneration power switched itself off.

The third floor appeared to be the way they'd left it, except much darker. Margaret stubbed her toe on the metal lunchbox and cursed it. Literally.

"That's probably why the tomato soup was hot," Zinnia said. "It's because you cursed it just now, in the past."

"I might be drunk, but I'm pretty good at understanding time travel when I'm doing it." Margaret paused and then mused, "That is a phrase I never expected to hear myself say."

Zinnia aimed the light downward and carefully moved the lunchbox back to where it had been.

"No, wait. That doesn't work out," Margaret said, shaking her head. "We were already here, and the soup was already hot. Before now."

"That's what I thought, but check this out." Zinnia picked up a corded power tool and blew across it at Margaret.

Margaret said, "You need to plug it in, dummy. Blowing on tools doesn't do anything, not even with your booze breath."

Zinnia sighed. "There was no dust. This place hasn't gotten dusty yet." She waved her hands around to indicate the whole space. "There must be a stasis field in here. I think it rolled back in time when we went outside the building. Or maybe just now, when we came in through the fire exit instead of the elevator."

"Stop talking," Margaret said. "I thought I could handle time travel math, but my brain is going to explode."

"We wouldn't want that." Zinnia led the way to the elevator.

Once there, they encountered a problem they should have anticipated. Because the building wasn't finished yet, the electricity wasn't running to the elevator. Pressing the call button did nothing but make the mechanism emit a tiny click. A flame of panic ignited in Zinnia's belly. Were they trapped? This was what she'd feared could happen. Her worst fear. And it was happening. She kept pressing the call button, kept making the tiny clicks as the panic rose inside her.

"Oh, well," Margaret said with what sounded like fake disappointment. "I guess we'll have to stay here forever. You can go ahead and have Piero. I liked the sound of his friend, Enzo." She walked away from the elevator, back toward the stairwell again. "I guess we'll just have to live out our days right here, and hope that everyone back home carries on without us."

"Not so fast."

Zinnia used the light from her phone to search the area surrounding the elevator. Something dark caught her eye. Could it be? She thrust her fingertip at it. Yes. The dark hole appeared to be a keyhole.

She pulled the key from her purse. With a hand that was unsteady due to both nerves and wine, she gently slid the key in. She gave it a turn.

The elevator let out a cheerful ding that resounded through the empty floor. The doors opened in a rectangular patch of impossible brightness. The interior walls of the elevator came into view.

"Oh, good," Margaret said flatly. She sounded more than a little disappointed. "It worked. Time to go home to our regular lives."

Zinnia put her foot in the door again while she grabbed the key.

Margaret trudged forward like a robot.

Zinnia linked her arm through Margaret's. It seemed like an adventure-y thing to do, plus Margaret was having some difficulties staying upright. They both stepped into the elevator. Zinnia pressed the button for the ground floor. Margaret slumped into the corner with a resigned sigh.

In no time at all, the doors opened.

They were back. The building hummed around them with activity.

A man in a rumpled suit stood on the other side of the doors. It was Karl Kormac, the manager of the Wisteria Permits Department. His eyebrows shot up above his yellow computer-glare glasses when he saw who was in the elevator.

"There you two are," Karl said, taking off his glasses to better glare at them. "Why are you an hour late for work?"

Margaret straightened up. "It's not what you think," she said, followed by a hiccup.

Karl glowered as he looked them up and down. "It's not what I think? I think you've been having a wild party. Look at yourselves."

They did. He had a point about them being filthy.

Karl continued stating the obvious. "You're both covered in dirt, and you smell like a winery." He took a step back and waved for them to exit the elevator. "Don't bother trying to explain yourselves. I don't even want to know. I'm heading upstairs for a department-heads meeting on the fifth floor. Get yourselves cleaned up and sobered up by the time I get back."

"A meeting for department heads?" Zinnia asked. "Shouldn't I be at this meeting?"

He fixed her with a serious look. "Zinnia Riddle, do you want to be at this meeting which starts in five minutes?"

"Not really."

"Didn't think so." He gave them one more sour look as he stepped into the elevator, put his yellow-lensed glasses back on, and pressed a button.

The elevator doors closed.

Margaret and Zinnia looked at each other.

"We have temporal jetlag," Zinnia said.

"Oh? How does that work?"

"I don't know. I just made it up."

"Temporal jetlag," Margaret repeated. "It's making my head ache."

"That was the wine," Zinnia said. She quickly did the math. "If time passed at the same rate, we should have gotten back here at three or four in the morning. We've lost five or six hours."

"I guess this answers your theory about the time not matching up."

"It also might explain why the cleaning lady watched herself clean." Zinnia frowned and rubbed her chin. "Except she didn't say anything about a trip to 1955." Zinnia realized how dirty her hands were and stopped rubbing her chin.

Margaret said, "If that portal thing is kicking out stray monsters willy-nilly, it might be kicking out time wave-y-waves."

"You mean temporal aftershocks?"

Margaret sighed. "Fine. You can name all the things."

Zinnia looked down at herself. She hadn't looked too bad, not until they'd fallen on the pile of dirt on the way back.

"Let's get to the bathroom so we can remove this dirt," Zinnia said. "Then we'll see about getting some coffee."

"Dibs on sleeping under your desk."

"I'm sure you'll perk up once we get some coffee in you. About three pots should do the trick."

"Challenge accepted." Margaret yawned and rubbed her face, spreading more dirt around.

CHAPTER 22

Zinnia and Margaret put a Closed for Maintenance sign on the ladies' washroom, and then used magic spells to wash and dry their clothes.

"We need to cover our tracks," Margaret said. She was using her finger to brush her teeth at the washroom counter. "Voo voo vava chee?"

"I beg your pardon?"

Margaret took her finger out of her mouth. "Do you have the key?"

"You saw me put it in my purse less than twenty minutes ago."

Margaret gave her teeth one more rub. "We need to switch it back. Liza can't know that we figured out what she's been up to."

"Sure. We can switch it back. She'll probably go there again at lunch time with Xavier, but I suppose that will be okay. We'll call a meeting of the coven tonight."

Margaret groaned. "Do we have to?"

"Four heads are better than one."

"Even if one of the heads is Fatima's?"

Zinnia regarded her friend for a moment. "You know, Margaret, I never realized how ageist you are. Are there any young people you're not suspicious of?"

"Young people are loose cannons."

Talk about the pot calling the kettle black. "In any case, I do believe it's time to involve the others. And possibly my niece as well, if it comes to that."

Margaret patted her gray curls dry. "I knew that Gilbert girl was too cheerful. Nobody her age is that happy. She's been up to something really evil."

"I'm not so sure of that," Zinnia said. "She's just a kid. I'm not ageist, or at least I try not to be, but it's true they don't have as much life experience. It's possible they have no idea it's a stasis field, or a time tunnel, or whatever it is. I believe they've simply been using the vacant floor to spend time together."

Margaret frowned. "They must know more than that."

"It did fool both of us. It's a lucky thing we took the stairs down, or we might never have figured it out."

"Oh, I would have noticed right away on our next visit," Margaret said. "Nothing gets past me." She started for the washroom door.

Zinnia cleared her throat.

Margaret gave her a tired look. "What?"

"Your clothes?"

Margaret looked down at herself. She was wearing only her underwear.

* * *

Shortly before lunch time, they swapped the real key with the fake one Liza had been wearing on a chain around her neck. The two keys were so similar that the witches couldn't help but question whether they'd made the correct swap despite being super-careful.

At 12:05, Liza left the office, followed by Xavier at 12:10.

The two witches met in Zinnia's office.

"I've got an idea," Margaret said. "We don't need to bring the whole coven into this. We could just talk to the Gilbert girl about sharing the key with us. We shouldn't have to steal it from her whenever we need it."

Zinnia frowned. "I don't like any part of what you just said."

"It's not always bad to keep secrets."

"Depends on the secrets."

Margaret narrowed her eyes at Zinnia. "Speaking of which, what were you doing with Piero last night? When Francesca and I got back with the food, you had a goofy look on your face."

"Me?"

"Yes, you. The same goofy face you're making right now. What were you doing with Piero?"

"Nothing you wouldn't have done."

Margaret squeezed her eyes into the narrowest of slits. "Ri-i-i-ight." She turned on her heel and clomped out of the office.

Zinnia leaned back in her chair and looked over at the surge detector in the corner. It was no longer glowing yellow. It was now a fiery orange.

Zinnia stared at the orange glow and rubbed her temples. She was in such a tough position. The key was powerful. Too powerful. That meant the witches couldn't allow Liza to keep using it and unwittingly letting monsters pass through to Earth. But on the other hand, if the coven met and decided to turn the key over to the DWM, then the DWM would have it, and that organization's reputation wasn't exactly pristine. The recent events with Chessa Wakeful made it clear that Margaret's paranoia about the shadowy organization was not unfounded.

Zinnia pulled her gaze away from the glowfish and looked at the directory on her phone. She could pick up the handset right now, and in ten seconds, she could be talking to Mayor Paladini. The mayor was certainly interested in the Gilbert family, if not the key specifically. Was she the person Zinnia ought to be reporting to? If only Zinnia knew who she could trust.

Something else pecked at the back of her mind. She was forgetting something.

She took another sip of coffee. She usually preferred tea, but after no sleep, plus wine and time travel jetlag, she needed all the help she could get. If she'd been at home, she could have whipped up something stronger. Then again, if she'd been at home, she could have climbed into her soft, comfortable bed.

Her eyelids felt heavy. She leaned all the way back in her chair. Since her eyelids were so heavy, she would allow them to rest for a minute. Just for a minute.

* * *

Zinnia woke up, disoriented from her chair nap.

Karl was in her office, repeating her name and clearing his throat.

"You're awake," he said.

"I was just resting my eyes." She checked the time. It was two o'clock, which meant she'd been asleep for over an hour. She leaned to the side to see if Liza was back at her desk. She wasn't. Neither was Xavier. Zinnia's pulse quickened. Her mouth tasted sour. They should have been back by now. They'd always returned by one o'clock. Something was wrong.

Karl followed Zinnia's gaze and asked, "Is there something going on that I should know about? Something to do with the new hires?"

Zinnia kept her voice calm and breezy. "Nothing work-related, I'm sure." She had to get rid of Karl so she could track down Liza, but how? She picked up her coffee mug and took a sip of the cold drink to clear the acrid taste of panic from her mouth.

Karl went to the door, as if to leave, but he didn't exit. He pulled the office door closed. Then he slowly pulled Zinnia's guest chair away from the wall, pushed it up snug to the other side of her desk, and took a seat. He groaned loudly as he sat, as usual.

Zinnia swept away her worries about Liza and Xavier to focus on the current problem. Karl wanted to talk to her. In private.

Karl Kormac was the sort of older man whose quirks you had to laugh at, if only to keep from crying for him out of pity. Karl was easily flummoxed by things like computers and email, yet he had gotten himself into a management position at City Hall. He was eagerly awaiting his retirement date in less than two years. Then, he promised, he would start pursuing his dreams, whatever those were.

When Zinnia had started working at the department, Karl had secretly been referred to as the Coworker Most Likely to Have a Heart Attack While Screaming at the Photocopier. Zinnia had observed his lack of patience with electronic devices first-hand, so it was no mystery to her why the photocopier never worked for Karl. She'd also seen him inadvertently jinx the coffee maker—something regular, non-magical people could do by accident if they used the right words and tone of voice.

Karl was average height and portly in build. He had a full head of hair, mostly brown, which was perpetually in need of a haircut. His wife had passed a few years back, so he didn't have anyone to remind him to visit the barber. He had squinty eyes, a bulbous nose, and a ruddy complexion that easily turned beet red when his ego was insulted, which happened at least once a week. He dressed exclusively in off-the-rack suits, even on Casual Fridays, and wore yellow-tinted glasses when he worked on the computer. When a coworker had used Karl as inspiration for a fictional book character, she'd cast him as Lark, the troll. Trolls weren't real, as far as Zinnia knew, but she did suspect Karl might have some supernatural powers. The man was a wicked good bowler, could drink scorching hot coffee without wincing, plus he was*really good* at jinxing the office appliances.

Karl spoke first. "Technically, we are both equals now, Zinnia."

"I suppose that's true, though you have subordinates and I'm only the boss of myself."

"Zinnia..." He trailed off and looked down. His cheeks reddened.

Zinnia's mind raced. She'd seen Karl Kormac look bashful before. On her first day at the office, she'd realized he had a crush on their coworker, Annette Scholem. Zinnia had encouraged Karl to act on his crush and spend time outside of work with Annette. Unfortunately, that advice hadn't worked out so well. Karl had been rejected as a suitor—Annette was understandably wary about romantic relationships—and he hadn't taken it well. At one point he'd suffered a meltdown and attempted to fire everyone in the office.

Zinnia remembered Karl telling her once that she wasn't "his type," but people changed. Seeing her dirty and inebriated might have ignited something in the older man.

Zinnia held her breath and waited for him to finish his thought. *Please don't ask me on a date.* She had certainly enjoyed the attention of Piero last night—or this morning, or back in 1955, or whenever it had happened—but she wasn't looking for a relationship right now, especially not with Karl Kormac.

"Zinnia, we all have our... demons," he said.

"Oh?" She took another sip of the cold coffee.

He gave her a sage look. "I want you to know that you can talk to me. I'm your friend."

"Thank you. That's very kind."

Karl rubbed his bulbous nose and squinted at her with his beady eyes. "What do you know about demons?"

Zinnia was slow to answer. "Demons? As in *personal* demons? Well, there's gambling, and drugs, and alcohol." She waved a hand, interrupting herself. "Karl, I realize my appearance this morning may have caused you some concern, and I appreciate your caring, I really do, but I assure you I do not have demons making me consume alcohol." No, she had consumed the wine of her own free volition. She had even encouraged Margaret to do the same.

"There are many kinds of demons," he said, running a hand through his mostly-brown, thick head of hair. As he did so, he knocked the pair of yellow-tinted glasses off the top of his head. He leaned forward, groaning, picked up the glasses, and sat upright, groaning some more. His face was red from the effort. His face didn't usually turn that red unless he'd had his ego insulted. She hadn't offended him, as far as she knew. Was something wrong with Karl? An illness?

Zinnia asked, "Karl, are you feeling all right?"

"Honestly, I don't know," he said matter-of-factly. "I've been feeling funny." He turned his head and stared at the glowing surge detector in the corner. "What is that thing, and why is it glowing red?"

She looked. Sure enough, the globe had moved beyond yellow and orange, and was now glowing an alarming shade of red.

"It's a decorative thing," she said. "For relaxation."

"That red isn't very relaxing."

"I can take it home with me tonight if it's bothering you."

"Of course not." He made a blustery sound. "It's your subdepartment, your office. You can decorate it," he waved at the wallpaper and curled his upper lip, "however you like."

"Thanks." She gathered some papers from her desk and stacked them together in a tidying-up motion that she hoped would signal completion of the conversation and send Karl on his way.

Karl didn't budge. *Lark didn't budge*, she thought. She had read that line in Annette's book, about the troll character who'd been based on Karl. Annette had been right about Karl's ability to not budge. The one and only time Zinnia had seen Karl move quickly and lightly was when he'd skipped his way up a grassy hill to play on a children's swing set. He'd been under the influence of two conflicting magic spells at the time, and he'd suffered greatly due to the bad reaction, yet remembering the sight of Karl skipping up the grassy hill never failed to put a smile on Zinnia's lips.

Since he wasn't going to budge, Zinnia decided to go ahead and *lance the boil*, so to speak.

"Karl, tell me about your demons," Zinnia said.

He made a HARUMPH sound and fidgeted with his computer glasses. "Me? You're the one who showed up to work drunk and covered in dirt."

She said nothing.

"Fine," he said. "Can you promise to keep an open mind?"

"My mind is very open."

"But can you keep a secret?"

Zinnia smiled and repeated a phrase she'd learned from her mentor. "Only the dead keep secrets, and even they aren't perfect."

"True," Karl said. "But I think you'll keep my secret. It's a big one. The sort of thing you'll keep to yourself because if you tried to tell someone, they'd think you were crazy."

Zinnia rested her elbow on her desk and leaned forward. "What is it, Karl?" She batted her eyelashes playfully to lighten the mood. It was something she'd seen her niece do before making a wildly inappropriate comment. "Was there some truth to what Annette wrote about you in her book? Are you actually descended from a long line of magical creatures some might call trolls?"

Karl maintained steady eye contact. "That depends. Are you and Margaret both witches?"

She stopped batting her eyelashes. "Good one," she said. "Very funny."

"Is it funny?" He looked down at her blouse. "How did you get all the dirt out of that light-colored shirt?"

She pursed her lips. "Just because I buy durable fabrics and I'm handy with the cleaning supplies available in the ground floor women's restroom, that does not make me a witch."

Karl adjusted his seat in the chair and groaned from the effort. He loosened his tie and unbuttoned his collar.

"All right," he said. "If you won't go first, I suppose I can. But first..." He turned his head and looked at the surge detector on the bookshelf again. It was no longer glowing red. The color had shifted all the way to white, and it was emitting more light than ever.

Zinnia lifted a hand to shield her eyes. Witches didn't suffer hangovers, or at least not bad ones, yet the light was bright enough to make her head ache.

Gruffly, he asked, "What the devil is that thing?" He got up with a groan and walked over to it.

"Karl, don't—" Before Zinnia could finish her warning, there was a cracking sound. Karl turned away just as the glass ball burst. Glass fragments and glowfish radiated out. The glass fell to the carpet and the glowfish hovered in midair.

Zinnia jumped to her feet. "Karl, are you okay?" He'd been close to the blast zone.

He rubbed the back of his neck and looked down at his hand. There was something dark on his fingers. Blood.

Karl looked around, blinking. "I, uh, what are those?" He reached out and poked his finger at one of the floating glowfish. It simply swam away. Through the air.

Zinnia grabbed some tissues from her desk and dabbed at the back of Karl's neck. Luckily for Karl, he'd turned away in time to avoid getting any glass shards in his eyes. The worst of the damage appeared to be the back of his neck, though she hadn't yet inspected his scalp. The fact that the surge detector had exploded did concern her, but there was another matter that was more pressing.

Karl's blood. It wasn't red. His blood was *black*.

"Karl," she said slowly. "Your blood isn't red."

"I know. That's what I was trying to tell you before your mood lamp exploded."

"It's not a mood lamp. It's a..." Based on the appearance of his blood, she made the decision to trust him with the truth. "It's a surge detector."

"Fair enough," he said. "And that explosion must mean it detected a surge?"

"Something like that."

He winced. "My neck really stings."

"Hang on. Let me do something about that." Using a light touch with her fingertips, she sent healing energy into the cuts on the back of Karl's neck. The wounds closed immediately. The strange black blood disappeared, as thought it had seeped back through his skin. "I'm just checking your scalp now, if that's all right." He didn't refuse. She threaded her fingers through the back of his hair, found three more wounds from the broken glass, and healed them as well.

"There," she said when it was done. "You're not bleeding anymore."

He turned around and faced her. "That was fast," he said in a deadpan voice. "And why is it, Zinnia Riddle, that I am no longer bleeding?"

She narrowed her eyes and pinched her lips. He knew darn well why he wasn't bleeding anymore. It was because she'd used her witch powers to heal him. She had told him the truth about the surge detector, but she wasn't about to say the words he was digging for. No witch gave away her secrets easily. As much as she wanted to know why Karl's blood was black, she wasn't going to admit her powers first.

"Well, well, well," Karl said, eerily calm considering there were glowfish wriggling through the air around them, defying all laws of physics. "It seems as though we are at an impasse."

She kept her silence.

There was a pounding on the door that startled both of them out of their staring contest. The door burst open.

Liza Gilbert stood there, eyes wide with panic. Half of her blonde hair had come loose from her ponytail and was hanging down the side of her face. She was breathing raggedly, and her face gleamed with sweat.

"Help," Liza said between gasps. "Help me. It's got Xavier."

CHAPTER 23

ALL CONCERNS ABOUT the exploding glowfish and Karl's black blood were pushed aside by Liza's appearance and declaration.

Karl demanded, "What happened to Xavier?"

Liza clung to the door handle, her honey-brown eyes darting left and right. "It... took him," she said, still breathing heavily. "There was... nothing I could do."

Karl moved quickly, putting himself between Liza and Zinnia.

"I'm glad you came to me," he said gruffly. Liza had actually come to Zinnia's office, but it was just like Karl to assume she'd been looking for him.

"This is bad," Liza said. "So bad." She kept clinging to the door handle. A rivulet of sweat streaked down the side of her temple.

"I'll handle this situation at once," Karl blustered. "Nobody takes one of my employees without my permission." He buttoned up his collar and straightened his tie. "Who was it?"

"Not a who," Liza wheezed. Her eyes glistened, and then tears streamed down both cheeks. She choked back a sob. "Not a who," she repeated softly.

Karl didn't bat an eyelash. "Take me to where it happened."

Zinnia cut in, "Did something happen to you on the third floor?" She noted that Liza was still in possession of the key, worn around her neck.

Liza looked at Zinnia as the color drained from her cheeks. She whispered hoarsely, "You know about the third floor?"

"We can talk about all of this later," Zinnia said. "After we locate Xavier."

Liza nodded mutely.

"We're going to the third floor," Zinnia said to Karl.

"You'd better believe we are," he said, as though it had been his idea all along.

Zinnia hoisted her purse onto her shoulder and shooed the other two out of her office.

As they entered the main area, their coworkers Carrot, Dawna, and Gavin stared at them with interest. Someone in the room was snoring. Margaret. Zinnia grabbed Margaret by the arm and forcibly removed her from her chair. Margaret gave Zinnia a dirty look but was immediately alert. She grabbed her own purse and nodded, as if to say she was ready for anything.

As the four of them proceeded toward the hallway, Gavin called out from his desk, "What's going on?"

Karl barked at him, "Nothing that concerns you, Mr. Gorman. You focus on those reports."

Gavin, who'd started to rise from his chair, sat down immediately. He gave Zinnia a creepy, knowing grin. Again, Zinnia got the feeling she was forgetting something important. But it probably didn't matter, compared to whatever had made Liza so frightened.

On the walk to the elevator, Zinnia held back to cast a narrow sound bubble and say to Margaret, "Karl has black blood. I saw it just now."

"I knew it! Is he a troll?"

"He was going to tell me about his powers, but he wanted me to go first, and I wouldn't."

"That sounds like you," Margaret agreed. "You can be so stubborn."

Talk about the pot calling the kettle black. Again. "Also, the surge detector went supernova," Zinnia said. "It turned orange, then red, then bright white, and it exploded in my office."

"Surge detected!" Margaret adjusted her purse strap. "Where are we going?"

"Third floor."

"All four of us? I shouldn't have rested my eyes. What time is it?"

"It's just past two o'clock. I fell asleep, too. I didn't notice Liza was late getting back from her lunch break. She finally showed up just a few minutes ago, looking like a mess. According to her, something has taken Xavier. Something on the third floor."

Margaret said, with a pout, "I miss all the good stuff."

"You haven't missed it yet. Open your eyes. It's all happening right now."

"Oh!" Margaret cheered up.

Zinnia popped the sound bubble just as Karl turned around to stare at them with suspicion.

Liza pressed the call button for the elevator. The doors opened immediately. The three of them followed Liza in.

"Was it the mayor?" Karl asked. "Is that who detained Xavier? That woman is so bossy. She's always putting her pointy nose in everything."

Liza's mouth moved silently before she spat out, "The mayor didn't take Xavier."

He demanded, "Then who did?"

Liza said, "I told you. It wasn't a who." She unfastened the clasp of her necklace, gripped the magical key, and slid the blade into the elevator's control panel.

Karl demanded, "Who gave you that key?"

"My grandmother," Liza said. "Except she didn't give it to me. I found it when I was packing up some things to take to her at the hospital."

The elevator suddenly plunged.

Karl gripped the handrail and looked around wildly. "What are you doing to the elevator?"

Before Liza answered, the elevator stopped plunging and the doors opened.

Beyond the elevator was the same abandoned, incomplete floor Zinnia and Margaret had visited the previous day.

Karl ducked his head out, looked left and right, then pulled his head back into the elevator.

"I can't believe it," he said, his tone wondrous. "It's an accordion floor." He turned to the witches with an excited, boy-like expression. "An accordion floor! Right here in City Hall!"

Zinnia said, "Can you explain to the rest of us what an accordion floor is, boss?" Karl liked being called boss.

Karl waved his hands with a childlike glee Zinnia hadn't witnessed since their time playing on the swing set at the park.

"It's a wrinkle in space," Karl said. "A floor that exists between floors, in a space that expands from within yet doesn't displace. City Hall has five floors, but it also has six." He peered out at the floor again. "Unless it has more than six." He frowned and scratched his head. "If there's one accordion floor, there could be a thousand."

"But why?" Zinnia asked.

Margaret cut in, "It's used for time travel. We know about that."

Karl chortled. "Time travel?" He chortled right at Margaret. "There's no such thing as time travel. It's just a wrinkle in space, not a wrinkle in time."

Zinnia raised an eyebrow. "Don't be so sure about that, boss."

Liza whimpered. The other three stopped talking about wrinkles and turned to look at her.

"Listen," Liza said. "Do you hear that? It's coming back."

In unison, the other three asked, "What's coming back?"

Liza opened her mouth but no sound came out. There was, however, a rumbling noise, and the shatter of glass breaking.

Suddenly, the giant head of a creature burst through one of the floor's milky windows and shot directly toward the elevator. The head extended on what appeared to be a neck, a very long neck. Except the neck never turned into shoulders. A head with a neck and no shoulders was something else.

"Sandworm," Zinnia managed to say.

Its mouth—if you could call it a mouth—split open along three seams as it came rushing toward the elevator.

Everyone screamed, even Karl.

A long, pink tendril shot from the sandworm's maw and grabbed hold of Liza, who'd been standing closest to the door. The tongue lashed around her like a whip, and then reeled her into the darkness of its terrible mouth.

Zinnia wasn't quite ready, but the defensive magic was already pooling in her hands. She widened her stance, braced herself, and shot her blue plasma fireballs at the creature. Margaret stood at Zinnia's side and followed suit with her equally powerful green-colored plasma fireballs.

The blue and green electricity crackled over the creature.

The sandworm's mouth closed around Liza, muting her screams.

Karl shook his fist at the creature. "Let her go! That's my employee. Put her down at once, whoever you are!"

Margaret leaned into Zinnia and gasped, "It's not working. That thing is too big!"

Karl continued to berate the sandworm, and the witches kept zapping it. Neither approach was having any effect.

Zinnia felt her strength draining rapidly. Even so, she gave all she had, holding nothing in reserve.

CHAPTER 24

THE TWO WITCHES' plasma was failing, sputtering out, when the elevator made a ding sound. With a metallic clang and whir, suddenly the elevator doors were closing. The view of the menacing sandworm was closed off by metal doors.

Both witches dropped their arms to their sides to avoid ricochet plasma within the elevator cage. They turned to Karl, who had his finger on the Close Doors button.

Margaret demanded, "Why did you do that?"

Karl puffed up his chest. "Sometimes the department supervisor has to make difficult decisions. I've already lost two employees to that thing, and I wasn't about to lose another one. I did it to protect the two of you."

The elevator was already moving upward rapidly.

Zinnia said, "We can't leave Liza behind."

"Of course we won't," Karl blustered. "I wasn't planning on leaving her there. But we need, uh, backup."

Zinnia spotted something on the floor. Liza's key. Shattered to pieces. She groaned as she crouched down and picked up the remnants. It had been crushed to smithereens.

"We have a problem," Zinnia said.

Margaret dropped to her knees beside Zinnia and wailed, "How are we ever going to get back to 1955?"

Karl and Zinnia looked at Margaret.

She quickly said, "I mean, how are we going to rescue Liza now? And the other one?"

"His name is Xavier," Zinnia said.

Margaret straightened up and huffed, "Why are you both looking at me like that? I'm not the one who smashed the key to smithereens."

Both witches looked at Karl.

He made a harumph sound then said, "I didn't smash the key. It must have been you two witches and your magic lightning zaps."

"But you did hit the button to close the elevator doors," Zinnia said.

He gave her an incredulous look. "Did you see the size of that thing? It would have taken all of us! Not just the new girl."

The new girl. Zinnia noted that the way Karl called Liza "the new girl" made it sound like Liza was expendable, like a crew member who wore red in a classic *Star Trek* episode. If a sandworm had attacked the *Star Trek* crew, it would have gobbled a Red Shirt first.

The elevator stopped moving. With another ding, the doors slid open.

All three turned to the doorway, bracing themselves for another round with the sandworm.

Instead, they were back on the ground floor again. They immediately saw who had pressed the call button. There were two people standing in the hallway: Dawna and Gavin.

"Great," Karl said. "Now the whole office is here. Is there any work getting done today at all?"

"Carrot's not here," Dawna said.

Margaret muttered, "And neither are the two of us who got eaten by sandworms."

Karl asked, "Where's Carrot? Is she in trouble?"

Dawna gave Karl a squinty look. "Not that I know of. She was sitting at her desk when we came out to..." She shook her head. "You two are both witches, aren't you?"

Zinnia and Margaret looked up from the shattered bits of key they were trying to piece together. In unison, they said, "No."

Dawna shook her head. "Deny it all you want, but now that I can see it, I see it all." She looked directly at Karl. "Boss, are these two witches?"

Karl said nothing.

Dawna took that as an answer in the affirmative. "Busted," she said, grinning.

"The game's up, ladies," Gavin said. He crossed his arms and looked smug, giving Zinnia his creepy grin again. "Your cover is blown, and you have only yourselves to blame."

Zinnia gave the gnome a dirty look. He already knew about the two of them being witches. He'd known for months. But they had an understanding about mutual secrecy. Why had he told Dawna? Why now?

Dawna, meanwhile, was unfolding a piece of paper. She showed the handwritten note to the witches.

"I found this crazy note on Gavin's desk this morning," Dawna explained. "At first, I thought it was a practical joke. All this talk about you two having a magic key and going to some other world."

Zinnia suddenly remembered the thing she'd been forgetting. The note they'd left on Gavin's desk the night before. They hadn't gotten back in time to remove it.

Dawna continued, "But then I thought maybe it wasn't a joke. When I looked at it that way, all sorts of things started to make sense. The way you two always talk so quiet inside the break room. Then I thought about all that stuff Annette wrote in her book, about the two teen witches..." She slowly turned her head to the side. "Did you hear that?"

The ground rumbled and the elevator shook. The witches and Karl exchanged panicked looks. The sandworm? Had it followed them through?

Dawna and Gavin, who were still outside the elevator in the hallway, turned to look at something. In unison, both of their jaws dropped open.

Zinnia, Margaret, and Karl leaned out of the elevator and followed their gaze.

Zinnia had expected—no, feared—she would see the sandworm rushing toward them through the hallway. But there was no sandworm. There was, however, a teeming mass of crawling creatures. They were moving on multiple legs, like spiders, but the size of crabs.

Margaret cried out, "Bone-crawlers!" She clutched Zinnia's arm and dug in her fingernails.

Dawna managed to tear her gaze off the wave of bone-crawlers and turn toward the witches, her eyes huge. "Did you two do this? Did you mix up one of your witch potions and make those things?"

"We did no such thing," Zinnia said. "Those are bone-crawlers, and—" She cut off her explanation, grabbed Gavin and Dawna by their arms, and yanked them into the elevator. As she did so, she caught a glance of two men in body armor coming toward them, chasing the bone-crawlers.

The larger of the two men yelled at her, "Take cover!"

She did so, ducking back into the elevator.

Karl was already pushing the button to close the doors.

The doors closed, and they started moving up. All five of them spaced themselves out evenly.

They looked at each other in stunned silence. Everyone looked horrified, except for one person, who looked happier than a kid at her own surprise birthday party.

Dawna Jones bobbed her head from side to side, grinning. In a sing-song voice, she sang, "You two are witches. You two are witches. I know your secret. I read your no-ote." The word*note* didn't have two syllables, but she stretched it out for the rhythm.

As she paused to take a breath, there was a skittering, scratching sound that filled the elevator. Everyone looked around and then down.

Dawna screamed.

One of the bone-crawlers had made it into the elevator. There was more skittering. It was actually three bone-crawlers. It was always difficult to count bone-crawlers, on account of how they were asymmetrical and sometimes clung together, looking like bits of burned meat on stiletto legs.

Karl loosened his tie and unbuttoned his collar again. "Everyone stay calm," he barked.

Zinnia tried to pool blue defensive plasma in her palms, but she was still spent from her efforts on the third floor. And by the look of Margaret's hands, the other witch was in the same position.

"I said stay calm," Karl barked. "Don't you dare electrocute me, you two witches."

Dawna screamed again. Or maybe she'd never stopped screaming.

Karl tilted his head left and right, cracking his neck. The skittering paused, and all was quiet. Dawna inhaled for another scream. Zinnia's ears were ringing.

And then Karl Kormac, manager of the Wisteria Permits Department, opened his mouth wider than it should have been possible for any human to open their mouth. Karl's tongue shot out. And out. And out. His tongue was as long and flexible as the tongue of the sandworm.

In less than ten seconds, Karl had snapped up not just one, but all three bone-crawlers and... eaten them.

CHAPTER 25

THE OTHER FOUR people in the elevator stared at Karl Kormac, the cheap-suit-wearing, coffee-machine-cursing, fart-bombing supervisor of the Wisteria Permits Department. Unless they were all sharing a group hallucination, Karl had just eaten three bone-crawlers.

Karl cracked his neck again and let out a burp. "Tasty," he said. The seven-foot-long tongue had retracted and his mouth looked perfectly normal.

Margaret waved a shaky finger at Karl. "You just ate three of those horrible creatures." She turned to the others. "You all saw that, right?"

The others nodded.

Zinnia said, "Is that your big secret, boss? You can eat anything?"

"That's *part of* my secret," Karl said. "It all falls under the major headline."

Dawna covered her mouth with both hands and made a hiccup-burp sound. "I'm gonna be sick," she said. "Is Karl a witch, too? Or a warlock or something?" More hiccups.

Zinnia patted Dawna on the shoulder. "Just keep breathing."

Margaret asked Karl, "And what exactly is the major headline? What are you?"

Karl wiped the corner of his mouth. "Haven't you guessed already?"

The two witches exchanged a look. Zinnia had an idea, but it felt rude to say the word out loud.

"Troll," Margaret said. "Karl, you're a troll."

Karl winced and clutched his hands to his heart. "Ouch. Margaret! How can you say that? And after I saved everyone from a trio of ferocious bone-crawlers?"

Margaret gave him a confused look. "You're *not* a troll?"

Karl bobbed his head from one side to the other, as if to say she was neither right nor wrong. "We prefer the term *sprites*," he said. "Whenever legends are translated to different languages, there's a tendency for translators to call any creature whose name they don't have a word for yet, trolls. Several family lines are unfairly labeled as trolls. It's a term that's both offensive and vague."

Stunned silence.

"I'm a sprite," Karl said. "S-P-R-I-T-E."

Dawna made another hiccup-burp sound. "This is all too much," she said hoarsely. "My boss thinks he's a sprite."

Karl made a HARUMPH sound and adjusted his tie. "I don't *think* I'm a sprite, Ms. Jones. I am one." His face reddened. "I know what I am."

Dawna kept one hand over her mouth and used the other to point at Zinnia. "You're a witch." She pointed at Margaret. "You're a witch." She pointed at Karl. "And you're a sprite?"

Karl pointed at Gavin. "Gnome," he said. "Your boyfriend's a gnome."

Dawna turned to Gavin. "A gnome? Seriously? You told me you were a wizard!"

Gavin's cheeks reddened to match Karl's. "I didn't tell you that," Gavin said. "You made an assumption, and I didn't correct you."

None of them noticed the elevator had stopped moving until the doors opened.

All five occupants wheeled to face the opening. Would it be the sandworm again? Or more bone-crawlers?' Zinnia cupped her hands and prepared to shoot what was left of her blue plasma.

A man in head-to-toe protective gear threw up both hands. "Hold your fire," he said.

Zinnia recognized him through his protective goggles.

"Agent Rob," she said.

"That's me," he said. "Agent Rob is here to save the day! And hopefully not become lunch for a nest of hungry bone-crawlers."

Zinnia turned to see her coworkers in various states of alarm. Margaret had green plasma dripping from her fingers.

"At ease," Zinnia said to the group. "This is Agent Rob. He's with..." Her discretion stopped her from naming the DWM. "He's with pest control," she said.

"I'm with the good guys," Rob said. "You can call us pest control."

Karl pushed his way to the front of the group, taking charge as usual. "Good to see you here," he said to the agent. "I've already taken care of three juveniles that got into the elevator." He sniffed the air. "Did you find the queen? If you take out the queen, the rest will fall in line." He licked his lips. "I'd be happy to help with that."

Agent Rob held up one armored hand. "No need, Mr. Kormac. We've already taken care of the queen. We're moving on to clean-up. Speaking of which, did any of you nice folks happen to see anything strange that you'd like to speak to one of our helpful members of staff about?"

"Don't say anything," Margaret whispered to Dawna. "If you say you saw something, they wipe your mind."

Karl, who was still standing at the front of the group, leaned in toward the agent and said something. Zinnia couldn't hear him over the echoing screams and thumps coming from further down the ground floor hallway. According to the ruckus, the DWM hadn't quite taken care of the entire mess yet.

"You got it, man," Rob said as he backed away from Karl, nodding. He gave the group two thumbs up, then turned and ran toward the noise.

Zinnia started to run after Rob, but Karl stopped her with a heavy hand on her shoulder. "Where do you think you're going?"

"I have to tell them about the third floor," Zinnia explained. "They need to send in a team to get Liza and Xavier. Maybe they have a way of getting through."

Karl seemed to consider this a moment.

"No," said Dawna. Her face was sweaty. She didn't look entirely well, but she'd calmed down her hiccup-burps. "They aren't the ones who do it," she said. "They're not the Chosen."

Gavin gave her a skeptical look. "Are you messing with us? Is this your way of getting back at me for not telling you everything sooner?"

The elevator doors tried to close on the group. Margaret stopped the doors with her foot and shooed everyone out. "Let's talk about this somewhere else," Margaret said. "Somewhere not inside this cramped elevator."

The group stepped out. Zinnia ran back to get the remaining bits of crushed key off the floor of the elevator, then stepped out and let it go.

Dawna was saying, "I know I'm new to the whole supernatural thing, but I've been practicing with my tarot cards, and, you guys, I think I can tell the future."

"Of course you can," Margaret said. "You're a cartomancer."

"Exactly," Dawna said. "I'm a fortune-teller. Same thing."

"No, no, no," Margaret said. "Not the same thing. You're a card mage, Dawna."

For once, Gavin agreed with Margaret. "It's true," he told Dawna. "If you call yourself a fortune-teller, none of the cool supernaturals will be friends with you."

Dawna put one hand on her hip. "Maybe I don't want to be friends with them."

"You want to have powerful friends," Gavin said. "Trust me."

"Like you? What does a gnome do, anyway?"

Gavin looked around furtively and muttered, "Where's a bone-crawler when you need one?"

Karl blustered, "That's enough chatter! Back to the business at hand. Dawna, you were telling us you saw something in the cards?"

Dawna scratched her dark cheek with one long fingernail and glanced around. They were still in the hallway near the elevator, and nobody else was nearby. "Where are the new kids? Where are Liza and Xavier?"

Zinnia put her hand on Dawna's shoulder and looked the woman straight in the eyes. "They need our help," Zinnia said. "We'll explain everything soon, but you were saying something about seeing the future? About people who are Chosen?"

Dawna stared back at Zinnia, her orange, cat-like eyes gradually relaxing. "The cards keep telling me that two people are in danger, and the only ones who can save them are a group of five wizards."

"Well, we're not wizards," Gavin said, brushing his hands. "Guess that leaves us out. Maybe it's five of the pest control guys."

Zinnia ignored Gavin and asked Dawna, "What else did the cards tell you?" Out of the corners of her eyes, she saw the other three leaning in to listen.

"There's a giant snake," Dawna said. "Enormous."

Margaret gasped. "She knows about the sandworm! Dawna, you really are a cartomancer!"

Zinnia prompted, "What else?"

Dawna's voice was soft, unsteady. "The giant snake swallowed two people, but it's a magic snake, so the people didn't die."

"That's good news," Margaret said. "They're still alive."

"But they're in terrible danger," Dawna said, her eyes glistening. "So the five wizards—or, I guess they're actually five people with supernatural powers—have to find a magical key and rescue them."

Gavin asked, "How?"

Karl cleared his throat. "What's the plan, Dawna?"

Dawna took a step back from the group, shaking her black curls. "That's all I know," she said. "Five people use the key." She put her hand on her hip again. "Please tell me one of you has this magic key."

Zinnia lifted her hand to show everyone the broken key fragments in her palm.

"We need an alternate plan," Zinnia said. "This is the only magic key we know of, and it's broken."

Karl said, "That can't be the only key. There must be another one. Dawna, think! Where's the other one?"

"I don't know," she said, her voice shaking. "I mean, I could try reading the cards again, but..." She held both hands to her mouth and hiccupped. "Oh, no. I'm going to be sick. I can still smell those creepy-crawly things."

"Me, too," Gavin said, wrinkling his nose. "What's that pest control crew doing? Having a barbecue?"

Karl burped. "It might be my breath," he said.

That set off a chain reaction that included more hiccupping from Dawna, and everyone talking about the smell of burnt bone-crawlers and each other's powers.

Zinnia tuned out the conversation and stared at the crumbled bits of key in her hand.

She didn't know Liza and Xavier very well. She wasn't even particularly attached to them. But they were still people! They weren't Red Shirts in a *Star Trek* episode. They had lives and futures that weren't going to happen if they were stuck inside magical snakes on another plane of reality.

She had to think. How could the five of them mount a rescue without the key?

She started to get an idea, fuzzy around the edges.

Karl burped again, and the stench of bone-crawler meat set Zinnia's thinking back by a minute.

Soon, she was back on track. They didn't have the magical key, but they did have a physical duplicate of it.

She couldn't shake the mental image of Karl's long, chameleon-like tongue snaking out of his mouth. However, the visual wasn't entirely bad, because it made her think of chameleons, and then she remembered a specific potion she'd read about in one of her books.

That was it! She had a plan, and it was thanks to Karl's smelly burps and freaky tongue.

Zinnia interrupted the conversation and said, "I have an idea. We might not have the right key, but I believe we can make one."

Everyone stared at her.

"We can make one," she repeated. "Maybe. I don't know if I can do it."

"Zinnia, you can do it," Margaret said, clapping her hands together. To the others, she said, "Zinnia can do it. She's amazing with potions. We just need to get her home, where she keeps all her good ingredients."

"Great," Karl said. "It's settled. We'll all go to Zinnia's house straight after work."

"All of us?" Zinnia tried not to let the horror show on her face.

"You heard the card mage," Karl said, gesturing at Dawna. "This is a five-wizard job."

"A five-man job," Gavin corrected.

"A five-person job," Margaret then corrected.

Karl checked his watch. "We'll head out to Zinnia's residence in a couple of hours, as soon as the department is closed." He shooed them down the hallway in the direction of their office. "Back to work with all of you. Chop chop. Don't make me tongue-lash anyone."

Dawna shrieked a little at the idea of Karl's chameleon tongue making another appearance. She ran ahead of the group, leading the way.

CHAPTER 26

THREE HOURS LATER

ZINNIA FOUND HERSELF alone in her kitchen with her least favorite coworker, Gavin Gorman. Previous to today, she would have said Karl was her least favorite coworker, but ever since the department boss had munched a trio of nasty monsters, Zinnia's opinion of the older man had been upgraded. Gavin was in the kitchen because he had insisted on helping Zinnia brew up a pot of coffee. So far, he hadn't been much help.

The others, Karl, Dawna, and Margaret, were stationed in Zinnia's living room, debating pizza toppings for their dinner takeout order.

Zinnia handed Gavin some of the freshly ground coffee she kept on hand for guests.

Gavin was sneering at her coffee maker. "This old thing is practically an antique," Gavin said. He wrinkled his nose and banged on the top of it. Zinnia wondered how he'd like it if someone banged on the top of Gavin. Zinnia was, to her surprise, kind of protective of her appliances.

"Does it even work?" Gavin asked.

"Yes," she sighed. "Antique or not, it still heats water and dribbles it through the beans. You ought to be able to make do."

"If you say so." He added the coffee and water, then grabbed a chair and sat right in front of the coffee maker, watching the drips come down.

"It doesn't need supervision," she said.

He grunted.

"The whole point of appliances is they do the work for you."

He didn't budge.

Zinnia leaned back against the kitchen counter and watched her coworker watch the coffee.

Gavin Gorman was a gnome who looked nothing like the gnomes in fairy tales. For starters, he was over six foot two. He wore stylish clothes that were, in Zinnia's opinion, always a size too small. Then again, Zinnia didn't read magazines about men's fashion, so what did she know? Wearing shoes without socks would drive her nuts, but Gavin did so regularly.

The forty-something man had a square face, a cleft chin, a short nose, and close-set, hazel eyes. His skin was bronze from frequent spray-tanning and his teeth were blue-white from frequent laser whitening. He wore his sandy brown hair in a conservative cut, and was always clean-shaven. The man couldn't walk past a mirror without pausing to admire himself, nor could he let a coworker's verbal mistake go uncorrected, but he wasn't all bad. Sure, back in January he had ransacked his murdered coworker's corpse looking for a pen, but he hadn't killed the woman for it.

Being a gnome, Gavin was naturally attracted to items of value. The one "item of value" he couldn't stay away from was Dawna Jones. The couple was always getting together and breaking up again. Nobody but the two of them cared, yet lately they had been making announcements about their current state of entanglement. They were under the impression their coworkers were interested. What Gavin and Dawna didn't realize was that people only cared to gossip about office romances that were secret or, better yet, taboo.

The last time Zinnia had been alone with Gavin, they'd been at his apartment at the Candy Factory. He had ingested an herbal compound, and she'd tricked him into believing the combination was going to have disastrous consequences for his love life. He'd then given her the information she needed, but the biggest breakthrough had come courtesy of a painting he had hanging in his living room. It was a painting of a nude redhead who bore more than a passing resemblance to Zinnia herself.

As Zinnia watched Gavin watching the coffee drip, she thought about the painting in a whole new light.

"Gavin," she said hesitantly. "That painting of the nude redhead you have in your apartment, where did you get it?"

He didn't take his eyes off the dripping coffee. "The one that looks just like you? I got it at a yard sale a few years back. It's really old. The frame is vintage. I mainly bought it for the frame, but then Raquel grew on me."

"Raquel?"

"That's the name I gave her, on account of how she reminded me of Raquel Welch."

Zinnia felt her pulse race. Could it be? Last night when she'd been alone with Piero in 1955, he'd shown her his beautiful paintings and asked that she pose for him sometime. The wine had gone to her head, and Piero was so charming. She'd thrown caution to the wind and offered to pose for him right then and there.

Zinnia's mouth was dry. When she spoke again, her speech wasn't so crisp. "Was there anything written on the back of the painting?"

"Just the date and the artist's name."

The tremble in her voice betrayed her nerves. "And what was the date?"

Gavin turned and gave her a confused look. "Since when are you so interested in an old painting? I'll sell it to you, if you want."

"No need. I'm just curious about the artist."

"I don't remember. I haven't looked at the back side of that painting since I hung it there." Gavin leaned to the side in his chair, looked down at his feet, and tapped the floor with the toes of one foot. "If it's really that important to you, I could teleport to my apartment right now and check."

Zinnia clapped her hands. "Would you? That would be wonderful."

He frowned. "I would... except teleportation is really exhausting. Plus, it only goes one direction, straight to the pre-defined safe spot. I'd have to call a taxi to get a ride back here to your house, assuming I had the strength to leave the apartment right away."

Zinnia tilted her head to the side. "Gavin, the last time we talked about teleportation, you told me it was just a myth about gnomes. You denied it."

Gavin shrugged and returned his gaze to the coffee maker. "Yeah, well, we weren't exactly friends back then."

"And we are now?"

He turned his head and gave her a hurt look. "Are you saying we aren't?"

"Of course not," she said quickly. "I suppose I haven't given it much thought."

"We go bowling together on Friday nights, even though Annette isn't around anymore to guilt us into it. That makes us friends. All of us."

Just then, a chorus of laughter filtered in from the living room. Zinnia realized that Gavin was right. They were more than coworkers. They were friends.

Even so, she wasn't about to tell Gavin that the painting that graced his living room was, quite possibly, a nude Zinnia Riddle.

"Speaking of friends," she said, "how do you feel about Dawna knowing you're a gnome?"

Gavin scoffed. "It's not ideal."

"But it's only fair that she knows the truth."

He scoffed again. "Whatever respect she had for me went out the window. Nobody wants to date a gnome. Not even other gnomes. My kind doesn't exactly have a stellar reputation."

"The only gnomes I know are you and your uncle, Griebel."

Gavin gave Zinnia a raised eyebrow.

"Oh," she said, recalling what she knew about Griebel and his scheming ways. "I see what you mean."

"If only I'd been born into one of the sexy supernatural families," he said. "Like shifters. Everyone thinks shifters are so dreamy."

Now it was Zinnia's turn to scoff. "Not all shifters are dreamy."

"You've never dated a shifter? But witches and shifters are supposed to hate each other, which only makes it hotter for them to date. It's sexy and scandalous, like star-crossed lovers."

Zinnia took a breath to settle the feelings that had flooded up. Gavin didn't know the truth about her time with a shifter, or how it had ended.

Or did he? Gavin was staring at her intently.

"Never mind about supernatural politics," Zinnia said. "There will be plenty of time for you to speculate about my nonexistent love life after we get Liza and Xavier back. Those poor kids." She grabbed mugs for everyone from her cupboard. "I just hope Dawna is right about her cards, and they're still alive."

"Dawna's the real deal," Gavin said. "I'd put my faith in her."

"And yet you wouldn't tell her the truth about who you were. Karl told her." It had been wrong of Karl to tell anyone, but that was beside the point.

Gavin didn't say anything.

Zinnia turned her attention inward, asking herself why she even cared about Gavin telling Dawna he was a gnome. Dawna had only just learned about the existence of supernatural powers that morning, when she'd read the note intended for Gavin. She hadn't even had a single night to sleep on the news.

Gavin grabbed the coffee pot, which was now full, and started toward the living room. "I'll take care of the crew," he said. "Do you want me to send your partner in crime back here to help you with that potion you were talking about? The, uh... what was it called again?"

"Chameleon potion," she said, getting excited about her project. "It sprays off a rainbow assortment of magic. Using it on a charmed object is a bit like hitting an infected patient with a raft of various antibiotics rather than a targeted strain."

He gave her an appreciative look. "And the key is the infected patient?" He and Dawna had both been brought up

ANGELA PEPPER

to speed about the accordion floor and the manner of Xavier's and Liza's abductions.

"Following the metaphor through, the keyhole in the elevator control panel is the infected patient."

"Very clever," Gavin said. "And if your chameleon potion doesn't work, we'll just call Uncle Griebel. I bet he can hotwire the thing."

"Your uncle is not my favorite person right now. Ever since one of his contraptions nearly electrocuted my niece."

"Huh. Uncle Griebel never mentioned that to me." He gave her a knowing look. "See? This is why gnomes have a bad reputation."

"Then it's up to you to be the changed gnome you wish to see in the world," she said, mangling the famous quote.

"Huh?"

"Never mind." She waved him to go join the others and take the coffee.

* * *

Half an hour later, Margaret Mills came into the kitchen for the fourth time that evening. "The pizza is here," she said.

"Not hungry." Zinnia barely looked up from her magical ingredients and cauldron full of bubbling potion. She was dimly aware of how she must have appeared at that moment—perfectly ready for the cover photo of Kitchen Bewitched Magazine!

Margaret did a double take. "Zinnia, is that an honest-to-goodness cauldron you're using?"

"Cauldrons have the exact right shape, and their materials don't interact. You can't mix this stuff in any old jar. You'd bruise the potion. If you were Kitchen Bewitched, you'd know that."

"Bruise the potion? But it's a liquid. I don't understand how it would get bruised."

"Of course you don't understand. And that's why I'm mixing the chameleon potion and you're keeping an eye on things out there, making sure nobody..." She searched her memory for a phrase she'd learned from the younger

202

Riddles. "Making sure nobody wipes their *pepperoni fingers* on my upholstery."

"Nobody wiped their pepperoni fingers on the sofa, but they are getting antsy about going through the elevator." She leaned forward and peered into the cauldron. As she did so, a single pale eyelash fluttered loose from her cheek and fell toward the cauldron's contents. Zinnia deftly grabbed the eyelash using magic and floated it safely over to the kitchen sink, where it wouldn't contaminate the entire batch. Margaret didn't even notice the close call. And this was exactly why Zinnia had sent Margaret out of the kitchen three times already.

"Step away from the cauldron," Zinnia said in her most authoritative voice.

Margaret backed up, waving both hands in the air. "Fine, I'll leave you to it, Ms. Kitchen Cursed."

"Kitchen Bewitched."

"Tomay-to, tomah-to."

Zinnia rolled her shoulders back, and cast the spell that would give Margaret a chomp on the hindquarters.

Margaret squealed and ran from the kitchen.

CHAPTER 27

WHILE ZINNIA PUT the finishing touches on the chameleon potion, she listened to her coworkers chatting amiably in the living room.

Dawna had a million questions about magic, and the others were eager to tell her about aspects of their lives that had been secret until now. Despite the shadow of disaster looming over them, the mood was cheerful, not unlike the moments they'd shared at the bowling alley whenever Karl bowled one of his high-scoring games.

The discussion turned to the one remaining coworker who wasn't accounted for: Carrot Greyson. Not one person had said a word to her about what they'd seen on the third floor or in the ground floor hallway. The crew from the DWM had done an excellent job of containing and cleaning up the bone-crawlers before the infestation had become a building-wide panic. Carrot Greyson had no idea what was going on around her.

"Carrot's just like me," Dawna said. "I bet she's got powers, but she doesn't know it yet."

Margaret made a vague noise.

Dawna immediately whooped. "She does? Margaret, tell me more!"

Margaret said nothing. Zinnia couldn't see the witch, but imagined Margaret was miming zipping her lips shut.

"Fine, don't tell me," Dawna said. "But you have to tell her. Poor Carrot can't be sitting there every day, working side by side with the rest of us, not knowing."

Karl said, "We don't know about Carrot. Just because Annette made her a rune mage in that silly book, that doesn't mean anything." He snorted. "The woman actually cast me as a troll."

Nobody said anything.

Karl went HARUMPH.

Gavin said, "Carrot is quite happy to live her life not knowing. I vote that we leave her out of this."

"I vote we tell her," Dawna said. "Come on, people. You're not going to take Gavin's side, are you?"

There was some muttering. Despite how they might have felt about telling Carrot about magic, none of them wanted to take sides in a Dawna-Gavin standoff.

"I could just ask Carrot," Dawna said.

"No," Margaret replied sternly. "First of all, not everyone is supernatural, Dawna. Keep that in mind at all times. And secondly, remember that it's extremely rude to ask."

"It's way beyond rude," Karl said. "Dawna, you don't ask. You don't. Not ever. Whenever you ask someone, you're putting yourself at risk, as well as everyone you consort with." He made a huffy noise. "As your supervisor, I forbid you from disclosing your gifts to anyone except those currently present."

"What?" Dawna sounded outraged. "You can't do that. You're not my supervisor in*everything*."

Karl made another HARUMPH, and the room fell silent. Zinnia guessed that by Dawna's lack of quibbling, Karl had flicked out his terrifying chameleon tongue.

"Okay," Dawna said meekly. "I see what you did there with your tongue." Her voice became nasal. "Ew. That thing smells nasty."

"It's the bone-crawlers," he said. "They take a long time to ferment."

"I didn't want an explanation," Dawna said.

"Me, neither," said Gavin.

"I'm interested in the fermentation process, but perhaps another time," Margaret said. "And I'd rather you tell me than show me."

There was a smattering of amused laughter.

Dawna spoke again. "All right, Karl. You can be my supervisor when it comes to magic stuff, but only if you're Gavin's supervisor, too. That way we're all at the same level."

"I already am his supervisor," Karl said.

"It's true," Gavin said. "I've known about Karl's powers for a long time, and he knows about mine. That's why I work at the department."

The revelation triggered a dozen more questions. Dawna spit out queries at a rapid pace. Soon, everyone was talking at once.

In the kitchen, Zinnia realized that was why Gavin always listened to Karl's orders despite giving off the impression he didn't respect the older man. It was a mentor thing.

While the conversation in the living room continued, Zinnia tuned them out and reviewed her notes and procedures for the potion.

So far, everything was coming together perfectly. She'd been short a few ingredients, but she'd consulted some of Tansy Wick's notes for substitutions, and she felt confident in her choices. There were some aspects of Zinnia's life where she didn't have the utmost confidence, such as when she was trying to impress lessons upon her niece, but Zinnia did know her potions.

From an early age, she'd shown an intuitive grasp for combining organic and inorganic materials to create powerful compounds. For every Witch Tongue word there was a color, a texture, a taste. Once she'd learned the language, she could "speak" in potions. With each year of experience, she'd become more fluent. This chameleon potion, to be used on the look-alike key, felt like it could be her final examination. Her thesis paper, so to speak. She'd been tested before, but never like this. The lives of two people hung in the balance.

She stepped back from the cauldron and rubbed her eyes.

She heard a knocking sound. Someone was at the front door.

Zinnia tuned in again to the voices in the living room.

Gavin said, "Who could that be? Everyone's here."

"I'll get it," Margaret said. "It might be one of the other Riddles. Zinnia's always helping her niece out of trouble."

Everyone went quiet.

Zinnia stayed where she was in the kitchen. She stared at the entryway, expecting to see her niece, Zara Riddle, come bursting in wearing something technicolor. Zara would launch into the story of some new catastrophe, talking a mile a minute, pausing only to demand to know who all the people in the living room were, as well as their respective powers.

But the redheaded librarian witch didn't show up. Who had been knocking at the front door?

Zinnia went to the living room. Her coworkers barely glanced up. One of them was missing. The other witch, Margaret.

"Where's Margaret?" Zinnia asked.

Gavin grinned up at Zinnia from his seat on her favorite reading chair. "Her ball and chain came by with some sort of family crisis."

Dawna shot Gavin a dirty look. "Don't say ball and chain. He's a person. His name is..." She scrunched up her face.

"Mike," Zinnia said. "Margaret's husband is Mike, and he's a very nice man." Nice was a substitute for the first word she'd thought of to describe Mike, which was *boring*.

Zinnia parted the front window's curtains and peered out at the porch. Mike and Margaret weren't there.

Zinnia asked, "Did she leave? Was there an emergency with the kids?" More importantly, was Zinnia going to have to use the key and walk through the time portal and face menacing sandworms without another witch to back her up?

"I don't know," Dawna said. "She didn't say anything to us."

Zinnia walked toward the front door to go check on Margaret. She paused, turned back, held up a finger, and gave the group a serious look. "Nobody go into the kitchen. Don't breathe in the direction of the kitchen. Don't even think about how much you shouldn't go into the kitchen. Just... don't."

The three, who were seated comfortably, agreed to heed her warning, and immediately went back to talking about magic.

Zinnia stepped outside and squinted from the brightness of the light. The sun was low on the horizon, and the whole sky was orange. For a moment, she wasn't sure if it was sunrise or sunset. Her internal clock had been thrown off by the visit to the past and a missed sleep. Catnapping at her desk for an hour was no substitute for a full night's rest.

She heard Margaret's distinctive voice. She followed it down the sidewalk and up the street. Margaret and her husband, Mike, were having a heated conversation about something. Zinnia didn't want to eavesdrop, and yet she felt an overwhelming urge to do so. Margaret had been dropping hints for weeks about something going on in her life, and whatever it was had better not be taking Margaret out of tonight's plans.

Zinnia picked up a leaf, a blade of grass, and a pinch of dirt. She rolled the items in the palm of her hand, whispered her spell in Witch Tongue, and relaxed as the glamour took hold. It was just a simple foliage-cover spell. To non-magical eyes, Zinnia would appear to be a green bush that matched her height and width. The species of bush was like nothing in existence on Earth, yet it blended readily with any environment. When she had last used the spell, which was on her niece, Zara had reported birds landing on her shoulders, attempting to roost on her. Zinnia had since modified the spell to make the false foliage less enticing to feathered friends. Even so, there was one bird, a blue jay, who seemed to be watching her from its perch on a fence post.

Zinnia ignored the curious blue jay and shuffled closer to Margaret and her husband.

Mike Mills, like his wife Margaret, had frizzy gray hair —just not as much of it. The top of his head was bald enough to be dry and shiny in the winter and sunburned in the summer. As it was late spring now, the top of his head was both shiny and pink. Mike's face was oblong, with a prominent brow bone and a square jaw. His head had a rectangular, boxy shape to it, and his nose was a smaller version of that box. He had small eyes, thin lips, and big teeth. When he wasn't actively engaged in conversation, he could look a bit like Frankenstein's monster standing out in the rain. But if you got him smiling, or, better yet, talking about his favorite hobby—flying remote-control airplanes —Mike Mills could turn on the charm.

Mike wasn't a large man, but he looked taller when standing next to his stout wife. Mike worked as a software engineer, and could wear whatever he wanted to the office. His usual ensemble was a pair of well-worn jeans and a tropical-print, button-down shirt with short sleeves. He'd put on a few pounds somewhere between his first kid and his fourth, plus a few more after that. The tropical shirts did nothing to minimize his expanding waistline, but he didn't seem bothered by this. In fact, with the way his head jutted forward at all times, Mike Mills gave the impression he was only vaguely aware of his body's existence. It was simply the vehicle in which his brain rode around, getting from the computer at work to the computer at home.

Mike was evidently agitated by something, jutting his head forward even more as he spoke to Margaret.

"You treat me like a nobody," Mike said, spittle raining from his mouth. "No. It's worse than that. You treat me like I'm one of the children."

Margaret, who had her arms crossed, jutted her chin up at him defiantly. "I wouldn't treat you like a child if you didn't act like one."

"What's that supposed to mean?"

"You know exactly what I'm talking about. You're a grown man, Mike. Why do you have to spend so much time and money on toys?"

"Toys? My computers aren't toys. They're how I earn a living to support our family."

She flung her arms out in frustration. "Oh! So that's how you want to play this? What about my contribution? My salary is almost as much as yours, and my job is the only one with benefits. Your boss is your old buddy who knows he can take advantage of you and pay you less."

"Don't you dare say that about Carter. He's going to bump up my pay once the next program gets through testing."

"For crying out loud! You've been saying that for ten years now. *Carter needs another year to get everything in place. Carter this. Carter that.* I'm sick of hearing about Carter's plans for the company's future. What about *your* future, Mike? When are you going to take some control over your life?"

"Why?" He looked for a moment like he might laugh. "Why would I take control just to have you snap it away again?"

"Are you saying that I'm controlling?"

"If the shirt fits, wear it."

"The shoe," she said. "The saying goes, *if the shoe fits, wear it.*"

He groaned and made a gesture of pulling his hair out, even though he didn't have any on the top of his head where he pretended to grasp. "Why?" His posture buckled, and he fell to his knees. "Why must you always correct me?"

"Why are you so content with being wrong?"

He groaned, got back to his feet limply, and then turned away with a heavy sigh.

"You win," he said. "I give up. There's just no winning with you, Margaret."

"Who said anything about winning? Do you think I want to win? Do you think I want to spend my life married to a loser?"

The word *loser* hung in the air like a curse that couldn't be taken back.

Mike slumped even more. "I'm done," he said, sounding like a broken man.

"Don't say that." Margaret crossed her arms again. "I'm, uh, I should not have said what I was thinking."

Zinnia, who'd been watching in horror from inside the bush glamour, thought, *Margaret, the word you're looking for is sorry. Tell him you're sorry!*

Margaret uncrossed her arms and placed her hands on her hips. "I'm not sorry," she said, responding to Zinnia's silent suggestion. "It's about time we were honest with each other, Michael."

Mike wouldn't meet her gaze. He waved a hand and took a step back.

"I'll be at my sister's," he said, turning his torso away from his wife, giving her the shoulder. "The kids are already there."

"But what about our plans? The schedule? We've got picnics, and barbecues, and mini-golf. You love mini-golf!"

"We all love mini-golf. But it's not enough to keep a family together."

"Don't say that."

"We can still do things together, as a family. We can still mini-golf."

"But it won't be the same. How can we be a family if we don't live together?"

"We'll figure it out. People get divorced all the time. It's a perfectly normal thing."

Margaret said nothing.

Mike took another step back, pulling further away. "We can stick to the schedule, mini-golf and all. If you want to set up some other time to see the kids without me, you can speak to my lawyer." He turned and walked away.

Margaret's mouth moved but no sound came out. Her eyelashes fluttered. Mike was already three houses away when she squeaked out, "Lawyer?"

Zinnia stood very still.

Mike disappeared out of sight around the corner.

Zinnia's heart pounded. This wasn't as bad as seeing her other coworker being snapped up by an interdimensional sandworm, but it was bad. Should she reveal herself and let Margaret know she'd heard everything? It could feel supportive to Margaret. But then again, it could make Zinnia the target of Margaret's wrath.

Margaret answered the question for her. She turned to the bush and kicked it. Hard.

"Ow!" Zinnia dropped the glamour all at once. "How did you know it was me?"

Margaret blinked rapidly. "I didn't. I felt like kicking something, and that ugly bush was right there."

Zinnia didn't believe her. "You felt my thoughts, didn't you?"

"Maybe." Margaret started walking back toward the house.

There was a rumble as a family van with a broken muffler started up. It lurched noisily out onto the street and zoomed by. Mike was at the wheel. Parked behind where the van had been was a compact sedan, the other Mills family vehicle. Zinnia realized Mike must have come there to exchange vehicles, since he had the four kids with him at his sister's place and would need the van.

Zinnia felt, yet again, that it was time for her to comfort her friend. She was almost getting good at it. She reached out and patted Margaret on the shoulder. "I'm sorry about —"

Margaret twisted quickly, yanking her shoulder away. "Don't be sorry," she snapped. "And don't look at me like that."

"Like how?"

Margaret scrunched up her whole face. Her eyes were glistening. "Like you feel sorry for me. It's disgusting."

Zinnia averted her gaze, looking up at the sky, which was now turning from orange to red. She loved being outside for sunset, but not like this.

Margaret asked, still snappy, "Did you at least get that pot of soup mixed up? And by soup, I mean... you know what I mean."

"It's ready."

"Well? What are we waiting for? A telegram from Liza and Xavier? An engraved invitation?"

Zinnia felt her irritation at Margaret rising. She had been the one waiting for Margaret, waiting for her to finish blowing up her marriage and get back on track with their plan. Why was Zinnia being yelled at? She hadn't done anything wrong... other than eavesdropping. But it was something witches did! Why else had they developed so many types of glamours?

Zinnia wanted to give Margaret an earful about how she wasn't the easiest person to get along with. Mike had actually made a few good points. But even as she mentally formed the words in her head, another part of her advised caution and compassion. Margaret was already hurting enough. Plus they did have a mission ahead of them.

Zinnia nodded and repeated her response. "The soup is ready."

"Good." Margaret turned and clomped toward the house.

She didn't have to tell Zinnia not to say a word to the others about what had just happened. Zinnia knew. Even when the two witches were furious, they still understood and trusted each other.

They returned to the house and got ready with minimal talking. They gathered supplies and split into two groups for the car ride back to their workplace. There was no point in taking all the cars. It would be suspicious to have the entire department's vehicles in the parking lot.

Both carpools arrived at City Hall just as the building's exterior lights were flickering on. The lights were immediately smothered by the problem insects. There seemed to be more of the moth-like bugs than ever.

CHAPTER 28

CITY HALL WAS eerily empty inside.

The cleaning crew, who'd been spooked by one creepy thing too many that week, had made good on their threat to go on strike. An all-staff memo from the mayor's office had gone out that afternoon, along with the request that all departments pitch in by cleaning their own offices until the "minor negotiation issues" had been resolved.

As the group of five entered the elevator, Margaret held back.

Dawna asked, "What's wrong, Margaret?"

"I don't know," Margaret said, frowning. She'd been quiet since her fight with her husband. She looked uncertain, which was anything but normal for the woman.

"We need five of us," Dawna said. "I've got my cards with me, and I'll try to figure out more, but I'm pretty sure we all need to stick together."

"Maybe someone should stay behind," Margaret said. "For safety."

Gavin said, "If you're too chicken to go, just say so."

Margaret gave him an indignant look. "Oh, I'm going! I was thinking Zinnia should stay behind."

Everyone turned to look at Zinnia, who said, "Why me?"

"Your family needs you," Margaret said. Her expression was inscrutable.

Dawna said, "What about your family? You've got those four kids of yours who are always gettin' in trouble. Zinnia doesn't have any kids." Dawna looked around the group. "None of us have kids except you, Margaret."

The others glanced around the elevator and murmured agreement. It was true. None of them had kids.

The elevator doors started to close.

Margaret jumped forward, squeezing past the doors.

"Not so chicken after all," Gavin said.

"If the prophecy is for five people, I don't have any choice," she said.

Zinnia gave Margaret a puzzled look. Since when were they referring to Dawna's card reading as a prophecy? She'd missed that memo.

Margaret avoided meeting Zinnia's eyes. They hadn't exchanged more than a couple of words since the house.

Dawna asked, "What about your kids, Margaret?"

Margaret snorted. "Having four kids just gives me four reasons to take a one-way ticket to 1955 and never come back."

Dawna chuckled, and soon Karl and Gavin joined in. Zinnia stayed quiet. The others thought Margaret was joking, complaining about her obnoxious children in her usual manner. They hadn't been outside with Zinnia. They hadn't witnessed the sad spectacle of Margaret's home life crumbling.

The elevator rose. The doors opened on the third floor. It was the regular third floor, with the boardroom, glass hallway, and cubicles. An overflowing garbage bin sat next to the wall across from the elevator.

Gavin stepped out, saying, "It doesn't look very magic to me." He turned to ask Karl, "Is this really an accordion floor?"

Dawna joked, "Quick, someone press the button to close the doors. We can get rid of Gavin for good."

"Hey!" Gavin gave his on-again, off-again girlfriend a dirty look. "Everyone saw that, right?" He waved one hand jerkily. "Dawna thinks it's funny to be mean to me."

Dawna leaned out and peered left and right. "I don't see any sandworms," she said.

"Me, neither," said Gavin.

Zinnia looked over at Karl. She held up the white key, which she hadn't used. They couldn't be on the accordion floor, assuming it was even possible to reach it again, because they hadn't tried the key yet.

Karl held his fingers to his lips in a shush gesture. It wasn't like Karl to play a prank. Zinnia caught on that he wasn't doing it to be funny. He was teaching Gavin and Dawna a lesson about paying attention.

"Tell me what you do see," Karl said to Gavin gruffly.

Gavin looked around. "I don't see anything, but it does smell a bit funny." He inhaled audibly. "Yes. With my keen supernatural senses, I can tell this is a different plane of existence."

"That's the garbage you're smelling," Dawna said.

Gavin walked over to the opposite wall and took a good, hard look at the pile of garbage. "Do you think there's a clue in here about where those sandworms have taken Liza and Xavier?"

Karl started to snigger. He wasn't just teaching the two of them a lesson. He was also enjoying himself.

Zinnia decided to put a stop to it. They'd wasted so much time already. She'd voted against sticking around the office until closing time, but Karl had promised to make some phone calls to his contacts to see if any of the other sprites knew about the floor. He hadn't found out anything, and the time had been wasted. If Karl wanted to remain in charge of the group, he was going to have to make better judgment calls.

Zinnia waved Gavin back to the elevator. "Gavin, get back in here, you ding-dong," Zinnia said. "This is the regular third floor. We haven't used the key yet."

"Oh. Right. I knew that." Gavin turned around and got back into the elevator. "I was making sure the regular third floor was okay. Like a control group in an experiment."

"Sure, you were," she muttered. "Ding-dong."

Gavin shot Zinnia a puzzled look. "Did you just call me a ding-dong? Twice?"

"Yes." Zinnia was more focused on getting the key into the chameleon potion from her purse than worrying about Gavin's feelings.

"Take it as a compliment," Margaret said. "She only calls people that if she likes them. She calls me a ding-dong all the time!"

"That's because you are a ding-dong," Zinnia muttered.

"Ouch," Margaret said. "I hope you cheer up once we're back in 1955." She said to the others, "You should have seen her last night. We met this lovely Italian-American family, and—"

Zinnia flicked Margaret a warning look. She thought, very clearly, *Margaret, if you tell them my business, I'll tell them yours.*

Margaret pointed to her temple and nodded. "That's a ten-four, good buddy."

Zinnia wasn't sure why Margaret had chosen to use CB radio slang to communicate, but she was pleased her message had been received. She wouldn't need to follow it up with a magical bite in the buttocks.

"Now watch closely," Karl instructed Gavin and Dawna. "You're getting to see a genuine witch at work, close up. Witches are typically secretive—for good reason —so this is a rare privilege."

The others watched as Zinnia carefully dipped the key in the chameleon potion. She slowly brought it over to the keyhole next to the control panel.

"It's dripping," Dawna said. "Is it supposed to be dripping like that?" She turned to Karl.

"Hold your questions until the end," Karl said gruffly. In other words, he didn't know.

Zinnia crouched down to be eye level with the keyhole so she could insert the key cleanly.

"Yes, it's supposed to be dripping," Zinnia said to Dawna out of the corner of her mouth. "Try not to step on the drips."

Dawna asked, "Will it ruin the potion?"

"No," Zinnia said. "But it is slippery, and if one of us falls down in this tiny elevator, they might take down the rest of us."

Gavin asked, "Was that a genuine witch joke?" He clapped slowly. "Nicely done."

Zinnia looked back over her shoulder. "Would you like to do the key insertion, Mr. Gorman?"

Gavin stopped grinning and cleared his throat. "Uh, no. Go ahead, Zinnia. I'm sure you know what you're doing."

Dawna crouched down and put a hand on Zinnia's arm. "Wait," she said. "Are we really going to 1955? I don't know if you noticed, but I'm kind of a different color than you folks. The nineteen-fifties weren't such a jolly old time for my people."

Gavin puffed up his chest. "I'll protect you," he said.

Karl said, "You'll be fine. You're with us."

Dawna didn't look very reassured. "It sure would be ironic if we were all looking out for sandworms and one of us got lynched."

The others exchanged uncomfortable glances.

Dawna went on. "It's just, what if we go through and it's night time there, and we find out Wisteria used to be one of those sundown towns, where black people couldn't be out after dark."

Nobody spoke, not even Gavin.

Finally, Margaret said, "If worst comes to worst, we'll put a magic glamour on you, Dawna. Zinnia has an excellent spell for disguising a person as a green, leafy bush."

"I do," Zinnia said. "I'm so sorry we have to plan this as an option, but I can protect you with a glamour."

Dawna pondered this for a thoughtful moment before nodding. "I'm in," she said. "Slide that key in there, Zinnia. Let's do this thing."

Let's do this thing.

Zinnia slid the key in. There was a hum, like white noise but prettier, that filled the elevator. She tried turning the key. It wouldn't turn.

"Wiggle it," Margaret said. "You've got to wiggle it."

Dawna asked, "Is that a magic thing?"

Margaret shrugged. "Just a basic key thing."

The key wouldn't turn. Zinnia's heart sunk. Wiggling the key wasn't helping. The chameleon potion had its limits. It was a general all-purpose potion that could do many things, but it wouldn't open interdimensional portals. There was no hope. Their hare-brained scheme wasn't going to work after all. They should have called the DWM. Why had they been so eager to believe Dawna's prophecy was about the five of them? Were they all so desperate to be heroes that they had screwed up any chance of getting the Red Shirts—make that *the new hires*—rescued?

Just as Zinnia's flame of hope guttered, she felt a tingle in her fingertips.

She wiggled the key. The tingle grew stronger. The chameleon potion was working! It had just needed some time to take hold. Ah, the oldest magic that ever was. The passage of time, which always changed everything with its spell.

She turned the key.

The elevator lights flickered.

Everyone had been quiet, but now they became even more quiet. Not one muscle twitched.

The elevator cage lurched. There was the sensation of smooth, fast movement, despite the elevator already being positioned on the third floor.

The movement, which seemed to be neither up nor down but both at once, stopped with a second lurch.

The elevator dinged and the doors opened.

Everyone who'd been holding their breath—which was all five of them—gasped.

CHAPTER 29

THE TWO PREVIOUS times Zinnia had been to the otherworldly third floor, the elevator had opened on an abandoned construction site. This third visit, the bare concrete space was still there, along with the objects she'd seen during her first visit: piles of lumber, a vintage lunchbox, and old tools. However, this time the entire floor was bathed in bright orange light, and the view through the windows was very different.

Before, the windows had been milky, filtering bright light that matched daytime blue sky. Now all the windows had been smashed. Some fragments remained in the frames, and the glass fragments showed pale blue sky. However, the view, as seen through the smashed holes, was not Wisteria as they knew it. Not the current version, and not the 1955 version.

It was daytime here, but daytime in the desert... if that desert were also on a different planet. Two pale daytime moons hung in the orange sky.

Dawna stepped forward, leading the way out of the elevator. "Two moons," she said. "I thought it was a mistake, but the cards told me to follow the two moons, and here they are."

Margaret was the second person to step out of the elevator. She craned her neck, looking left and right. "What's going on? When we came through here yesterday, we walked down the stairs and out into a regular-looking world. It was Wisteria, in 1955. I think I would have remembered seeing sand dunes and two moons in the sky."

Karl stepped out third, making a mild HARUMPH sound to get everyone's attention.

"Just as I suspected," Karl said. "This is a three-way connection. If we take the stairs down, we'll corkscrew through the portal and go into the past. But the world outside the windows is a different one. Remarkable."

Dawna asked, "You mean this is a portal with three doors? Like a three-way traffic stop?"

"Yes," Karl said.

"You mean a three-way *intersection*," Gavin said. "Because sometimes there's a yield sign one way."

Ignoring him, Karl said, "There can be all manner of connections. I told you that an accordion floor is known for its elasticity."

Had he? The group looked at each other.

Gavin stepped out of the elevator. "No, boss. You didn't tell us any of that stuff."

Zinnia chimed in, "And you told me that time travel was impossible."

Karl tugged at one ear. "Did I? Well, we sprites can't be expected to know everything."

Gavin waved at the twin moons. "Do you sprites know about alien planets?"

Karl breathed in and out. "The air seems breathable."

"But you didn't know that before we got here," Gavin said. "It might have been handy to know more about the place we were going to. The way you talked about accordion floors, I thought you knew all about them."

Karl's face reddened. He made a blustery sound.

"Go easy on our boss," Dawna said to Gavin. "This is uncharted territory for all of us."

"Thank you," Karl said to Dawna.

Gavin pointed at Dawna. "Teacher's pet!"

"Good grief," Margaret said. "Are we going to hit the clean streets of 1955, or what?" She was already heading toward the stairwell.

"Not so fast," Zinnia called out. "I didn't see any sandworms in 1955. Doesn't that sandy desert outside the windows seem like the more appropriate place to look for the Red Shirts? I mean, Liza and Xavier?"

Gavin cracked up. "Did you actually call them Red Shirts?" He rubbed the corners of his eyes. "That is priceless. Especially coming from you, Zinnia."

Dawna elbowed him. "Don't be nasty. Just because the cards say they're not dead doesn't mean they aren't in danger."

Gavin shrugged. "Lighten up! If your prophecy says we'll rescue them, then it's destined to happen no matter what, whether we have a few laughs along the way or not."

Dawna said nothing.

Karl said, "Dawna? Is there something you haven't told us?"

"I'm sure it's nothing," she said, waving a hand. "But depending on how you interpret the cards, it's not exactly a sure thing that we succeed. There may be a slim chance the five heroes are..." She trailed off.

The elevator dinged, and the doors tried to close. Zinnia was still inside the elevator, the last to leave. She had held back in order to package up the key and the remaining chameleon potion. The magical compound wouldn't do them much good if it were to become contaminated with dry desert dust. Extra silica was not ideal, let alone silica from an alien planet.

Margaret waved at Zinnia. "Hold the elevator," she said to Zinnia. To Dawna, she said, "There's a slim chance the five heroes are what? Eaten by sandworms?"

"Thrown into a volcano," Dawna said. "But that only came up once in a hundred readings." She winced.

Karl said, "That's not bad odds. We have a one percent chance of failure. I can live with that."

Margaret raised her eyebrows at Zinnia, who was still inside the elevator cage, holding the door. The ding was becoming more insistent.

"One percent isn't bad," Zinnia said.

The others nodded in agreement. Margaret sighed.

Zinnia took one final look around the elevator, and then stepped out. The doors closed, and there was a hum as it sped away.

She already felt homesick for her cozy house with its floral wallpaper and comfortable furnishings. If she didn't return, what would happen to her home and all her things? It would go to Zara. But what would happen to Zara? If

Zara went to the DWM for answers, she'd be fed one of their usual cover stories. It would have to be a good one, to explain the disappearance of 87.5 percent of the Wisteria Permits Department. Perhaps a structural collapse. But Zara would know better. She would look for the truth. She would...

Zinnia's dark daydreams about her niece searching for her were interrupted by Dawna's voice.

"Everybody, come over this way," Dawna called out. She was standing by one of the broken windows. "We can climb out right here." She leaned out, looked left and right, her curly black hair waving in a breeze, then leaned back in. "Would you believe this building is growing out of the side of a mountain?"

Gavin corrected her immediately. "Buildings don't grow. What you mean is it's carved *into* a mountain. Or *embedded* in a mountain."

"Magic buildings can grow," Margaret said, correcting the corrector.

Dawna waved them over. "You guys gotta see this! For real!"

Everyone joined Dawna by the broken windows and looked out at the orange desert, then down, at a stone path that ran just below the windows.

Dawna kicked the broken glass out of the bottom of the window frame and straddled the window ledge. "It's real," she said, testing the path with her toes. "Not one of those magic illusion things." She stepped all the way out. "Let's go find those nasty sandworm bullies and get our friends back."

"Hang on." Karl raised both hands to halt the group. "First, do we have our supplies?" Margaret patted her purse. "Sure do, boss. Those sandworms will get some serious indigestion if they try to eat any more of us."

"Good," Karl said. "Everyone stick together." He made hand motions like a runway traffic director. "We are exiting the building this way, everyone."

One at a time, everyone stepped out, except Zinnia. "Be there in a minute," she said. "Just checking my supplies."

She opened her purse and thumbed through the assortment of offense and self-defense potions. She wished she had brought more explosives, but everything took time, and the chameleon potion had been fussy. She went over the weapons one more time, mentally rehearsing the implementation of each.

There was a sound nearby, like sand being softly crushed under a bicycle tire.

A female voice asked, "What'ssss in that sssstrange bag?"

The voice was coming from inside the empty third floor. The others were already out the window and walking down the path.

"Who's there?" Zinnia wrapped her fingers around one of the weaponized potion balls. "Show yourself before I make you."

"Such boldnessss," came the voice again. "Is that a bag of yours called a pursssssse? I've heard of pursessss." The soft, sand-crushing sound was closer now.

Zinnia looked down to see, less than four feet from where she stood, the largest snake she'd ever seen outside of a zoo. It was a shimmering copper and yellow reptile, at least ten feet long. The sight was shocking, and yet, she had seen much scarier things in this same location. This snake was tiny compared to the monstrous sandworm that had taken Liza.

"Hello," Zinnia said to the snake. "Yes, this is my purse." Her fear instinct told her to blast the snake repeatedly with magic, but there were two reasons not to do so. For one, she had to save her limited supply of spells in case the sandworm came back. For another, it was extremely rude to blast magic at a creature who simply wanted to know more about your purse.

The snake lifted its head up, up, up, until its eyes were eye level with Zinnia.

"Greetingssss," it replied. "You're not from around here, are you?"

"What gave me away?"

"You're not kneeling in terror before me," it said casually.

Zinnia swallowed the lump in her throat. The situation wasn't entirely bad. At least the snake spoke English.

"I like your pursssse," the snake said. "What'ssss your name, human?"

"My name is Zinnia Riddle. I've come from far away. I'm here looking for two of my colleagues. Their names are —"

The tail of the snake rattled, cutting off Zinnia. "What are colleaguesssss?" The snake seemed genuinely curious.

"That's just another word for coworkers."

"Co... workers?" The snake tilted its head in what seemed to Zinnia to be a very human gesture. "You mean slavessss?"

"Sure," Zinnia said. She was not one to toss around the word *slaves* casually, but going along with the snake seemed to be the lesser of two evils, given the situation. "I'm here looking for two slaves, Liza and Xavier. They, uh, escaped this way a few hours ago. Have you seen them?"

"Let'ssss say I know where your slaves are. What payment will I receive for showing you where your slaves might be found?"

Payment? She hadn't brought payment, not unless the snake liked explosives.

"I would be willing to pay the usual fee," Zinnia said, bluffing. Sure, why not?

The snake made a sound halfway between a hiss and a human laugh.

Zinnia stood up straighter.

"Double the usual fee," Zinnia said. When in doubt, double down!

The snake stopped laughing. "Follow me," it said. The snake slithered out the window and down the mountain path.

Zinnia followed. As she stepped outside, she caught her first full breath of the air belonging to the alien landscape. It was hotter than she expected, and fragrant. And familiar.

It was the same air that had been coming out of the hand dryers in the washrooms at City Hall, a blend of cinnamon, flowers, and something sweet.

Zinnia followed the snake past a blossoming and fruit-bearing cacti. She paused to smell the flowers and fruit, careful not to contact the cactus needles. Yes, that was the scent, all right. And the flowers on the cactus were stunning. She committed the petal pattern to memory. The flowers would make a stunning custom wallpaper print.

Zinnia kept walking, careful to keep up with, but not step on the tail of, the ten-foot-long talking snake. As much as she was concerned about what was going to happen next, and the one percent chance she might be thrown in a volcano, she was excited that some of the puzzle pieces were falling into place.

CHAPTER 30

ZINNIA AND THE snake caught up with the others halfway down the mountain.

"There you are," Dawna said to Zinnia. "I thought someone was missing from our motley crew of adven..." Dawna spotted the ten-foot-long copper and yellow snake. Her eyes bulged. She shrieked and jumped up on a boulder. "Giant snake!"

"That'sss better," said the snake. "That'sss how humansss should react in my presence."

Gavin stamped his foot on the path once, twice, then paused with his food it mid-air. "Are we safe, Zinnia? Margaret? What's going on?"

Karl grunted, and his freakishly long sprite tongue flicked out of his mouth. His tongue whipped left and right, snapping in the air between the snake and his employees.

Dawna screamed again, her gaze darting between the giant snake and Karl's tongue, as though her brain was confused over which one was more frightening.

Margaret held very still, her hand inside her purse, ready to draw. She reminded Zinnia of a gunslinger in an old Western movie.

"These trigger-happy people are my friends," Zinnia said to the snake.

"Are they also slavessss?"

"They all work for something called City Hall," Zinnia said.

Dawna, who'd stopped screaming, said, "What's this about slaves?"

"Just a translation glitch," Zinnia said. "Calm down, everyone."

Karl slowly reeled in his bug-catching tongue.

Gavin gently placed his raised foot on the path, heel first, then toes.

Zinnia turned to the snake. "As I was saying, these are my friends." She pointed at them in turn. "Dawna Jones, Gavin Gorman, Margaret Mills, and Karl Kormac. Everyone, meet..." She looked at the snake. "I'm sorry, but I don't know your name."

The snake said, in its hissy voice, "You may call me Snake."

Karl, who had reeled in his tongue but was still regarding the snake with suspicion, said, "That's not a name."

"Actually, it could be a name," Gavin said. "Just not for a snake. That's like me saying my name is Person."

Margaret didn't say anything. She still had her hand in her purse, and one eye was twitching.

"Then you may call me Gavin Gorman," the snake said.

"No," Gavin said. "That's my name."

"You can be Person," the snake said. "We shall call you Person, so that nobody is confussssssed."

Gavin was, for once, speechless.

"Susan," Karl said to the talking snake. "We'll call you Susan."

"You can call me that," the snake—Susan—said. "But it'ssss not my name."

"I understand what's happening here," Karl said. He explained to the others, "I've heard about this from my elders. Sprites used to travel between worlds all the time. In many of the magic realms, a creature's true name holds its power."

Gavin groaned and shook his head at Zinnia. "And you just told the talking snake all of our names, Zinnia. Good one."

Dawna elbowed Gavin. "You weren't exactly jumping up to stop her."

"Because I was getting ready to protect you," he said. "Keeping you safe is my number one priority."

It hadn't looked that way to Zinnia, or to the snake, apparently.

Susan slithered up to Gavin and flicked her forked tongue at him. "Interessssting," she hissed. "You deceive this female mate of yours."

Dawna used Gavin's shoulder to steady herself as she climbed down from the boulder. She said to Susan, "This man deceives me all the time. I put a three-quarters-full ice cream cake in his freezer and wouldn't you know it, Gavin claimed there was a power failure so he had to eat it all before it melted."

Susan asked, "What issss ice cream cake?"

"Only the best thing ever invented!" Dawna used the back of her hand to pat the sweat from her brow. "It's sweet and cold, and it melts in your mouth with just the right amount of crunch. It's better than regular cake, because you can't eat it too fast or you get brain freeze." Dawna reached out and flicked Gavin's bicep with one of her long orange fingernails. "Unless you're this guy, who can eat half a cake in the time it takes me to run out to get chocolate syrup."

Susan rattled her tail. "What issss chocolate syrup?"

Dawna tried to explain chocolate syrup to the snake, but it was very difficult, since Susan didn't know what chocolate was. When Dawna gave up, she looked at the others and said, "That answers the question of where we are. We must be in Hell, because they don't have ice cream or chocolate here."

Karl looked skyward. "Hell doesn't have two pale moons you can see in the daytime."

All the humans looked at Karl.

Margaret asked, "And how many moons are there in Hell, boss?"

Karl's face reddened and he made a HARUMPH sound. "Never mind about that," he said, wiping sweat from his brow with the back of one hand. "It's hot out here in this desert. That giant red sun is higher now than it was a few minutes ago, which means it's only going to get hotter." He removed his suit jacket and slung it over his shoulder. His dress shirt had dark rings of sweat under each armpit. "We need to take cover, and we need to find the kids."

Zinnia explained to Susan, "By *kids*, he means the two people we're looking for. The young man and woman who were taken by the sandworms."

"They weren't taken by sandworms," Susan said.

Margaret finally spoke directly to the talking snake. "Yes, they were. Or at least Liza was. I saw it with my own two eyes."

"They were taken, but not by sandworms," Susan said. "Sandworms are very small. You must check your shoes regularly for them. The ones you call *kids* were taken by timewyrms. They are the holy keepers of time."

Gavin threw his hands up in the air. "Oh! Well, that explains everything!"

"Timewyrms," Margaret said, twirling the gray curl that hung down the center of her forehead. "Never heard of them."

"I have," Karl said, scratching his chin. "I believe they're a sort of guardian that keeps realms from contaminating each other." He looked around at the dry desert landscape. "That makes me the first one in multiple generations of my family who's had the privilege of seeing a timewyrm." His face had an uncharacteristic look of openness and wonder, like the expression Zinnia had seen that day on the swing set. "My great-grandfather wasn't pulling my leg after all."

Everyone was quiet for a moment.

Dawna broke the silence. She waved at the snake and said, "Is anyone besides me getting kind of a biblical, Adam-and-Eve feeling from this talking snake?"

Zinnia said, "If Susan offers us any fruit, let's not take it." She waited for the others to laugh at her joke but they did not.

Margaret said solemnly, "The fruit mentioned in the Bible was a metaphor."

Susan said, in a helpful tone, "Would you like me to offer you fruit?"

In unison, all of them said, "No."

Karl cleared his throat. "Forgive our ignorance, Susan, but we need to know why the timewyrm took our people."

"Your people are anachronisms. They do not belong in this time or place. The timewyrms keep everything as it should be. Do not weep for them. Your people are among the living. For now. But you must take them away before they come to harm."

"What about us?" Dawna asked. "We don't belong here, either."

"Stay by my ssside and you'll be sssafe." Susan flicked her forked tongue and then slithered ahead of them, down the mountain path.

After a minimal amount of quibbling, the group was off again, following their talking snake guide.

* * *

They finally passed from the hot, dry desert into terrain with some shade from scruffy trees just as the enormous orange sun was hitting its apex. The sky was now so bright that the two moons were no longer visible. Zinnia's eyes had adjusted to the orange cast of the local light, and while she couldn't forget entirely that she was in another world, it was no longer her topmost thought.

Margaret fell in step beside her just as they passed from the scruffy trees to a denser, cooler forest. The desert behind them immediately felt like a false memory. The forest was not only cooler, but filled with foggy mist and the sound of frogs. Two raccoon-sized rodents ambled across the path in front of the witches, showing no fear of people whatsoever.

The two walked in silence for several minutes until Margaret said, "You know it's a trap, right?"

They were at the back of the group. They hadn't cast a sound bubble, but Margaret had kept her volume down low enough so the others wouldn't hear them.

"Of course it's a trap," Zinnia said. "A talking snake shows up right when we pass through, and just happens to know where our friends are? I wasn't born yesterday."

"So, what's your plan? We're just going to follow this snake right into a trap?"

"We're prepared." Zinnia patted her purse. "I've got enough magical explosives in here to blow up a City Hall–sized mountain."

"It's always good for a witch to be prepared for anything. I'm just glad I brought this." Margaret dug into her purse and pulled out what appeared to be a pack of gum. She offered it to Zinnia.

"What's this?" Zinnia asked. It wasn't one of the items they'd packed back at her house on Earth. "It this a neurotoxin that paralyzes the user?"

"It's gum," Margaret said. "Peppermint."

"Also good to have on a trip to another world." Zinnia took a piece and chewed it thoughtfully.

Margaret said, "Dawna's taking this really well. She just found out about magic today, but she's adapting a lot better than I did. It must be different when magic comes to you in adulthood. Was your niece this easy?"

Zinnia chuckled. "Nothing about Zara is ever easy, but I suppose she did accept magic readily." Thinking about Zara made Zinnia desperately homesick again. She'd never been this far from home before. Most humans hadn't been.

Zinnia looked around at the misty forest that was now surrounding them. Something about the leaves on the trees caught her eye. She stopped and gathered some branches in her hand.

"Look at this," she said to Margaret. "Does the shape of these leaves look familiar to you?"

The gray-haired witch studied the leaves a moment before looking up with a surprised expression. "It's your bush glamour," she said. "And I just figured out what's so strange about that spell. The leaves aren't symmetrical. One side is jagged and the other side has smooth curves."

"I never could identify the bush, but it appears to be commonplace here. Do you suppose...?"

The witches stared at each other, then looked at the foliage surrounding them.

Zinnia chewed her peppermint gum for a moment, then tried again to express her thought. "Do you suppose this place is the source of our magic?"

"Hmm."

"And that it leaks into Wisteria through some sort of opening on the third floor of City Hall?"

Margaret blinked. "No. I hadn't thought of it until just now. The opening must be a sort of fistule."

Zinnia wrinkled her nose. "Did you say *fistule*?"

"Yes. Mike had a fistule a while back," Margaret said. "It's an abnormal channel that creates a passageway between two things that don't normally connect. Mike's was enterovesicular, so it directed into his bladder."

"That's awful. I had no idea. I'm sorry you and your husband had to deal with that."

"He's fine now. Since it was going into his bladder, we took him to see his favorite surgeon, who got him fixed right up. Since the surgery, he hasn't had any bladder infections." She frowned. "Which is too bad, because they really made him suffer."

"And you want Mike to suffer?"

Margaret said nothing.

Zinnia looked at the forest floor for a moment before looking over at her friend. "I'm sorry about what's going on with you two."

Margaret scowled. "Don't look at me like that."

"Like what? I'm not giving you the pitying look again, am I?"

"No." Margaret tossed aside the asymmetrical leaves and started walking again. "You're giving me the look that says I'm mean and rotten to Mike. Your look says I'm a nasty little witch, and he should have left me years ago."

"You might be projecting just a wee bit. If I was looking at you with any emotion at all, it was only concern." Zinnia easily caught up to Margaret.

"I don't like this forest," Margaret said. "Did you see those rodents? They were as big as house cats."

"I guess we know what's been eating the bags of grain in the cafeteria back home."

"This is all Liza's fault. It's because of that silly new girl that we're all here."

"We don't know that for sure. It might have been Xavier. He was the first one to get captured by a timewyrm. I bet he saw one and challenged it to a fight."

Margaret grunted.

"You remember what he was like in the swamp that night," Zinnia said. "He drew first blood on the cougar, and then he tried to fight the First Responders. The kid doesn't know when to back down."

"Men are all fools, but it's the selfish girls who make them even stupider."

"Who are you talking about? Xavier? Or someone else?"

"Xavier," Margaret snapped. "He's an idiot who deserves what he gets."

"And yet you risked your life to come here and rescue two people you claim you don't care about."

"I haven't been on a vacation in almost twenty years. I wasn't going to turn down a free trip."

"Is that all this is to you? A free vacation?"

"Sure. It's like visiting the Grand Canyon, except—"

Zinnia put a hand on Margaret's shoulder to stop her. There was a buzzing, zipping sound in the air. A flock of multicolored birds swooped across the trail in front of them, snapping their way through a cloud of moth-like insects. The birds had fast wings, like hummingbirds, but were the size of parrots. Once the insects were gone, the birds flew away again, their wings buzzing as they zipped through the air.

"You don't see those in the Grand Canyon," Zinnia said.

"Mike loves birds," Margaret said. Her eyes glistened.

"Did something happen? You two seemed happy enough with each other the last time I saw you together."

Margaret blinked away the moisture in her eyes and stuck her nose in the air. "Appearances can be deceiving."

Zinnia looked around at the forest with the strangely shaped leaves. Yes, appearances could be deceiving. For all she knew, the whole forest could be an illusion. They could be treading across the skin of some planet-sized creature.

It was times like these that her creative imagination was of little comfort.

* * *

After another hour of walking, the party of six—or five plus one snake—exited the woods and found themselves at the outskirts of a village.

Dawna clapped her hands excitedly. "This looks just like that medieval town I used to go to when I was little." She explained to the group, "My parents were really into this stuff. My mom sewed costumes for everyone, and my dad made chainmail armor."

Gavin seemed surprised by this information. "Really?"

The others were also surprised. Dawna was a private person when it came to her life outside the office, so any details at all about her childhood were news to the group.

The giant copper and yellow snake, who hadn't spoken in a while, coiled up. All of Susan's scales seemed to catch the sunlight at the same moment, and then, in a flash of light, she changed.

Susan looked as human as any of them. She was a beautiful woman, her curves and her face soft with the freshness of youth. She had long, golden hair that fell in waves down to her knees, covering her. In fact, her hair was the only thing covering her. She was completely naked.

Karl whipped his suit jacket off his shoulder and handed it to her while averting his eyes.

Susan said with a light laugh, "I don't want your sweaty jacket, troll."

"Sprite," he said peevishly, taking back the jacket and clutching it to his chest. "I'm a sprite, not a troll."

"You are what you are," the snake who was now a woman said. She snapped her fingers, and was instantly clad in a shimmering, silver-hued gown.

Dawna rubbed her eyes and asked Zinnia, "Did that just happen? Did our talking snake turn into a beautiful goddess?"

Susan heard the question and smiled. "Thank you," she said. "I *am* a beautiful goddess. I'm glad you noticed. The villagers around here are too terrified of me to offer any honest compliments."

"Uh-oh," Dawna said. She leaned over to Zinnia and whispered, "If she's a goddess, we've got a problem."

Zinnia already had her hand inside her purse, her fingers wrapped around a grenade-sized magic explosive. She had been on high alert since the moment they'd approached the village.

Zinnia said to Dawna, "Let me guess. Was there something in your cards about a goddess?"

"She only came up once," Dawna said, gulping audibly. "In the reading with the volcano."

"That can't be good," Zinnia said.

An unbearably loud whistle rang through the group. It was coming from Susan, who had two fingers in her mouth and was blowing fiercely.

All around them, doors popped open and people jumped out, armed with crudely-forged yet deadly-looking weaponry. Most of the people were human sized, but a few were tiny and a couple were very large. A giant man— nearly twelve feet tall—grabbed both Karl and Gavin in two swoops of his meaty arms. Karl's long tongue lashed around ineffectively.

Zinnia took aim and threw her magical grenade at the former snake's feet. A plume of dust rose up, but that was all. The grenade didn't explode.

Meanwhile, the tiny people had thrown a net over Margaret and were working together to wrestle her to the ground. Margaret was cursing them and flailing her arms and legs, but she wasn't zapping them with magic. Why wasn't she putting her green lightning to use?

The blonde goddess stopped whistling and calmly laid one fair hand on Dawna's shoulder.

"Sleep now, mage," Susan said.

Dawna's eyes rolled up. She dropped to the ground as though boneless.

Zinnia pelted the second grenade directly at the goddess. It hit her in the torso and bounced off. Still no explosion.

Zinnia tried to cast a motion disruption spell, but the Witch Tongue seemed to tangle up her actual tongue.

She used a wordless spell, with gestures alone, designed to kick and bite the goddess, but Susan showed no reaction whatsoever.

Zinnia felt within herself and found that she was empty. There was no familiar tug of magic pooling within her and dispersing. She directed her telekinesis to lift a rock. Nothing.

Her magic was dead.

Had she been dosed with witchbane without realizing it? She hadn't ingested anything in this realm, except some bottled water they'd packed, and Margaret's peppermint gum.

Margaret made angry rhino noises within her net. "It's this world," she choked out. "Zinnia, this whole world is poison!"

Zinnia looked around. The world didn't look or smell like poison, but then again, the last time she'd eaten witchbane she hadn't noticed until it was too late. Appearances could be deceiving.

Two pale hands came toward Zinnia. They parted, landing on her shoulders as a face swam into view. It was the goddess. The nameless, powerful one they'd called Susan. As she drew nearer, her eyes were so cold, so stone-like, so familiar.

"I know you," Zinnia said woozily.

The snake-woman hissed, "Witch, you do not know me. Do you still wish to see the ones called Liza and Xavier? You shall see them." A coolness passed from her hands into Zinnia's shoulders and through the witch's body. "You will see them soon enough."

Zinnia slipped down into the coolness. She fought it and resurfaced.

"No," she said through gritted teeth. "You will regret taking us. Our mage has seen the future. Release us at once, or your fate is sealed."

"Rest now," the goddess said. "Rest your weary eyes."

Zinnia tried to fight, but the coolness was so much more appealing than the fire that burned in her shoulder and smoldered in her thumb. Her eyelids were so heavy. She would rest them, just for a moment, then she would destroy this goddess. How dare she pose as a snake pretending to be their friend! How dare she! How...

CHAPTER 31

ZINNIA WOKE TO the sound of water running. She listened before opening her eyes. There was trickling water, chirping birds, and distant voices—both female, laughing merrily. She also heard her mentor's voice inside her head: *Zinnia, what do you know to be true?*

The last thing she remembered was being knocked out by the snake-woman. She knew that time had passed, but not how much. She was lying on her side. Her body was whole, unbroken, and the air around her was a comfortable temperature. No breeze. She cracked open her eyelids.

It was bright. She squinted as the world swam into focus. She expected to see the stone walls of a dungeon and a filthy dirt floor beneath her cheek. Instead, she saw beautiful flowers. A garden? No. The flowers were too regular. It was wallpaper. And beneath her cheek was a soft surface. Red. Velvet upholstery. Hope swelled in her chest. Was she home again?

She lifted her head. Her vision blurred as her head throbbed. Her arm was numb. Or just plain gone. Had she been wrong when she'd perceived herself as being whole? Thankfully, she found the arm under her torso. She was whole. Her arm had simply fallen asleep from being pinched beneath her body. A wave of relief and gratitude washed over her. She clasped her hands in front of her, rubbing one wrist and then the other. She wasn't tied up. Wherever she was, at least she wasn't tied up.

She pushed herself upright, swung her legs down from what she now recognized as a red velvet couch with taut upholstery. She blinked away the stars that swam in her vision.

She was in a grand room with a high ceiling—three stories, maybe more. The floor was gleaming marble, the furnishings were both crisp and sumptuous at the same time, and there were grand columns supporting the lofty ceiling. It might have been an art gallery, except there wasn't quite enough art on the wallpapered walls. There was, however, a large fountain gurgling at the center of the room, under a grand chandelier. She was in either a luxurious hotel lobby or a castle's sitting room. She looked around for a concierge desk. There was no desk, no concierge. Castle it was.

Zinnia got to her feet and looked around to see if her travel companions were slumbering on the other couches. They were not. However, if they were also being detained in a place half as pleasant as this one, they were fine for now.

Now what? She didn't have her purse or any of her magical supplies. What had Margaret yelled while she was being captured? The whole world was poison. Their witch powers didn't work here. To test this hypothesis again, Zinnia directed her levitation at a small, ornate table. It didn't budge. Just like the rock she'd attempted to lift during the ambush.

But levitation was just one of her skills.

Next, Zinnia used Witch Tongue to cast an object-location spell on her purse. The words tangled her tongue and deflated inside her mouth before she could utter them. Her powers were not working.

"Hello," came a calm female voice behind her.

Zinnia whipped around to see a familiar-looking young woman with blonde hair and honey-brown eyes.

"Liza!" Zinnia was so happy to see her coworker alive that she ran toward who she thought was Liza Gilbert, arms extended.

The woman took a step backward and said, "Nobody calls me that."

Zinnia halted her approach. She could have sworn the woman was Liza, but now that she was closer, there were differences. This woman had the same eyes and hair, but her face was narrower, her cheeks hollower.

The blonde continued in a friendly, conversational tone. "I suppose some of us go by Liza, but not me. My family has called me Beth ever since I was a baby, and it stuck, so I'm just plain ol' Beth."

"Beth," Zinnia repeated. "I'm Zinnia, Zinnia Riddle."

Beth gave her a curious look. "Zinnia? What's that short for?"

"It's not short for anything. It's a type of flower."

Beth tilted her head back and let out a merry laugh. "Of course it is. I've been gone from Earth for so long now that I've forgotten entire ranges of vocabulary."

Zinnia pieced together the clues in her head. "As for your name, is Beth short for Elizabeth?"

"Yes. Don't you know that? I thought you were from Earth."

"I am from Earth. I was just checking."

"My name's Elizabeth, all right." She walked over to one of the red velvet couches and perched delicately on the arm. "Why were people of my parents' generation so lacking in imagination? In school, every second one of us was named Elizabeth. Either that or Margaret, or Mary. I actually had a friend named Mary-Margaret Elizabeth. Poor thing."

"And what is your last name? Is it Gilbert?"

Beth wrinkled her nose. "No." She languidly stretched back on her couch-arm perch. "That's a funny question." She smiled, as though the two of them were new friends meeting for tea, and not captive and captor.

Zinnia politely mirrored Beth's smile. "If you enjoyed that, you'll be happy to hear I have many funny questions."

Beth pointed at her playfully. "I did know a boy with the last name of Gilbert. He was a fine young man. I think he might have pursued me if I hadn't come here."

Zinnia figured as much, as she'd already connected the dots. The woman standing before her was Queenie Gilbert, before she became Queenie Gilbert.

Beth asked, "Do you know him? The Gilbert boy? How is he? Did he even notice I was gone?" She rubbed her chin with both hands and frowned as she looked down. "Wait. Never mind. I've been here for hundreds of years. He's probably dead and gone, along with everyone else I ever knew or loved."

"Not exactly," Zinnia said slowly. "Some time has passed, but not hundreds of years."

"Oh?"

"It's a complicated story, but I do know you, Beth. We've met before."

"We have?" Beth cocked her head.

"From your perspective, we haven't met before, but we will." Zinnia winced and waved a hand. Time travel was confusing to talk about. "Other than right now, that is. When we do meet, it will be the first time for me."

Beth batted her eyelashes. "Is that what your cartomancer has foretold?" She went on to identify Dawna Jones by an outdated label. Beth was from 1955, all right.

"Her name is Dawna Jones," Zinnia said. "Dawna didn't have to tell me about meeting you, because it happened already from my perspective. I remember it clearly. You and I have a mutual friend. Winona Vander Zalm."

"Winona! Why didn't you say so?" Beth slid off the arm of the sofa and walked toward Zinnia, rounding the other furnishings. She stopped with one sofa between them —a purple one—and frowned. "Did Winona send you here? I thought her powers were limited to..." The blonde with the honey-brown eyes gave Zinnia a questioning look. Zinnia knew when she was being tested, and this was a test.

"Her powers are limited to healing," Zinnia said, answering the test question. "Winona Vander Zalm was a nurse during the war, which is when she discovered her abilities. I know about it because we were friends." Winona had also been in Zinnia and Margaret's coven for a while, as a non-witch member.

Beth was no slouch. She pounced on Zinnia's statement. "You *were* friends? Were? What happened?"

"We *are* friends," Zinnia said, lying just a little. "In fact, I recently helped her with a dispute she had with a real estate agent. Just a few months ago in my time." That part was true. Winona had been a ghost already, but the statement was technically not a lie.

Beth smiled and nodded. Test passed. "And what are you, Zinnia Riddle? My high priestess tells me you're a witch."

Zinnia lifted both hands in a gesture of helplessness. "I'm nothing in this world of yours. My magic doesn't work here."

Beth's eyes twinkled. "Oh, there is abundant magic all around." She winked. "Who knows? In time, you may learn to use it. Once you learn how to pull..." She smiled. "You'll see."

"I'm looking forward to it. Forgive my ignorance, but where exactly is *here*?"

Beth pressed her lips together in a mirthful smile. "This ol' place? We're in my castle, as you probably already guessed. As for the land that surrounds it, the land is what you make of it. Some call it Heaven. Others call it Hell." She wrinkled her nose. "But people don't call it Hell quite as much as they used to in the old days. When I first met my husband, he wasn't a very nice man." She paused and rolled her eyes. "Men."

"You're married?"

Beth climbed onto the purple velvet couch between them, sitting on her knees in a childlike gesture. She thrust her left hand toward Zinnia, wiggling her fingers so that the enormous diamond on her ring finger caught the light.

"Beautiful," Zinnia said. "It must have been quite the engagement party, with a ring like that."

Beth picked at the ring casually. "The funny thing is, diamonds aren't scarce here at all, but I suppose I'm an old-fashioned girl. The king likes to keep me happy."

"You're the queen," Zinnia said. "Queenie Gilbert."

Beth squinted. "That's a curious thing for you to say. I'm Queen Beth. We don't have last names here."

"Queenie Gilbert is your name in the future. After you come back to Earth."

Her honey-brown eyes widened. "Oh, I could never leave this place. You must be mistaken."

"People change," Zinnia said. "You might not be ready to leave now, but you will eventually." Zinnia looked more closely at the young woman. Beth didn't look a day over twenty-five. "Have you really been here for hundreds of years?"

"Something like that. I stopped counting a while back."

"How are you still so young? Does the orange sun in this land keep you from aging?"

"The locals age, but my beloved king keeps me from changing. He wants me to stay exactly how I am."

"He must be very powerful. Is he some kind of sorcerer?"

Again, Beth's eyes twinkled. "You could say that." She whispered, "He's a god, actually." She giggled as she patted the seat of the couch next to her. "Come and sit. I'm dying to hear gossip about what's happening on Earth."

Zinnia looked at the couch seat but didn't take Queen Beth's invitation. She did want to soak up as much knowledge as possible, but she had to stay on mission. Plus she didn't trust the queen, who was displaying a careless attitude about the captives, as though Zinnia and the others were nothing but playthings for the bored royal.

"I'd love to chat more," Zinnia said diplomatically, "but I need to know about the others who came through with me. Where are my friends?"

Beth's posture slumped as her head rolled from side to side in an expression of boredom that struck Zinnia as particularly childish. The queen had been spoiled by hundreds of years of marriage to a powerful god-king, and she expected her playthings to not ask so many questions.

Zinnia repeated, "Where are my friends?"

In a bored, monotone voice, the queen said, "I assure you that the other humans from the future, or the past, or from wherever it is you call *now*, are all quite comfortable. They are being fed."

"Being fed?" Zinnia hoped they were not *being fed...* to monsters.

"They're in the dining hall enjoying a feast," Queen Beth said with limp posture and vague hand waves. "My personal chef wasn't happy about the short notice, but he's a good ogre. He does try his best with his big, brutish hands." She perked a little and clapped her hands girlishly. "Want to know a secret about ogres? If you talk in a really high voice like this," she pitched up her voice to cartoon-fairy levels, "they can't hear a word you're saying."

"That's a fascinating fact about ogres, but I should go meet up with the others." Zinnia glanced around. "Which way is the dining hall?"

Just then, the white marble floor moved, rippling like water. Then the white marble became a snake—a sparkling, pure-white snake. The snake coiled, extended its head up, and turned once more into its female human form. This time the woman they'd dubbed Susan had hair that was pure white.

"Hello, again," the snake-woman said to Zinnia. She offered a smile that might have been friendly if her teeth weren't pointed like those of a barracuda. She was nude again, but not for long. With another shimmer, she was wearing a dress made of lace. The dress was cornflower blue, and matched her eyes in their current hue. As she continued smiling, her sharp teeth turned square and human-looking.

Queen Beth squealed with excitement. "There you are!" She swatted the snake-woman on the arm. "You're always sneaking up on people, you naughty girl."

The snake-woman gracefully flipped her long, shimmering white curtain of hair over one shoulder. "I have to do something to amuse myself," she said haughtily. "Since you don't allow me to torture the villagers these days."

They both laughed like two old friends sharing a private joke. Zinnia didn't find the idea of villagers being tortured very amusing.

The snake-woman stopped giggling long enough to point at Zinnia and tell the queen, "I actually told her people that we didn't know about chocolate."

Queen Beth slapped her own knee with apparent delight. "You're so naughty!" She said to Zinnia, "Of course we have chocolate. Duh."

"But we don't have ice cream cakes," the snake-woman said to Zinnia. "Or at least we didn't until now. Fortunately, your companions were able to explain them to the chef. The gnome with the white teeth offered to help, but the chef wouldn't allow it. Gnomes in the kitchen ruin everything with their fussy ways. They can't simply let a thing be as it is. They always have to change one thing."

Zinnia noted to herself that the snake-woman was not wrong about Gavin's ways. She hadn't realized it was a gnome thing.

"What about the troll?" Queen Beth asked. "He thinks he's a sprite!"

Susan snorted. "We should roast him on a spit for dinner, and see if he tastes like a sprite."

The two laughed some more.

"That's not funny," Zinnia said. "Karl is my friend. He's a person."

The blondes stared at Zinnia.

Zinnia turned to the more human one. "Beth, have you been here for so long that you think it's amusing to joke about eating people?"

"It was just a joke," the queen said.

The snake-woman asked, "Why are you defending a troll?"

"He's a sprite, and his name is Karl."

Two blank stares.

"He's my friend," Zinnia said.

The two started giggling again.

Zinnia shook her head, picked a doorway, and started walking toward it. "I'll find the dining hall myself," she muttered.

As she left the palatial sitting room, Zinnia heard the words of her mentor in her head. *A little diplomacy never hurt any relationship, especially the delicate kind of relationship that exists between two powerful beings who can easily destroy each other.*

Zinnia mentally thumbed her nose at her mentor. She'd been kidnapped. Again. Perhaps the ambush and capture had been a test, or cautionary measures, or simply for the amusement of the queen. Regardless, she didn't care. She wasn't going to play the role of the simpering victim. She was getting her friends and going home, with magic powers or without.

A witch could be down, but she was never out. Fate had a way of turning things around in the blink of an eye.

CHAPTER 32

THE BANQUET HALL was as large and palatial as Zinnia had expected.

She found her coworkers enjoying a sumptuous feast along with a dozen people from the village, all regular-sized humans, as well as another dozen of the tiny people who'd captured Margaret under their net. The ambush had happened quickly, but Zinnia recognized a few of the people.

Zinnia approached cautiously, even though her coworkers didn't appear to be in any distress.

Dawna was eating with enthusiasm. Gavin was picking at his food, pulling it apart with a single utensil that was both spoon and fork—a spork. Margaret and Karl were both eating as though in a contest to see who could put away more food.

Zinnia was disappointed to note that Xavier and Liza were not present.

When Zinnia reached the table, the locals introduced themselves one by one, by name, and invited her to join them in the feast.

The tiny people were sitting on special chairs that had higher seats as well as access ladders.

In addition to the thirty people seated at the long table, there were a half-dozen attendants dressed in black and white. Most appeared to be human, although two were strange colors—green and blue. Zinnia tried not to stare at the people who came in colors she wasn't accustomed to.

Karl paused his inhaling of a black-colored pudding long enough to grunt, "Pull up a chair. These people are okay."

"How quickly things change," Zinnia said. "The last I saw everyone here, some of us were being ambushed and captured by the others."

The tiny people tittered in their tiny voices.

"We hope there are no hard feelings," said the tiny person who'd introduced herself as Tippi. She had a high, squeaky voice that matched her appearance. "We love our queen—"

She was interrupted by a chorus of "Long live Queen Beth! Long may she rule!" Glasses and goblets clinked in toasts.

Tippi continued, "We love our queen and will do anything to protect her. We had to test your abilities to make sure you couldn't harm our beloved and benevolent queen." She raised her thimble-sized goblet and started off another cheer as the others joined in. "Long live Queen Beth! Long may she rule!"

A tiny man to Tippi's left, Tottothot, asked Zinnia eagerly, "No hard feelings?"

"No hard feelings," Zinnia said, which wasn't entirely true. "But you could have tried talking to us. I wouldn't have reached for my supplies if your group hadn't attacked us first."

"We had no choice," Tottothot said. "Look how small we are compared to you."

Tippi shook her head. "The worst enemies are the ones who talk their way in through your front door."

Zinnia thought of Jesse, which made her thumb ache. Tippi and Tottothot made a good point. The worst enemies really did talk their way in through the front door.

Margaret caught Zinnia's eye. "Over here," Margaret said, using an enormous piece of food that looked like a turkey leg, except much larger, to point at the chair beside her. "Come and sit with me."

One of the attendants, a blue-skinned man who was dressed in a traditional Earth-style tuxedo, pulled out the chair for Zinnia. "Be seated," he said. "Enjoy the queen's hospitality. We have sent for the other two humans from Earth."

Tippi said, "As soon as we can figure out where the timewyrms have stashed them!"

All the tiny people laughed.

Tuxedo Man said, "The timewyrms mean well, but they cling to the old ways."

"Stupid brainless timewyrms," Tippi said with evident distaste.

"They are brainless," Tottothot agreed.

Tippi continued, "They're as troublesome as the giant ravens who try to steal our young." Tippi looked across the table at the drumstick in Margaret's hand. Cheerfully, she added, "But at least the ravens taste excellent when roasted. I can't say the same for grilled timewyrm."

Margaret paused in her chewing, looked down at the raven drumstick in her fist, shrugged, and continued eating.

Zinnia said to Tuxedo Man, "I guess if you haven't located Liza and Xavier yet, the queen hasn't met either of them." What she meant was, the queen hadn't met her own granddaughter.

"Not yet." Tuxedo Man frowned. "Why do you ask with that tone? Your friends are not assassins, are they?" His eyes widened, and an array of sharp spikes suddenly erupted from his blue face. "Your people swore to me the first two came here by accident. If I find out you're plotting to kill the queen and seize the throne, my mistress will have you chopped to pieces and fed to the bone-crawlers."

The table went quiet. Everyone stared at Zinnia, awaiting a response.

"They came here by accident," Zinnia said. "The two of them were using the hidden floor and came here by accident."

Tuxedo Man, or Pufferfish Man, slowly pulled in his face spikes. The Earth people gave him wary looks and slowed their eating.

Tippi asked Zinnia, "What were they using the portal for?"

Zinnia felt herself blushing. "We believe they were, um, *hooking up*."

Everyone at the table who wasn't from Earth looked confused. A few of the human-sized villagers muttered to each other in a language Zinnia didn't understand.

"That means kissing," Zinnia explained.

Tippi put her tiny hands on her tiny hips. "Then why didn't you say they were kissing? Are you trying to deceive us?"

"Hooking up means kissing plus other stuff."

Tippi got to her feet, which only made her a few inches taller. "They were practicing sex magic?"

The human-sized villagers gasped. They understood English, even if they weren't speaking it.

"No," Zinnia said. "Not sex magic. They were kissing for their own amusement."

"Sex magic," Tippi said, nodding.

"No..." Zinnia became aware of her coworkers hanging on her every word. Of course. This was exactly the sort of thing they would enjoy—watching their forty-eight-year-old spinster coworker explain *hooking up* to people from a foreign land.

One of the other tiny people ran across the table to Tippi and whispered something in her ear. Both tiny people blushed.

"Now I understand," Tippi said. "They didn't realize they were engaging in sex magic. That must have been the magic signature that attracted the timewyrms. The timewyrms do love to interrupt mating rituals." She waved for Zinnia to take the chair next to Margaret. "Be comfortable," she said. "The staff will return with your friends soon."

Zinnia walked around the thirty-foot-long table and took a seat next to Margaret. She hadn't realized how hungry she was until the smell of the food hit her nostrils.

* * *

Considering the chef was an ogre who'd never made an ice cream cake before, the results were truly impressive.

Gavin moaned and held his stomach with both hands. "Somebody stop me before I take a fourth helping and explode."

"Go ahead and take another helping," said the green-skinned attendant dressed in what could have been a French maid Halloween costume. "I will sew you back together," she said. "My stitches are the neatest in all this great land."

Gavin didn't look pleased at the idea of being sewn back together at all, let alone by a green-skinned woman, but he did take another slice of the ice cream cake.

Further up the table, Karl made a HARUMPH sound. "Since you're having another piece, Gavin, I'd better have some, too."

"It's not a contest," Dawna said.

Tippi clapped her hands and jumped up and down on the table. "We love eating contests! It's one of the main things we do now that we don't battle to the death for the enjoyment of the king."

Zinnia asked Tippi, "When did that practice stop?"

Tippi held her chin between two impossibly small fingers and looked up—way, way, up—at the high ceiling. "Two hundred and seven years ago," she said. "I was just a little girl at the time."

Zinnia did a double take. "How long do your people live?"

Tippi shrugged. "Nobody knows. Most of my people used to die in sport-battle or being fed to the king. Our beloved queen stopped the rituals, and now we are..." She smiled. "Living our days and nights without certainty."

Her male companion Tottothot, who had the familiarity of a spouse, raised his thimble-sized goblet in a toast. "To living our days and nights without certainty. Long live our beautiful and wise queen!"

The others cheered in agreement.

Zinnia and Margaret exchanged a look. It sounded like Beth's arrival in the land had benefited its people greatly.

One of the other tiny people, a man with a black goatee and a bald head, said, "I'm not so sure about life without certainty. Call me old-fashioned, but the nice thing about being eaten by the king at his weekly party was knowing death would be quick and certain. I have lived to see my father's father become weak and feeble of mind."

"Oh, shut up, Riollobo," said one of the other tiny people. "You don't speak for us."

The goateed man, Riollobo, grabbed a piece of cake bigger than his whole head and slunk off to the corner of his chair with it.

"Don't listen to him," Tippi said to Zinnia. "There is always someone who is unhappy no matter what."

"So it goes on Earth," Zinnia said.

Margaret raised her glass, spilling red wine as she did so. "A toast to the queen! Long live the queen!"

People of all sizes and origins joined the toast.

Zinnia clinked her glass with as many people as she could reach, and resumed eating.

While they dined, Zinnia looked around at the villagers. She knew that a person's outer appearance didn't necessarily reflect what was going on in their lives, but the people of this world certainly seemed happy enough— other than grumpy Riollobo—and it was all thanks to their Earthly queen.

Some day their queen would have to leave her people to return to her own time and land. She had to become Queenie Gilbert, and have children who would have Liza, who would bring the people from Earth back here.

Beth's fate was inescapable, because it had already happened.

Tippi and Tottothot began teaching the Earth visitors a traditional song. The melody was rather catchy.

Zinnia wondered, when their queen left them, what would happen to all of these people? Without Beth around to change the king's behavior, the villagers might go back to the certainty of dying in sport-battle or being fed to the king.

Zinnia glanced around at the smiling, laughing faces gathered around the long banquet table.

Good times don't last forever, she thought sadly.

* * *

The ogre who had prepared their meal came out to accept their accolades. He was the same giant man who'd captured Gavin and Karl so easily in the ambush. His name was Bill, and though he didn't speak much English, he seemed to have a sweet, pleasant disposition.

Zinnia was thinking about how kind Bill seemed, and then worrying about Liza and Xavier, when Tippi walked across the table to her.

Tippi leaned casually against Zinnia's after-dinner coffee mug, and said, "Want to hear something interesting about the chef?"

"You mean Bill? Sure." Zinnia had noticed that gossiping seemed to be the main pastime of the people in this world, right behind eating.

Tippi said, "Back in the old days, Bill's job was handicapping people before the sport-battles."

"Do you mean he adjusted the numbers for betting purposes?" That didn't fit. The ogre hadn't seemed like much of a math whiz, but perhaps Zinnia was being prejudiced.

Tippi laughed. "Bill's job was to *handicap*. You don't know this word? It's when one of the people in the battle doesn't have a leg, so to make things even, you have an ogre bite off the opponent's leg."

Zinnia's jaw dropped open. She quickly closed her mouth, lest it seem threatening to Tippi, whom Zinnia could have eaten in three bites.

"He didn't like it, either," Tippi said. "Bill is actually a really nice guy, for an ogre."

"It sounds like things were terrible here before your queen arrived."

"We didn't know any better," Tippi said. "If everything's terrible, then nothing is terrible." She circled around Zinnia's mug and grabbed hold of the spoon to stir it, using the edge of the cup as a rest, the way one might row a boat.

"Thank you," Zinnia said, unsure of the local customs.

"The queen enjoys it when we stir her coffee. She says it reminds her of a man called Gulliver. Do you know him?"

That would be *Gulliver's Travels*, from the storybooks. "I know *of* him," Zinnia said with a smile.

There was a commotion at one of the entrances.

Xavier and Liza came in at a jogging pace. They looked thinner than the last time Zinnia had seen them, which had been yesterday from Zinnia's perspective. Both were very dirty, covered in a gray-green grime.

Liza locked her gaze on Zinnia. She stammered, "Yo-o-ou're eating? I can't believe you people!"

Blue Pufferfish Man in a Tuxedo displayed his face spikes. "Please join your friends now," he said in a bristly tone. "We have several more courses."

Tippi raised her goblet and cried out, "Several more courses! Long live the queen!" The other villagers joined in with their own toasts.

Liza and Xavier stayed where they were, both looking aghast.

Xavier pointed to the small villagers, "Are those people?"

Tippi made what Zinnia guessed was a rude gesture using both of her arms. "Of course we're people, you big lummox!"

The other tiny people started chanting drunkenly, "Big lummox! Big lummox!" The whole party descended into chaos.

Zinnia pushed her chair back and caught Margaret's eye.

Margaret nodded at Zinnia, and said to Karl, "Time for us to move on, boss."

Karl said, "Let me see if I can get a doggie bag." He rubbed his fingers together greedily.

Margaret got to her feet. "Never mind a doggie bag, boss. I'll buy you an ice cream sundae as soon as we hit 1955."

Karl got up right away and barked at Gavin to do the same.

CHAPTER 33

ALL SEVEN WISTERIA Permits Department employees prepared to leave the castle together. Liza and Xavier were tight-lipped about their experience with the timewyrms, but their eyes and behavior told so much. The two stuffed their pockets with food from the banquet table and avoided making eye contact with the local villagers. They startled at loud noises and kept their heads ducked down.

The attendant in the French maid outfit returned with Zinnia's purse, as well as the others' bags and supplies. Zinnia immediately checked her purse contents. Everything she'd packed for the journey was replaceable except the key. Luckily, the key and remaining chameleon potion were tucked away inside the interior pocket right where she'd left them. Most of her supplies and potions were there as well.

"We had to be cautious," little Tippi said apologetically from her perch on the edge of the long banquet table.

"I understand," Zinnia said. "Thank you for returning our things. And thank you for conducting a relatively mild kidnapping."

"You're welcome!"

Zinnia had been sarcastic, but the tiny person had taken her words at face value.

Tippi danced around Zinnia's purse flirtatiously. "Maybe you can take me with you? I've always wanted to see other worlds."

"I'm afraid you would have some difficulties on Earth. We don't have any people your size, so you wouldn't be able to blend in at all."

Tippi danced some more. "Who wants to blend in?"

Zinnia tugged at the collar of her floral-patterned blouse. "Some people like to keep a low profile."

"But why?"

"To avoid trouble."

"By trouble, do you mean being forced to fight to the death with a similar opponent?"

Zinnia thought about it for a moment. "Something like that," she agreed.

The conversation was interrupted by the servant in the tuxedo. He came to let Zinnia know that Bill, the former leg-munching ogre who was now a chef, had volunteered to pack food and water canteens for the group's voyage back to the mountainside portal.

While the ogre prepared their supplies, the WPD crew made use of the castle's exquisite washroom facilities before heading out.

* * *

Karl met Zinnia in the hallway when she came out of the washroom. Karl's poor suit was looking rumpled and dirty beyond salvage. The cheap fabric had practically sucked up the red sand of the desert. He was a mess. The man swore he was a sprite, yet he seemed to be morphing into a storybook troll before Zinnia's eyes.

"I heard a rumor that you met the queen," Karl said, sweeping his hand through his mostly-brown hair, which looked even more badly in need of a trim than usual. "You'd think she would have wanted to talk to the group's leader."

Zinnia was tempted to point out that Karl didn't exactly look like a leader. Her own clothing, by comparison, was still crisp and fresh. Her floral-patterned blouse, green slacks, and sensible shoes looked as tidy as they'd been at the start of their journey. There was something to be said for durable fabrics, bold patterns, and quality materials.

Karl grumbled, "I don't know why they thought you were the leader."

"You did specifically come to my office to talk about how we were equals," Zinnia said. "Both of us are department heads now."

Karl went HARUMPH. "How would the queen even know about that? Did you tell the snake?"

"Relax, boss." Karl Kormac was no longer her boss, but it soothed him to be called by the title, so Zinnia had kept up the practice. "You didn't miss much. Picture a spoiled brat who's easily bored. The type who might suggest, upon hearing that the villagers have no bread, that they ought to eat cake."

He frowned. "Is she human?"

Zinnia looked around to make sure they were alone in the hallway by the castle washrooms. They were, but even so, she wasn't sure if she ought to tell Karl the queen's identity. They were technically in the past, sort of, and she didn't want to create even more chaos that could put the future in jeopardy.

"Out with it," Karl barked gruffly. "You know something."

"The queen, the one her devoted subjects call Queen Beth, is Liza Gilbert's grandmother."

"That frail old woman?" He sucked in a breath. "It's always the one you least expect. But that makes sense. The first creatures started showing up around City Hall after that day Queenie Gilbert was at the office for lunch with her daughter." He did a double take. "That's why her name is Queenie! She's a double agent!"

His volume had been rising, so Zinnia shushed him. "There's another twist," she whispered. "She's not Queenie yet. The queen that's here is the 1955 version of Beth, before she married the Gilbert boy."

"Ah. So we have to send her back to the past, through the third floor and down the stairwell to 1955. That's why we're here. That must be our mission."

Zinnia scratched her head. She'd washed her face in the palatial ladies' room, but two days of interdimensional travel and no regular sleep was making her itchy. Plus she was troubled by Karl's insistence that they might need to meddle with the timeline more than they had.

"I'm not so sure about that," Zinnia said. "She'll go back on her own eventually. Once she gets bored here."

"But what if the portal closes before she does?"

"It won't." Zinnia shook her head. "It can't. She'll make it through because she already has. It's inevitable. We both met the older version of Queenie, so we know it has to happen."

"Not if we're in an alternate timeline now, in one of an infinite number of parallel dimensions. The Queenie we met returned home, but we might be on a new timeline now."

Zinnia scratched her head some more. This business of thinking through time travel paradoxes and parallel dimensions was literally a head-scratcher. Karl might be right. If they'd jumped over to some parallel dimension, that could explain young Liza's nightmares about ceasing to exist. In some realities, she'd never existed in the first place. But how could Liza exist to have the dreams if she wasn't meant to be? This line of thinking only led to more head scratching.

"We'll tell the queen she has to go back now," Karl said. "I'll talk some sense into her."

"The queen doesn't strike me as the type to take orders from anyone, not even the king. It sounds like she has him wrapped around her little finger, and he's a god. An actual god."

"What about the snake? Can we explain everything to her?"

"I wouldn't trust that one at all. She's not human. I wouldn't even trust her to return a library book on time."

"So, we're just going to leave here, go home, and hope for the best." Karl spoke with grim determination, as though it had been his idea right from the start.

"We got what we came for. We found Liza and Xavier. I believe the rest is up to fate." Zinnia grabbed an elastic band from her purse and tied up her hair. "Speaking of fate, did Dawna get any new readings with the cards? Please tell me she sees a future that doesn't involve volcanoes."

Just then, Dawna emerged from the washroom. "Ooh, you guys!" Dawna was rubbing her elbows. "Listen to this. All this dry air, and I'm not getting ashy. I'm going to book my next vacation here."

Zinnia repeated to Dawna the questions she'd just asked Karl.

"The good news is that I didn't see any more volcanoes," Dawna said.

Zinnia sighed with relief.

"The bad news is I actually didn't see anything at all, because the cards don't work here," Dawna said. "I keep trying to get that magic spark, but it feels like striking a wet match."

"I expected as much," Karl said gruffly. "Our powers don't work here."

"But your tongue works," Zinnia said. "I saw it thrashing around when the ogre grabbed you and Gavin."

Karl shook his head. "It wasn't at full power. If my tongue had been working, that ogre would have dropped us and run away screaming."

Dawna held up one hand and wrinkled her nose. "Ew."

Karl's face reddened. "At least I took charge and did something. What were you planning to do? Throw up on them?"

"That's enough," Zinnia said, holding up both hands. "Karl, Dawna didn't mean to shame you for being who you are. She's new at this." Zinnia held a warning finger up at Dawna. "And Dawna, we do not say 'ew' when one of our own uses their powers." *No matter how gross it is*.

"I promise to be a better fortune-teller," Dawna said, adjusting the headband that was holding back her black curls.

"Cartomancer," Karl and Zinnia said in unison, correcting her.

"Whatever," Dawna said.

"You're a cartomancer or card mage, not a fortune-teller," Karl said. "And I'm a sprite. Names matter." He glanced up at the castle hallway's high ceiling. "Especially in a place like this."

"Okay, okay," Dawna said. "I hear what you both are saying."

Karl straightened his tie, gave both women an exasperated look, and left to check with the ogre about the supplies.

Dawna whispered to Zinnia, "That man is a troll, right? Who's he kidding with that sprite nonsense?"

"He might be a sprite," Zinnia said. "I've never met a troll before, or a sprite, so who knows? People have always told me trolls aren't real." She pointed at Dawna. "Regardless, we ought to be more accepting, weird tongue and all."

"Don't worry. I can humor the grumpy sprite. I've got plenty of practice humoring Mr. Karl Kormac."

Zinnia looked into Dawna's orange, cat-like eyes. "And how are you doing? This must be a lot for you to take in."

Dawna responded with enthusiasm. "I'm fine, girl! How are you? Did you really meet the queen? That's what the itty bitty people told me."

"I did meet the queen."

"How was that? Did you curtsy?"

"No, but only because she didn't identify herself as a queen right away."

"She wasn't wearing one of those tiaras? I'm telling you, if I was queen of this place, I'd have a real nice tiara. Or a whole bunch, to go with all my outfits. Plus a servant whose job it is to get my curls untangled from all the diamonds."

"You'd make a beautiful queen," Zinnia said.

"Thank you! And they have people here in all sorts of colors, so you know that's not gonna be a problem."

"True enough. Even so, I think we're wise to get out of here soon, before something comes up and we get in more trouble."

"You don't have to tell me twice," Dawna said. "I was just kidding about coming back here on vacation. I don't ever want to go any place that's not on Earth. Never again."

"It will be good to go home. When we were still on Earth, the cards you read said we'd make it home safely, right?"

"As long as we steer clear of any volcanoes." They stared into each other's eyes for a moment. "The volcano thing was only one reading," Dawna said. "I'm sure we have nothing to worry about."

"Karl said so himself, those are very good odds."

"Very good odds," Dawna agreed. "Actually, it was more like three readings out of a hundred."

"Oh, Dawna."

She raised both hands. "Don't shoot the messenger!"

CHAPTER 34

THE JOURNEY BACK to the mountain took the group through the village, then the misty forest, and finally through the dry, sandy desert. The magical realm had some very tight microclimates that would have made an Earth meteorologist's eyes bug out.

As they traveled, Zinnia noted that morale of the group was mixed.

Dawna and Gavin were the most enthusiastic ones. Dawna claimed she didn't want to come back, yet she wasn't in any particular hurry to leave. She and Gavin carried on like happy tourists on a honeymoon, stopping periodically to take in the sights. They tried taking photographs, but none of the group's phones would power up. Whatever energy was in the air that stopped the witches' magic from working also stopped the electronics.

Karl and Margaret were more subdued, alternating between complaining about blisters on their feet and talking about the great food they'd consumed at the castle.

Unlike Zinnia, the other four had not been unconscious for long after the ambush. They'd all been loaded into a wagon and taken, fully awake and aware, to the castle. They'd been eating for at least two hours before Zinnia had woken up and joined them. None of the four had been terribly concerned about Zinnia, which gave the witch mixed feelings. She was glad they were confident in her ability to look after herself, but... seriously?

It had to be something in the air. Everyone was way too laid-back about having been kidnapped, albeit briefly, in a strange world.

Zinnia, who was the fifth person in their brigade, was also getting blisters on her feet. She hadn't gotten a blister since becoming a witch, due to her regenerative powers, so it was a novel experience for her.

She limped as she looked around the desert. The shadows being cast by the flowering cactus were growing longer. Night would be upon them soon, and night time in the desert would be cold. They had been given lanterns by the villagers, and had been assured that they would travel unharmed by the timewyrms or anything else, but all the same, Zinnia would be glad to put this world and its novel experiences behind her.

Eventually, the blisters became too distracting. Zinnia stopped to sit on a rock and take off her shoes to survey the damage. She tried to soothe her heels with items from her purse, which didn't go well, since most of the magical compounds were weapons.

The giant red sun was setting. Zinnia forgot her blisters temporarily as she gazed at the alien world's two moons above the mountain peak. She had seen many wondrous things in her life as a witch, but never two moons during a blazing scarlet sunset in a foreign land. It was a shame her phone wouldn't take a photo, but it probably didn't matter. Who would she ever show such a thing to? People would assume the image was a fake.

An idea struck her, and she chuckled under her breath. If she could take a photo here, she'd have it printed as a postcard, which she would mail to Detective Ethan Fung. *Having a wonderful adventure in a Hell dimension. Wish you were here. Best, Zinnia.*

The youngest of their not-so-merry band of adventurers, Liza and Xavier, who'd been trailing behind, caught up to Zinnia as she sat on the rock rubbing salve on her heel blisters.

Liza told Xavier, "Go on ahead without me. I want to talk to Zinnia."

Xavier rubbed the tip of his broad nose. He seemed reluctant to leave Liza. His light-green eyes darted along the horizon as he stayed at her side. Xavier seemed different here, out in the desert. His usual cockiness had turned into vigilance. He'd been walking with a sharpened stick. With the way he held the stick, his muscles tense as he surveyed their surroundings, he looked every bit a man. A warrior.

"Don't sit still for too long," Xavier said gruffly. "And yell for me at the first sign of trouble."

"I will," Liza said tiredly.

Xavier grinned at Zinnia. "I can't believe you're a witch," he said. "That's so surreal."

Zinnia nodded. When the group had used the washrooms, Liza and Xavier had been debriefed about their coworkers. As much as the witches, gnome, cartomancer, and sprite valued their secrecy, they agreed that interdimensional travel was enough of a trust bond between all parties present. Liza and Xavier did not, as far as anyone knew, have any supernatural powers. But then again, even if they did, it was probable their powers wouldn't work in this other world.

Liza did not know her grandmother was in charge of this world, including the creatures who'd imprisoned her. Only Karl and Zinnia knew so far, though if Zinnia had it in her head, that meant Margaret already knew or would soon.

Once Xavier had walked out of hearing range, Zinnia asked Liza, "What's wrong?"

"Nothing new," Liza said, sitting cross-legged on the red sand in front of Zinnia. "I just got tired of hearing Xavier talking. Did you know we were trapped in that timewyrm holding cell for five days?"

"I suspected as much."

"You abandoned us here for five days!"

"We didn't know it would be so long. The time dilation between the worlds isn't consistent. When Margaret and I came through the first time, we experienced less time passing than the hours we were gone, not more."

"But you went to the nineteen-fifties, not to this Hell world."

"The key didn't come with a chart of time differences. We couldn't have known. We came for you as soon as we could."

"Margaret said you went back to the office and worked until five o'clock."

"We did," Zinnia said with a sigh, regretting the wasted time. "And then we went to my house to get supplies. We couldn't have come for you without the potion that made the duplicate key work, but in hindsight, I should have made an excuse to leave the office early. I'm sorry we left you as long as we did."

Liza sniffed. "Those hours turned into days that felt like an eternity."

"I'm sorry that happened to you," Zinnia said. "It shouldn't have happened. I want you to know that it wasn't your fault."

Liza frowned. "Why would I think it was *my* fault?"

"Sometimes people blame themselves when bad things happen."

Liza looked down at Zinnia's feet.

Somewhere in the distance, a bird cawed.

"Double your socks over," Liza said, still looking at Zinnia's feet. "Like this." She shook the sand off Zinnia's sock, put it on her blistered foot, and then pulled the top of the sock down as a second layer over Zinnia's heel. "You're getting those blisters because the shoe's too loose for hiking. Now the two layers will slide past each other rather than across your foot. You're stuck with the blisters you've already got, but this should prevent more."

Zinnia did the same treatment with her other sock, pulled her shoes back on, and stood to test them. "That works," she said, taking a few cautious steps. "You're a genius!"

Liza's eyes glistened with tears. "There's no need to be sarcastic." Her lips pouted.

Zinnia put her hands on Liza's shoulders and looked into her wide-set, honey-brown eyes. "I wasn't being sarcastic. You're a clever girl, and I'm glad to have you on our team."

Liza shrugged off Zinnia's hands. "But none of us would even be here if it wasn't for my genius move to stick my grandma's key into that elevator panel. I don't know what I was thinking."

"You might not have had a choice. Magic has a mind of its own."

"Are you saying someone made me use the key?"

"Not someone. Magic itself. It's a force, with a personality of its own. Another witch I know claims that magic has a perverse sense of humor."

"But why me? Why did Grandma Queenie have that key at her house?"

Zinnia looked around. The light was disappearing rapidly, the desert landscape turning midnight blue. Zinnia wanted to tell Liza the truth about her grandmother. Now that they were on their way back home, it should be safe enough.

"Liza, can you keep a secret?"

"A secret?" Liza snorted. "You know I can't. If it wasn't for me blabbing, Margaret's marriage wouldn't be on the rocks right now."

Zinnia was confused. Why were they talking about Mike and Margaret's marriage? What did that have to do with anything?

Liza's eyes widened. "You didn't know?" She shook her head. "Mike's been cheating on her, with a junior programmer at his office. The girl is friends with one of my friends, who told me about it, but only because she didn't know I work with Margaret. I put two and two together, and figured out it was Mike. It was pretty obvious after that. Whenever Margaret's kids' school couldn't get through to Mr. Mills at work, I'd find out the next day it was because he took a long 'business meeting' with his junior programmer." Liza's face scrunched up. "I didn't like knowing he was treating her like that. Margaret's not easy to get along with, but she's a decent person. She didn't deserve that. So I told her."

Zinnia could only blink. Why hadn't Margaret told Zinnia that Mike was cheating on her? Why had she allowed Zinnia to believe Margaret was the one pushing him away?

Zinnia asked, "When? When did you tell her?"

"A month ago," Liza said. "Ever since then she's been in complete denial. She pretends I never told her. That's why I didn't want to hang out with everyone in the break room at lunch time. That's why I was riding the elevator at lunch until I got bored and stuck that key in."

"That's..." Zinnia was at a loss for words.

"So, maybe everything bad that's happening right now is my fault," Liza said angrily, getting her feet and kicking a stone off the path. "Everyone would have been better off if I'd never existed in the first place."

"Don't say that," Zinnia said. "You can't..."

Liza wasn't listening. She was already jogging away, hurrying to catch up with Xavier and the others.

Zinnia grabbed her purse and started running as well.

* * *

As they trudged toward the mountain, Zinnia kept thinking about an old poem, the one where a single missing horseshoe nail caused a war to be lost.

The group wouldn't be there if Liza hadn't stuck her grandmother's key in the elevator control panel. And she wouldn't have done so if Margaret had made Liza feel more welcome in the office. But it wasn't Margaret's fault. Not entirely. Margaret wouldn't have turned on Liza if Mike hadn't been cheating on her.

The group was trudging across a desert in a possible Hell dimension because a married man couldn't keep his hands to himself. Perhaps some of the blame belonged to the young woman he was carrying on with. Or was the woman the victim? Was he her boss who'd been taking advantage? Or was she a shameless hussy who didn't care about destroying a family? It was hard not to hate them both for what they'd done to Margaret and the kids.

Zinnia unclenched her fists and tried to think about something else. Anything else. Playing the mental blame game, shifting the fault between a man and a woman—it only made her feel sick to her stomach. She had been in Margaret's shoes herself. It was not a good place to be. She needed something to take her mind off the vicious blame game circling in her head.

Zinnia caught up with Xavier, who was ambling on his own, and fell in stride next to him. He was carrying one of the lanterns they'd been given by the castle staff. The sky was not yet entirely dark—perhaps it wouldn't be, thanks to the two bright moons—but the lanterns gave a cozy feeling of light bubbles around the travelers.

"Talk to me," Zinnia said tiredly to Xavier. "What do you think of all this?"

"I don't care for the desert," he said, spitting out grit and wiping his full lips with the back of his hand. "The tropical forest wasn't my favorite, either. This place is like all of Mexico crammed into a few square miles."

"And you don't like that?"

"No. I guess that doesn't make me much of a half-Mexican, does it?" He grinned and waggled his bushy eyebrows.

Zinnia smiled. Xavier did have his charm, especially when he made fun of himself.

"You are your own person," she said. "What about the village and the castle? Did your Irish side enjoy that?"

He didn't answer. He stopped walking and looked at her. "What's the deal, Zinnia? How do I find my magic?"

Down to brass tacks already!

"Not everyone has powers," she said.

He set the glowing lantern on the path and crossed his arms. "But you do. And Margaret, and Gavin, and Dawna. Even Karl. Why not me?"

Zinnia was reminded of the many why-not-me conversations she'd had with her great-niece, whose powers hadn't manifested yet—assuming she had any.

"Tell me about your family," Zinnia said. "These things run in families. If you do have supernatural lineage, there will be clues. Perhaps you can think of a family legend involving unusual skills?"

He grinned. "Is that a crack about Irish people and their legendary drinking abilities?" He shook his head. "Zinnia, I expected better from you than lazy stereotypes."

"Be serious for a minute," she said. "Is there something your grandparents joke about? Any unusual nicknames?"

His rubbery features grew serious. "Now you've got me thinking," he said.

"Thinking isn't such a bad thing."

He looked down, stroking the stubble on his chin. He really had been trapped with the timewyrms for five days, if not longer, based on the darkness of the beard he had growing in.

He flicked his light-green eyes up at Zinnia. "Is it true you guys were calling us the Red Shirts?"

"That's not how we truly feel about you," she said. "It was just..." She had no excuse. "It was said in poor taste, I'm afraid."

He waved a hand. "Nah. It's actually the best part. I got to be part of something, part of a bigger story. Maybe next time I'll be the hero, and not the damsel in distress."

"Perhaps," she said. "With that beard of yours, you don't make a very good damsel."

He laughed and pointed at her. "A joke! This whole wacky adventure has given you a sense of humor."

She put her hands on her hips. "It's always been here, Xavier."

He picked up the lantern and skipped energetically to get moving toward the rest of the group. "Good talk," he said.

"Good talk," she agreed.

"One of my grandfathers has some great stories," he said after a moment of walking. "I always thought he was making stuff up, but now you've got me wondering."

"Oh?"

They sped up their pace to catch up with the group, and continued talking about Xavier's family.

* * *

As the group reached the mountain, Zinnia saw something moving at the side of the mountain. She blinked. Was it a trick of the moonlight, or was something traveling up there?

Zinnia fell in step next to Margaret, pointing ahead. "Do you see something up there?"

"I see the broken windows for the accordion floor," Margaret said.

Zinnia saw the movement again. The two big moons gave off a considerable amount of light in the night sky. "Look! There it goes again."

Margaret stopped walking and squinted. "That looks like one of those..." Her voice died in her throat. The thing made itself visible, wrapping its long, sinuous body around the front of the peak. It was a timewyrm, and it looked even bigger than Zinnia remembered.

The others were taking notice of the creature as well. Everyone was talking, pointing, looking.

Liza screamed at the top of her lungs.

In the time Liza took to catch her breath, Xavier yelled, "Timewyrm! Take cover!"

They were completely exposed, walking on a path in the middle of the desert. There was nothing to take cover under. Zinnia tested her powers with an illumination spell. Nothing happened. Her powers were still on the blink.

Karl blustered, "Calm down, everyone! They're not coming for us. We have the queen's promise."

Liza screamed again. Xavier, who was at her side, tried to calm her.

Dawna said, "I think Karl's right. If they wanted to gobble us up, they would have done it already. Plus I didn't get any card readings with us getting eaten by those things."

The group fell silent, watching the enormous timewyrm slither down the mountain toward the broken windows.

Margaret asked in a whisper, "What are they doing? Did they come to make sure we got safely home and didn't stick around to mess up their world?"

Nobody had an answer.

The group watched as the timewyrm was joined by two more of its kind. The three enormous creatures plunged in through the broken windows all at once. These ones were too big for the windows, though. Their bodies obliterated the walls between the windows, ripping a huge hole in the side of the mountain. The ground beneath Zinnia's feet shook. As the timewyrms disappeared from sight, the mountain rumbled as though being hollowed out by explosives.

The noise continued for about ten minutes.

And then, all at once, the timewyrms wriggled out of the side of the mountain and slithered away. A cloud of dust wafted down from the dark hole.

Thirty minutes later, the group had wordlessly climbed the mountain path. They entered the cave anxiously, holding up their borrowed lanterns so they could survey the damage.

It was exactly as bad as Zinnia had expected.

The timewyrms had obliterated the walls, the ceiling, and the floor. What had once been a floor abandoned during construction was now a cave full of rubble, broken support rods, and scraps of metal.

Zinnia set down her lantern and ran toward the elevator doors. The sliding metal doors had been eviscerated. They lay on the floor in ruins. Where the doors and the call button with the keyhole had previously been, now there was only solid rock and more rubble. No keyhole, no way to open the elevator portal. No portal, no going home.

Behind Zinnia, everyone was talking at once, coming to the same conclusion with varying levels of panic and dismay.

Zinnia sank to her knees.

Their only way home had been destroyed by the timewyrms.

She picked up a rock and threw it with all her strength against the wall.

CHAPTER 35

"CALM DOWN, EVERYONE," blustered Karl, spit flying from his mouth. "We won't solve this problem if everyone's talking at once."

Everyone ignored Karl's blustering and continued to argue.

"This is the volcano ending," Gavin said. "The bad outcome that Dawna foresaw with her reading on the tarot cards."

"That can't be," Margaret said, dumbfounded. "This can't be how it all ends."

"Look around," Gavin said. "We're inside a mountain, which is basically a volcano. Same shape."

"But there's no lava," Margaret said. "This is not going to be the volcano ending." She stamped her foot. "I have to get home for my kids. They can't grow up without a mother."

"The lava will be along any minute now," Gavin said. "Then we'll see who's right and who's wrong."

"You'd like that, wouldn't you?" Margaret glared at the gnome. "You'd love for lava to come shooting up from the floor of this cave right now, just to prove you're right."

"We've got to stay calm," blustered Karl, not that anyone was listening.

"I know the difference between a volcano and a mountain," Dawna said. "If the cards had told me about a mountain, I would have said it was a mountain. I might be new at this stuff, but I know what a volcano is."

"A volcano can look like an ordinary mountain before it erupts," Gavin insisted.

"Stop jinxing us," Margaret said, waving her arms frantically. "Haven't you ever heard of a self-fulfilling prophecy? If you keep saying this mountain is going to be a volcano, you might make it happen. We don't know how magic works in this place!"

"Stop yelling, both of you," Dawna said. "You're upsetting the youngsters."

They turned to look at Liza and Xavier.

Liza sat near the edge of the cave, rocking back and forth with her hands covering her ears. "I won't go back there," she chanted. "I won't. They can't make me go back."

Xavier also looked upset, his face grim and shining with sweat as he worked silently, kneeling in the debris and digging through the rubble with both hands. One of his fingers was bleeding.

Karl looked over Xavier's shoulder. "What are you doing, son? You've cut your hand. You should be wearing gloves."

"We don't have any gloves," Xavier muttered. "We don't have anything useful. You came to rescue us, and all you brought was useless potions."

The others exchanged serious looks.

Liza dropped her hands from her ears. "Xavier, what are you digging for?"

"There are metal rods in here," he said. "They might come in handy as weapons for when those timewyrms come back."

Karl dropped a hand on Xavier's shoulder. "Good thinking, son. Keep digging." He pointed down at Xavier and told the others, "If everyone pitches in, we'll have this business cleared up in no time."

Dawna said, "Karl, snap out of it! This isn't a boardroom meeting about reports. Putting our heads down isn't gonna cut it."

Margaret whimpered. "We don't even know what time it is back home. I need to check on my kids." She took out her phone and shook it. "Stupid thing!"

"This is definitely the volcano ending," Gavin said, starting the argument over again.

Dawna yelled, "I know the difference between a volcano and a mountain!"

All of them yelled over each other, digging into the pointless argument about volcanoes versus mountains.

Everyone was arguing except Zinnia, who was sifting through the rubble near the ruined elevator doors. She was searching for the patch of wall that had held the call button and keyhole. It was a long shot, but she hoped she might be able to use the keyhole to open the portal despite the ruined structure. It wasn't a true elevator, anyway. It was just the magical entrance to the elevator that existed in Wisteria. They could get home if they could activate the portal. All they needed was a bit of luck.

The voices of Zinnia's coworkers faded into the background. She struggled, physically, to sort through the ruined pieces of wall and stone. She dropped an awkward-shaped boulder, narrowly missing her toes. Everything was so much heavier without magic to help with the lifting.

Zinnia was so focused on her task that she didn't notice when the group fell silent. She didn't realize that Queen Beth and the snake-woman, Susan for lack of a better name, had joined them inside the lantern-lit cave. Not until someone tapped her on the shoulder.

Zinnia whipped around, ready to tell Gavin to either help her or shut up and leave her to it. But it wasn't Gavin interrupting her work. It was the queen, looking somber. And guilty.

"You did this," Zinnia growled at Queen Beth. "Is this how you amuse yourself? I thought that was your husband's game, toying with people like they're playthings. I thought you were the*good one*."

The queen took one look at the fury in Zinnia's hazel eyes and jumped back.

"It wasn't me, I swear," Queen Beth said.

"You didn't send your creatures to destroy this place?"

"I only ordered the timewyrms to leave you alone." She shook her head, her perfect blonde waves whipping with the movement. Her honey-brown eyes were wide and gleaming in the lantern light within the cave. "I forbade them from coming anywhere near you, but..." She trailed off, her eyes brimming with tears. A sob cracked in her throat. "Now what will we do?"

Zinnia put her hands on her hips. "Why are you acting like you're the one who's had something bad happen to you? We're the ones stuck here without a way home."

The queen sniffed pitifully. "If you can't leave, how am *I* supposed to get home again?"

There was a thunk as she dropped something. A suitcase.

The murderous rage gradually drained from Zinnia. The queen wasn't lying. The tears were real.

"You changed your mind about going home?" Zinnia asked.

The queen nodded mutely.

"You even packed your suitcase," Zinnia said. By the looks of it, the queen had indeed intended to return to her home in 1955 via the staircase. No wonder she was as distraught as any of them over the portal being ruined.

"I thought about what you told me." Queen Beth sniffed and smiled through her tears. "Honestly, the truth is I couldn't stop thinking about the Gilbert boy. I've had fun here with the king, but it's impossible to love a god the same way you can love a human."

Coldly, Zinnia said, "I'm glad you had your moment of self-actualization, but nobody's going anywhere." Zinnia picked up the two pieces that had once formed the panel that fit on the wall. "This was our way out of here. I still have the key, but what good is a key without a lock?"

The two women stared at each other.

Gavin interrupted, "Your, uh, highness, did you say something about *the Gilbert boy*?"

Liza had stopped rocking and was standing, staring at the queen with saucer eyes.

Xavier's eyes were nearly as large. He whipped his head back and forth between the queen and her look-alike granddaughter fast enough to give himself whiplash.

"Two moons," Dawna said breathlessly, waving a finger and swishing her head. "I knew it! The two moons symbolize the two women. I knew there was more going on to those double moons that kept coming up every time I read the cards."

Gavin pointed at the queen. "You're Queenie Gilbert. How did you turn yourself young again?"

"She didn't," Margaret said, catching on quickly. "Queenie Gilbert is in a hospital bed. This woman is either an impostor or..." Margaret turned to Zinnia and gave her an incredulous look. "You knew? You met her and you found out who she was, and you didn't tell me?"

"Zinnia told me," Karl said gruffly. "The rest of you are on a need-to-know basis."

Xavier grabbed Liza by the shoulder. "Is that your grandma?"

Liza's mouth wobbled before she said, "Grandma?"

Susan, who had been quiet up until now, sidled up to Liza. She practically slithered despite being in human form, and slung one arm around the younger Gilbert's shoulders. "She's not your grandma, petulant child," Susan said, her tone mocking. "And she never will be if your group can't find the way out of this world."

Liza didn't seem to notice the snake-woman's arm across her shoulders. Her focus was riveted on her young grandmother.

The group waited with bated breath to see what the two relatives would do next.

"Look at me," Liza said to the queen. "Grandma, why won't you look at me?"

The queen looked anywhere but at Liza. She leaned down and fidgeted with the handle of her suitcase.

Liza cried out, "If you don't go home to where you belong, I'm not going to be born!"

Everyone stared at the queen.

Beth wouldn't look up from her suitcase. "That's why I can't look at you," she said. "That's why..." She trailed off.

Margaret gasped. "You knew!" She pointed at the queen. "You knew the timewyrms had captured your granddaughter."

Everyone else gasped.

Liza walked up to the queen and grasped her shoulders. "Is it true? Look at me, Grandma! You have to see me!"

The queen looked left and right, avoiding eye contact with her descendant.

"We were locked up for five days in a pile of filth," Liza said. "How could you do that to family? How could you do that to me? I love you."

The queen looked up at the ruined ceiling. "I don't know you. I don't have any children, let alone grandchildren. Look at us. We're the same age."

Liza released the other woman with a push.

The queen stumbled backward, tripped over her suitcase, and fell onto the rubble.

The cave was so silent, Zinnia could hear a trickle of water dripping deep within the mountain.

The queen buried her face in her hands. "I didn't know it was you," she sobbed. "I didn't know I had a granddaughter. I thought—" Her voice hitched on a sob. "When they told me one of the humans they captured looked like me, I thought it was my sister coming to take me home. I didn't know it was..."

Liza put her hands on her hips and glared down at the queen. "You thought it was Great-Aunt Katie, and you were happy to let her rot in that festering dump? You're not the person I thought you were." Liza turned her back on the woman. "You're dead to me," she said.

The queen sobbed.

Susan watched the exchange silently, her eyes flicking back and forth between the two blondes.

The others looked around, communicating through glances. Most of them were surprised. Shocked, even. Liza was always such a sweet, happy-go-lucky person around the office. She loved her grandmother, and spoke highly of her. She didn't tell her grandmother she was *dead to her*.

Gavin broke the silence. "This is a paradox," he said. "We're standing in the middle of a paradox. Present, past, and future are all meeting up here."

"Two moons in the sky," Dawna said enigmatically. "We stand in the company of two moons traveling at different speeds."

"I don't know what any of this means, but I'm going home," Margaret said. "The elevator might not work, but we should be able to dig out the stairs. Once we get to 1955, we'll figure it out from there."

"The stairs," Karl said confidently, striking his finger in the air. "Our next order of business is digging out the stairs. I need a committee chairperson to report back on progress."

"This is crazy," Xavier said.

Karl nudged the young man toward the corner where the stairs had been. "Let's get you digging over there."

"All right," Xavier said, shrugging as he picked up a lantern and brought it over to the stairwell area. He pulled away one stone. "Nobody's going to believe us when we get home."

"I'm not going home," Liza said softly. "I'm not going home, because I was never here."

"Liza?" Dawna grabbed her by the shoulders and looked into her eyes. Dawna turned and said to Margaret, "Something's wrong with Liza."

Margaret climbed over the rubble and took a close look at Liza. "Something is happening," Margaret said, directing her comment mainly toward Zinnia. "Liza's not entirely here."

Karl wasn't paying any attention to the business with Liza. "We have to get to work clearing the stairwell access," Karl said. "We'll get home and take her to a doctor."

"Girl, you're fading on us," Dawna said.

Margaret agreed, "She is fading. Someone hold up the lantern behind her."

Karl and Xavier were moving rubble in the corner, so Margaret circled around and lifted the lantern herself.

Liza's lips trembled. "What's happening to me?"

"She's literally fading away," Dawna said.

"You mean figuratively," Gavin corrected. He stood halfway between the women and the men working in the corner, arms crossed. "You meant to say Liza is *figuratively* fading away."

"I know what literally means, you silly gnome," Dawna said. "Look at her!"

Everyone looked, including Xavier and Karl. It was true. The lantern Margaret was holding up behind Liza could be seen through Liza's body. The young woman was fading, becoming a ghost.

All nine people—or eight plus the snake-woman—went silent. Liza was still there, but she was fading away before their eyes. If the queen couldn't return to the past, she wouldn't get married and have children who would later have more children. Liza's nightmares about ceasing to exist would become true.

An eerie animal sound came in from the desert. It sounded like a hooting owl, only lonelier.

Zinnia looked down at the smashed pieces of elevator panel in her hands. She couldn't give up hope yet. The split between the two pieces had a curved, snake-like shape.

The idea hit Zinnia, flaring up hope.

The snake-woman had powers. According to the villagers, there was magic everywhere in this strange land. It couldn't be accessed by the Earth witches, but perhaps all hope wasn't lost yet. The cave hadn't filled with lava, after all. Not yet.

Zinnia said, "Susan?"

The snake-woman turned her head, her eyes briefly flashing red with annoyance at being addressed as Susan—or possibly at being addressed at all.

Sullenly, Susan said, "What do you want of me, witch?"

"Do you know of another portal? Another place where our key might fit so we can travel home?"

Susan scowled. "This is the only place."

The queen, who'd gotten to her feet and wiped most of the tears from her cheeks frowned at her companion. "You're not lying to us, are you?"

Susan shook her head.

The queen explained to the group, "She didn't want me to leave." The queen turned back to Susan and said, "Give us the truth, and give us your word."

Susan hissed and then spat on the ground. The saliva sizzled as it landed and emitted a cloud of steam.

"My word is my bond," the snake-woman said, walking up to stand nose-to-nose with the queen.

Margaret and Zinnia exchanged a look. Some things, apparently, were the same in this world.

"Is there another portal?" Queen Beth asked.

"There is no other portal," Susan said. "This is the only place like this that I know of." Susan stepped back from the queen and turned her head stiffly and slowly, taking in the whole group. "I was here when the artifact appeared in the mountain." Her head didn't bob at all when she spoke, which made her appear powerful and snake-like. "I watched our future queen arrive. It was because of my protection that she survived her first battle."

The queen closed the gap between herself and Susan, and touched the snake-woman's cheek tenderly. "You are my dearest friend. If I can't go home, at least that means we'll stay together."

Zinnia dropped the broken elevator pieces with a noisy clatter. "I hope you're happy now, Susan," she said with grit in her voice. "You had your monsters destroy this place. You ruined the lives of eight people so your best friend won't leave you." Zinnia spat the dust from her mouth and wiped her lips with the back of her hand. "You're a despicable, selfish creature."

Susan turned toward Zinnia and changed into a snake. This time she was at least thirty feet long, and gleaming silver. Her body coiled around everyone gathered. Gavin and Xavier scrambled to high ground on the rubble to keep from being knocked over by Susan's twitching tail.

Susan's hissing head rose until it touched the jagged roof of the cave.

"You sssspeak liessss," she hissed. "You think I ordered this destruction? I love my friend. I love her."

"Exactly," Zinnia said. "You love her so much that you didn't want her to leave. Where I come from, we have a saying. If you love something, set it free. But I guess you didn't learn about that here, in your godforsaken Hell world."

The snake pulled back her lips, baring fangs that were a foot long. "You are the falssssse one. You are born of demonssss. You are the godforsaken one, witch."

Zinnia marched up to the hissing, towering snake. In the back of her mind, she knew she was putting herself in grave danger with not even enough magic to give off a static electricity shock, but she had nothing left to lose. All of them were trapped in this strange world. They were unfathomably far away from everyone they'd ever known and loved. How much worse could things get?

Zinnia spat her words into the mouth of the hissing, towering snake. "Susan, if you didn't send those monstrosities to destroy this place, who did?"

The ground beneath their feet began to rumble. The mountain that enclosed them shook and growled. Chunks of stone fell from the former ceiling and crashed around them.

Liza screamed, and Dawna joined in.

Xavier yelled, "Earthquake!"

Gavin said dully, "Volcano. It's got to be the volcano erupting, right on time."

Karl shouted above the din, "Single file everyone! Proceed to the exit in an orderly fashion!" He grabbed Zinnia's lantern and used it to light the path to the cave entrance. "Form a human chain! Grab one person's hand with each of yours! Everyone's getting out of here if we work together! Remember the fire drills, people. Remember your safety training!"

An avalanche of rocks tumbled down on Zinnia. She was being buried alive. She tried to use magic to push away the crumbling stone, but she had no magic, and she didn't have enough physical strength in her human body. The darkness closed in.

CHAPTER 36

EVERYTHING WENT DARK, and then, someone was grabbing Zinnia by the hand. Zinnia was pulled free of the tumbling rocks, and dragged to the cave entrance and out into the cool, night air. Zinnia gasped a thank-you to her rescuers, Queen Beth and Susan, who was back in human form again.

"And there's my number seven," said Karl Kormac, nodding at the sight of Zinnia. Karl was standing on the mountain path in all his wrinkled-suit glory, lit from below by lanterns and from above by two glowing moons.

The rumbling of the mountain had ceased, and Zinnia's ears were ringing in the silence.

Susan, who still had one of Zinnia's hands in hers, looked the witch in the eyes and said, "I didn't send the timewyrms to destroy this place, but I know who did."

Zinnia pulled her hands away from the two women. She spat cave grit from her mouth, along with some blood and part of what might be a tooth. She looked into the woman's cool blue eyes and demanded, "Who sent the timewyrms?"

"My brother," Susan said, almost whispering. "The king."

Zinnia looked from Susan to Beth and back again. The two were close friends, and apparently they were also related by marriage. If the king was a god, that made his sister Susan a goddess. But judging by the fearful look in her eyes, she was not as powerful as her brother.

Zinnia glanced behind her to survey the wreckage inside the cave. The timewyrms had done a fine job destroying the portal, but the recent earthquake had certainly finished the job.

Zinnia turned back to Susan and said, "When you say it was your brother, the king, do you mean the same one who spent millennia torturing the people of this world for his own amusement?"

Susan nodded.

Zinnia spat again. The chunks were definitely tooth. "Why am I not surprised?"

Susan and Beth exchanged a worried look, then both jerked their heads to look at something at the peak of the mountain. The two blonde women gasped in unison as their eyes widened.

The ground rumbled again. Zinnia turned around slowly, following their gazes. The peak of the mountain, a black triangle against the purple sky, was smoking.

There was another rumble, and the ground shook hard enough to topple every one of the group to their knees. Zinnia reached out both hands to catch herself, and felt the jolt in her wrists. Getting knocked around without her witch powers was as inconvenient as it was painful. She felt helpless, which only stoked her rage. She heard her emotions being echoed by Margaret, who let out an animalistic growl further down the path.

Zinnia picked small pebbles from her palms and stared up, powerless, as the smoke at the peak became bubbling lava. The hot molten rock poured out, incinerating the scant shrubs that grew along the mountainsides.

"KNEEL," boomed a voice. "KNEEL BEFORE YOUR KING."

Zinnia heard Gavin muttering, "We're already kneeling."

The lava continued to bubble up, and something red, glowing, and person-shaped emerged. The lava was not pouring out of the tip of the mountain so much as it was *climbing out*. The figure had broad, muscular shoulders and sinewy legs. It was a man, made of red-hot lava. The king.

The lava man strode down the side of the mountain toward them.

"HOW DARE YOU," he boomed. "HOW DARE YOU LEAVE ME, BETH? AFTER EVERYTHING I'VE DONE FOR YOU. AFTER I'VE CHANGED. AFTER—"

"Enough!" The queen tossed a rock directly at his looming head. The rock soared in a high arc, much higher than a human could have thrown it. Beth had powers? Her rock sunk into the man's enormous molten head with a tiny hiss.

The bubbling figure's face smoothed enough to show facial expressions. He appeared to be confused. The sight of the giant lava man frowning and scratching his molten brow with his lava hand struck Zinnia as comically absurd. She heard her sentiments voiced by Margaret, who let out a sharp, "Hah!"

The queen picked up another rock, tossed it in an impossibly powerful arc, and nailed him right between the eyes.

"HOW COULD YOU," he boomed. "BETH, YOU CAN'T TREAT ME—"

"Stop yelling!" She lobbed another rock. This one sunk into his eye, melting upon contact. "Everyone can hear you!"

The molten-lava king's posture slumped.

"I'M NOT yelling," he said, his volume lowering as he spoke. "I'm not. You were the one yelling."

She yelled back, "I have to yell because you don't listen!"

His frown became so pronounced that bits of lava splashed out of his forehead wrinkles. "I listen," he said.

The mountainside was silent except for the hissing of shrubs being incinerated by the lava dripping from the king. He was over twenty feet tall, and radiating heat greater than the biggest bonfire Zinnia had ever felt. Thankfully he had stopped far enough away from them that their clothes weren't about to burst into flames.

The silence was broken by Gavin commenting, "This is the volcano ending. I told you so."

Dawna said, "Not now. You don't know when to shut up, do you?"

Karl said, "Everyone, be quiet. Let the lava man speak."

Margaret said, "Let the lava man speak? Excuse me? How about we let the *woman* speak?"

Xavier said, "Uh, has anyone seen Liza? Where's Liza?"

"She made it out of the cave," Karl said. "I counted her. Zinnia was the last one out."

Dawna said, "She was right here a minute ago. Liza?"

Zinnia was about to join her friends to help locate Liza when the queen spoke again to her flaming spouse.

"You're the one who sent the timewyrms to destroy this place," Beth said.

With a petulant tone, the giant lava monster replied, "I couldn't let you leave me. What about our children?"

"We don't have any children," the queen shot back. "Remember? You didn't want any. You said you weren't ready."

"I might be ready now."

She waved at the destroyed mountainside. "Look at this," she spat out, gesturing wildly. "This is not the work of a man who is ready for children."

"I'm sorry," he said. "Sorry you're so mad."

The queen didn't respond.

"I'm sorry," he repeated, pouting his molten-lava lower lip. His body shrunk by ten percent, but he was still a giant, still radiating a tremendous amount of heat.

The queen put her hands on her hips and tapped her foot. "You should be sorry."

Margaret suddenly broke from the group, raced up the path, and placed herself squarely between the queen and the molten-lava king.

"Typical man," Margaret said, waving her arm at the lava giant, her voice dripping with contempt. "You stomp around, doing whatever you want, and then you think two little words are going to let you off the hook? *I'm sorry?* Nope. That doesn't cut it!"

Zinnia ran to Margaret's side and tugged on her arm. It was to no avail. Margaret's stout form gave her the advantage of holding her place when she wanted to. She would not budge. Instead of heeding Zinnia's whispered warnings, or, really, any common sense whatsoever, the gray-haired witch continued to berate the smoldering king.

"You think you can do whatever you please!" Margaret's hands flapped around like angry birds. "You think the whole world revolves around you! That you're the only person who matters! You think everyone else will just pick up the pieces!"

The king looked from Margaret to his queen and back to Margaret again. "Who dares speak to the king with such disrespect?" He frowned, and more lava squirted out of his forehead wrinkles.

Margaret yelled up at him, "This witch! That's who!"

"A witch?" He shriveled visibly and backed away from her by two large steps, setting off a small avalanche that narrowly missed the group. He turned his flaming face toward Susan. "Sister, you did not say the visitors were witches."

"They're no threat," Susan replied, tension making her voice high and squeaky. "Do not bother harming the witches from Earth. They haven't found the way to access the magic here." Susan shot Zinnia a quick, meaningful look, eyebrows raised, as if to say there *was* a way to access the magic, if the witches kept trying.

"I don't like witches," the king said. "Too bossy."

"That's how people are. They're imperfect. You can't eat them all or there won't be any left."

"But I don't like the things that are happening right now," he said. "The old ways were better."

"You weren't happy then, either," Susan said.

The lava man scratched his head. "I don't remember."

While Susan had been trying to talk civility into her giant, fiery brother, Margaret had picked up a big rock. Margaret heaved it back and chucked it at the king. As she whipped her arm to follow through, a stream of sparkling magic shot from her fingertips. The flung rock turned an icy, glowing blue in the air before it struck the king in the shin. There was a crack that reverberated through the desert landscape.

"Ow," the king said. "She is a witch."

Margaret turned to Zinnia, her face contorted with delight. "The magic," she said breathlessly. "It's everywhere, Zinnia! You don't have to wrap it around your tongue, because it's everywhere!" She raised both arms in a triumphant Y shape. "Can't you feel it? Oh, Zinnia, it's magnificent! It's—"

Margaret stopped speaking because she was no longer Margaret. She was a stone statue, frozen with her arms raised in a triumphant Y. Susan was touching her elbow.

"For her own protection," Susan said hurriedly to Zinnia. "She's still in there."

Zinnia nodded slowly. She'd seen living things turned to stone before, and back again. The others from the office, however, had not. Pandemonium ensued. Liza still hadn't been found, and now Margaret had been turned to stone.

Meanwhile, the queen had started a dialog with her lava-king. They were arguing about which one of them had the right to end their relationship, as well as who was to blame for their ongoing conflicts. Despite them being the rulers of a magical world, the words they used and the emotions behind them were no different from the kind that could be heard in the aisles of any home improvement store on a Saturday afternoon.

Zinnia tuned them out, because she was trying to focus on only two things: the magic that apparently hung in the air all around them, and the goddess.

"I know your name," Zinnia said to Susan, who wasn't really Susan.

The king's sister rolled her lovely eyes. "No, you don't."

"Oh, no? Come here and I'll whisper it in your ear."

She narrowed her eyes but reluctantly came over to where Zinnia stood on the mountain path. She leaned forward. Zinnia turned her bruised and bleeding mouth toward the woman's ear.

"Diablo," she said. "Your name is Diablo."

The goddess reeled backward, sucking in air audibly. "Witch," she gasped. "You have beaten me, witch." She began to choke, held her throat, and coughed. She was trying to expel something. After much coughing, a glowing ball of light fell from her mouth. The ball floated, bubble-like, straight to Zinnia.

Zinnia caught the ball, crushed it in her fist, and felt magic flooding through her once again. She could see the magic that hung in the air all around them. Now that she knew where to look, it was so obvious!

Zinnia turned to her coworkers. They were all in such a panic, they hadn't seen Zinnia get her powers back. But they had found Liza.

Liza was hysterical. "I don't exist," Liza cried. "This is my nightmare, and it's happening. Look! I'm fading away!" She held up one hand. It was even more transparent than it had been in the cave. Liza let out one last wail, shot a pleading, pathetic look at Zinnia, and blinked out of existence.

Zinnia looked around and counted up everything that was wrong. Their only way home lay in ruins. The queen was arguing with the king, who was made of lava and three times her size. Margaret was a statue. Karl was sitting on an overturned log with a blank look on his face. Xavier and Dawna were digging at the sandy ground with their bare hands, calling for Liza. Gavin was staring at Zinnia.

"You have to do something," Gavin said. "Zinnia, you have to save us."

She held up one finger, twirling the airborne magic around it. "I'm trying."

"Try harder."

"Yessss," said the goddess, whose true name was Diablo. She had turned back into a snake—a sapphire-blue ten-footer this time—and slithered around the edge of the group. "You musssst try harder," the goddess hissed.

Zinnia looked down at her hands. They were dirty and bleeding, but the magic that was in the air was running through her fingers like water. What could she do with all this strange power?

CHAPTER 37

WHAT COULD ZINNIA do with the magical realm's abundant power? Plenty!

Her first task was to clear the corner where the stairs had been.

Not only was her levitation working again, but it was working better than it ever had on Earth. Back home, she'd been limited to levitating objects that weighed no more than what she could lift manually. But here, she was tossing boulders out of the corner as if they were Styrofoam set pieces from an early episode of *Star Trek*.

The others offered to help, but after a few close calls, they decided the best way of helping was to stay out of Zinnia's way.

Unfortunately, despite a fantastic effort clearing the corner, no stairs were found, magical or otherwise. Zinnia had suspected as much, so it wasn't a crushing disappointment.

Next, she got to work fixing the elevator doors and the keyhole.

Using a combination of brute force plus a myriad of spells, including a souped-up steadfast spell, she managed to reassemble what might have, to a casual observer, passed for an elevator entrance.

Zinnia stepped back and admired her handiwork. It was now the dead of night, and most of her coworkers were either asleep or watching quietly. Liza was still missing. Zinnia hoped that once the portal reopened, the young Gilbert would turn up. Margaret was still a statue. The goddess, Diablo, had tried to return Margaret to human form once the king had been distracted away from the loudmouthed witch, but Diablo's powers hadn't yet recovered from the transfer that had taken place when Zinnia spoke Diablo's name. Zinnia tried not to worry too much about Margaret. Her main focus was getting the elevator up and running, so to speak.

She took a deep breath, prepared the key with the chameleon potion, and tried it in the lock.

Nothing happened.

She wiggled the key, like she had before.

Still nothing. She fought the urge to curse under her breath, lest she accidentally jinx the lock even more.

"That cover plate is cracked," said Gavin.

Zinnia startled. She hadn't heard the gnome approaching. "I know it's cracked," she snapped. "This poor elevator has been ripped to shreds by monsters and then battered in an earthquake. It's not exactly showroom-fresh."

Gavin threw both hands in the air defensively. "Excuuuuse me for trying to help," he said. "I forgot that Ms. Zinnia Riddle is now a department of one person only, top to bottom. Nobody else can work with her because nobody else measures up."

Zinnia let out an exasperated sigh. "That's not true. I only sent you away from the stairwell project because you were going to hurt yourselves."

"We could have been done hours ago if you'd let me and the guys help clear the stones."

"I did finish that hours ago," she said. "Haven't you seen? I've been working this whole time on the elevator. Do you know how hard it is to unwrinkle metal?"

He pointed his chin at the cracked panel. "Did you try wiggling the key?"

She resisted the urge to send a magical bite to Gavin's posterior. With the way her magic was supercharged in this world, the spell was liable to chomp through muscle.

"I wiggled it," she said.

"The cover plate is cracked," he said, stating the obvious for a second time. "That's why it won't work."

She gave the key another wiggle, then pulled it out of the hole wearily. She put her back to the wall and slid down until she was sitting. Exhaustion suddenly hit her like, well, a crumbling cave roof.

"Come on, Zinnia," Gavin said. "You can't give up now."

"I'm not giving up," she lied. "I just need a moment to rest."

"You can't stop," he said. "You're the witch. I'm just a gnome. The tiny bit of magic I can do is a drop in the bucket compared to what you have access to."

Dawna, who'd been sitting by the campfire near the mouth of the cave, came over and joined them.

"The cover plate has a crack in it," Dawna said.

Zinnia said nothing.

"You should do another reading," Gavin said to Dawna. "Zinnia's got her powers back. You should, too."

Dawna gave him a sad look and shook her head. "I keep trying, but I've got nothing."

"You've got to try something," Gavin said. "Zinnia's broken, and I'm just a gnome."

"What?" Dawna scrunched her face. "Did you say you were *just a gnome*? You told me gnomes had amazing powers!"

Gavin hunched his shoulders and stuck his grimy hands into his pockets. His designer trousers were stained and torn in multiple places.

"I'm not amazing after all," Gavin said sheepishly. "I'm just a gnome. All I can do is sniff out items of value, and escape home, like a coward."

"That's it!" Dawna clapped her hands together. "Gavin, you can go home! All you have to do is stamp your foot three times."

"I don't know about that," he said warily. "Teleportation doesn't work across different worlds, different dimensions."

"Why not?"

Zinnia got to her feet again, and chimed in, "Why not?"

He freed one hand from his pocket and itched the back of his neck. "Uh, I don't know." He looked down and scuffed the floor of the cave with the toe of one shoe. "I could try, but it's a one-way ticket. What about the rest of you?"

Dawna grabbed his arm. "Good thinking. I don't want to be stuck here without you." She quickly added to Zinnia, "No offense."

Gavin kissed her, then turned to Zinnia, his chin lifted defiantly. "You heard Dawna. I won't leave her, even if I could." He shrugged. "We'll just have to make the best of our lives here on this side. We can keep working on getting the elevator fixed, even if it takes years."

He continued to talk, trying to make the best out of a bad situation, but Zinnia didn't hear a word he was saying. She had already decided on a different outcome for their adventure.

Zinnia handed both the key and the remaining chameleon potion to Gavin.

"You were right," Zinnia said. "I'm not a department of one. I'm part of a team, and so are you."

He stared stupidly at the key. "You want me to try the key? I'm not going to have any better luck than you, Zinnia."

"You can, and you will." She grinned at him as hope bloomed in her heart. "Gavin, Dawna, this is the volcano ending."

They both blinked.

Gavin spoke hesitantly. "This is the volcano ending?"

Zinnia nodded. She was exhausted, but she could see the loop clearly in her mind. "We've already been thrown into the volcano, but it's a good thing. This is the best outcome from the tarot cards, not the bad one."

Dawna gasped in understanding. "This is the volcano ending," she exclaimed. "The lava has come out, and now we go in and through."

Gavin frowned at the key and potion. "But there's no use. The cover plate is cracked."

Zinnia reached out and closed his grimy fingers around the key. He wasn't catching on as quickly as Dawna, but he'd get there.

Zinnia was almost too excited to say the words. Almost, but not quite. "You teleport home, and you open the portal from the other side."

He immediately tried to give the key back to Zinnia. "I don't know," he said. "Let me think about it. Traveling between dimensions is the kind of thing that gets a gnome turned into a red spray of liquid gnome, if you know what I mean."

Zinnia refused to take the items back. "We must be brave," she said. "We must do what ought to be done."

Gavin frowned. "I'm no hero."

"That's what all the good heroes say."

He shook his head. "I don't see this working out."

"You don't see it, because you're not the card mage," Zinnia said. She pointed at Dawna. "But our card mage foresaw a future with the group going into a volcano, so we have to do our part to make it come true."

Dawna grabbed Gavin by the shoulders. "You have to go, Gavin. You have to open the portal from the other side so we can get through. Who's going to feed my cats if I don't get back?"

Gavin turned to Zinnia and gave her a defeated look. "The cats," he said dully. "I'm going to stamp my foot three times, and I may rematerialize inside my apartment on Earth, or I may have my atoms scattered to the winds, but I'll do it." He swallowed and looked even more defeated. "I'll do it for Dawna's cats."

"That's true love," Zinnia said. "We should check with the others and make sure we're all in agreement."

Gavin shook his head. "It's now or never," he said. "I don't want to wait." He cleared his throat. "Nobody likes long goodbyes." He lifted his foot and prepared to stamp it three times.

Zinnia waved her hands at Gavin. "Wait! Before you go. There's one more thing."

"One more thing?"

She leaned in close and whispered something into Gavin's ear.

He backed away, shaking his head. "I don't like that idea," he said. "This is getting complicated."

"Do it," she implored. "You have to."

He kept shaking his head. "Messing with fate and timelines... We could get more than we bargained for."

"We must be brave and do what ought to be done."

Gavin took a deep breath. And then, before he could change his mind or be talked out of it, he stamped his foot on the ground three times.

There was no puff of smoke or change in the air. He was just gone.

CHAPTER 38

Hours passed.

The otherworldly sky, with its unfamiliar pattern of stars, turned purple, then burgundy. The red sun was rising after a long night.

The remaining, non-statue members of the Wisteria Permits Department, Zinnia, Dawna, Karl, and Xavier, were making the best of their stay inside the cave. It wasn't exactly hospitable, but it kept them out of the dusty winds that had picked up shortly after Gavin had teleported away.

The lanterns were subdued, their fuel source nearly burned out. The wrinkled remains of the elevator doors were fastened to the wall from which they'd been torn. The broken pieces of the control panel had been reaffixed at the correct height, give or take a few inches. Zinnia hoped everything was close enough to match and work when the portal opened from the other side. That was, *if* the portal opened.

It had been three hours since Gavin had disappeared, but given the rate-of-time differences between the two places, it was possible he was only now leaving his apartment to return to City Hall. It was a shame that gnomes could only teleport to one predetermined spot, but then again, if gnomes were able to travel anywhere at any time, that would have made them much more than gnomes. They would be wizards.

Throughout the whole night, the king and queen had continued to argue about absolutely everything. Argue, make up, and argue again. They reminded some of the WPD crew of Gavin and Dawna. Both royals were sitting now, just outside the cave entrance. The king had shrunk in size and was only twice the size of the queen. He was still smoldering, though—both his mood and his physical body.

They had come to an agreement that they were going to stick together and work on their issues.

"I won't leave you," Beth said, for the umpteenth time. "I give you my word. My word is my bond. I will not leave your side."

"Then why are we still here at the mountain?" The king sounded grumpy and doubtful.

"You can go back to the castle without me. I'm staying to see if the Earth people can return home."

"I'm not leaving without you," he said. "And you're not leaving with them."

"I already promised I won't go!"

"If you play a trick on me and you leave, I'm going to start eating the villagers. I will eat one every minute until they're all gone."

"This is exactly what you always do. You and your threats. It's emotional blackmail!"

"You told me that all is fair in love and war."

"That's not what that saying means."

He growled, shaking the ground once again. A few loose pebbles fell from the cave ceiling.

"Don't be like that," Beth said. "The Earth people are listening. They're going to think we're in an abusive relationship."

More like codependent, Zinnia thought to herself. But also abusive, to some degree. At least that was how it looked from the outside.

The king said something in a low voice Zinnia couldn't hear. Beth giggled.

After a moment, Beth called back into the cave, "We're going for a walk, but we'll be back. Do you need anything?"

Zinnia replied, "If you pass by a Starbucks, I'd love a latte. Get one for everyone, my treat."

Beth giggled. "What are you talking about?"

Zinnia waved a hand. "Never mind."

It was a real shame all Zinnia's coworkers were asleep; they'd missed her lightening the mood with anachronisms.

Beth and the king walked off, leaving Zinnia the only person awake at the camp.

The snake-goddess, Diablo, was still there, albeit in her blue snake form. She was currently draped around the shoulders of the statue of Margaret. The statue appeared to be wearing the snake as a scarf. Margaret wouldn't have liked that, since she was dead-set against the wearing of fur or animal skins, other than as shoes.

Xavier had fallen asleep hours earlier, curled up in a ball near the cave entrance. He'd been inconsolable about the disappearance of Liza. It had been a relief to the whole group when he'd finally fallen asleep. Dawna dozed with her head on Xavier's shoe. She couldn't have been too comfortable, but Karl had put his wrinkled suit jacket over her as a makeshift blanket, and she appeared to be sleeping.

Karl was sleeping next to the fire in a seated position, with his back propped up on a boulder. When Zinnia walked over to stoke the fire, he woke and mumbled a greeting.

An hour later, Karl and Zinnia sat across from each other on boulders. The fire burned brightly between them. Zinnia had been cautious about using the magic in the air. The source energy didn't behave the way Witch Tongue did back on Earth.

She had, however, used the abundant magic to split some of the combustible building materials into firewood, and she'd also used magic to light the fire. A third spell redirected all of the campfire smoke back out of the cave so they wouldn't be smoked out. Zinnia was grateful for her camping trips with her mentor, where she'd learned these basic spells.

Karl, who had removed his tie entirely and rolled up his shirt sleeves, gazed into the flames.

"Good job on the fire," he said to Zinnia.

"Thanks, boss."

"I told you before. I'm not your boss anymore. You and I are equals. We're both the heads of our own departments."

"Then I suppose that makes me the head of the Department of Cave Fires." Zinnia smiled and tossed another chunk of lumber onto the fire. The cave was already toasty warm, but she had to do something to keep her mind off her worries. Was Gavin on his way back? Would the plan work? Did he even survive the interdimensional teleportation?

Karl smiled back at Zinnia. "If you're head of the Department of Cave Fires, that makes me the head of..." He looked around them. "I don't know what."

"Safety," she said. "You did a fine job getting everyone out of here in one piece when the king was shaking the mountain."

"Not quite all in one piece." He leaned forward and studied her face. "But it looks like your busted teeth have already grown back in."

Zinnia rubbed her teeth. The two in the front felt shorter than they should have been. They were still regrowing. Bemusedly, she said, "Ah! So those were the ones I was spitting out after the king caused the earthquake."

"You were spittin' mad after that. Like a tough guy in a fighting movie."

"I really was spittin' mad. I don't take it very well when my powers get stolen."

"At least you won't need to see a dentist as soon as we get back."

She chuckled. "Having to see a dentist was the least of my worries."

"It must be nice to have those witch powers. You're sort of a superhero."

"What about you? What powers do trolls—er, I mean *sprites* have?"

Karl gave her a rare grin. "We're very good at collecting tolls for bridges, and eating billy goats."

"Ha ha," she said. "But seriously. Tell me a little more about your people."

"You go first. Your powers must have some limits. What's your weakness?"

"You mean my Kryptonite?" She batted her eyelashes. It was witchbane, but she wasn't going to tell him that. "Microwave pizza."

Karl narrowed his small, squinty eyes. "Something tells me that's not true."

"Have you ever seen me eat microwave pizza?"

"Come to think of it, no."

"Exactly. Now you tell me your Kryptonite."

He glanced around the cave. "Diamonds," he said mischievously. "If you throw diamonds at me, I'm beaten. But you have to use a lot of diamonds."

Zinnia crossed her arms. "Fine. Don't tell me about sprites. Be mysterious." She thought of the book her niece referred to as the Monster Manual. She would be looking up sprites—as well as trolls—as soon as she got home.

"Sprites love being mysterious," he said.

Zinnia rubbed her chin thoughtfully. "I do know you've got that long tongue, and you snacked on those bone-crawlers like they were candied apples."

Karl twitched his bulbous nose. "Candied apples would have tasted a lot better." He leaned back and rubbed his stomach. "But I can't say I'm any worse off for having munched on some otherworldly vermin. Sprites have unusual digestion issues, especially in regard to gases."

Zinnia kept a straight face, thinking about the vast number of times Karl had irradiated parts of the office with his gases. Dryly, she said, "You don't say."

"We require a lot of chitin," he said. "The long-chain polymer is a vital protein for us. We sprites need far more chitin than we get in the standard American diet."

"I had no idea. Chitin. As in the protein that's in lobster shells?"

"Oh, yes. I do love lobster, shells and all."

"I'll keep that in mind for the next office potluck." She glanced over at the battered elevator doors. "Assuming there is a next potluck."

Karl followed her gaze to the portal area. He and the others had been told about the current plan. Karl had seemed miffed about not being consulted, but had congratulated Zinnia for taking charge with the plan anyway.

"There will be another potluck," Karl said. "Gavin Gorman puts on an act, but he's a good worker. Deep down, he's a solid team player."

Zinnia chuckled. "And a snappy dresser. I mean, if we're handing out compliments willy-nilly, I'll give him that."

"Do you think so? I always felt his clothes were on the tight side. Perhaps one size too small."

"It's true! I thought it was just me who felt that way."

Karl picked up another piece of lumber and tossed it onto the roaring fire. "Zinnia, it sounds like you and I have a lot more in common than we thought."

"Indeed," she said.

Something bright flitted through her field of view. She leaned back and looked up. Outside the cave entrance, the sun was rising and already baking the desert in warm red light. Inside the cave, the ceiling was still dark. Against the darkness were spots of light. Hundreds of them. Thousands. Something inside the cave was glowing.

"Look at that," Zinnia said. She got to her feet and examined one of the bright spots.

"What's that?" Karl got to his feet, came around the roaring fire, and joined her. "Fireflies?" He squinted at the dark ceiling. "I'll be! It's one of those things that flew out of that snow globe in your office."

"It's a glowfish," she said. "Some of them are clinging to the ceiling, and some are swimming through the air."

Karl gently blew on one of the glowfish, sending it swimming away even faster. "Tiny fish that swim through the air," he said with wonder. "Now I've seen everything."

Another voice rang through the cave. "Does that mean you're ready to go home now?"

CHAPTER 39

KARL AND ZINNIA turned to see Gavin standing within a bright box of light at the side of the cave. Zinnia rushed forward and threw her arms around the gnome. She'd never been so happy to see Gavin. She'd never been so happy to see *anyone*.

"Easy now," Gavin said. "I already have a girlfriend."

Zinnia pulled away quickly, shot him a look, and went to wake Dawna and Xavier.

"You made it," Karl said to Gavin. "Good work. You're a real team player."

Gavin ducked his head impishly. "Thanks, boss. I would have been here sooner, but I had some issues with security at the hospital." He nodded over his shoulder at the other occupant of the elevator—an elderly woman with white hair, propped up in a wheelchair.

Gavin rolled the wheelchair out of the elevator, then quickly ran back inside it, where he used his foot to prop open the door.

The white-haired woman surveyed the scene with bugged-out eyes.

Gavin said to Zinnia, "I'll stay here holding the door, if you don't mind. Would you mind waking everyone?"

Zinnia and Karl managed to get Dawna awake easily. Xavier was harder to rouse.

Dawna's gaze fell on the old woman. "The crone!" She grabbed Zinnia's arm excitedly. "That's the crone! I didn't think she was important, since she only came up in the readings with the volcano ending."

"Gavin found her for us," Zinnia said. "Well, for Liza."

Dawna held her hand over her mouth shyly. "When I got the crone, I thought it was either you or Margaret."

Zinnia raised an eyebrow. "Excuse me?"

"No offense," Dawna said.

307

"Too late," Zinnia muttered.

Xavier made a beeline for the elderly woman, looked at her, then demanded of Gavin, "Who's this? Why'd you drag some old lady into this mess? We're trying to get out of here, not start a colony." They had explained the whole plan to Xavier, but either he hadn't been listening or hadn't retained the information. The poor young man had been a mess since Liza's disappearance.

The woman in the wheelchair spoke up. "I'm not *some old lady*, dear. That's no way to speak to your elder."

Dawna elbowed Xavier. "This is Liza's grandmother. We told you she might be coming. She's here for Liza."

Queenie Gilbert said, "I *am* Liza's grandmother. Where is she?"

Xavier muttered, "I'm asleep. This is all a dream."

Dawna said to Queenie, "He's just confused because the last time he saw you, you were standing on the side of the mountain yelling at the king, who happens to be a giant made of glowing lava."

"The king?" Queenie held her pale, skeletal hand to her mouth. She'd lost a lot of weight since her visit to City Hall, and was now painfully thin. "Oh, dear. You must have me confused with someone else."

Zinnia walked over to the woman's wheelchair and crouched to be at eye level. The cords at the sides of Queenie's neck were taut, and she seemed to be straining to get out of her wheelchair but too weak to do so.

Zinnia said softly, "Queenie, can you remember the time when you were last here?"

"I don't know this place," she said, her voice trembling.

"Do you remember the last time people called you Beth?"

The woman's wide-set, honey-brown eyes brightened. "Oh, yes. It was before my big vacation. I went to the most beautiful places."

"And where were those places?"

The white-haired woman let out a nervous laugh. "They weren't on another planet, if that's what you mean! It was just Europe. Italy, Spain, France. That sort of thing."

Zinnia held her gaze. "Are you sure about that?"

Queenie nodded. "Yes, dear. When I was on vacation, I made the most wonderful friend, and she started calling me Queenie."

Zinnia glanced back over her shoulder, then back at the elderly woman. "Queenie, how many pale moons do you see hanging in the sky behind me?"

The woman looked. "Two." She pulled her head back. "Two? I'm sorry. I must be confused. I haven't been feeling well lately."

Zinnia patted her on the knee. "I understand your time on Earth is drawing to a close. How do you feel about... moving on to a different place?"

"Sweetheart, we all move on to a different place, whether we feel like it or not. We all..." She frowned, looked down at her lap, and cleared her throat. "That's odd. I can feel my feet." She kicked at the blanket that covered her legs. "I can feel my feet. I think maybe I can walk."

Karl cut in. "Your hair!" He turned to the others, gesticulating excitedly. "Look at her hair! It's growing, and changing color!"

Sure enough, Queenie Gilbert's hair was lengthening. The white strands were turning a golden blonde. Her wrinkles disappeared. Her face smoothed and took on more color. Her eyes remained the same, but less sunken. With each breath, her youth returned. In a matter of minutes, she appeared to be exactly the same age as the woman who was currently outside arguing with a petulant king made of lava.

"I'm back," Queenie said, patting herself. "Have I died? This must be heaven." She pushed the blanket off her lap and sprang out of the wheelchair. She was still wearing a hospital gown and disposable slippers—not exactly queenly attire, but her posture became more regal as she approached the cave opening and peered outside.

Zinnia joined her at the cave opening. The others held back, watching and murmuring to each other.

Queenie looked out over the desert of her kingdom. Her eyes glistened.

ANGELA PEPPER

"I'm home," Queenie said. "I never thought I'd find my way home again."

Zinnia felt a sympathetic rush of emotion, mixed with the almost overwhelming urge to run full speed for the elevator and press the button to go back to her own home.

"Thank you so much," Queenie said to Zinnia. Her voice was raspy, but not from age. "I don't know what I did to deserve this. I barely know you."

"I have to confess something," Zinnia said. "We brought you here so that you could save someone else. Your granddaughter, Liza."

Queenie's eyelashes fluttered and her expression grew pained. "Liza's in trouble?"

Zinnia swallowed hard. There'd been no sign of Liza since her disappearance last night. This ploy was a long shot, but it was all they had.

"She might be in trouble," Zinnia said. "But we have an idea. Do you see those two arguing over there?" She pointed to the side of the mountain.

Another version of the woman, dressed in a regal gown, was still arguing with the lava king.

Queenie chuckled. "I remember him, all right. It's all coming back to me. He's such a stubborn man! It takes him decades to admit when he's wrong, you know." She squinted at the two figures on the mountainside. The sun had risen, and the sky was red and clear, but there was a cloud of smoke surrounding the arguing royals. "Who's that he's arguing with? Is it Liza?"

"That's... you. I don't know if it's all come back to you yet, if you even remember, but this is the part where you've circled back. There's an overlap."

"An overlap?"

The woman was understandably confused, but Zinnia understood it perfectly. The overlap was similar to what had happened back at City Hall, when the cleaning lady had watched herself clean the top floor. How could Zinnia explain it to Queenie?

"You've traveled back in time," Zinnia said. "It's 1955 again, more or less, but in a different world."

310

"It is? How can that be?"

"Magic," Zinnia said.

Recognition flickered across Queenie's honey-brown eyes. "I know about magic," she said. "This land with the red sun is full of magic."

"So, you believe me that you've traveled back in time?"

Queenie nodded slowly. "This is the overlap. That's me over there." She looked down at her hospital gown and patted herself. "I can't talk to myself looking like this. I'll be so frightened."

"We'll get you a change of clothes. All you need to do is convince the version of yourself who's arguing with the king to trade places. She'll come back here and go down the stairs, which are..." Zinnia realized she hadn't checked the stairs yet.

Dawna, who'd been listening attentively, interjected, "The stairs are right here, Zinnia. As long as Gavin keeps the elevator open, I think they'll stay. There's a hole in the cave with stairs going down. I already went to have a peek. It's 1955 down there, all right. I came back here fast, before anyone got any ideas."

"Thank you," Zinnia said. "I guess we're ready to make the exchange."

When she turned back to Queenie, the woman looked more alert than ever. She started to step out of the cave onto the pathway.

"Wait," Zinnia said. "Your clothes. I'm sure we can rustle up something." She glanced around the cave, searching for extra clothing.

Something scraped the dust behind her. A blue snake slithered into sight, then changed into a woman again. Diablo. She was nude, and holding out a blue dress and a pair of sparkling shoes.

"Take these, my queen," Diablo said.

Queenie cried out and hugged her friend. "Diablo! I thought I'd never see you again! I thought you were dead!"

Diablo looked at Zinnia and asked, "What is she talking about? A goddess does not die."

Zinnia took in a deep breath. This was the tricky part. "Diablo, you're going to go through to 1955 with your friend." She pointed to the royal couple arguing on the mountainside. "You're going with the one who's arguing with the king over which one of them starts all the arguments." She gestured to the rejuvenated Queenie. "And this version is going to stay here with the king to fulfill her promise, and to make sure he doesn't go back to torturing everyone."

The women stared at Zinnia as though expecting more explanation.

"That queen gave her word that she wouldn't leave this land," Zinnia said. "That's why Queenie has to take her placc. Whether or not you tell the king about the switch, that's up to you."

Diablo looked unconvinced. "We could send this one to your Earth past." She pointed at the new arrival.

"We can't do that," Zinnia said. "If we did, this Queenie would experience the same sixty-odd years of life over and over again with her memories intact. She would have to make all the same choices, knowing the outcomes, good or bad. She would live that existence over and over in a loop. We can't do that to a person. It could be heaven, or it could be hell."

Diablo frowned. "It would be hell," she said. "But why do I have to go?"

"Because you did," Zinnia said plainly. "I know it sounds far-fetched, but it's what you're going to do. I know, because it's already happened." She paused, unsure if she should say the next part, then decided to go for it. "I know because I've met your grandchildren."

"Liesss," Diablo hissed. "I cannot have children."

"Maybe not here, but you can have them on Earth. And you will. When you go down those stairs, you'll meet a wonderful man who's already a bit mad, and..." She smiled. "I wouldn't want to spoil it for you."

Diablo had a faraway look in her eyes. "Children," she said. "And grandchildren."

"Powerful ones," Zinnia said.

Diablo's nostrils flared. "Others will try to harm my children. That is why gods and goddesses cannot have descendants."

Zinnia said nothing. People *would* try to harm Diablo's offspring. It happened to everyone's offspring, gods or otherwise. She could offer no consolation or reassurances otherwise.

Queenie had already stripped off the hospital gown and was pulling on the sparkly dress provided by Diablo. She and her best friend, whom she would not be reunited with for long if everything went according to plan, began making a plan to draw the other queen away from the king so they could convince her to make the switch.

Zinnia turned back to her coworkers, who were all watching with big eyes.

"Everything's taken care of," Zinnia said. "Why do I feel like I'm forgetting something?" She felt a scratch inside her brain, like the needle on a record player scratching. She whipped her head around, her gaze landing on the statue of Margaret. The witch's stone arms were still raised in a victory long forgotten.

"Oh, Margaret," Zinnia said. "I didn't forget about you!" It wasn't true. She had forgotten about Margaret momentarily, but she told herself she would have remembered before the elevator doors had closed.

* * *

The statue of Margaret was quite useful for holding the elevator doors open while everyone said their goodbyes.

Zinnia carefully removed the magic key from the elevator's control panel and gave it to Queen Beth, who would soon return to Earth and be known as Queenie. To everyone's relief, the queen had been happy to trade positions with the more experienced version of herself.

Zinnia said, "Take this key with you to 1955, and keep it close. When it's time, you'll return to City Hall, where you'll use the key to open the connection."

Gavin interjected, "Doesn't she need chameleon potion?"

"No," Zinnia said. "This is no longer the duplicate key. It's now the original."

"What?"

Zinnia waved at him to never mind. The whole paradox thing was as mystifying as magic itself, but in that moment, with the world's magic flowing all around her in the air, Zinnia understood the plan completely. All the pieces fit. This exchange was a paradox, the snake eating its own tail, yet it was also real. She'd been blessed to have been a part of it. They all had been.

She continued explaining the plan to the young queen, who looked worn out from arguing with her molten husband all night.

"I understand," the queen said. "But you must think I'm a terrible person, the way I treated all of you."

"You have a long life ahead of you," Zinnia said. "A very long life. I know you will make the most of it."

The queen nodded. "I will."

Zinnia pointed to her gnome coworker. "Remember the face of that man, Gavin Gorman. When he finally comes for you, that's when you'll make the journey. Don't go through on your own the first time you open the portal, or it might mess everything up."

She gave the group a solemn look. "I understand." She glanced over at the cave opening and the red vista beyond. "I'm going to miss this place."

Diablo slung an arm around her shoulders. "You'll be back before you know it, my queen." She gave Zinnia a dirty look. "I'm not so sure about what's going to happen to me, but I'll be by your side as long as you'll let me."

The elevator dinged. The doors banged against the stone statue of Margaret.

"Uh oh," Dawna said. "It never dinged like that before. We'd better get going."

"Now," Zinnia said. "It's time for all of us to continue."

People muttered their goodbyes. The queen and the snake-goddess would leave down the stairs. After a one-minute count, the people in the elevator—Karl, Dawna, Gavin, Zinnia, Xavier, plus the statue of Margaret—would press the button for the ground floor and return to City Hall.

A figure appeared, silhouetted in the cave opening. It was Queenie, looking regal in her sparkling dress. "Goodbye!" She waved and blew them all kisses. "Enjoy the past, and the future! I know you can't send a postcard, but please think of me fondly!"

Zinnia stepped into the elevator with her coworkers.

They all tugged on the statue of Margaret to get her inside, and then the elevator doors closed.

A little voice from the back corner said, "Hey! You're squishing me!"

Everyone turned around.

There in the corner was Liza Gilbert, looking annoyed.

Everyone cried out with relief and hugged her.

She groaned from the onslaught of hugs. "I've been here the whole time. You couldn't see me or hear me. I guess I was a ghost or something."

They pulled away, and everyone started talking at once.

The elevator dinged, and everyone fell silent.

The doors opened on a regular floor of City Hall.

City Hall! Boring white walls and gray commercial carpet! What a relief to not see a red sky or the inside of a cave!

Someone stood in the hallway, facing the elevator. It was the mayor herself, Paula Paladini, standing with her arms crossed, looking stern in her pinstripe suit.

"I see you all made it back," she said coolly.

CHAPTER 40

MAYOR PAULA PALADINI stood behind her desk in her private office on the top floor, where she'd taken the crew from the elevator.

Paladini looked the same as the last time Zinnia had seen her at the hospital, and the same as she'd looked every time before that. The sixty-something woman had her icy blonde and white hair pulled back in a tight knot. Against her pale skin, her lips were a shocking dark red, and her dark-brown eyes looked nearly black. Her pinstriped pantsuit and crisp, white blouse looked brand-new and freshly pressed. The mayor was wearing flats, as usual, but with her tall, skinny frame, she towered over the group of filthy, tired Permits Department employees. She gave off no scent at all, or perhaps the group simply couldn't smell her over their own stink.

"Wheel that statue into the corner," the mayor said to the employees who were currently using a commercial dolly to wheel in the statue of Margaret Mills with her arms raised triumphantly.

The trio of employees did as they were told. One of them muttered, "Hey, I know this lady. She works on the ground floor. I left my dog in the car by accident on a hot day, and when I came back, she'd busted my window."

Another of the guys said, "I know her, too. She's a real piece of work."

The first one glared at his coworker. "Shut your mouth. This lady saved my dog's life."

The third one asked, "Is that why they made a statue of her? Because she saved a dog's life?"

Paladini barked at them, "That's enough! Leave the statue on the dolly. Just go."

The employees nearly tipped over the dolly and Margaret in their hurry to get away from the mayor.

Once they'd exited, closing the office door behind them, Paladini turned her attention to the group. They were milling aimlessly near the visitor seating area inside the palatial office with its fifth-floor corner views of both the forest and the town of Wisteria. All were still jubilant from their victory and reunion with Liza, yet subdued by the mayor's intimidating presence.

"Sit," Paladini commanded.

Everyone either took a chair or squeezed onto the sofa. Zinnia sunk into the plush cushion on the end. She remembered what the cleaning lady, Ruth, had said about taking naps in the mayor's office. No wonder! The comfortable sofa was long and luxurious, hard to resist.

Paladini began pacing in the space behind her desk. She wrung her hands in a nervous gesture Zinnia hadn't been expecting. She reminded Zinnia of a parent whose teenager has finally made it home after a break in curfew. Paladini looked nervous, angry, and relieved, all at the same time.

Paladini barked at the group, "Do you people even know what time it is? Or what day?"

Zinnia, Karl, Dawna, Gavin, Xavier, and Liza exchanged furtive glances. Nobody spoke up.

"It's Friday," Paladini said. "After Gavin Gorman opened the portal from this side, things started slipping quickly. I was able to put the brakes on by throwing a few control switches, but you did lose a full day."

The group made non-verbal surprised noises. The mayor knew about their time-traveling, world-jumping adventures. Zinnia glanced around at the others. They were all making thoughtful, concerned faces.

"What a mess," Paladini said. "What a colossal mess."

Gavin raised his hand. "There's no mess anymore," he said. "We fixed everything."

He was about to say more, but Paladini's nearly black eyes bore into him, and whatever the gnome had been about to utter died in his throat.

Paladini gave them a forced smile, revealing the black gap between her front teeth. "I know you thought you were helping," she said, as though trying to convince herself to go easier on them. "You did what seemed right." She shook her head, paced some more, and muttered, "The key was here for a month and I never saw it." She wheeled around to face the group. "Where was the key?"

Everyone looked at Liza.

Liza gulped. In a hoarse voice, she answered, "It was on my necklace."

The mayor nodded. "Touching your skin. That explains it. That explains why the scans didn't work."

Karl piped up. "She didn't know. Liza Gilbert is a fine employee. She would never intentionally deceive her superiors."

The mayor snapped her fingers and pointed at Karl. "That's enough, troll."

Karl's face reddened.

Zinnia jumped up from the sofa. "He's a sprite," she said.

The mayor looked taken aback, blinking at Zinnia before she spoke. "Yes," she said icily. "I do understand they prefer to be called sprites these days. I'm not a dinosaur. It was a slip of the tongue."

Karl said, "Apology accepted."

Gavin said, "But she didn't apol—" He was silenced by Dawna digging her elbow into his side.

"Not now," Dawna hissed.

Zinnia, who was still standing, addressed the mayor on behalf of the group. "With all due respect, Mayor Paladini, we did the best we could, considering the circumstances."

The mayor regarded her coolly. "You had no idea what you were doing," she said.

"Oh, no, you don't," Dawna said, waving her hand full of busted nails as she struggled to free herself from the sumptuous sofa. "Zinnia does not deserve to get in trouble. If anyone should take the blame, it's me."

Everyone turned to Dawna.

Dawna said, "You see, it all started because I was being snoopy. I took a note off Gavin's desk and read it when I shouldn't have. This is all my fault."

"No," Liza said, the third one to extract herself from the plush sofa. "It's all my fault. I was the one who had the brilliant idea to stick a key into a hole in the elevator panel. I didn't even know it was a portal. I thought it was an abandoned floor." She made a tsk sound and looked down at her filthy toes sticking out of the ends of her strange boot-sandals. "And instead of turning the key over to the authorities, I started going there on my lunch breaks."

Gavin asked, "Why did you go there for lunch? Why didn't you eat with us?"

Liza glanced over at Zinnia, then at the statue of Margaret. "Long story," she said.

"It's all my fault," Xavier said, rising from one of the chairs and stepping forward. "Liza, you didn't want to keep going. It was all me." He took another step toward the mayor and held out his hands as though expecting to be handcuffed. "I kept bugging her to go because I liked spending time with her. I was being selfish."

Gavin, who was still seated, said, "Xavier's right. It is his fault. He should have told someone." Gavin gave Xavier a hurt look. "What's the deal, man? I invited you to my poker game. You didn't think I'd want to see a secret floor?"

Karl groaned as he got up from his chair. "Calm down, everyone," he said. "None of us did anything immoral or illegal. In hindsight, perhaps it was foolhardy for us to go through without appropriate backup, but in our defense, we didn't know who to trust." He addressed the mayor directly. "My kind have faced endless discrimination over the years. We sprites have been chased out of many places."

The mayor pursed her lips.

Xavier stopped holding his hands out to be handcuffed and tucked them behind his back.

Dawna looked right at Zinnia and asked, "Did you know the mayor was some kind of wizard?"

"I'm not a wizard," the mayor said.

Xavier asked, "If you're not a wizard, then how do you know about where we went?"

The mayor pursed her blood-red lips again.

Xavier wasn't cowed at all. "If you knew about the third floor, you should have done something." He puffed up his chest. "If you knew about those giant timewyrms, you should have done something to block off the access." He made a fist with one hand and punched it into his palm. "I should get a lawyer and sue you. I should sue the whole city."

Liza grabbed Xavier's fist and held it at her side. "Easy now," she said to him. "The floor was blocked off, and would have stayed that way if I hadn't taken my grandmother's key. You're not going to sue me, are you?"

Xavier's fight energy calmed down, thanks to Liza's sweet stare.

Zinnia cleared her throat. "Mayor Paladini, you don't have to tell us what you are, but you ought to give us some sort of explanation."

Everyone turned to the mayor. The only sound was the hum of the air conditioner.

After a moment, the mayor plainly stated, "I come from a long line of time paladins."

The words settled on the group.

Dawna said to her coworkers, "Is it just me who doesn't know what that means?"

Zinnia exchanged looks with Karl and Gavin, who both shrugged.

The mayor said, "You wouldn't know of my kind. There are few of us left."

Dawna said, "I'll bite. What's a time paladin?"

The mayor seemed to relax a little. "Do any of you watch *Dr. Who*?"

The group was too stunned to answer.

"Well, we are nothing like Dr. Who," the mayor said quickly. A genuine smile was curling her dark-red lips. "I do not have a Tardis, and I do not travel around with a companion having adventures. However, like Dr. Who, my people are concerned with preserving the timeline."

Everyone nodded and pretended to understand.

She continued, "My superiors dispatched me here, to this town, after the rift formed in 1955. That was when many types of creatures came through from another world and terrorized the construction workers, as well as some townspeople." She gestured for them to be seated again, and she walked around to the front of her desk, where she perched on the edge. Everyone settled back into their seats.

The mayor smiled at the memory. "A small group of us managed to repair the damage in 1955, but I must confess that I didn't know how." She shook her head and looked down at her swinging feet, which made her appear young, and not nearly as imposing. "I was much younger then, and inexperienced."

Dawna waved her hand. "Excuse me, but wouldn't you have been a baby in 1955?"

The others chortled.

"I'm older than I look," Paladini answered, exactly as Zinnia knew she would.

"Back to the story," Gavin said. "How did you fix a rift between worlds?"

"I can't go into the technical details," Paladini said. "Not because you don't deserve to know, but because your minds couldn't comprehend it. In layman's terms, I tugged at a thread, and pulled through a fate line from the distant future. I created a loop and tied it with a knot. The repair seemed stable enough, but to be safe, I have remained stationed here to witness the other end of that thread I pulled."

Karl said gruffly, "That's perfectly understandable. It sounds to me like you took charge and did the best you could to keep control under the circumstances."

"Lawdy, lawd," Dawna said, shaking her head and waving both hands, broken nails and all. "That's what my grandma would say if she was here right now. Lawdy, lawd, that's a big ol' whopper. Are you for real? You're really a time wizard?"

"Time paladin," the mayor said patiently.

Dawna asked, "Isn't a paladin a type of soldier?"

"Actually, it's a knight," Gavin corrected. "Paladins were the twelve peers of Charlemagne's court. The count palatine was their chief."

Everyone began talking at once about paladins and time travel.

The mayor waited patiently before clearing her throat to get their attention. "I'm glad everything's been cleared up," she said. "I hope I can count on your discretion. You are forbidden to mention any of this to any person not currently present." She glanced over at Margaret. "The other witch can know, once we revive her, but nobody else."

Dawna laughed. "Who'd believe us?"

The mayor leaned back from her perch on her desk, picked up the phone handset, and hovered her hand over the buttons. "If you're not in agreement about secrecy, I shall have your memory wiped as a group. I'm afraid this is an all-or-nothing deal."

"We're in agreement," Karl said vehemently. "All of us. Right?" He looked around at the group. Everyone nodded, except Margaret, who was still a statue.

"Good." The mayor set down the phone handset with a resounding clunk. "By the way, why is Margaret Mills a statue?"

"She started yelling at the lava king," Zinnia said.

The mayor raised an eyebrow. "And he turned her to stone?"

"That was the work of a snake-goddess," Zinnia said. "I believe she did it to protect Margaret."

"Why didn't she change her back before you left?"

Dawna said, in a tattle-tale voice, "Because Zinnia sucked all her magic powers out of her by saying her name."

The mayor gave Zinnia a look of surprised reverence. "Nicely done," she said. "Your mentor would be very proud." She gave Margaret another look. "We shouldn't leave her like this for long. Do you have a way to change her back, or do I need to make some calls?"

"I know a couple of gorgons," Zinnia said.

Dawna gasped. "Gorgons are real?"

ANGELA PEPPER

* * *

The group discussed a few more details with the mayor before she had to leave on other important business. Zinnia couldn't imagine what sort of business might be more important than the resolution of the current situation, but it was probably for the best she didn't find out.

Paladini allowed Zinnia to stay behind in the mayor's private office with the statue until one of the gorgons could come by to restore Margaret. The others—Karl, Gavin, Dawna, Xavier, and Liza, returned to the Permits Department office on the ground floor.

Zinnia got comfortable on the mayor's sofa, but found herself unable to doze off. It was hard to relax with Margaret Mills doing a permanent cheer in the corner.

Eventually, there was a knock on the door.

It was Chloe Taub who had come to the witches' rescue. She was dressed in faded jeans and a white T-shirt, carrying her newborn baby in a sling. Since the last time Zinnia had seen Chloe, Zinnia and her niece had learned the secret about Jordan Junior. It was Chloe's desire for a baby that had set in motion so many events, both good and bad.

Zinnia stared at Chloe, amazed at her resemblance to her grandmother, Diablo. Zinnia wished she could tell the blonde gorgon about meeting her goddess ancestor in the other world, but she couldn't. She was sworn to secrecy.

Instead, Zinnia asked, "How is your grandmother these days? I must admit I became intrigued with her after seeing her name mentioned in the City Hall construction logs."

"She's dead," Chloe said.

That was fast. From Zinnia's perspective, Diablo had been young and vital, crossing into her new Earth life only hours ago.

"I'm sorry for your loss," Zinnia said.

"Thanks. Please tell your coworker, Liza Gilbert, that I'm sorry for her loss. I heard about her grandmother passing away last night. I know she was a special woman. My own grandmother spoke very highly of her best friend."

"I'll pass that along," Zinnia said. Queenie Gilbert had technically been kidnapped from the hospital, so the news about her passing must have been a cover story arranged by the mayor.

Chloe sniffed Zinnia. "You smell like you've been camping."

"That's because we were camping." Sort of.

The gorgon narrowed her eyes at the statue of Margaret, her arms still raised in a Y. "You didn't say over the phone how this happened."

"It's classified," Zinnia said with a shrug. "Let's just chalk it up to the worst camping trip ever." She made a hopeful face. "You can turn Margaret back, right?"

"I'll try," Chloe said, taking a moment to adjust her baby in the sling that was attached to her.

"Do you want me to hold Jordan Junior?"

"No need," Chloe said casually. She looked up at Margaret, who was a few inches taller than the gorgon, thanks to being on the dolly. Chloe placed her hands on Margaret's cheeks, and then pressed her mouth to Margaret's. She appeared to be breathing life into the statue, blowing it from her mouth into Margaret's.

There was a creaking sound, the air electrified, and then Margaret was flesh and blood again, her arms windmilling as she struggled to catch her balance.

"Susan," Margaret said. "Let me talk! I have to finish telling that stupid man how stupid he is or he'll never know! I have a..." She looked around the mayor's clean, modern office. She spotted Zinnia and made a choking sound.

"Take it slowly," Chloe said. "You were a statue, Margaret. Solid granite. It will take a few minutes for all of your cellular function to return to normal."

Margaret jumped back, falling off the dolly. Zinnia had anticipated that particular move, and was there to catch her friend.

"Easy now," Zinnia said softly. "Do you remember what happened?"

"Of course I do," Margaret said indignantly. "The timewyrms wrecked the portal home, and then the big idiot made of lava showed up, and..." She frowned. "We're back on Earth again? That was fast."

Chloe was watching quietly.

Zinnia clamped a hand over Margaret's mouth and mentally implored her to be quiet, lest she spill any more classified secrets.

Chloe said, "She called me Susan."

"She's confused," Zinnia said.

Chloe frowned. "That's the name Queenie Gilbert used to call my grandmother sometimes." She tilted her head thoughtfully. "She's still alive," Chloe said wistfully. "I knew it."

Zinnia kept her hand clamped over Margaret's mouth.

"Thanks so much for your help," Zinnia said to the gorgon. "We are in your debt. Please don't hesitate to call on us, Chloe."

Margaret mumbled something similarly positive, albeit muffled, through Zinnia's hand.

Chloe picked up her diaper bag. "You're welcome," she said dreamily, and headed for the door. She was smiling.

* * *

The two witches returned to their office, expecting to find Carrot in a panic, or at the very least confused by whatever cover story the mayor's office had sent down.

Instead, they found her desk empty, and a resignation letter on her keyboard. It was dated Thursday morning. The group had gone through the elevator portal on Wednesday night. Carrot had only stopped in briefly to drop off the note, so she hadn't even realized they were missing.

Karl read the personal part of the note aloud to the two witches. "*I'm sorry for the short notice, but my great-uncle came through with the loan, and I have to meet the landlord this morning for the building before he rents it to someone else. I will keep you posted, and of course you'll all be invited to the grand opening.*" He looked up. "And there are three exclamation points."

"I'm happy for her," said Dawna, who had read the note an hour earlier. "This is a good change for her."

Gavin rubbed his chin and glanced over at the customer service counter. "It won't be the same around here without Carrot."

Dawna rolled her eyes. "You mean it won't be the same without Carrot handling all the walk-ins. You'll have to pitch in until we get a replacement."

"A replacement?" Gavin looked around at the group. "You mean someone we don't know? I don't like the sound of that."

Everyone looked at Karl.

Karl rubbed the stubble on his jaw. "You know, it would be easier for all of us if we could be ourselves around each other."

Margaret, who'd been clutching an ice pack to her head and looking wan, suddenly perked up. "I could do spells!"

Zinnia said, "You already do spells."

Margaret stuck her tongue out like a brat. "I could do them out in the open."

Xavier said, "If I hang out with all of you magical people, do you think some of the magic will rub off on me?"

Liza chimed in. "Does magic work that way?"

"Careful what you wish for," Zinnia said. "You two are in the enviable position of being in the know of a huge secret, yet because you don't have any powers yourselves, you don't have any responsibilities."

Xavier puffed up his chest. "I'm responsible."

Margaret studied Xavier. "You sure are willing to fight. Maybe you have some kind of talent you haven't discovered yet."

"I could read your cards," Dawna said to the young man.

Liza jumped up and down, clapping her hands excitedly. "Dawna! Dawna! Do mine first!"

Karl shut down the conversation with a mighty HARUMPH. "It's only two o'clock," he said. "This office has been closed for a full day and a half. We probably have a million voicemail messages. Everyone needs to get to work." He gave them his most serious, authoritative scowl. "Now."

Nobody moved.

"We must maintain the status quo," Karl said. "That's lesson one of being a supernatural." He stared at Dawna in particular.

"I need to visit the nail salon," Dawna said. "It's a status quo for me, personally."

Gavin said, "Our boss has a good point. We should keep up our routine. Between the monster infestations and the cleaning crew's strike, there's a good chance nobody noticed we were closed, but we can't slack off forever. Let's power through our voicemail and email, then everyone can come over to my place for beer."

"It's Friday," Karl said. "We have to go bowling. We must maintain the status quo!"

"No bowling tonight," Xavier said. "I just got an alert on my phone. They're fumigating Shady Lanes." Xavier grinned. "Someone found some extra-large termites under the lanes."

Everyone chuckled. There would be a few more fumigations around town before all the strange creatures had been dealt with.

"Beer at my place," Gavin said.

The others murmured uncertainly. Wouldn't it be better to return home and shower off the campfire and cave grime?

Gavin waggled his eyebrows. "I've got a naked-lady painting of Zinnia." He beamed, very proud of himself for having figured out why Zinnia had been curious about the date on the back of his painting.

Zinnia felt her cheeks flush. "That's not a painting of me," she said. "Don't be ridiculous. It's vintage."

Margaret gasped. "Zinnia! When we were in the past, we met that guy, Piero! Wasn't he an artist? A painter?"

Gavin snickered.

Zinnia said nothing, but the rest of the office erupted in hysterics. It only settled down after Karl took off his shoe and banged it on one of the desks.

"Get to work, people!" His face reddened, and he released a smell that could have wilted a house plant.

Everyone ran for cover and got to work.

* * *

Later that night, they all gathered at Gavin's apartment in the Candy Factory. They prepared a feast that was nearly as good as the banquet some of them had enjoyed at the palace. They fought off exhaustion to stay awake and talk about everything that had happened.

At some point, Margaret turned on the television and started playing the classic Disney animated movie, *101 Dalmatians*. Everyone agreed that Mayor Paladini did resemble Cruella De Vil, even though her hair wasn't half black and half white. There were other differences, too. The mayor was a secret time paladin who valiantly kept order in the universe, whereas Cruella De Vil tried to murder Dalmatian puppies to make a fur coat.

They didn't get to see the end of the movie, because everyone fell asleep sprawled around Gavin's apartment, like kids at a sleepover.

Nobody saw the apartment door open and the mayor enter the apartment, use an instrument with flashing lights to take readings of the air above each of them, and then leave quietly, like a mixed-up version of Santa Claus.

Nobody saw except Zinnia Riddle, who watched the whole procedure through the fringe of her eyelashes.

CHAPTER 41

FOURTEEN DAYS LATER

ZINNIA SPENT OVER an hour picking out the right outfit to wear to brunch at her niece's house.

She'd fully recovered from the trip through time and the other world. Her new front teeth seemed brighter than the others, but she couldn't complain about that. The pain in her shoulder was completely gone now, and the ache in her thumb rarely flared up—only when she thought about Jesse. It was an emotional ache, not a physical one, so it was probably there permanently. And she was okay with that. Gone were the days she froze her feelings, sealing them in with magic. These days, Zinnia let herself feel everything. Good. Bad. Whatever.

That morning, she was feeling two things.

For one, she was concerned about her longtime associate, Tansy Wick. The woman was a recluse, preferring the company of her plants and her two dogs, so her absence hadn't been noticed immediately, but lately people had become concerned. Zinnia planned to drive out to the woman's property at the outskirts of town to check on her later that day, after brunch.

The other thing Zinnia was having feelings about was seeing Zara's father again. The man, Rhys Quarry, had shown up without any warning whatsoever, and he'd also revealed his supernatural ability to his daughter and granddaughter. He was a shifter. One of *them*. One of the people who hated witches. However, rumor had it fox shifters weren't as disgusted by witches as other types of shifters. Some even attracted to witches. Rhys certainly hadn't minded getting close to Zara's mother, Zirconia.

That might have happened due to Zirconia not being the typical witch. She had denied her magic. She had denied it to the point of renouncing her powers, and taking a poison to suppress her abilities. The worst part of it all was that the woman had probably gone to an early grave due to that poison. It wasn't healthy for a witch to deny her powers.

Zinnia finally settled on the perfect ensemble: a cute pair of flower-dotted leggings, paired with a paisley-and-floral tunic. The tunic didn't have much of a shape to it, so she cinched it at the waist with a braided cord that she'd had a few extra feet of after making curtain tiebacks. She wasn't sure how to wear her hair. Up? Down? She split the difference and plaited it back in a loose braid. It was a perfect summery look.

She tidied her bedroom, and went downstairs to prepare the food she'd promised to bring—bagels, cream cheese, lox, and a nice fruit platter. Zinnia used a spell she didn't have much practice with yet to make perfectly round melon balls. With each perfect melon ball produced, she felt more and more at ease, more like herself.

Once she'd prepared enough food to feed a small army —and her niece and great-niece did resemble a small army when it came to the amount of food they could put away— she gathered everything in bags and headed out.

The weather was perfectly sunny, which was typical for the middle of June in Wisteria. Warm breezes blew the scent of flowering bushes in through the car windows on the drive over. Zinnia wondered how Liza's grandmother was doing in the other world. Had sixty-some years of experience on Earth prepared her to better handle her responsibilities as the queen? Or given her the perspective to better manage disagreements with her hot-blooded husband? Had they come to some agreement about having children together?

Zinnia parked the car and let all her wondering drift away on the warm summer breezes.

The key was gone now. Depending on one's perspective, the key had either been smashed to pieces or was still making its way through time in an endless loop, being duplicated and becoming the original.

Either way, there would be no traveling back to the accordion floor. The mayor had assured them of that, in no uncertain terms. Her job as a time paladin was to keep the timeline secure. Now that Queenie and Diablo had completed their journey to 1955, there would be no need of an opening between the dimensions. Probably. In Wisteria, it was best to never say *never*, lest you be proven a liar in the next breath.

Zinnia walked up to Zara's front door and rang the doorbell. She stood there patiently while the usual ruckus ensued on the other side of the door, with everyone yelling "doorbell!" at the top of their lungs.

Zoey answered the door. She looked smart and adorable, as usual. Zinnia's heart swelled with love for her great-niece.

Before Zinnia could get her boots off, Zara's grandfather, Rhys Quarry, had pounced. He hugged her. Zinnia was so unprepared for his enthusiastic greeting that she could do nothing but stand there helplessly, her arms flopping limply at her sides.

Something bright and striped moved toward Zinnia. It was Zara, dressed in a striped blouse that would have looked right at home on a circus clown. She'd paired the blouse with a navy pencil skirt.

Rhys finally released Zinnia from his tight embrace. "Little Ziti Noodles, it's been too long!" He stepped back and looked her over. "And you're not so little anymore. I'll have to call you Zirconia!"

Zinnia felt herself die a little. "You mean Zinnia," she said, horrified. "I'm not Zirconia."

"Slip of the tongue," he said, his green eyes teasing. It had not been a slip of the tongue at all.

"Rhys Quarry, I'm not like my sister. Not at all." She wished she had worn more of a serious ensemble, perhaps entirely black. Maybe then Rhys wouldn't tease her so mercilessly.

Rhys asked his granddaughter, "Zozo, did you know that your aunt was about your age when we first met? She was such a shy little thing, compared to you. I wonder if it's a generational thing?"

"I wasn't shy," Zinnia said, defending herself. "I was younger than Zoey, and I was raised to have manners. I knew better than to—" She cut herself off. She'd only been in the door a few minutes. This was exactly how Rhys always got under her skin! He wouldn't make a fool of her this time. She changed her tone and said sweetly, "It's lovely to see you again, Rhys."

"And under better circumstances," he agreed. "A brunch beats a funeral every time." He sniffed the air. "Bagels?"

"Yes!" She was happy for a topic change. "I've brought a dozen fresh bagels, along with a selection of cream cheese flavors, as well as the world's most perfectly round melon balls. They're like marbles."

Zoey grabbed the bags with a happy whoop. "You had me at bagels," she called over her shoulder on the way to the kitchen.

Zinnia gave her niece, Zara, a warm smile. "Like mother, like daughter."

The three adults continued their pleasant interactions for a few minutes, still standing by the doorway. Rhys made a joke about the family of redheads play-fighting like fox pups tumbling around.

Zinnia admitted that she hadn't known Rhys was a fox shifter until Zara told her.

Rhys immediately turned the conversation, as he often did, to himself. He grinned at Zinnia, his green eyes twinkling, and accused Zinnia of flirting with him.

Zinnia nearly died, for the second time that morning.

Zara uttered the word "gross," and immediately ran off to the kitchen to help her daughter prepare the brunch.

Zinnia and Rhys stood alone together at the entrance.

"And here we are," Zinnia said. "Funny how time passes but some things never change."

"You've changed," he said. "You've become even more lovely than ever."

She shook her head. "You and your flattery, Rhys Quarry. How did I never know you were a fox?"

He grinned. The sounds of Zara and Zoey happily arguing over food preparation in the kitchen drifted over. Rhys tilted his head and took another good, long look at Zinnia. She did the same to him.

From the moment Zinnia Riddle had first met Rhys Quarry, all those years ago, she'd been smitten. She'd been a teen at the time, and he was a grownup of twenty-two, but he hadn't fully crossed over into adulthood. He'd always talked to Zinnia in a way that made her feel like a lady, not a kid. He'd always been respectful and mindful of her innocence, which naturally ignited her wild, teen-hormone-fueled imagination. Her crush on the young man had been fierce and painful. The worst heartbreak of Zinnia's young life had been when her older sister revealed she had become pregnant by Rhys. Their parents were furious. Rhys had been hired by the family as a matchmaker. His job had been to find a suitable husband for Zirconia, not to sully her with his own child—out of wedlock, no less. Zinnia had also been furious, but for different reasons. Her careful plans to marry Rhys herself after she reached eighteen had been dashed by this new development. She eventually got over it, as teenagers always do, yet seeing him now triggered those old longings.

Rhys Quarry was not conventionally handsome. He was shorter than average, and slight of build. His hair was a rusty red. He had a weak chin, a slightly bulbous nose, and rubbery facial expressions. But he had those mischievous gold-green eyes. When he looked at you, you felt seen. Paid attention to. That was why the man was so successful as a matchmaker. And probably why Zinnia's older sister had seduced *him*—or so Zinnia believed. Zirconia had pled innocence at the time, of course, implying that Rhys had been the one doing the seducing. But Zinnia knew her older sister better than their parents did. Zinnia had a pretty good idea about exactly what went down around the time Zara was conceived. That was all ancient history now, thirty-three years later, but being in the presence of Rhys brought back Zinnia's feelings of heartbreak and outrage.

After a few minutes of awkward silence by the entryway, they made their way through the house and then to the back yard, where Zoey had done a wonderful job decorating the overgrown jungle of a yard. The younger Riddles served brunch, and everyone talked a mile a minute, fighting to get a word in edgewise. Zinnia took it all in.

As she watched Rhys eat brunch, there was a moment where Zinnia's shoulders suddenly hunched up defensively. An unexpected emotion had come out of nowhere, the way these things do. She felt a hot rush of grief for the life she never had the chance to live. The life where she and Rhys were married, and the parents of a big brood of redheaded babies. Babies? No, their imaginary children would be fully grown by now, possibly having babies of their own. Zinnia could have been a grandmother at this very moment, in the other unlived life.

Her shoulders relaxed again. Being a grandmother? No, thank you! She was much too young for that.

This new realization gave her a different feeling. Relief. She wasn't a grandmother, or a mother, or even a wife. She was only responsible for herself, thank you very much, and that was just fine. She had her work, her coven, her other group of supernatural teammates at the office, and now her niece and great-niece. She had enough. More than enough.

She looked across the cheerfully-decorated folding card table at all of their smiling faces. If any stone had remained around her heart, her family's joy at being reunited was now melting it away. Zinnia took a breath of fragrant summer air and took it all in. She was on Earth, in her own time, where she belonged. She had all of this, and it was... enough.

For now.

For a full list of books in this
series and other titles by
Angela Pepper, visit

www.angelapepper.com

Made in the USA
Las Vegas, NV
07 September 2021

29810483R00186